TWO-SEVEN
REMAINDER

TWO-SEVEN REMAINDER

MATT HADER

A NOVEL

BOOKS BY MATT HADER

Two-Seven Remainder
Amika Press

Bad Reputation: The Complete Collection
The Core
West Bound
Breaking
Balmoral
Bad Reputation
Thinkbox Entertainment

Confessions of a Rock Star
Famous Monsters Music

First Edition   ISBN 13: 978-1-937484-40-8

AMIKA PRESS   466 Central AVE #23 Northfield IL 60093   847 920 8084
info@amikapress.com   Available for purchase on amikapress.com

Edited by John Manos and Ann Wambach. Cover design by Sarah Koz and John Rose. Designed and typeset by Sarah Koz. Body in Maiola, designed by Veronika Burian in 2005. Titles in Modesto Condensed & Balboa Condensed, designed by Jim Parkinson in 2000 and 2001. Thanks to Nathan Matteson.

FOR ART

1

Jakub "Pies" Jakubowski gulped back the acidic slurry of formerly chewed breakfast sausage that rose in his throat. Beads of sweat sprouted along his hairline, and he fidgeted with the bottom of the three buttons on his large and ill-fitting, dark-blue golf shirt. He couldn't stop his fingers from gently twisting the button back and forth.

Pies Jakubowski was literally in the belly of the beast, the large, windowless room where he sat presently—and he wanted out.

He sought to implement his ultimate escape-from-Chicago plan sooner than later, but he had to continually remind himself to be patient so that everything would work without complication.

Pies glanced down and noticed the emblazoned gold-threaded badge that was woven into his shirt, and his breath caught in his throat for a moment. He never dreamed he'd wear a badge, not even one made from stitching.

And this was certainly not the type of job he had ever planned to take on. Against his objections, and his better judgment, he was ordered—forced, really—to accept the assignment.

Pies would have to muster some real courage to make it all work out as drawn up, because his freedom was on the line.

He watched as his training officer, Naomi Gott—the woman who had taken him through two days of intensive classroom instruction before she shifted his schooling to their current location—toggled the switch to deactivate the phone console. Once the small switch was thrown, no further administrative or emergency 9-1-1 calls would be routed to her police and fire communications pod.

Naomi had warm green eyes and wore her dark hair bluntly styled. Her lovely smile and high cheekbones worked to only enhance her overall charm. She carried some extra roundness on her midsection and hips, but Pies thought that she was utterly beautiful in every other way, especially in her personality and demeanor.

Naomi was a gentle soul and the perfect choice to train new employees into such stressful positions under equally stressful workplace conditions. Patient. With a voice like liquid silk, she was soft-spoken, yet somewhat direct—a classic earth-mother type.

Naomi Gott might have been a bit older than Pies, but he thought to himself that if he were here under different circumstances, and the woman he had loved so deeply for his entire life ultimately rejected him, Naomi would probably be the sort of woman he'd ask out. Any potential date would also hinge on whether Pies had been found out and arrested by that time. As soon as he recognized that he was lost in thought over Naomi, he forced himself back on task.

The communications pod where they sat was one of ten newly constructed, high-tech desk units, all of which formed the foundation of the systematized assortment of phones, emergency radio consoles, and computer monitors that filled the space of the massive room. The twenty-two-foot ceiling and the airy glass-and-glossy-white-walled-dominated construction of the interior in the brand-new building dwarfed the equally spaced communications pods.

Six of the ten communications pods were designed as phone positions where emergency and nonemergency calls from the public would be received. Three pods were radio positions where a communications officer would dispatch the police to various calls, and the last pod was for the fire/EMS radio dispatcher to occupy. The fire/EMS radio position was always manned, and at least two of the three police radio positions were occupied, depending on shift needs.

Eight-foot-high, clear, sound-dampening walls constructed of beveled one-inch, tempered glass divided the individual communications pods. Each glass partition had "Northcomm" etched into it in twenty-inch-tall letters. Some sounds from other communications officers and radio traffic carried about the room just the same, especially if one of the communications officers happened to lean back and away from the glass partitions. Mostly, though, the sounds were muffled, and the sharp edges of the sometimes-frenzied police and fire communications were somewhat muted.

"Your mommy won't wake up? Oh, honey, it'll be okay. I need you to go and open the front door. Can you do that, sweetie?"

"Evanston 2 is requesting back up at his traffic stop. Evanston 7 and 8, can you break away?"

"Sir, if you don't hang up now, you'll be arrested. This is a 9-1-1 line for emergencies only."

"Northbrook Ladder 2 reporting fully engulfed, single-story structure."

"Kenilworth 2, report of accident at Sheridan and Oxford."

"I'll show you available Skokie 5."

Street-side, the Northcomm 9-1-1 police and fire communications center looked like any other brick-constructed, commercial warehouse on the industrial frontage road along I-294 in Northbrook, Illinois. Passing motorists wouldn't realize that the interior of the structure was visually more in line with a futuristic J.J. Abrams movie set than a place where emergency services were dispatched.

In the recent past each suburban municipality of the Chicago's North Shore had its own small emergency radio room that was relegated to a tiny, closet-sized space somewhere in the individual police department building—a place where a dispatcher, or maybe two, could operate at a time and take phone and radio calls, so as to lord over the safety of the suburb's pampered residents.

The recent amalgamation of local municipalities' police and fire communications rooms into the one fantastic space that was Northcomm was the direct consequence of a smooth-talking Cincinnati native's ability to schmooze his way into the civic pocketbooks of every suburban mayor and city manager north of Howard Street, south of Lake Cook Road, east of I-294, and west of Lake Michigan.

The Cincinnatian successfully convinced the civic executives that launching a new communications center would be a prudent decision for the safety of their citizens and the health of each town's coffers.

And if the Cincinnatian's personal wallet expanded during the process, so be it. Privatization was in the air.

That newly installed director of communications for Northcomm had only four years prior established a similar communications center in the suburbs of his southwestern Ohio city. An emergency communications center that, on the surface, with its utilization of floating glass walls and high-tech gear, seemed like a total misuse of public funds but, in fact, had saved the taxpayers millions and millions of dollars each year since its inception—even as it lined the pockets of some of the notables who made the deal happen.

The new director achieved all of this when he slashed salaries of new hires by one third, shrank the overall number of dispatchers on each shift, and forced communications officers with more than twenty years on the job out the door through the utilization of a meager, but mandatory, "buyout" package.

For his latest operation in the Chicago area, it also didn't hurt that the new director of communication's brother-in-law owned the land on the frontage road in Northbrook where the building was constructed.

Through his daily dealings, the brother-in-law, a local lawyer, had enough personal and professional muck on nearly each and every mayor and city manager on the North Shore that the 9-1-1 center was a done deal before the municipal executives even knew they needed a new communications facility.

In the cases of both the suburban Cincinnati center and North-comm, the pooling of communications personnel and services was a winning combination for all the municipalities involved—at least for the time being, and until the books would be reviewed five years down the road. Only then would the auditors begin to get a sniff that their citizens would not see the savings they were first promised.

One year after that first whiff of impropriety, the auditors would also figure out where a hefty percentage of the municipalities' money savings was actually going, and it wasn't into the towns' treasuries. But that was going to happen further down the road—both in Cincinnati and on Chicago's North Shore. It would become a story for the newspapers and television investigative teams to cover on another day in the future.

Comparable to the massive Chicago 9-1-1 Emergency Communications Center located near the United Center sports arena on the West Side of the city, suburban Northcomm 9-1-1 Center was equal in state-of-the-art equipment, but not in workforce size. Whereas Chicago's center would typically have a few dozen communications officers working on a shift at any given time, the recently opened Northcomm 9-1-1 Center had shift sizes of only six to ten civilian communications officers—depending on the day of the week and the time of the day.

And since the suburban "public safety answering point," or PSAP, was responsible for providing emergency service communications to the several exclusive and moneyed communities on the North Shore, their hiring practices and personnel guidelines were quite stringent. Only the finest of the civilian applicants who took the battery of tests (written and psychological) required for the job were considered. Candidates had to have spotless criminal records, as well.

Pies Jakubowski fit that bill perfectly—on paper.

It wasn't really evident this day as he received his training, but Pies had a sardonic sense of humor. He was typically a fairly quiet man who kept his thoughts to himself. But sometimes—rarely—he would blurt out witticisms that hit the mark with those around him, at least those whose sense of irony was sharp enough to get his jokes. If anyone were here presently to explain to him how Northcomm actually came to be and how it would one day be caught up in a criminal controversy, he'd get a decent laugh out of the story. Pies disliked politicians, but overall he had a sort of strange loathing/respect for white-collar criminals and the way they'd accomplish their rip-offs while wearing expensive suits and operating in the daytime, not skulking around in the shadows like he usually did to make money.

Maybe someday Pies's dry sense of humor would fully return, but for now he was on a solemn and dangerous mission. There was not a lot of room in his life for levity.

Naomi said, "I'll be back in five. You should take a walk and stretch your legs. If it gets busy, you may not get a chance." She rose and gently twisted her waist from one side to the other. Pies heard an audible "pop" when she twisted to her right. They locked eyes, and Naomi blurted out a giggle—Pies remained silent and just stared.

"You okay, Jakub? You seem off today. I know that there's a lot to cover, but you're doing great." Naomi called him by his birth name because that was the name on the reams of paper forms that he had filled out when he applied for the position several months back. Anyone who truly knew the man called him by only one name, though: Pies.

Pies shrugged and said, "I don't want to mess this up. Folks could get hurt."

"It hasn't even been a week yet. Take it all in. There's no rush," said Naomi. "When I first started at the Evanston PD, it took about three months to get comfortable with the job. You'll move through faster, I'm sure of it."

Naomi actually enjoyed training Pies because the twenty-eight-year-old seemed to pick things up rather quickly, as if he'd worked in, or was extremely familiar with, law enforcement and emergency communications.

And if Naomi were being honest with herself, she'd acknowledge that she enjoyed looking into Pies's clear, intense, hazel-colored eyes. She thought his eyes were stunning, like none she had seen before. He wasn't rugged or muscular, and he more resembled an awkward catalogue model, but there was something about those eyes that she couldn't get enough of. To Naomi, Pies was the male equivalent of the sexy librarian. And that alone intrigued her to no end.

Pies's own late mother, in her more sober and lucid moments, would call Pies her *lis,* or "fox" in Polish, for the simple reason that her son was sneaky like a fox, not because he was particularly handsome. He'd bat those hazel eyes whenever he found himself in a childhood jam—and it usually got him out of trouble.

"I think we're going to start having you take calls while I do the computer commands," said Naomi. "You do the talking, I'll do everything else."

"Really? It's only been…"

When he stopped and glanced down, Naomi added, "You're going to be fine. A little baptism by fire won't hurt too much."

Pies nodded uneasily at that remark and remained seated. Naomi peeled the radio/telephone headset off her ear and placed it on the desktop of their communications pod.

Pies, adorned with his very own headset, watched as the similarly golf-shirt-adorned Naomi stepped toward the main door that led to the hallway, outer offices, bathrooms, and break room. She pushed open the glass door, which quickly swung closed as she exited.

A muscular, uniformed, male cop angled out of one of the offices with a stack of paperwork in hand and moved right alongside Naomi. They carried on a pleasant if inaudible conversation as they disappeared around a corner.

Pies made sure that none of the other police and fire 9-1-1 communications officers in the room were paying attention to him. All the others were busy speaking into their headsets and tapping away on the computer keyboards of the communications pods in front of them.

Pies went to work.

Through the fabric of his pants, he pushed the tiny rubberized on/off switch of the cell-phone-sized, mini-DVR control unit that was concealed in his right front pocket. As he turned the mini-DVR unit on, he gently pinched the bottom button of his golf shirt—which was actually a button camera—between his left thumb and forefinger and aimed it at the middle of the four twenty-two-inch computer monitors on the desk in front of him.

Pies kept his left forefinger and thumb on the shirt-button camera and used his right forefinger to hunt and peck in a quick command on the computer terminal keyboard. It was a command he'd seen Naomi use several times since he started his training to be a 9-1-1 dispatcher.

The screen instantly displayed a list of data and business names and addresses, with notations on the right column of the page next to each entry.

The heading on the computer page read: Alarms Out of Service Log.

The computer pages listed each and every alarm system, both business and residential, that was out of service in the North Shore area of Chicago. The information was provided to the police so that if any errant alarms activated at those locations, the police could choose to ignore the activation knowing that there was a malfunction in the system. But it also allowed the police on patrol to pay a little extra attention, as time permitted during their hectic shifts, to the places where the alarms were on the fritz.

Pies did his best to act casual. He didn't want to attract any undue attention as he used the button lens on his golf shirt to record the screen. He hit the "down" arrow on the keyboard, and the computer page changed—and he kept recording. Three pages later, Pies tapped his right front pocket once again and turned off the mini-DVR device, let go of the shirt button, and pressed the Escape key on the keyboard to clear the computer screen of the Alarms Out of Service Log information.

He leaned back and let out the deep breath that he hadn't realized he was holding—and that's when he noticed that Naomi had not completely toggled the switch to deactivate their phone console.

The button should have flashed red to show that the deactivation mode was locked into place. The button was half-toggled and still green—the color it displays if the pod operator is available to take emergency calls from the public.

As he leaned forward to completely deactivate the communications position, he heard three abrupt tones in his ear through his headset and the low whisper of a terrified woman who said, "Oh my God, we're being robbed. Help us..."

Pies peered toward the hall, but there was no sign of Naomi. The other communications officers in the room were all occupied with their own phone and radio calls and didn't notice that Pies needed help. After only a few days on the job, mostly spent in a classroom or listening in to Naomi as she took call after call, he wasn't ready for this.

Immediately he saw the caller's location and business name information automatically displayed in a single line of data at the bottom of all his computer-aided dispatch monitors: Happy Sammies, 3511 Lake Avenue, Wilmette, IL.

"Hello...hello? Is anyone there?" asked the terrified woman's whispered voice on the other end of the phone line.

"Yeah. Yeah, I'm here," said Pies as his eyes searched again for Naomi. When he couldn't locate her, he placed a finger over the end of the clear plastic tube that was the microphone of his headset and said, "Hey! Somebody! I need help here." But none of the other communications officers heard him. All of them were hunched over their own pods, busy with other calls. The well-designed tempered glass was beautiful, but the sound-deadening properties acted as his nemesis at that moment.

"My God, help me..."

Pies slid his finger off of the microphone and said, "Um, does he have a gun or...like...a weapon or something?"

The lack of confidence in his voice frightened the caller even more.

"Yes. A gun. Linda's with him. He doesn't know I'm here in back. We're not open for business yet. She unlocked the door to sweep the sidewalk, and then..."

In the background, Pies could hear the robber scream, "The money, you bitch."

"He's going to shoot her," whispered the woman.

"Happy Sammies. The sandwich place, right?" asked Pies, know-ing he'd seen it before in his travels. It was on the border of Wilmette and Glenview—right smack-dab between two different police de-partments' shared borders.

Criminals know that police get lazy from time to time and tend to ignore the far fringes of their own municipal boundaries while out on patrol. The small sandwich shop would be the perfect place to score a few hundred bucks in a lightning-fast armed robbery. You could be in and out in an instant before either police department could accurately determine jurisdiction.

Pies knew this because it was the type of thing he'd set up him-self, on rare occasion, for the crews working for his boss Stan Zie-linski out of their Edison Park neighborhood criminal operation.

Pies asked, "You have a drive-thru there, right?"

"Are you sending someone?"

"Um, sure. Do you have a drive-thru window?"

"Stop saying stupid things."

"I think I can help, okay?" Said Pies.

"He's going to shoot her," she frantically whispered.

*

NEAR THE corner of Lake and Laramie Avenues in Wilmette sat Happy Sammies, a quaint business housed in the one-story husk of a former Dairy Queen franchise. The place catered to the wealthy high school students at nearby Loyola Academy, so business was usually good—during the school year.

Because of the morning sun that reflected off of the front win-dows, from the street a person who passed by wouldn't see the black T-shirt and blue jeans of the fetid and fidgety white man who point-ed a cheap .22 revolver at the female employee inside the doorway. The employee held a broomstick in her hand and was terrified to the point of frozen rigidity.

"You got two seconds, bitch. The cash. Now," screamed the robber, through a patchwork of rotted and crooked meth-altered teeth. He grabbed the terrified woman's arm and led her toward the counter.

"Hey!" said the woman in back, a short and skinny lady of fifty, the one who spoke with Pies on the phone. She stood behind the main counter next to the drive-thru window, and she held a thick and heavy-looking, blue-colored, bank deposit bag. The robber couldn't help but lick his cracked lips as he took notice of the crinkled fan of dollar bills that messily stuck out of the overstuffed bag.

When the thief shakily angled the gun in her direction, the woman violently shoved open the small drive-thru window and tossed the bag outside and onto the parking lot where it landed with an audible plop.

"Son of a...," yelped the robber as he backpedaled and barged through the front door and around to the side of the building.

The employee with the broomstick stood immobilized in shock as the woman in back raced around the counter and up to the front door. She instantly shoved her key into the lock and slammed the deadbolt home. Once she and her workmate were safe, she took the employee by the wrist and led her into a crouched position on the opposite side of the eatery.

Outside, the robber had heard the front door lock, but he didn't give a shit. He got what he came for. He tried as best he could to act casual as he nodded about like a peacock to make sure that no one witnessed the robbery. He tucked the small gun into his front pants pocket, only the butt of the pistol visible, and pulled his sweat-stained shirt down to cover it as he advanced closer and leaned over to retrieve the fat bank deposit bag from under the drive-thru window.

He grinned at his easily achieved windfall. But as he lifted the bag closer he could see that there were only three one-dollar bills tucked into the top of the semi-opened, zippered bank bag. He hastily unzipped the bag the rest of the way—and the thing was jammed full of folded sandwich wrapping paper.

He said, "Shit."

He grabbed the three one-dollar bills, tossed the bag aside, and ran.

2

T HE EDISON Park neighborhood, on the northwestern edge of
the city of Chicago, was always one of the go-to places for city
employees to reside. Streets & Sanitation workers, Park District staff,
plumbers, carpenters, and the like were required to live within the
boundaries of the city, and Edison Park—wedged in on two sides by
the well-established suburbs of Niles, a blue-collar town, and Park
Ridge, an upscale community—fit the bill.

Edison Park was a cramped area, with row upon row of Chicago
bungalows, Cape Cods, and tiny Georgian-style homes all jammed
together, one right on top of the next. For most of the residents,
though, they loved it that way—cozy and comfortable. Some people assume that in city neighborhoods no one knows their neighbors,
but that wasn't the case here. People had a sense of community in
Edison Park. They were proud to call the city neighborhood their
home. Over the years, with its quaint and vibrant business district
chock-full of eateries and taverns, the area, like its counterparts Bev-
erly and Mount Greenwood on the Southwest Side, even became the
home turf for many Chicago police officers and firefighters.

But along with the law-abiders residing in the cute, boxy little
homes, there were the criminals, too. An organized criminal element
was able to operate and flourish, really, while hiding in plain sight.
They'd been in the area for years.

Edison Park is where Pies Jakubowski was born and raised. He was a quiet but extremely intelligent kid who was keenly interested in mechanical contraptions. He was the kind of boy who always self-educated and who constantly kept up on advances in technology. It was a good thing that Pies was so curious and sought knowledge whenever and wherever he could, because he never actually graduated from high school, much less attended college.

He had in his possession a diploma from a prestigious Catholic high school in the suburbs and another from a respectable small college in the western suburbs, but, in reality, Pies stopped attending school halfway through his sophomore year of high school.

As a kid, Pies had a knack for finding salvageable old televisions and appliances in the trash of the alleyways in his neighborhood. Once discovered, he'd fix and sell the repaired electronics and machines. It wasn't only the money earned from the sales that interested young Pies, it was the thrill of accomplishment he felt by bringing the broken technology back to life.

With his father's guidance, Pies was able to sidestep any trouble he encountered with a local gang known as the Popes. Pies's father, a sergeant with the Chicago PD, schooled his son on the areas to avoid in Edison Park, and the boy learned to steer clear of the gang's territorial alleyways where the buildings were tagged with "IP," for Insane Popes.

Unfortunately for Pies, his father, suffering through years of depression, would eventually drive himself to the densely forested Dam No. 4 Woods-East across Dee Road from Maine Township High School in Park Ridge and eat a fast-moving round from his service weapon. This happened shortly after Pies's mother drank herself to death at the age of thirty-seven. Her death certificate noted that she expired from a massive heart attack. However, that was not the case at all. Pies's father bullied the Cook County medical examiner to erase the actual reason for her death, a gastrointestinal hemorrhage caused by alcohol abuse, and change it to the more natural sounding heart attack so as to ease the embarrassment of the terrible circumstances.

After his father's unexpected, self-inflicted, exit, fourteen-year-old Pies had been left to live alone. There were no aunts or uncles to live with, no family at all. Pies's father was an only child of immigrants, and his parents had died years before. Pies's mother emigrated from Poland two years before he was born, and she had no living relatives in the United States.

Pies had no other family, but the house was paid for, so he stayed—with the help of neighbors.

That was all fourteen years ago.

Among the possessions his father had accumulated over the years was a small cache of weapons hidden in an attic compartment—mostly handguns that Pies's father had taken off suspects while on the job. No one other than Pies knew of the handguns' existence. If he were having a day where he felt too afraid to be alone, he'd sometimes take one of the guns from the hiding spot in the attic and keep it nearby in case of trouble. The guns, all of them with the serial numbers removed, oddly enough, also comforted Pies at times. His thoughts were so confused after his father left him that he sometimes wondered if he should join him. The weapons held so much power in Pies's mind at that time. They could instantly stop the fierce hurt that he continued to endure.

Child Protective Services snooped around for a time shortly after his father's death, but they evaporated one day after Pies's across-the-street neighbor, Mr. Stan Zielinski, met with the agents after a visit to the house. Stan spoke with Pies later that same day after he witnessed the young Pies break down and say he didn't want to leave his house. Stan advised him that if anyone asked who was looking out for him now that he was orphaned, to lie and say it was his non-existent aunt and uncle. The neighbors wondered for a while how a fourteen-year-old kid could live by himself, but even their musings faded and never returned as Pies eventually edged closer to his eighteenth birthday.

The Zielinski family, who lived in a Georgian-style brick home that looked a lot like Pies's house, kept an eye on him. They made sure he had groceries to eat and new clothes to wear. Mr. Zielinski even showed Pies how to pay his utility bills and real estate taxes with the money left over in his father's accounts. His father's money wouldn't last all too long, but in the end everything would work out, financially, for young Pies.

When his father was alive, he had a deep distrust of the Zielinskis. He would constantly caution his son that they were up to no good. Pies's father never got any more specific than that with his young son, and the warnings never carried much weight, anyway, because Pies hung out with the Zielinski's own boy.

After his father's death, Pies had only respect and admiration for Mr. Stan Zielinski. He never understood his father's trepidations about the Zielinski family at all. They'd always been so nice to him.

Sebastian "Bast" Zielinski was a year older than Pies. Growing up, Bast treated Pies like the little brother he never had—meaning, he tormented the crap out of the skinny Pies on a near-daily basis. Pies endured the abuse because he didn't have any siblings of his own, and he truly saw a brother in Bast—warts and all.

Bast's father Stan quickly became a second father to Pies. The elder Zielinski never called Pies by his nickname, though. Stan always referred to him as Jakub and showed the young man nothing but fatherly respect, love, and guidance. Pies became so enamored with Stan's parental attention that after his own father died, he began doing side jobs for Mr. Zielinski. Felonious jobs.

Stan Zielinski was the man who directly controlled the organized criminal activity in Edison Park. He'd taken over for his own father, Emi Zielinski, after the older man dropped dead of a heart attack in the late 1980s.

Stan did report to a Chicago Mob, or Outfit, lieutenant named Donny Noretti who was based in Oak Park. Noretti ran the show for the extreme North Side of Chicago and also the entire North Shore area for the Outfit—and business was good.

As long as he paid his percentage to the Outfit, Stan Zielinski had the interference-free run of the Edison Park area mostly due to the fact that the majority of residents in the neighborhood, excepting some of the Irish cops and firefighters living there, were of similar eastern European ancestry.

Stan Zielinski enjoyed familial shorthand with the residents and earned their trust through the utilization of both good deeds and intimidation, depending on which was needed at the time.

The Zielinskis were seemingly trusted business people in their community. They gladly sponsored peewee football, Little League baseball, and youth basketball teams each and every year. It was their admission fee for appearing socially legitimate. And even if a slim majority of the residents understood what the Zielinskis were truly up to, they looked the other way out of fear.

After escaping Communism with his wife and infant son from the Wawer section of Warsaw, Poland, in 1963, Emi Zielinski started a little off-brand insurance agency on Northwest Highway as a criminal front shortly after his arrival in the United States. The elder Zielinski would've liked to start his life in the United States a bit farther southeast on busy Milwaukee Avenue, the long-established home of other recent emigrants from his Warsaw neighborhood, but that territory was already being controlled by another Warsaw resident who had come to the states thirty years prior.

Emi knew the insurance business inside and out, as his son Stan would. Their legitimate association with their chosen industry was a stroke of genius of the elder Zielinski's. The more they served their community with insurance products, the less the police would suspect them of any wrongdoing.

But that's where the insurance expertise stopped. Young Bast Zielinski, who didn't remember his grandfather because the man had died when Bast was an infant, would never have any real working knowledge of the industry. He found the insurance business mind-numbingly boring. Bast was now making a great living without the cloak of being a legitimate businessman, and he was fine with that.

Emi Zielinski, and then Stan after him, was an expert in locating potential moneyed homeowners and businesses to burglarize. That was the family specialty. The Zielinskis were very good at gleaning pertinent data from insurance applications and making judgment calls on whom to burgle and when—never overusing any fruitful orchard they happened upon.

But they did their most inspired work burglarizing files of other insurance agents' offices that were located in their Outfit-approved area of operation—where they would learn who was worth what, how much life insurance this man had, which woman had recently purchased an expensive piece of jewelry, etc., etc. Business was good.

The Zielinski men never did the actual burglaries themselves, not after Stan had been in the family business for a few years, anyway. This was Stan's organizational innovation in their chosen field, which changed some of the working standards and added another layer of protection to the ones operating at the top of the food chain.

They hired out for the dirty work so that the Zielinskis would not be the ones at the scene of an active burglary if the police ever showed up. Sure, Bast Zielinski went on jobs from time to time, but he acted only as a lookout and drove a vehicle not used in the actual burglary itself. Bast would never physically operate within the confines of the building the burglary team was taking care of.

A decade or so ago, the cops were hot on Stan Zielinski. The investigators, part of a joint property-crimes, task-force group of suburban and Chicago PD detectives, were finally able to identify Stan as the possible man in charge of the burglary crew, and they applied so much pressure that two of his soldiers turned state's evidence on him. Stan Zielinski wound up doing a brief jolt at Menard Correctional Center and paying a hefty fine for feloniously receiving stolen property. It was the only charge that the police could pin on him at the time. When Stan was released, he forged the new operational methods that he still used.

In the beginning of the Zielinskis' burglary dynasty, gathering information on which places to plunder was incredibly easy because there was no real computer tracking of any sort. They could operate with impunity. As computerized security measures were added to data systems, finding choice businesses and homes to strike became a more nuanced pursuit.

A burglary crew wouldn't want to incriminate themselves in any way, so various methods were employed so that money would still be made and the proper percentage would continue to flow up the chain of command. It was always healthier for the Zielinski crew to remain in the good graces of their Outfit overlords. But they were top earners in their field, so the Outfit mostly left them alone to do what they did best.

Stan Zielinski learned through the trial and, mostly, error of being caught and incarcerated that the crew needed to cover their tracks as best they could without getting pinched. And they did just that by utilizing young men with no serious criminal records, men like Pies, to apply for and get jobs that required them to be inside of businesses and homes—trades like carpet cleaners, window washers, dog sitters, and, yes, Pies's specialty of appliance repair. Occupations that allowed for firsthand reconnaissance of the properties they intended to burgle.

Bast Zielinski and fellow crew members Andy Peters and Crick Mazur, both Edison Park born and bred, had all been arrested from time to time for petty crimes—property damage, DUIs, misdemeanor assaults, and the like—but nothing too serious.

The exception was Crick, the one crew member with an actual burglary arrest—which was later tossed when an Outfit lawyer named DiNizio got him cleared on a technicality. The technicality being that the prosecutor in charge of the case needed a new and rather expensive kitchen-remodel job. The other minor offenses the crew members got pinched for were not crimes they ever served hard time for. There was nothing on Bast's, Crick's, or Andy's records that would keep them from getting hired by a service industry company. However, they would be excluded from working at a secure police and fire 9-1-1 communications center.

That's where Pies came in.

Pies was the only one on the burglary crew with a spotless record.

If it weren't for his stupidly flippant remark several months ago to Bast about how cool it would be to have an insider at the new North-comm center to feed the Zielinski crew alarms-out-of-service information, Pies wouldn't be in his currently precarious position.

The Zielinski's crew was extremely professional—never rushing into jobs they didn't have topflight recon on. Sometimes it would take months to set up even the simplest heists. But they juggled so many jobs in the air at one time that the cash never ceased to flow.

Pies, Andy, and Crick, and sometimes Bast as their lookout driver, worked, alternatively, as the burglary crews' surveillance teams—letting the boss know where the good stuff was being kept—and as the burglars themselves.

The Zielinskis were geniuses in their lucrative criminal pursuits. If one of the crew members worked the legitimate job to gather the initial intelligence, that same crew member would never be on the team that actually pulled off the burglary of that same property. This way there was always plausible deniability in play. "Gee, officer, I was at the big fancy house cleaning the drapes last week, is all. I don't know nothing." Pies and the others would hold a few of these part-time, service-industry jobs at once for better recon coverage.

And Pies was so quiet and unassuming in most of his personal and professional interactions that people who would come in contact with him would forget about him mere moments after the interaction. He was seemingly a docile human chameleon.

Pies Jakubowski was also an expert at keeping up with security systems technology. If the systems he encountered seemed impenetrable, Pies had a way of crafting an ingenious workaround that would allow a crew member to get in and out of a building in minutes—even if the alarm was activated. The majority of his workarounds were rudimentary, involving physical obstructions and misdirections. Misdirections like bringing along Andy's sister's leashed and über-friendly black Labrador retriever to a burglary so that if Pies or the others were spotted, the police would think twice about stopping a friendly guy out walking his loveable black Lab. The obstructions employed were very low-tech and mostly involved wearing pull-down balaclava and rubber gloves and spray-painting the lens of any surveillance camera angled toward their field of operation.

There was so much genius in the simplicity of Pies's planning. So much so that Bast would, more times than not, try to take credit for Pies's work so as to impress his own father. Stan Zielinski deeply loved his son but was aware that Pies was probably the one responsible for most of the brainwork going on in the Zielinski burglary crew.

Pies was smarter, Bast was tougher.

Many a time would come when Stan knew that he would need brawn over brain, so his son, Bast, was very much appreciated.

Over the years, a slow-moving rift opened in Bast's mind between himself and Pies. It was a chasm that Pies would never fully recognize, or truly comprehend. And all of the strife was a direct result of Bast's jealously over the more intelligent man's aptitude, and his own father's appreciation for that prowess.

3

DRESSED IN a dark-blue, button-up, long-sleeved shirt and the
same pants he'd worn to work, Pies quick-stepped down the
stairs from the second floor of his tiny brick Georgian-style home
and moved through the plainly decorated living room—white-on-
off-white with tan furnishings—through the dining area and into
the miniscule similarly decorated kitchen.

He stood and seesawed between the fridge and the cabinet next
to the sink to gather the ingredients for a quick ham sandwich on
rye with stone-ground mustard. He dispensed a glass of water from
the sink tap and took a long gulp.

On the small kitchen table was a hodgepodge of papers, pens, envelopes, and stamps. Two passports and two passport-renewal applications were center table—one application with Pies's legal name on
top, the other inscribed with the name Wicktoria Chlebek.

Next to the applications were two separate money orders. On top
of the applications were simple headshot photos of Pies and of a
stunningly beautiful twenty-eight-year old woman with dark hair,
crystal-blue eyes, and a gorgeous jawline.

Pies's expression in his photo was staid and plain. Wicktoria Chlebek had the hint of a flirtatious smirk on her face—showing a deep
dimple on her left cheek. Mischievous. Each photo had a dull white
background with the individual face perfectly centered in the frame.

Opened next to the applications were Pies's and Wicktoria's expiring passports—both with their teenaged photos displayed. Alongside the passport items there was a long handwritten list of business names and addresses—the ones that Pies secretly had taken from the alarms-out-of-service log at his new job. A few of the names on the list had been circled.

After Pies slapped the sandwich together, he began to stuff it into his mouth and chew as quickly as he could. He was late for a meeting at Zielinski's Insurance Agency on Northwest Highway.

As he chewed he looked over the passport applications to make sure they were filled out completely and correctly. He took the last bite from his sandwich, sloshed down another chug of water from his glass, picked up a pen that was resting on the table next to the pile of papers, signed his passport application, and pushed it aside.

Pies took in a couple of deep breaths, shook his hands vigorously, and switched the pen from his right hand to his left. He leaned over Wicktoria's old passport and studied her signature for a moment and then effortlessly signed her application in very different handwriting than his own—one with a more feminine flourish. The signature didn't quite perfectly match Wicktoria's teenage version, but it didn't matter. Signatures change over time.

Pies shoved all of the application materials—old passports, papers, and photos—into their respective pre-addressed manila envelopes, sealed them, and placed a row of self-adhesive postage stamps on each. The return address on each envelope was the same one Pies had written on each application: 101 Seymour Street, Unit 7, Half Moon Bay, CA 94019.

He'd never been to the street on the applications and envelopes, or Half Moon Bay, or even California, for that matter, but a few days ago he finalized an agreement, online, to rent the condo on Seymour Street for the next six months. He overnighted a money order the day he finalized the agreement to make sure there were no hiccups. He could've used an electronic transferring service to move the money for the apartment, but lately he had been attempting to limit his electronic footprint as much as he could. The California apartment was his now.

He took one last swig of water, picked up and folded the list of deactivated alarms, and wedged the paper into his back left pocket.

Envelopes in hand, Pies exited the house. But as soon as the door closed and locked, the latch flipped back open, and Pies pushed his way into the kitchen. He had forgotten something.

He placed the envelopes on the kitchen table and made his way to the basement doorway. He bounded down the creaky steps and into a cramped finished area that was chock-full of electronic equipment, new and old alike, computers and monitors. The image frozen on the main twenty-six-inch monitor on his workbench was that of the alarms-out-of-service log page, an image taken from the button camera while Pies was at the 9-1-1 communications center.

Pies sidestepped past a door that opened into a closet-sized darkroom that was filled with shelves, old cameras, boxes of unused 35mm film, jugs of development chemicals, and development trays. The room hadn't seen a lot of use since his father's demise.

Pies shuffled his way to another workbench—ten feet away—that was crammed with hand-tools, wires, spools of nylon filament, and other electronic repair items. There were wall-mounted storage units on all three sides of this workbench. The storage units were comprised of row after row of see-through plastic drawers, which extended from floor to ceiling and were filled with fasteners and electrical and plumbing parts. Pies's father had maintained what was basically a mini parts center for any home improvement job he needed to tackle. He always purchased way more supplies than he needed for the jobs, and he kept the overage in the neat, little shelved box system for later use.

Once Pies moved to this workbench area, he picked up a cell-phone-sized device that had a two-foot wire and button camera attached by a USB connection.

He undid his pants and gently slipped the mini-DVR operating system into his front right pocket. Then he proceeded to snake the wire with the tiny button camera attached at the end through a hole on the inside of his pants pocket. He fished the wire under his shirt and refastened his pants. He then worked the wire under his shirt and popped the minute camera through the buttonhole three down from the top of his shirt. He had removed the original shirt button and cut a small slit in the fabric closest to his skin so that the camera fit better. He pushed his hands downward and smoothed the fabric of his shirt and bolted up the stairs.

Only now was Pies truly ready for his meeting at Zielinski's Insurance Agency on Northwest Highway.

4

Stan Zielinski was fifty-five years old and had a thick mop of honey-brown hair. He was in incredible physical shape. Dressed in an expensive, black-with-neon-green-accents, athletic getup, he glided along like a trim high school kid out for a brisk afternoon jog. He ran south along the Metra tracks on Olmsted Avenue and passed the row of bars and eateries that were situated across from the tiny brick Edison Park train station. Then he accelerated his pace just as he turned right onto Oliphant Avenue and crossed over the tracks.

A slow-moving BMW honked playfully, and Stan gave a pleasant wave.

He angled right again and cut through the postage-stamp-sized park on the other side of the railroad tracks, and as he emerged from the park, he could see a sixty-year-old, stern-looking woman staring at him as she stood in her yard on North Shore Avenue. From the garden implements scattered about her lawn, he figured that she was elbow-deep in yard work, but the woman had suddenly lost her interest in the task. She held a metal rake in her hand and flung an ireful, laser-like look through Stan as he glided along and approached.

Stan slowed his pace, began to walk, and waved, "Hello, Mrs. Chlebek. How are you? Beautiful day."

Milena Chlebek was in no mood for Stan this day—or any other day of late. She knew exactly what he was about. Even more so, she knew precisely what Stan's son Bast was into, as well.

"Tell him to leave her be," she said, rather forcefully, nearly spitting the words out, in her clipped, Polish-accented English.

Stan shrugged and tried on a little smile that had no chance of working on the woman. "They're grown people, what can we do?"

"We look other way most times for you, you know. Don't make the waves, as you say. But he's a married man, for God's sake. *Dupek* he is. *Dupek!*"

"There's no need for that, Mrs. Chlebek," said Stan, who resumed a slow jog. He now wanted nothing more than to be inside his own home, located only a few houses in from Ozanam Avenue, and far enough away from the angry woman with the rake in her hand.

"The heart wants, Mrs. Chlebek," he said over his shoulder.

But Stan knew that if someone like Milena Chlebek was unhappy, it could come back to bite him on the ass. Hard.

Stan Zielinski operated the criminal enterprises in Edison Park, sure, but Milena and a few other strong women like her—all first-generation immigrants—would stop looking the other way and quite possibly impede him and his crew, if and when their family members were involved, or if the women had even the whiff of their family members being in danger of any involvement in all things Zielinski.

Wicktoria "Vicki" Chlebek, Milena and Blaze Chlebek's daughter, was just such a possibly, potentially, peripherally involved person. Vicki and Bast Zielinski had a thing going on—very casual, extremely sexual—and Milena was not happy about it, especially since, as she had stated, Stan's son Bast was married with a couple of kids of his own.

An angry Milena Chlebek could simply plant a few choice words into the ears of various neighbors and cause untold difficulties for Stan. Suddenly the Zielinski crew would no longer have access to the backrooms and basements of some of the empty neighborhood-owned buildings along Northwest Highway, in which they most times needed to temporarily store the stolen goods they procured.

The sixty-year-old woman was one of the legitimate thought leaders in the Edison Park neighborhood. She had been for years. Milena was instrumental in petitioning and securing from the city of Chicago the ordinance that limited the annoying street parking that used to crowd the area. The ordinance involved the issuing of special parking permits for local residents so that they could resume parking in front of their own properties. If a car without a permit took a spot reserved for a resident, the vehicle would be immediately towed.

With the influx of even more eateries, taverns, and bars in the 1990s, Edison Park had to do something to maintain the quaint, cozy, tree-lined residential area south of the train station. The parking situation had gotten so bad that on many occasions the Chlebek family and their immediate neighbors would find the parked cars of bar and restaurant patrons blocking their driveways and sometimes, incredibly enough, even parked in their private driveways.

These days the patrons of the late-night taverns and eateries were guided toward paid parking lots and metered spots along the railroad tracks. If they chose not to comply, their cars would be towed with happy and expensive malice.

Stan knew that a pissed-off Milena Chlebek could easily plant nuggets of vital information about his dealings into the ears of Chicago PD members, too, some of whom lived on her block, and for that reason as well, he wanted very much not to make her angry.

*

"YOU DON'T flaunt it, okay. You just don't do that," said a concerned Stan Zielinski as he paced in the living room of his home. He shifted his direction to a coffee table and retrieved a towel to wipe his sweaty forehead.

The house—four bedrooms, three baths, with a gourmet, French-country-influenced kitchen—was very tastefully decorated, but not too flashy. The décor was subdued with mellow sage and milk chocolate colors on the walls. This was not the same small Georgian-style house that had been across from Pies's childhood home.

Stan had decorated the place himself shortly after his wife passed away from cancer three years earlier, when the Zielinskis moved a few blocks and literally to the other side of the Metra rail tracks, into this grander home on a side streets off Ozanam Avenue—right across the Chicago border from Park Ridge.

Stan Zielinski loved to poke fun at the suburb of Park Ridge, even though he shopped for groceries there and frequented the beautiful Pickwick Theater from time to time. He'd often say to his friends and cohorts, "They consider themselves so superior that they changed Ozanam Avenue on their side of the street to the hoity-toity Canfield Avenue. What the hell is a Canfield?"

Whether accurate or not, Stan liked to refer to folks who lived in the suburb across Ozanam Avenue as "cake eaters." He would always add to that invective, "Those cake eaters and their buying habits keep my lights on, though! They buy, I take." And he would laugh and laugh with anyone within earshot of his often-used insult.

His son Bast Zielinski was younger, of course, at twenty-nine years of age, and a much larger man than his father. Standing six feet four, weighing 230 pounds, Bast was not one to be trifled with—especially if you were familiar with his line of work, or his temper. Bast was also something of a fashion devotee. His hair was expertly coiffed, and he always wore the latest and most expensive clothing trends. He looked like a cross between a preened boy-band member and a beefy NFL linebacker. He sat in an antique wooden chair near the fireplace in the living room and said, "Rebecca won't find out, Pops. It's okay. It's good."

"It's good, huh? You have Noretti coming here now for a pickup and an update on how you're doing, and even he's hearing things about you. One of his guys overheard a regular at the Olmsted Inn talking shit about you and the girl. These are things that cause concern. Noretti was already worried about you taking over, but if he thinks that you're not ready, well. You'll be working nights from here on out, you get me?"

Bast leaned heavily against the squeaky chair back and let out a breath of exasperation. He wanted to keep his newly acquired reins of their criminal enterprise and not have to go back to working the strange hours of a burglary crew member, most of that time spent as a lookout. He liked the feeling of power that washed over him as he ran the operation from the back office of the insurance agency building.

"I don't give a shit if you keep something on the side, just keep it low-key is what I'm saying. We don't need the one raising your kids to find out about the other one with the rack. Things will go to hell quick if that happens. You understand?"

"I got it. It's not a problem, I swear."

"Because if…"

"I got it, Pops!"

Stan's eyes locked on and squinted at the larger Zielinski. Stan might be smaller, but he would "go" at the drop of a hat—even if to pummel his own son.

Bast saw the look in Stan's eyes. He softened and added, "I'll be careful. I will."

"Sebastian, I've been worried about you, okay? First the coke…"

"I'm done with that."

"And now the Chlebek girl. She's trouble, you know. I know that you do. Should Pies run the show to give you time to sort this out? He's good and he knows what to do. Pies can—"

Bast rose quickly to his feet. "Pies? Pies?"

"He's been good for us. Look at this thing he's got now. The dispatcher thing. That's smart thinking on his part. Let Pies run the show for a while and then you take it all back when things settle."

Stan's remarks hit Bast hard. It hurt him to the core. His lips tightened as he considered a response.

With a correct Polish inflection, he barked the true pronunciation of "Pies."

"P-yes? The dog. You want the dog to run the show? Pops…Pops, I made him take that new job. That was my idea. Give me a goddamn break."

"Bast?"

Bast settled some and took a few breaths. "I'm done with partying."

"But is she? You can't be around that stuff. I know, Bast. You know that I know."

The low muffled thump as a car door closed outside, and then another, stopped their conversation. They both peered through the front windows as two stocky men walked from a large BMW and up the steps to the front door of the house.

Stan gave Bast's muscular shoulder a gentle squeeze. "Okay, all right. It's your show. Let's move on to the business at hand, how's that sound? Should I call you 'Sport' now to make it all better?"

Bast smirked. The word "sport" was an inside joke between him and his father to calm things down when they got heated. He nodded just as the doorbell chimed.

"You got it, Sport," said Stan.

Stan walked over and yanked the door open, and Donny Noretti, forty-five years old, thickset with an honest face and trusting eyes, slid into the living room, followed by Luke, his tall and muscular bodyguard and driver. Luke was a quiet, twenty-seven-year-old man with all the mannerisms of a bird of prey on the hunt.

Noretti said, "What's the matter?" He leaned back a little and took in Stan first, and then Bast. "Whoa, it is fucking tense in here." As Noretti plopped into a chair near the window, he motioned to his body man. "Luke, get the thing and meet me in the car."

Stan turned, tossed his towel on the coffee table, and grabbed up a plain brown paper bag with the top sloppily rolled down tight. He handed it to the silent Luke, and the dangerous man exited.

Noretti studied both the Zielinski men for a beat or two. Finally.

"Crick and Andy? Are they still in? Or are they out now? Would hate to lose them. They're good."

Bast glanced at Stan and said, "Well, they're not in right now. The cops don't have a lot. It's skimpy, at best, so I'm guessing DiNizio will get them cleared in a few weeks. He's already filed a motion to get the charges dropped on a lack of evidence."

Noretti seemed concerned and added, "Let's hope so."

"They got snagged two blocks from the..." Bast began.

"Like a plumbing and kitchen fixtures place, right?" Noretti interrupted, and Bast yielded immediately and became silent. "Whoa, some of those fixtures run up there, believe me, I know. We just re-did the kitchen and first floor bath at home."

"They had nothing on them except a screwdriver when the cops grabbed them up," said Bast. "No merch at all. Nothing."

Stan added, "Pies dropped the stuff into a clothing donation box after he saw the cops closing in. We have a master key to those."

"Wait it out, go back later, sure," said Noretti. "So what went wrong?"

"Pies wound up getting away clean, but some asshole rookie saw Crick and Andy parked a block from the plumbing and kitchen supply place while Pies was inside, yanked 'em from the car, and ran Crick's name," Bast explained. "With his prior for B&E, they poked around the car and found the damned screwdriver in the trunk."

"Why were they in the car together, that's what I don't get?" asked Noretti.

Bast could only look at the Outfit boss. He had no response, because he knew that Andy and Crick had made a sloppy move. They had screwed up, and it cost them.

Noretti sensed that Bast was already beating himself up, so he moved on. "*Merda.* Okay, so Crick and Andy are sidelined for now. But we stay in business with the dog and his new 9-1-1 job, right? Talk about impeccable timing, huh?"

A proud Stan said, "Northcomm opened up for us just in time. Bast set that up."

Bast added, "I have a new guy stepping up for the heavy lifting until Crick and Andy get cleared. He's one of us. Crick and Andy will have to lay low for a while."

"Good. That'll be okay," said Noretti. "Nice work, Bast."

"The dog went back the next day with that key and got the merch, 150 boxes of faucet sets, so we have that in the pipeline. It was all that German-made stuff."

Noretti said, "We've gotten them before, I remember. That's great. Expensive, yes?"

"You cleared about fifteen," Bast said to Noretti.

Noretti motioned with his thumb outside, as if referring to the paper bag that just went out the door, and said, "Nice. Look at you. Stepping up here in your old man's retirement. Good thing, because this sack of shit probably wouldn't have lasted another day on this green earth. Look at this sick son of a bitch." Noretti leaned forward and playfully patted Stan's taut and toned belly. They all laughed.

As he laughed, though, Bast caught sight out the front window where a petite and pretty twenty-eight-year-old woman was frantically chasing a cute, little five-year-old girl in a dress up the sidewalk and toward Stan's house.

"Ah. Donny, give me a second, would you?"

Noretti looked a question at Stan, but said to Bast, "Sure. No problem."

Bast opened the front door and loped down the steps as the little girl, his daughter, who the family called Itty-Bitty, an adorable mini-me version of her beautiful mother, jumped happily into his arms.

"Daddy," screamed the little girl with utter delight.

"You look beautiful today, my Itty-Bitty." He held the little girl tightly and said to the pretty woman, "Hey, what's going on?"

Rebecca Zielinski, Bast's wife of six years, gave him a deadpan stare and said, "I went to the basement to get the clothes out of the dryer, and this. She knows where you're going and she just takes off."

Bast gently chucked Itty-Bitty's chin with his forefinger and thumb and said, "Did you do that? You have to stay at home with Mommy, honey. You'll get hurt out on the street."

"But I wanted to be with you," said Itty-Bitty as she tucked her face into Bast's neck and snuggled against him.

Rebecca let out a breath, shook her head, and said, "I have a hair appointment anyway. So she's all yours."

Bast leaned over, placed Itty-Bitty back on her feet, and saw that Luke eyed him from the driver's seat of Noretti's luxury car. Luke never bothered to even look away.

"I should only be two hours," said Rebecca.

Bast raised his gaze to his wife and said, "Honey, I have a meeting. I have work I have to do, you know that. They're waiting inside right now, and then I have to see the guys at the agency."

"Mother has Sebastian, so you don't have to worry about him. Keep her at the agency, and I'll be by after my appointment." When Bast didn't respond, she continued, "Bast?"

"Okay. Okay." Bast gently grabbed Itty-Bitty up in his arms again. "You're going to help Daddy at his work today."

Itty-Bitty squealed, "Yay, Daddy's work. Bye, Mommy."

"I'll see you soon, sweetie," said Rebecca as she turned and walked away.

Bast waved to his wife and then caught sight of Luke, again, as he stared at him from the car. Bast and Itty-Bitty made their way up the steps and into Stan's house.

As he opened the door, Stan could be heard from inside, "There's our Itty-Bitty. Come here, baby. Look at you? You're so pretty today."

Bast walked inside and the front door closed, which immediately shut off any further sounds from inside the house.

5

Naomi Gott tugged the windbreaker she had worn into the neon-lit building a bit tighter to cover the stitched badge on her golf shirt. She didn't want to zip it completely to the top because with so many warm bodies roaming about, and the excess heat they produced, it was too damned hot in the place. But she didn't want to chance having any of the employees or other gamblers at the casino on River Road know where she worked, or that she arrived here at the five-dollar slot machines directly from her job twenty minutes earlier. People with gambling troubles who work in any branch of law enforcement can be easy targets for extortionists.

The trip to this particular space was something she did nearly every working day. The staff at the casino knew her as a regular—they just didn't know her name or what she did for a living.

The din of the casino's electronic games did nothing to help Naomi's newly minted shitty disposition—the result of having only a fifteen-dollar credit remaining on the five-dollar machine she was perched in front of.

Naomi was not a "bet 1 credit on a maximum 3 credits machine" type of player. She would go for the maximum each and every time in the hopes her chances of winning would rise. Naomi was a serious slots gambler, and, being a serious gambler, she knew massive payoffs came only when you bet big. She hated this attribute of her own personality because it had caused so much pain for her and her family over the years, but she also did little to fight her urges. When she was hunkered down in front of a machine, like she was presently, her usual sweet exterior gave way to an inner demon who would screw anyone over for just one more press of the "play" button.

The machine she played was linked to a larger network that could possibly pay off on a progressive jackpot currently worth over a million dollars. And again, to win the full jackpot, you had to bet the maximum credits allowed.

The fingers of her right hand hovered over the "play" button, and she took in the sight of the slot machine's faceplate. The goofy frog cartoon characters plastered all over the machine seemed to mock her this day. So far she had shoved three hundred dollars into the thing in the past twenty minutes with only two winning spins to show for it. She was so much in the zone, though, that she hadn't even noticed the thirty or so players seated all around her and the hundreds of others milling about the large casino. But they were all keeping to themselves, too.

All she could focus on now was that she needed three tux-wearing, frog cartoon characters to line up in a row to win it all.

Three tuxes and she'd be golden.

With her decent salary from the Northcomm 9-1-1 Center, Naomi could afford a nice place to live in the city or the suburbs, but her habits here at the casino on River Road precluded her from living her life to the fullest.

At first glance, Naomi was an attractive and confident-looking woman with a job in which she literally saved lives. But deep down, she was damaged. If asked, she could easily pinpoint the source of her dark inner thoughts and corrosive personal habits, but she chose to emotionally swallow back the memories of her abuse at the hands of her older cousins.

The female family members, both teenagers at the time, had been entrusted to watch over young Naomi during the summer months when all of their parents were away at their jobs. It all began when Naomi was only five years old. The sexually abusive activities they forced her to do were so wrong, and so disturbing, that they confounded her even to this day. Eventually, the older cousins were caught in the act, but they were never criminally charged—and these days, the shitty memories of her past early summers ruined for Naomi what was supposed to be the best season of the year.

There was no denying it. The abuse that Naomi suffered early on in her life was the direct reason for her quest to work in law enforcement. In her mind, she knew that she could probably no longer help herself, but maybe someday she'd have a hand in saving someone else in a similar situation.

She also realized that her gambling problems were the direct result of her efforts to financially win her way out of the job that continued to remind her of her childhood abuse.

Naomi currently resided alone in a mobile-home park just off of Touhy Avenue on the northern edge of O'Hare airport. The noise-cancelling headphones she wore inside to retain her sanity from the awful aircraft blare outside were probably more expensive than the home itself.

As she lowered her hand to press the button that would bet her last fifteen dollars, Naomi closed her eyes and saw images of what the million dollar winnings could bring to her life. The fast moving images of a nice house and the trappings of financial security calmed her.

But flashes of Jakub "Pies" Jakubowski began to ping about in her mind. He'd been bouncing around in there a lot since they first met a few days ago. Naomi wasn't exactly sure why she'd become so enamored by the man with the brown hair and the hazel eyes. He was attractive enough, yes, but not her normal type. A stocky, muscular man usually caught her eye. Her ex-husband, a current Chicago police officer, had the build she normally desired. Jason, her wonderful four-year-old son they had together, was already molded in his father's image, very sturdy for his young age and larger than the other kids.

Naomi had been awarded custody of Jason but decided it would be best, at this time, if the boy lived with her ex-husband's parents. The ex-in-laws were recent retirees and extremely kind and caring —her ex-mother-in-law was a former school administrator, and her ex-father-in-law had been a high-ranking Chicago PD detective.

As Naomi sat there, eyes closed, fingers splayed out, and hovered over the slot machine "play" button, she thought that there was more to her trainee than his decent looks. He had a gentleness she'd not experienced with any other man—especially one she had to work so closely with.

They were so physically connected, seated knee to knee throughout their eight-hour shifts, that Naomi had the urge to lean in and hold the gentle man and to kiss him. At first, she couldn't even fully explain the urges to her own self. She was confused by the attraction. And then the sheer immediacy of the attraction confused her even further.

But then it came to her.

Jakub "Pies" Jakubowski was also damaged in some way. She was sure of it. She knew that if he allowed her to go into a deeper conversation, they'd learn that they were both in the same emotional boat. Fellow travelers, as it were. They were meant for one another.

It wouldn't be appropriate for her to date a new employee, so she had to fight the urge to be more than a trainer to the twenty-eight-year-old Jakub. In fact, it was strictly forbidden by Northcomm rules and regulations to fraternize with a subordinate.

But Naomi had skirted rules before.

Her life became quite complicated when she began an affair with her supervisor, a married police lieutenant, at her old job in Evanston. Once found out by the command of the department, it was Naomi who was forced out, not the supervisor.

She left, officially, under good circumstances so that she could secure another job, but it was small solace for the embarrassment caused to her reputation by the affair.

Her own marriage ended soon afterward.

She mentally shook the images of Pies away and got back to the business at hand. When she stopped fantasizing about the money, her lucid mind knew that a one-million-dollar, slot-machine wind-fall, after the taxes were stripped away, was not really all that much cash to actually achieve the fantastic success images in her mind's eye. She would do okay for a while, but the remaining $600,000 af-ter taxes in ethereal fantasy money wouldn't go all that far.

If she pressed the machine's button and lost, she wouldn't have any real food in her trailer until her next paycheck—which was still a few days away. She'd have to subsist on a quarter-jar of off-brand peanut butter and stale saltine crackers.

Eyes still closed, Naomi pressed the button anyway.

When she heard the machine make a playful frog croaking sound and annoying calliope music played, she knew she had won. Nao-mi opened her eyes to see two tux-wearing frogs and a smiling frog aligned in a row. She had not won the million dollars, but the $125 she snagged was okay.

She took a long cleansing breath—reached out to press the "play" button once again—and stopped herself.

Naomi pressed the "cash out" button instead, collected her ticket, and went to retrieve her $125 at the cashier's cage.

6

Busy Northwest Highway on Chicago's far Northwest Side, with its plethora of bars, restaurants, and specialty stores, was a mere three-block walk from both Pies's home, located to the north, and Bast's house, which was near his father Stan's home, across the tracks to the south.

Bast Zielinski also paid for a little apartment, a pied-à-terre, above the Polish bakery owned by the Chlebek family. It was a cozy, one-bedroom, second-floor walk-up. Vicki Chlebek's father, Blaze, owned the brick building and ran the business on the first floor, where her mother, Milena, would work the counter from time to time, especially in the buildup to Lent when she sold the neighborhood's finest raspberry-filled paczki.

Blaze Chlebek was a master baker who always added in a bit of grain alcohol to his paczki batter. The booze wasn't for flavoring, it was a baking secret not used by the grocery-store-chain bakers—a secret that halted the hot oil the pastry was fried in from penetrating and ruining the pillow-soft interior of the sweet treat.

Bast Zielinski paid the rent at the small apartment above the bakery, but the lease was in Vicki's name and she stayed there some of the time when not living at home with her parents. "Some of the time" meaning the occasions when she and Bast would rendezvous, which happened to be more often than not of late. What better location to hook up in than an apartment one block from Zielinski's Insurance Agency—and a few blocks from home?

Vicki Chlebek, who would proudly proclaim to anyone within earshot that she was not the "settling down type," was the object of affection for nearly all the young men who grew up alongside her in Edison Park. It was Bast, being the well-heeled boss's kid, who won her affections as they grew into adulthood.

Vicki knew Bast's wife, Rebecca—they had grown up together, as well—but she had no problem being romantically involved with the married man. She figured that Bast would never leave Rebecca. "That's fine with me," Vicki would say to anyone who inquired about her romantic affairs. "I can't be domesticated." Or so she would say.

Pies half-jogged along at a rapid pace toward Northwest Highway, late for his meeting at Zielinski's Insurance Agency. In his anxious state of mind, he no longer even recognized the beauty that was all around him—the tree-lined side streets with the dappled sunshine illuminating the well-maintained homes that dotted those streets and the people who milled about, the families who made Edison Park a socially solid, safe, city neighborhood. Because of his life's turmoil it had been a while since Pies had even noticed how lucky he was to be living in a wonderful urban area like this.

As he rounded the corner onto the busy thoroughfare, he nearly bumped into an elderly man who was out for a stroll. "Hiya, kid," said the friendly old man, but Pies ignored him and kept moving.

On the wide sidewalk, for as far as he could see, were retail business signs hanging over the doorways. A lively mix of young and older residents alike walked along doing their daily business.

Pies was very familiar with all of the buildings in the business district of Edison Park. He knew the retail spaces, the basements, and especially the rooftops that he and his childhood acquaintances had used as secret pathways to elude any trouble that bubbled up on the sidewalks below.

It was almost always trouble that they had brewed up themselves. Like on warm summer nights when a young Pies and his cohorts, led by Bast, would spit from the rooftops and onto the pedestrians walking below. After spitting, they'd scream out, "It's raining." It was a stupidly juvenile, and disgusting, move. But they fit the bill as disgusting juveniles. For the majority of those same kids, namely Crick, Andy, and Bast, even after growing into adulthood, the needle on the shit-heel meter didn't swing all that much.

The dominant neighborhood nationalities were represented by the various colors of their respective homeland flags, most prominently Polish, Irish, and Italian. The proudly displayed colors were visible in the signage that was attached above the doorways of the 1920s brick commercial buildings along busy Northwest Highway.

Among the most popular places there were Polish bakeries and restaurants, Italian bakeries and restaurants, and a few authentic Irish pubs, too.

The name of Northwest Highway always seemed like a misnomer to Pies. It didn't look anything like what most people would imagine a "highway" to be. The main street in the neighborhood was simply a two-lane Chicago city street with space to accommodate parallel parking on each side of the thoroughfare.

When Pies got close enough to recognize the Zielinski's Insurance Agency's white sign with red lettering hanging over the sidewalk one block away, he observed Bast as he drove up in his dark-blue BMW and parked. Bast got out of his car but kept his eyes on Pies, who now slowed to a casual walk. If Bast was late, Pies figured there was no longer a need to rush.

Bast looked away from Pies, as if he'd never seen him before. He opened the passenger door on his car and helped his daughter from her seat. He took the cute little girl by the hand and led her across the wide sidewalk and up to his office. He unlocked the door as Pies strode past the front of the agency. Bast and his daughter shuffled inside the business and the door locked from inside—all without a word spoken, and all by predetermined design.

That was the way these meetings played out. Usually, no two crew members would enter the insurance agency space from the front door at the same time, in case they were under surveillance by the police.

Pies casually opened the front door of the kitschy Broz Brothers Shoes store located directly next to the insurance agency and looked eastward.

A tall and dangerous-looking man with ropey muscles leaned with his back against the plate-glass window of the next business down, a signage outlet to the east of the crappy shoe store. The man twisted his neck from side to side and loosened up. When Pies disappeared from his view and inside the shoe store, the dangerous-looking man pushed away from the window, turned to his left, opened the signage outlet's door, and stepped inside the business.

Once in the shoe store, Pies's nose was assaulted by the smells of dust, sweat, and new leather. The shoe store, which appeared to not have been updated since the 1970s, was owned by a chubby sixty-five-year-old man, who was presently on all fours in front of an eighty-year-old woman who was trying on some sensible shoes. The owner looked away immediately after he recognized Pies. He was paid by the Zielinskis to allow crew members access to his back room, but that didn't mean he had to socialize with Pies, or whoever else encroached on his business.

Pies walked past another elderly woman in her seventies who had a single shoe in her hand. "I'd like these in a 7," she said to Pies, but when Pies ignored her and continued to the back room, she became perturbed. "Sir? You, there. Young man."

The back of the store was a dark and squared-off storage area. To the right was a metal door that led to the signage company, and then there was another metal door to the left.

Pies ducked between a couple of tall racks of shoeboxes and up to the battered, black metal door on the left wall and knocked once. The door was opened by Bast.

"Hey, let's do this," said Bast.

Pies slipped into the back room of the brightly lit space, and Bast closed the door. Bast was temporarily housing some inventory of his own, out of view of the public. Stacks of boxes with the fruit-related logo of a high-end computer company dotted the space.

When Pies noticed the boxes, Bast said, "The new kid's work. Nice, huh? Mostly tablets, but he grabbed a few desktop models in there too. Snatched as much as he could hold in his junked-out car."

The back room of the insurance agency was the same size as the shoe store's space—about twenty-five-by-twenty-five-feet—with a white metal door that led to the alley and a closed wooden door that led to the office area out front. There was a small bathroom in the corner with a toilet, sink, and a rudimentary shower stall inside.

The wooden door opened and Itty-Bitty stuck her pretty little face into the back room, "Daddy, I want to play with my babies."

The insurance agency portion in the front of the retail space was as sparse as could be. It was outfitted with two metal desks and faux-leather 1990s chairs. On the left wall out front were three pea-green-colored filing cabinets, and on the right, a copy machine—also a '90s model.

Passing pedestrians who happened to take a peek inside the office, which was usually closed these days, would think they were looking into a twenty-five-year-old, business-related time capsule.

Bast shifted over to a tall metal cabinet, opened the door, and revealed what amounted to an upright toy box stuffed full of dolls, coloring books, etc. Bast grabbed four dolls out of the metal cabinet and crossed the room to hand them to his daughter. She smiled and took the dolls, and Bast gently closed the wooden door to the front office behind her.

"Good score," said Pies, as he apprehensively looked over the boxed merchandise.

Pies's concern was immediately picked up by Bast. He waved away his subordinate's angst with a dismissive motion. "It is cool, Pies, okay."

Pies said, "I thought you were going to take the auto-parts place first."

"Too chancy. We don't think that the kid's ready to work that close to a busy street. It was right on Dempster, Pies. Come on. He'd probably freak out. We're working this all out. Don't you worry."

In the center of the room were two freestanding walls that were eight feet apart and positioned perpendicularly to the left sidewall. The freestanding walls formed an open office space.

Bast shuffled between stolen boxes of computers and around one of the partial walls. He pointed to an uncomfortable chair opposite his dented metal desk, and Pies took a seat.

Pies surreptitiously activated the video device through the fabric of his pants pocket and quickly adjusted his button camera. Bast didn't pick up on what appeared to be a man fiddling with his shirt button.

Bast slid into his own seat on the other side of the desk—an expensive, handmade Italian-leather executive chair. He said, "We think the kid's got the nads to get good at this. He's Crick's nephew, man. Come on. He's only nineteen, but we knew he'd fit in."

Pies's expression was so filled with worry that Bast tried to alleviate his trepidation. "We'll be good until Andy and Crick get out of the pound. Won't be too much longer. DiNizio's got the motions in at Skokie. Once these bullshit charges go away, Pops says you can go back to doing what you normally do."

Pies said, "You have to tell Mr. Zielinski not to pull these off all in a row. The police will figure it out, if we move too fast..."

"Relax, P-yes. My pops wanted to make sure the kid was a good fit. The computer place was a layup. No skill or finesse required." Bast winked after the jab at Pies's usual tactics—where skill outweighed brute force. He smiled even wider when he knew that his verbal blow landed, and then he piled on. "He completely trashed the door. The dude can handle a pry bar. We'll be fine. Wait until you meet him. He's a big kid, man. Tough."

"Without the finesse," said Pies—and that's when Bast's entire body fixed in instant anger. He stared long and hard at his subordinate.

The words Bast's father had said to him earlier about Pies taking over until he cleaned up his act began to viciously ricochet around in his mind. He tried to blink the thoughts away, but that only gave him a dull, throbbing pain over his right eye.

"You're paid to do what my old man tells you to do," said Bast.

Pies's eyes narrowed, but then he nodded that he understood. He was extremely anxious—especially knowing what Bast would do to him if he discovered he was actively recording this meeting.

Pies had been recording Zielinski crew members for a while now, but the sessions accelerated the day after he was accepted by North-comm to actually start the job. That day, two weeks ago, was the moment when Pies began planning his escape from the Zielinski family and their hold on him—a grasp that he hadn't been able to shake.

Pies had grown accustomed to working front jobs for the Zielinski crew to gain access to the places they would later burglarize. But working directly under the watchful eye of North Shore police departments and their representatives was an entirely different experience. Pies was terrified every time he set foot in the Northcomm building, believing that at any moment he'd be found out, arrested, convicted, and put away for a very long time.

When Bast advised Pies that Stan had ordered him into service at the 9-1-1 communications center to grab up the information on which alarms were out of service, Pies knew the end was upon him.

The new job was such a risky venture.

So risky in fact that Pies immediately began to think that maybe, just maybe, Stan Zielinski had gotten as much use out of Pies as he could. Was the boss simply exploiting Pies's clean criminal record one last time, for one major score? Was he going to toss him aside after Pies got what Stan wanted even if Pies wasn't found out and arrested?

Pies had good reason to worry. He had firsthand knowledge of the boss tossing players aside when their usefulness was over. When they were tossed, they were tossed for good.

Pies hadn't had a personal meeting with Stan Zielinski for a few months, and every time he'd try to set one up, Bast had put the stop to it. Had Pies done something wrong? He wondered...

Pies couldn't chance not planning to get away. He needed to be ready to make a move toward safety. He had to go somewhere that the Zielinski crew wouldn't look for him.

It was crazy to think about, even for Pies, but Vietnam was a seemingly counterintuitive choice to run to. All in all, though, it was an excellent destination, if you didn't mind the heat and humidity 365 days a year.

It was a good option because Pies and Vicki Chlebek, the woman he loved, both had an affinity to travel there. They had spoken of traveling to Southeast Asia many times in the past. It was an infatuation that had begun after they enjoyed a streetwise celebrity chef—a former-heroin-addict-made-good who they both found entertaining—do a television show about the country. The celebrity chef's infatuation became Pies's and Vicki's fascination, too.

Vietnam had recently waded into a renaissance of progressive and rapid upward socioeconomic change, but the most important reason for choosing the country, other than the fact that the Zielinskis probably wouldn't think of searching for them there, was that the country had no extradition to the United States. Not yet, anyway.

If the Zielinskis did find out where Pies had run to and dropped a dime on him to the FBI about his past criminal dealings, there would be absolutely nothing anyone could do to arrest him.

Could Pies and Vicki settle there, though, without going stir-crazy after a year's time? Would there be enough Western culture in Vietnam to get by until they grew more accustomed to their new home?

Pies saved the bulk of his earnings over the past years, and he had the will and the means to accomplish his ultimate goal. But there were some very high physical, and emotional, hurdles he still had to navigate before he could make his move.

For starters, Pies had to persuade Vicki to come with him—and convincing the beautiful and free-spirited Vicki Chlebek to do that was going to be the most difficult task of all.

Although Stan Zielinski had ordered Pies to do unimaginable tasks in the past when Pies was a teen, those dangerous undertakings were all one-time deals that ceased shortly before Pies turned seventeen. After sensing that the unspeakable job he'd ordered Pies to perform had somehow changed the young man's psyche—for the worse—Stan Zielinski knew it was time to allow the kid to go back to being a regular crew member.

Even after all the travails he had been through with the Zielinski family in the past—oddly—Pies still respected Stan and felt a deep regret for what he was about to do. Stan Zielinski was a father figure to Pies. The older Zielinski always seemed to treat Pies with respect, although as Pies grew more mature, he began to sense, correctly, that Stan had simply manipulated him when he was a teenager.

The pay for the tasks performed had been very good, but there were vicious cycles of emotional and physical abuse that needed to be halted. It was time for Pies to leave his home behind.

"I need a sit-down with Mr. Zielinski. About this new job. Face to face, me and him," said Pies, as he subconsciously touched the button camera on his shirt.

Bast studied Pies for a good long beat, because for very good reasons of his own, he didn't need Pies to find out that his father was not actually the one who ordered him to take the new 9-1-1 communications gig.

Bast had a simple goal: He wanted a few major scores using the alarms-out-of-service information from the 9-1-1 center under his belt before news spread, both in his own circles and possibly in the law enforcement world, that he was the new Zielinski crew boss.

Yes, Bast wanted to exploit Pies's new gig for as much money as he could before the authorities found out and shut the operation down, but, more importantly, the new boss wanted his audacious feat of getting an insider into the new 9-1-1 communications center to be the first thing his criminal cohorts in the Outfit heard about when he was officially announced as the new boss of the Zielinski crew. It would be a rather impressive introduction. If Pies fell into police custody during the process of Bast's spectacular unveiling, so be it. Bast had no problem with the notion that he would have to permanently silence Pies before Pies could testify against him or the other crew members.

"We need to rethink this thing," said Pies.

"Sure, okay. Now we're rethinking," said Bast.

"I've always done as he's instructed, and I'm happy for what I have. I am. But this job... This job is going to backfire on Mr. Zielinski. I can sense it."

"Okay. Rethink this. You're going to do the fucking job until my pops tells you not to do the fucking job. At that point, the fucking job will be over. Clear?"

Pies froze in place for a moment, then looked at his shoes and nodded. "Okay."

Both men could hear the back alley door of the business open and close, and then a second later the shared door with the shoe store opened and closed, as well.

Andy Peters, a tall and friendly-looking ex-Chicago police officer, and Crick Mazur, the dangerous man who had been leaning against the glass of the signage store, slipped into Bast's back office area in unison from the two separate doors.

"What's the haps, my fellas," said Andy, who sported a grin that seemed to be one tooth off of sincere.

Crick stared at Pies, grinned, and then mockingly barked at him, "Woof, woof!" Crick flicked his chin in Bast's direction and continued, "The dog get us a bone?" speaking as if Pies wasn't even in the room.

Pies lowered his gaze to between his feet again and his left eyelid twitched a little. He wanted so badly to spin and hammer Crick with a hard right to the mouth—but he did nothing.

Pies had sworn off violence since the time he was a teenager. Prior to his seventeenth birthday, Pies had done some very terrible things to some equally terrible people. As his seventeenth birthday neared, he softened his approach, and he changed rather dramatically. When confronted with a potentially violent situation these days, Pies would simply ignore the person or even walk away. He had

had enough violence for one lifetime—and Bast, Andy, and Crick all knew this about him, so they would mess with him from to time to see if they could get a rise out of their docile, fellow crew member.

Pies had been holding true to his nonviolent ways for the past twelve years, and he took much pride in that accomplishment. He settled his breath and felt for the button camera to make sure it was still angled in place and filming Bast.

Andy said, "Pies, we appreciate what you're doing with the new gig at the 9-1-1 center. You know, keeping us getting paid."

"It's pretty tricky, huh, what you're doing?" asked Crick.

Andy added, "Bast made the right call on this one, that's for sure. He's a smart dude too…"

Andy stopped mid-sentence when he noticed the look that Bast was launching his way.

"What do you mean? Bast?" asked Pies. "Mr. Zielinski's running…"

Crick said, "Yeah. Stan said your new gig will be paying us for a long time to come."

Bast, without Pies ever noticing, gave Andy a "what-the-fuck?" look. He then leaned toward Pies and said, "What do you have for us today?"

Pies didn't totally catch on to what had just been said—and he pushed no further. He stood and reached into his back left pocket to retrieve the list of alarms that were out of service for that day— and when he did, another folded paper fell out and onto the floor at the same time. Pies wasn't even aware that the second piece of paper dropped, but Andy and Crick were.

Pies handed the alarms-out-of-service page to Bast, who unfolded it and read with anticipation. "Choice. Yes. Yes. Very nice," said Bast, as his eyes scanned the paper. "Two jewelry places, one with expensive women's clothes. One's a diamond outlet. Nice…"

"Like I said before, the circled ones are the places to consider first. Those five there haven't worked in days. The cops stop going to those after so many activations," said Pies.

"Cool, cool," said Bast.

"You have to spread these jobs out. If they're all taken too quickly, it won't end well for us," said Pies.

"It'll be fine. Relax," said Bast.

Andy bent and grabbed up the other folded paper from the floor and unfurled it and read it. What Andy's eyes scanned was an expensive sheet of certificate paper, like that on which diplomas are printed. His facial expression went from slacked to more of a surprised look as he realized what he had read.

"Pies? Buddy? Did you have an eventful workday?" asked Andy.

Pies spun, saw the paper in Andy's hand, and snatched it back. He wadded it up and shoved it into his back pocket.

"What? What's going on?" asked Bast.

Pies offered nothing further, so Andy did. "Pies received a written commendation for handling an armed-robbery-in-progress call today. You're supposed to frame those, dude, not jam 'em into your pocket."

Even Crick made a little "I'm-impressed" face.

Bast, grin fixed, turned to take in Pies. "Keep them coming. This new job is going to be a gold mine."

Pies sat back down again and nodded once.

"Did three years in a two-man unit in the 16th and I never got one of those," said Andy.

"'Cause you were on the take?" sputtered Crick. He settled, looked Pies's way, and said, "Good going, dog."

"Crick. Andy. Give me and our friend a second, okay?"

When both Crick and Andy moved out of the back alleyway door, Bast again studied Pies closely. He leaned back in his expensive chair and said, "Has she caught on?"

"No. She doesn't know," said Pies, not at all comfortable with where this conversation was headed.

"It's Friday, so she'll probably be at the high school. You know the one, right?" asked Bast.

Pies knew. He also knew that Bast was being an asshole. The high school was across the street from where his father had killed himself.

"I don't know exactly what she gets out of it, but, eh. Inspiration, I guess. Who knows? Make sure she doesn't meet with anyone. If she does, I'll be with the wife, but you hit me up right away and I'll have Crick and Andy pay the asshole a visit. Follow her until she's back home or at the apartment. Got it?"

Pies sat there and offered nothing.

"And if she sees you, don't talk to her," continued Bast.

Pies locked eyes with Bast and didn't let go.

"You think I don't know about the crap you've planted in her ear over the years?" added Bast. "I have you do this thing for me because I know you'll look after her, but you don't mess with the merch on this one. You're not kids anymore. Let it go, dude. I don't trust Andy and Crick around her. Especially Andy since they had that thing going in school back in the day."

This was the one job that Pies despised more than anything—to keep tabs on the woman he loved for his scumbag boss.

Vicki Chlebek was far from perfect. Yes, she was a free-spirited person who dabbled in various illicit substances and had no qualms about playing around with the married Bast, but Pies still loved her. He had since they were five years old and she first moved to North Olcott Avenue, and later to North Shore Avenue when her parents' business became more successful.

Pies knew who she really was, a talented artist and painter, a loving daughter to her parents, a loyal friend—mostly. He understood her artistic quirks. He ignored her bad habits, because Pies usually only saw the good in Wicktoria "Vicki" Chlebek. He could never stop himself from loving her.

"Are we headed for a rough road?" asked Bast.

Pies let out an exasperated breath before Bast could continue.

"There are things, dog. Things that people could find out about you and what you did."

"Your father would go down, too," said Pies without hesitation.

Bast hardened his stance even further. "How many hitters pedal a Schwinn three-speed to a job site?" he said. "There's absolutely nothing that points to any involvement other than yours alone. And don't screw with me, numb nuts. It'll look like this 9-1-1 job was your idea, too. It kind of was, if I remember right. Yours alone, dog. Not my dad's."

"I can't do it anymore…"

Bast's expression quickly disintegrated into a hardness that Pies hadn't witnessed in a while. The large man took in an angry breath and said, "Why are you making this so difficult? Now go."

But Pies didn't move.

"Go!"

Pies finally stood and exited through the side door that led into the shoe store.

7

TWELVE YEARS *ago...*
Pies, very clean-cut and well-groomed for his sixteen years of age, hunched over the workbench and toiled away in the basement of his boxy, little home.

His and Stan Zielinski's conversation from the day before still echoed in his mind.

"It has to be clean, Jakub. You don't want me to go to prison, do you? If these guys talk to the police any more than they have, that's going to happen."

Pies said, "It'll be clean, Mr. Zielinski."

"If you get caught, it'll be over. We'll both be in a cage."

"I'll be careful."

"I don't want you getting hurt, either," said Stan Zielinski.

"I won't, I promise."

"You're a good boy. In a few days, you'll become a man."

Pies knew his way around electronic equipment—evident by the many complex projects displayed all about him. The projects were scattered nearby on his father's old workbenches. It had only been eighteen months since his father left him, and Pies would still sometimes sit in the workspace so he could be physically closer to the tools and materials they once used to complete household electrical and plumbing repair projects. Sitting there made him feel closer to his father. It was as simple as that.

A police scanner on a table squawked with some hurried voice transmissions.

"1610 with a male white subject on Milwaukee and Devon at the hot-dog-stand parking lot. He's got on a red T-shirt and blue jeans."

"Okay, 1610."

"I said hands! Get 'em behind your back! 1610, send me a car."

"1610 requesting backup at Milwaukee and Devon."

"1612 responding."

Pies would listen to the scanner his father purchased many years ago and pay attention to terminology and patterns that could be helpful to him in his new criminal pursuits with the Zielinski crew.

The various televisions and PC processors distributed about the workbench and the floor were mostly fixed and ready to be sold to other teenagers or to adults who couldn't afford new models. Pies still needed to do some quality control and spit-and-shine work to make sure all the merchandise looked nearly showroom ready, but other than that, the products were good to go. He took much pride in how his merchandise appeared when sold. It was a trait that garnered a lot of repeat business, and Pies, of course, enjoyed making the extra money.

But on this day, sixteen-year-old Pies worked on a different sort of project. The hardware in hand was crafted from sheet metal, one-inch-diameter copper tubing, springs, pieces of metal dowel, and super-thin nylon filament.

Pies carefully used an old rag to cover his hands as he placed two of the devices into his backpack and zipped it tight. He leaned away from the workbench but stopped himself. He grabbed another rag and used it to open the middle drawer of the workbench—inside were three boxes of shotgun shells. He popped one box open, again using the rag, and pinched two shells out of the box. He unzipped his backpack, gingerly placed the shotgun shells inside, and zipped it again. Only then did Pies turn and bound up the basement stairs two at a time.

He was so focused on his task that day, as he pushed his way out of the back door of his home and jumped down the three steps to where his three-speed bike rested, that he didn't even notice anything else going on around him. As he lifted his leg and straddled the bike, two hands grasped the handlebars.

"Hey, dog. Where you off to?" asked a seventeen-year-old Bast Zielinski. He was only one year older than Pies but nearly a foot taller. When Pies didn't answer, Bast violently rocked the handlebars back and forth and nearly knocked Pies to the ground.

"What does he have you doing? I saw you there at the house last week, and then yesterday. Pies?"

Pies remained tight-lipped.

"Speak, P-yes. Speak. Woof," said Bast with a faux-friendly smile plastered on his face. "You already had an old man. You goofed that up. That's on you."

Anger brewed in Pies, and he twisted the handlebars clean away from Bast and said, "I have to go, Bast."

"My pops isn't your family, dog. It's not happening. Don't try to get tight with him. You get me?"

"Bast? Leave him alone," said sixteen-year-old Vicki Chlebek as she stood in the open doorway of the privacy fence, in the alley behind Pies's home. To Pies, she was a vision of beauty in her simple white T-shirt and blue-jean coveralls.

Bast turned to see the pretty Vicki step into the yard through the open gate. He said, "Is she fighting your fights for you now, buddy? You're kind of pathetic."

Before Vicki could physically get between the boys though, Pies took off in the other direction, wedged quickly through the open gate that led to the front yard, and pedaled as fast as he could out onto the front sidewalk and away from the girl he loved and the brother figure that had, over the years, become his bully.

Pies directed his bike through his Edison Park neighborhood, across Ozanam Avenue and west on tree-lined Belle Plaine Avenue and into Park Ridge. He was headed a couple of miles away to Dam No. Four Woods-East.

Many years ago the civic planners in Cook County had the fore-sight to hold onto portions of the area's natural beauty by not allow-ing development in certain predetermined zones. Those areas were very delicately developed to allow for direct access, parking, and the like, but were mostly left to Mother Nature's care. The many more or less wild spaces of the Forest Preserve District of Cook County were popular natural havens for families to enjoy the year-round.

If Pies arrived early enough on this weekday morning he should have a deeper portion of the wooded area, where there were no trails, to himself for a few more hours without any interruptions or com-plications.

Stan had approached the young Pies for a side job—a very high-paying and secretive job—and confided in him that two men who had worked for him had to die. The men had gone to the police and gotten Mr. Zielinski into some serious trouble. It was trouble that would put Pies's new father into prison for a long, long time if the men weren't dealt with soon.

Pies knew both men in question from the neighborhood and had no reason not to believe every word his new father figure had told him.

Both of the doomed men had last names beginning with the letter B, and were known in the neighborhood as, simply, "the Bs." They were part of the Zielinski burglary crew at that time and worked ex-clusively as a two-man team—a very prolific and professional two-man burglary team.

Roman Bartosz was a very quiet man who kept to himself and never spoke when out in public. The best he would give a young Pies when they crossed paths in the neighborhood was a quick nod. No smile. No wave. No "hey, kid, how are you doing?" Just a nod. Pies had known Bartosz his entire life, but the man played it close to the vest and trusted no one. He lived in the eastern edge of the neighbor-hood on Oconto near Pratt Avenue. Bartosz had no family either—and probably for good reason. He was not a friendly sort in the least.

Lech Banasik, on the other hand, was seemingly a great guy. He was a large, gregarious man who loved to hug people, both men and women—it never mattered to Banasik. He treated everyone as if they were his best friends.

He often had huge summertime backyard barbeques for the neighbors and their kids at his home on Oriole Avenue near Ibsen Street, just a block or so away from Pies's own house.

Pies would, from time to time, take photos of the partygoers with the cheap Kodak 35mm camera his father had purchased in the 1980s. Back in the small basement darkroom at his house, Pies would go through the steps of processing some of those photos all on his own. It was something that he and his father had liked to do together as a family activity. Pies still took and processed his own photos, just not as frequently.

Pies had his camera with him at most of the Banasik events, but he would only take a couple of shots each time. He never felt very comfortable with the strange looks he got from some of the other partygoers when he clicked off random shots of the crowds, or of the smiling Dana Banasik—especially when others were in the background. From some of the glances he got, Pies felt like he was doing something wrong, and that's what led him to limiting the number of photos he took.

Lech Banasik would spare no expense at his huge gatherings. The grilled meats would be top-notch and the booze top-shelf.

But Banasik had a dark side that Pies witnessed himself shortly after his own father's death.

Pies recalled one such party, a summer ago, when a man from outside the neighborhood, presumably a buddy of Banasik's, kept crudely propositioning Banasik's daughter Dana. Pies recalled hearing the man say to the young woman, "You'll need a yardstick to get the right read, honey. I'm sure that's something you're interested in." Pies couldn't believe how brazen the man was.

Dana, a very pretty young lady who was only a year older than Pies, was a great kid—friendly, jovial, and whip smart.

The party in the Banasiks' yard that day was in honor of Dana's im-pending departure to Dartmouth. The Banasik family—Lech, his wife Angela, a nurse, and their only daughter Dana—were elated and proud.

When the man, who had to have been drinking heavily to act the way he did, would not stop his advances on Banasik's only child, Lech had done something that scared Pies very deeply. Lech slid two cigars from his shirt pocket, and, when the drunken man was near the keg pouring another beer, he motioned for the man to follow him to the alley for a friendly smoke.

The man said, "About goddamned time you got the good stuff out. Better be the Cubans. Cheap ass." Lech Banasik laughed right along at the drunken man's off-color response to the invitation.

No one else at the party seemed to notice that Banasik and the man walked down the strip of smooth cement that separated the two-car, detached garage from the six-foot-high, wooden privacy fence that bordered the neighbors' yards—except for Pies. The men quickly ducked into the alley behind the garage and out of view of the other guests.

Pies went to the other side of the garage and peeked through a gap in the fence in time to surreptitiously observe Lech Banasik give the drunken man a cigar and then gently take the beer cup away from him and place it on the ground at their feet. As the drunk man ad-mired the cigar in his fingers, without a word, or even a sound, an unemotional Lech Banasik quick punched the drunk man in the throat so hard that he rag-dolled to the ground, unconscious before his head bounced off the pavement.

Banasik then kicked the man's face as hard as he could. Just once. The drunken man's head snapped back, the cigar flew from his clenched teeth, and Pies could hear him gasp for breath.

Banasik straightened, took a couple of deep breaths of his own so to clear his murderous thoughts, and moseyed back to the party.

Pies had smartly backed away from the privacy fence and his van-tage point, and he noted as Banasik re-entered the yard; walked up to Bartosz, who seemed to be enjoying a glass of Scotch, alone as always; and spoke into his ear.

Bartosz stepped away from Banasik, walked into the house, and Pies could see through the kitchen window as he picked the phone off the counter. Bartosz dialed, waited, spoke what looked like two sentences, disconnected, and put the phone back. He immediately re-emerged from the house and gave Banasik a little nod as he descended the back stairs from the kitchen.

Pies recalled that about ten minutes later a panel van pulled up in the alley. He couldn't make out any occupants of the vehicle because he didn't have time to get to the fence—he could only see the top portion of the van as it arrived. The van was there for about fifteen seconds, and then it slowly drove away. By the time Pies got back to his original vantage point and peeked through the gap in the fence once again, the drunken man was gone.

Pies stepped back quietly into the middle of the party, and Banasik grasped him by the shoulder and said, "You having fun, Jakub?"

"Yes, sir," said the surprised Pies as he waited for a rebuke. A warning. Something.

"Good. Dana says that if you keep after it, you could end up at a place like Dartmouth, too. She thinks that you're smarter than she is."

Pies wanted nothing more to do with the conversation and said, "I don't know about that, sir."

Banasik gave Pies a quick embrace and said, "You're a good kid," and then he went back to his guests.

That was a year earlier.

At sixteen Pies had no actual hate for the Bs, but after what Mr. Zielinski had done for him—treating him like a son after his parents had died, basically taking him in, and teaching him certain skills that could make him more money than he had ever dreamed of in his short life—he'd do anything for Stan. He would kill for Mr. Zielinski—without a second thought, without hesitation.

A fear did still grip Pies, though. He was afraid for what would become of Dana Banasik. Once his side job was complete, he and Dana

would have something terrible in common. Both would be father-
less, belonging to a club that no one really wanted to join.

On his bike, he glanced back over his shoulder, but neither Bast
nor anyone else was following him into Park Ridge.

Belle Plaine Avenue ended at Talcott Road, and Pies pedaled fast
as a gap in the traffic opened and his bike sliced across the busy
street. He angled left down the long driveway that ran along the side
of the high school's football stadium and peeled right as he rounded
into the massive parking lot of the school. He pedaled through the
empty lot and headed due west toward the opening of the Dam No.
Four Woods-East across Dee Road on the other side of the school's
grounds.

At Dee Road, Pies had to wait for the traffic to open up before he
moved across the way. Once on the other side, though, he hopped off
his bike and lifted it up and over the high curb. He pushed the bike
through the tall, uncut grass that bordered the line of trees next to
the road. He propelled his way into the thicket of trees, and the grass
transitioned to hardened, packed earth. The thick forest of mature
trees seemed to gently envelop him.

Pies forced the bike along and meandered between the trees without much difficulty. He needed to get as far away as he could from
the visitors parking area to the south and Dee Road to the east.

There would be no real reason for a cop to stop the sixteen-year-old
Pies as he made his way on his bike, but if one had, and then searched
his battered bag, the cop would be in for a dangerous surprise.

The devices he'd tucked into his backpack were constructed from
household electric handy boxes, the type found on the shelves of every national hardware retailer—the same type of electrical box used
in nearly every home to contain the actual light switch and recepta-
cles used to plug appliances into.

These handy boxes looked markedly different, though. They
had been reshaped. All four of the sides were cut at the seams and
pinched toward the center of the backplate where they contacted,
and they held in place a two-inch-long piece of hollow one-inch-

diameter copper tubing that had been screwed into the enlarged, back access hole of the box. On the front edge of the copper tubing was another thinner copper fitting that threaded onto its open end —so as to hold a shotgun shell in place. At the rear of the copper tube, where it attached to the back of the handy box, was a small U-shaped piece of thicker sheet metal. This small U-shaped component housed a spring-loaded section of metal dowel that had the tip sharpened to a point.

Encompassing the entire outer backside of the handy box was a larger, arching, U-shaped, one-inch-wide strip of sheet metal. Small, nail-sized holes were drilled into the outside edges of this component, allowing the entire device to be attached to a stationary point —like a tree or a wall.

The entirety of the device would fit into a six-inch-square box. There were two of them.

Each device had a length of thin-gauged, nearly see-through, strong nylon filament attached to the back end of the spring-loaded, metal-dowel component, as well.

Pies planned it so that the items he toted into the wooded area in his backpack would be left there. Once the devices were activated, the remaining parts would cause no further danger to whomever found them—if they were ever found. Even the cheap hammer Pies had brought along to nail the devices to the trees he would attach them to would be left at the scene.

After he was finished with his experiment, and when he eventually biked away from the forest preserve, he would carry nothing more than an empty backpack and some rubber gloves.

Pies had fashioned the shotgun-shell, booby-trap devices from drawings he got off the Internet.

They were similar to the devices he saw on a cable television documentary and were used in rural Arkansas and Hawaii to rid the areas of pesky and quite dangerous feral hogs. Farmers in both of those locations had great success eliminating their four-legged problems before their children or livestock could be harmed.

Pies was hunting the two-legged sort of critter, and he believed that the contraption he fashioned in his basement would do the job properly without using a traceable gun, something Mr. Zielinski had insisted on.

When activated, the booby traps' accuracy, and ensuing lethality, were heightened by the addition of the one-inch-diameter copper tubing that housed the actual shotgun shell. This design addition was one that Pies thought up all on his own. The original design simply called for the modified sides of the handy box to hold the shotgun shell in place. Pies believed that the copper tubing would allow for the spray of double-ought buck to be delivered in a directed, focused pattern so as to get the job done correctly.

But Pies needed to test the devices first to make sure the weapons plan he had pitched to Stan Zielinski would actually work.

Most of the parts required for the shotgun-shell devices came from the workbench area in Pies's own basement—items left behind by his father's home repair projects. Mr. Jakubowski had all of the parts required for a working prototype except for the shotgun shells. Stan Zielinski provided those to Pies the day before his trek into the forest preserve. He had slid the three boxes of shells out of a plastic bag and never touched them with his own hands.

"You bring the gloves?" Stan asked at that moment in time.

Pies had nodded and produced a pair of yellow dishwashing gloves from his front pants pockets. They were ones he found under his kitchen sink. They still smelled faintly of his mother's perfume.

Then Stan said, "Don't touch anything with your bare hands. I mean nothing, okay?"

As Pies continued to push his bike along, he came to a spot deep in the woods where he no longer heard the traffic noise from Dee Road. He leaned his bike against a skinny tree and shrugged the backpack off his shoulders. He sized up the trees in his vicinity and liked the two closest to him, the pair only three feet apart from one another.

He unzipped the backpack, lifted the yellow rubber gloves into view, slipped them on, and gently took out the remainder of the backpack's contents, along with the hammer, some cheap needle-nose pliers, and a disposable plastic container filled with assorted nails and fasteners.

Pies went to work nailing one device on the inside edge of each tree, about four feet off the ground, so that the prototypes would face one another. He popped open the container of fasteners and chose two eyelet screws and twisted one into each tree, about one foot off the forest floor.

He then gently grabbed the nylon filament of the device that was attached to the left tree and pulled it downward. It was tough going with the gloves on, but he managed to fish the filament through the eyelet screw opening below. He gathered up a few feet worth of filament at the base of the tree and then pulled that toward the tree on the right, just shy of being completely taut. Using the needle-nose pliers, he tied the filament to the eyelet screw attached to the base of the tree on the right. He then replicated the process from the right tree's device to the left tree.

He took a step back and studied his setup. There were the two modified metal electrical handy boxes at about his shoulder height with nylon filament tracking down each tree and then crisscrossing over each other and connected to the opposite tree. The taut nylon lines were so sheer that they were barely visible.

"This has to work," said Pies, aloud. And then he heard a rustle in the trees about one hundred feet to the south. He instantly knelt and scanned his surroundings. If someone was out there, they'd have a tough time seeing him. Pies had worn a dark-brown shirt and dark-green pants for this occasion. He wanted to blend in as best he could without being noticed.

When there were no further noises, Pies righted himself and took the two shotgun shells out of his backpack. He gingerly handled the shells and placed one into the device on the right and then one into the device on the left. The shells easily slid into the two-inch sections of copper tubing. He secured each of them in place with the thin, threaded copper fitting. He pulled back the spring and plunger setup he had fashioned into each device, one at a time, carefully, until there were two more audible clicks. The devices were locked and loaded.

Pies took a hesitant step back, then another, and then about five more. He didn't want to be anywhere near the devices if they worked properly, or if they went off on their own before he tried to activate them.

He scanned the floor of the forest and found what he was looking for. It was a two-foot-long, thick tree branch. He lifted it and hefted the branch to make sure it would successfully trip the nylon-filament triggers on his devices.

All systems were a go.

Pies took a couple of breaths, cleared his mind, and delicately tossed the heavy branch toward the crisscrossed nylon filament that floated between the two trees.

The branch fell in a gentle arc, until—

The simultaneous shotgun-shell activation was loud, but not the deep, compressed explosive sound you would normally hear if it had been fired from an actual long-barreled gun. From a distance, Pies was sure the explosion would sound like nothing more than a big firecracker going off. Figuring that the sound wouldn't carry too far here in the lush forest was one of the main reasons Pies chose this spot. It was in the same general area where his father shot himself to death. In that instance no one heard the gunshot, and it took two days to locate Mr. Jakubowski's body.

For the first time that day Pies smiled. He knew his plan could work. He knew he would be able to save Mr. Zielinski from going to prison.

"What the hell are you doing, man?" barked a seventeen-year-old boy with long hair, who wore a heavy-looking army coat—and stood only fifty feet away—as he zipped his fly. He was with another seventeen-year-old boy, a fat kid who held a lit joint in one hand while he hoisted up his pants with the other.

Pies angled away, snatched his backpack off the ground, got on his bike, and pedaled as fast as he could. He panted out ragged breaths as he zigzagged between and around the trees and headed toward Dee Road and safety.

He didn't recognize either of the kids, and Pies knew that they probably wouldn't have known him, either. They were most likely Park Ridge teens. Park Ridge kids rarely ventured into Edison Park —not until they were of drinking age and frequented the bars on Olmsted Avenue. And these two teens wouldn't be any problem at all, because if they even tried to get Pies turned in to the cops, their own uncertain activities could be called into question during any investigation.

When Pies got to Dee Road he stopped and looked back. No one was on his tail. He took off the rubber gloves, stuffed them into his pants pockets, and pedaled toward Edison Park.

*

"I HAVE to fire it first, in the kiln," said sixteen-year-old Vicki as she pinched a petal into place on the soft-clay flower sculpture she currently worked on. "Otherwise it'll just fall apart when it air-dries. It's permanent once I fire it. Then I'll glaze it. You're going to like this, I promise."

Pies sat on a beanbag chair nearby and admired Vicki as she created away in the basement of her parents' house, only one block from his own home. She bent to the side of her workstation and turned on the small kiln that her parents had purchased for her after they recognized that she was serious about her art and that she actually had true talent.

The Chlebeks had also been spending extra tuition money, because they lived out of area, so that Vicki could attend the better school that was located in Park Ridge—across from where Pies tested the booby traps. The school had an excellent arts program that Vicki had been excelling in of late.

However, Pies couldn't help but admire her shapely figure as she worked away in her basement art studio. She had blossomed from a stick-thin girl to a woman in the matter of a year or so. Pies couldn't help but notice.

Vicki went back to forming the petals of the clay flower on her worktable, but she finally took notice of Pies and his expression.

"Quit gawking, perv. You've had your chance," she said.

Pies's eyes opened a little wider, and when Vicki caught sight of that she laughed loudly.

"You're just going to sit there, huh? Not talking today?" she asked. "You've been quiet lately."

Pies wanted so badly to tell another human, outside of Stan Zielinski, what he was about to do. That he was only a day away from killing—murdering—two men for their sins against his new father.

No harm could come to Mr. Zielinski, and Pies truly understood that. He had to do what had to be done. But what would Vicki think of him if she ever discovered that he was a killer? Would she condone the action because she knew how much Mr. Zielinski meant to Pies? Or would she be repulsed and never speak to him again? Would she turn him in to the police?

"Pies?"

Pies snapped out of his reverie, saw that Vicki had a goofy smirk on her face, and he said, "I think you should just paint and not do the sculpture stuff. The flowers are okay, I guess. But...I love your paintings."

"I suck at that."

"Oh, no, not at all. I think that's what you do best," Pies replied.

She got quiet now as she worked away, still with her back to Pies. After a long moment she said, "My mom made another comment the other day about never seeing your aunt or uncle around your house."

For the briefest of moments, Pies looked concerned. "What? What did you say?"

"Don't worry. Secret's safe with me," she said. "My parents are too busy these days. My mom's probably forgotten all about it already."

And that was that, another fleeting moment in the lives of self-absorbed teenagers. Pies went back to staring blankly, and Vicki went on to fire her new flower sculpture. Neither had to speak, really, because each was so comfortable with the other that there was no dialogue needed. They had always been this way, ever since they were five-year-old children.

∗

PIES HADN'T slept at all.

He puked up anything he consumed, even water. More notably, it had taken him longer than he expected, mostly due to his trembling hands, to put together the twelve additional devices need to kill the Bs. As he built the devices and loaded them into his backpack, he soon discovered the bag wasn't large enough to carry all the components at one time.

Shortly after 2 A.M. he had to bike to the site of the first proposed hit scene. There he hid six of the devices, each sans the shotgun shell, in an elderly neighbor's trashcan. Garbage collection was still three days off, so he knew the devices would almost certainly not be discovered or tampered with.

Pies needed sleep, but it wasn't going to come. Not this day. Mr. Zielinski advised him that Banasik and Bartosz were both scheduled to speak with investigators that very afternoon.

Bartosz was to be the first person the cops would interview, and Banasik would be the second. Both needed to be taken care of before they set foot in a police station.

Pies wasn't mindful enough to ask Mr. Zielinski how he knew all of this; he simply believed everything that came out of the man's mouth.

And as he stumbled around sleepless that morning, there was something else brewing that Pies had never counted on. It was a deep-seeded anger that kept bubbling up. Anger like he had never felt before, anger he could not accurately describe, even to himself. It was an animalistic hate that filled him when he began to ponder how the Bs were attempting to take away his father figure.

The night before as he built device after device, Pies felt like a new person was emerging from within—an angrier young man who could kill without hesitation. It was as if a murderous monster had been born within. He wasn't sure how he felt about this new personality trait, but he had work to do and not a second more to think about it. Time was running out for Mr. Zielinski. The police would arrest him soon if the Bs weren't taken care of.

Mr. Zielinski had provided Pies with inside information on the daily movements, habits, and quirks of the men who were marked for death. The main bit of information being that Banasik and Bartosz spent nearly every morning having breakfast together at a diner on Northwest Highway. And the time when they met, at about 7:30 each morning, would be the perfect chance to set his plan in motion.

The day that Pies murdered the two men was simply beautiful. It was a bright and sunny summer day with little humidity or chance of precipitation. While most teens Pies's age were home asleep, he was at work, hunting his prey.

Wearing his backpack, which felt much heavier this day, Pies pedaled his bike lazily up and down Northwest Highway, across the street from the diner from where the victims would eat and discuss their business.

It was 7:25 A.M., and he'd been rolling in what seemed to him to be an endless loop for hours on end. It had only been fifteen minutes.

At 7:32, Bartosz arrived on foot, and Pies stopped his bike to peer through the diner's sidewalk-facing windows as the unfriendly man took his usual seat in a booth near the front.

Pies knew from Mr. Zielinski that Bartosz had a car, but he always chose to walk the three blocks to the diner each day—rain or shine. His car, a 1965 black, ragtop over maroon-colored Oldsmobile 442 was cherry, with a mere 43,000 original miles. Bartosz drove his car only when necessary—or when he picked up high-end hookers at hotels near O'Hare airport—so that he could keep his baby as pristine as possible, and this beautiful sunny day did not necessitate a car ride.

Pies straddled his bike on the sidewalk across from the diner, but he felt exposed, so he slowly pedaled away, not too far down the block, before he u-turned and rode past again. This time, only a minute later, he observed as Banasik parked his brand-new Buick on the street and got out. Thirty seconds later both intended victims were seated in the booth—and Pies pedaled away as quickly as he could.

If Mr. Zielinski's information were accurate, Pies would have little more than an hour to set everything up and complete the day's work.

*

ROMAN BARTOSZ spent the last two minutes of his life walking down the alley behind Oconto Avenue that led to his backyard. The first of those two minutes were devoted to scraping dog shit off of the sole of his expensive Italian-made loafers as he cursed in Polish.

"*Kurwa!*"

He looked up from his messy shoe and noticed that his back privacy gate was popped open. Nearly every other house in the area had the same wooden privacy fences. That whole "good fences make good neighbors" mantra was definitely in play in Edison Park.

"Goddamn it," said Bartosz.

He angrily pushed the gate door wide open and plodded onto the three-foot-wide cement walkway that separated his outside garage wall from the privacy fence on the other side—and that's when he noticed that the side pedestrian door of his garage was jimmied open. His baby of a mint-condition car was inside the garage, and he instantly broke out in flop-sweats.

"Shit. *Gowno, gowno, gowno...*"

He hesitated at the jimmied door and listened intently to make sure the burglar wasn't still inside his garage. Bartosz was used to sneaking into other people's homes and businesses and screwing up their lives. Having that awful favor returned infuriated him to no end.

All was quiet.

Through the partially opened door, he could see that the trunk of his mint-condition Olds 442 had been opened and left in the up position.

"Kurwa!"

As Bartosz barged into the garage to inspect what damage had been done to his car and what may possibly had been stolen, he advanced through a crisscrossed labyrinth of nylon filament that interconnected six shotgun-shell, booby-trap devices—three attached to the inside edge of the doorjamb and the other three fastened and stacked one right on top of the other to the edge of the wood workbench to the left of the doorway. The nylon filament was strung an inch outside the arc of the small, opened pedestrian door.

Pies straddled his bike at the opening of the alley at Oconto Avenue and Pratt Avenue. He watched as Bartosz stepped into his yard and then caught sight of a pretty woman who was on a morning jog. The woman didn't even pay any attention to Pies as she cut a path between him and his target. And when Pies heard the muffled, yet distinctive, simultaneous explosions from the booby traps, the jogging woman never broke stride. She naïvely ran from view.

The explosion was loud, but it sounded more like someone dropping a couple of two-by-fours onto a cement floor in an enclosed space. It was not a sound that would garner any further interest from a nosy neighbor.

Pies gagged and almost vomited, but nothing came up, because his stomach was empty. He dry-heaved once again before he composed himself and slowly pedaled down the alley toward Bartosz's house to get a better look.

As he rolled deliberately past the open privacy gate, he could see the mangled body of Bartosz. He lay on his side, his head wedged and canted at a strange forty-five-degree angle against the privacy fence, and his eyes were fixed at half-mast and stared right at Pies as a pool of blood gathered all around him. The shotgun-shell blasts had spun him right back out of the garage and onto the walkway.

Pies looked away as tears completely filled his eyes, and he rode quickly toward Oriole Avenue. He listened, but didn't hear any sirens.

Not yet, anyway.

He utilized as many alleys as he could, and he soon found himself rolling up on the intersection of Oriole Avenue and Ibsen Street, only two blocks from his own home.

From his vantage point at the corner, he could see that Lech Banasik's Buick was not parked on the street, so he pedaled his bike down the alley in back of the house. It was something he did nearly every day, so it didn't look out of the ordinary. Pies peered through the long, horizontal and narrow windows of the Banasik's garage door as he rolled past and could see that the Buick wasn't there either. Banasik hadn't arrived home yet.

Earlier that morning, Pies surveilled the home as Mrs. Banasik walked to the bus stop on Northwest Highway near a tiny grocery store to catch her ride to the hospital where she worked.

Dana Banasik, who had recently finished her freshman year at Dartmouth, was in Lake Geneva, Wisconsin, with friends. Lech Banasik had told Mr. Zielinski about Dana's travel plans the week before—that was all prior to the police grabbing up the Bs and placing undue pressure on them to give up Stan Zielinski.

That's what Stan had told Pies, anyway.

Stan Zielinski had lied.

In reality the Bs had already done their damage. There were no meetings with the police planned for the day Pies killed the men. Those meetings had already happened the week before, when Banasik and Bartosz wore concealed wires and had a long conversation with Mr. Zielinski—a mix of talk about their illegal activities along with what their children were up to and how proud they were of them.

Stan Zielinski had already been arrested and had bonded out of jail by the time Pies was setting up his murderous booby traps. Pies, being a kid, never watched the news or paid attention to what other grown-ups were talking about, so he didn't even realize that Mr. Zielinski had been arrested. Bast never said anything, either.

Pies knew that only Lech Banasik would be coming back to the house sometime in the near future, so he pedaled up and down the alley and waited him out. He had to be sure his and Mr. Zielinski's plan worked. Mr. Zielinski made Pies promise he'd watch and see that both men were, indeed, dead.

Pies's teenage thoughts, of late, were so confusing. He felt like such a failure for going through with this murderous plan because he mostly thought of himself as a good kid. But at the same time, he could not allow for his new father to go to prison. He couldn't lose another parent. He'd already lost one father, and the thought of losing another was too much to bear. And then there were the angry, monstrous thoughts. The ones that began shortly after Mr. Zielinski came to him for help with his legal problems. The angry thoughts scared him the most.

As Pies rode another lazy loop in the alley, he stopped in the street on Ibsen and spotted Dana Banasik walking up the alley from Pratt Avenue.

"Oh, no..." he said.

Simultaneously, his eye caught on Lech Banasik's Buick rounding the corner from Oleander Avenue and heading toward his garage in the alley of Oriole Avenue.

Pies had to make a decision, and just as he stomped on the pedals of his bike to ride down the alley toward Dana, Lech Banasik gave Pies a little honk from his car horn, and a friendly wave. But Pies didn't see or hear any of that.

He anxiously pedaled and skidded to a stop a few feet in front of Dana Banasik, who looked tired from a long night of partying. She shrugged her heavy backpack off her shoulders.

"Whoa. Easy. Hey, Jakub. What's the hurry?" she asked.

"Hey, Dana. I was just, ah..."

Down the alley Lech Banasik opened the garage door with the automatic device and pulled his Buick into his garage space. The pedestrian door at the Banasik residence opened directly toward the house and not to the walkway at the side of the garage, which Pies knew from his own experiences.

Years ago Lech Banasik had built a workbench across the wall where that pedestrian door was located, thus he covered the opening, which made it useless—and Pies knew that, too.

There was now only one way to get from the interior of the garage to the back door of their home, and the walkway between the garage and the privacy fence was the only path.

Dana heaved her heavy backpack onto her shoulder once again, shifted around Pies's stopped bike, and kept walking toward her home, which was only three houses, a side street, and three more houses away.

"I am really hungover, Jakub. Sorry. I need some water and some sleep," she said as she kept trudging along.

Pies scrambled for something to ask, something that would stop her.

"I was thinking about going to Dartmouth," he lied.

Dana stopped again and made an "I'm-impressed" face. As she started to walk again though, she said, "How have your grades been? The admissions process is pretty brutal."

Pies didn't want to tell her that he no longer went to school and that Mr. Zielinski was paying an administrator at the private school he was enrolled in to make it appear as if Jakub Jakubowski was actually attending.

They slowly crossed over Ibsen Street and were only a couple of houses away from Lech Banasik as he circled out of the garage after parking his car. He spotted Pies and Dana, and said, "Hey, honey, I thought you'd be home later. Hey, Jakub."

Dana smiled at her father and shrugged.

Pies grabbed Dana's arm and stopped her in her tracks. "Straight As. I'm getting all As."

When Lech Banasik pushed opened his privacy gate and stepped forward the shotgun-shell booby traps all activated simultaneously with a loud explosion.

Dana was stunned by the sound and stood for a second and stared toward her garage—where Pies could now see a delicate red mist hover in the air over the top of the privacy fencing. The feet of the newly dead Lech Banasik protruded out into the alley.

"Daddy?"

Pies sucked in a deep and mournful breath, dropped his head, and tears rolled down his cheeks as Dana ran to her father's body.

"Daddy?... No!... No!" screamed Dana Banasik.

*

After the police spoke with him at the crime scene, and he was able to deflect any of their questions with, "I didn't see anyone or anything. I just heard it," the emotional Pies pedaled the few blocks to Vicki Chlebek's house. There, in the basement, he found the love of his life painting a beautiful landscape. She obviously did not hear the sirens and commotion that the two murders had brought to her neighborhood.

Once she opened the door for him, Vicki kept her eye on her easel and said, "So, what do you think?"

Pies didn't answer.

Vicki fully turned and saw the sheer exhaustion and deteriorated emotion on his face.

She put her paintbrush down and leaned closer to tenderly hug Pies. Pies, wary from his murderous activities, and the lack of sleep, gently pulled away and plopped into the beanbag chair.

He wept.

"Oh, no. What's wrong?" asked Vicki as she tucked into the chair next to him.

"Just thinking about my dad," lied Pies.

8

Now...

Pies, fresh from his acrimonious meeting with Bast at the insurance agency, sat in his parked car at the opening of the alley of Oriole Avenue where it met Ibsen Street.

It was a spot where he had been known to sit many, many times over the course of the past decade.

He was parked in the middle of the side street, blocking it for any traffic that might try to get by. But for now no cars had attempted to pass. All he could do was sit there and idly examine the privacy gate of the Banasiks' backyard.

Except for the two seconds when his eyes twitched to the left and tracked the old lady who pushed her personal shopping cart down the sidewalk on Ibsen, Pies saw no other activity in the area. It had been like this for the past seventeen minutes.

That's when he heard a woman scream. She was in distress and sounded as if she was in the fight of her life.

Pies got out of his car, pulled his cell phone from his pocket to call the police and listened a bit more closely to determine her exact whereabouts.

The screams came from the Banasiks' backyard.

Pies left his car in the middle of the street and ran as fast as he could down the alley and to the Banasiks' back gate. He tried the gate latch, but it was locked. He instantly knew he would have to scale the six-foot wooden fence so he could render assistance to the distressed woman—who continued to scream from inside the confines of the yard.

As he readied himself to grab ahold of the top of the wood structure and hoist himself up and over, he stopped to listen again—because something wasn't right. Something was off.

In all of the commotion, he only heard one voice. There was no sound of a struggle. Only one woman's voice as it screamed out in agony.

"Get the hell off, damn you. Get off," screamed the woman's voice again and again. Pies could tell that she was slurring her speech now that he was closer to her actual proximity.

Pies scrambled through the alley to the other side of the garage and peered through the gap in the fence—the same gap he had used years before to view Mr. Banasik ruthlessly assault the drunken man. Only this time he was on the outside looking in.

Pies adjusted to the sunlight streaming through the gap, and he could finally see Dana Banasik, now twenty-nine years old, alone in the yard.

The years had not been kind to Dana. Her daily intake of copious amounts of alcohol, the hard stuff, had plenty to do with that. She looked like she was in her fifties to Pies's eyes.

Pies observed as she continued to scream—at nothing. Well, not really nothing. Dana remained five feet from an empty bird feeder that was positioned on a shepherd's hook in the center of the yard. She angrily paced back and forth and simply screamed like hell at the inanimate object.

"Oh, man...," said Pies, quietly.

But then Dana caught sight of movement between the boards of the tall wooden fence.

"What the hell are you looking at?" she yelled in her drunken voice.

Pies pushed away from the fence and started to walk back to his parked car.

Pies heard the back door of the Banasiks' home open, and Mrs.

Banasik said, "Dana, baby, please come inside. The neighbors are going to call the police again. Dana?"

As Pies angled away, he could hear Dana shriek again—louder than before, "Leave me alone, damn it."

Pies got into his car, started it, and could still hear Dana saying, "What the hell are you looking at? Get out."

Pies put his car into gear and slowly rolled away.

9

FROM HIS perch in the metal bleacher seats, Pies surveyed the illuminated field fifty feet below. It was Friday night under the lights at Maine Township High School's football stadium, and both seating sections on each side of the field were filled to capacity with boisterous fans as the number-two-ranked home team took on the number-one team from the southwestern suburbs of Chicago in an early season game.

The repetitive, military-like drumming from both school's bands nearly drowned out the spoken audio seeping from the earbuds that were squeezed into Pies's ears.

"The people seem lovely, you know? Kind of docile," said Vicki's recorded voice.

"Yeah. They do. Gentle, huh?" said Pies's recorded voice. "Humble, you know?"

There was a pause in the recorded conversation, with only background television noises heard, but the home team's cheerleaders' rhythmic chant from below on the running track filled that audio space for a moment.

"There's something about the landscape. I mean, where the jungle meets the city," Vicki's voice said in Pies's ears. "It's enchanting. It's as if the plant life seems to have almost overgrow the buildings."

"Enchanting? Kind of like the Everglades," said Pies with a laugh.

"You goof. Florida sucks. Too many old people."

As Pies sat there among the high-school football fans, he couldn't help but smile at Vicki's response, and he remembered exactly when the conversation was secretly taped. He and Vicki Chlebek were in his living room sprawled out on his overstuffed, tan-colored sofa, one sitting on each side with their backs to each of the cushy sofa arms, their bare feet intertwined in the middle, as they enjoyed a travel show on TV.

The memory brought a spark of happiness to Pies as he watched the football game unfold below him. The home team was ahead by fourteen points in the second quarter and was looking strong.

The recording was made five years ago without Vicki's knowledge —like all of the recordings, both audio and video, that Pies produced over the past several years. The recordings were very personal and revealed quite a bit both from Pies's perspective and the subject he was recording at the time.

If the people he knew discovered he'd covertly recorded them, there would be trouble. Especially if any of the Zielinski crew found out. He would probably be dead. He only recently decided to use the recordings against his criminal cohorts to gain his freedom and create a buffer between himself and the Zielinski crew members. The recordings, in the very near future, would play an integral role in his ultimate escape-from-Chicago plan.

When he first began secretly taping people, Pies knew that it was wrong, but at that time it was a way for him to be able to study the subjects of the digital tapes over and over again so that he could look and listen for any traits or tells that could point to troubles down the road.

Like with the Bast recordings that he possessed. Pies learned the warning signs for when Bast was out-and-out lying, or if he was actually being sincere—which was not too often. After their discussion earlier that afternoon at the insurance office, Pies could tell that Bast was hiding something from him. It was in the way he tilted his head when he spoke. Pies knew this because he'd studied many videotapes of his boss.

With Vicki, it was an entirely different scenario though. Pies was so infatuated with her that if he could, he would sit and look at Vicki's face for hours on end. He knew it was strange, but he couldn't help himself. They had a deep emotional connection, and it was difficult for Pies to stay away from Vicki for too long a period.

That's how the tapes initially came to be.

If Pies could videotape Vicki, he could watch the tape over and over again without angering Bast for taking up too much of Vicki's time.

He wasn't necessarily proud of obtaining the recordings, but he had them. And he was going to use them the best way he knew how to get himself and Vicki out of Chicago for good.

"Florida's the only place I've seen the jungle meet civilization like that—when I went there that one time, you know," said Pies's recorded voice in the earbuds.

"Yeah, I guess, but I bet it's really different in this place here. The ugly suburban sprawl hasn't trashed their country yet. No bullshit fast-food places or tract houses messing things up. Have you been to the western suburbs lately? God..." Vicki's voice trailed off.

"Trashed their country...yet," laughed Pies's voice. "I think we already did that."

"You know what I mean. It's more natural looking in Vietnam," her recorded voice giggled.

"It's a long way from Chicago," said Pies's five-years-ago voice.

The audio of the television show they were viewing was a mix of the host's New Jersey accented voiceover along with a jazzy sound track, and it could be plainly heard in the background of the recording.

"This guy here," Vicki's voice said, referring to the television host, as Pies remembered, "he's kind of a dick, but he is all about the food. That's it, really. I mean the food, right? Our neighbor was there when the war was going on and he said it was a shit hole with dead people lying everywhere he looked. But when they could get it from the locals, the food was really good. Like French food, and stuff like that.

French food. Weird, right? You wouldn't expect French food in a place like Vietnam."

"You weren't paying attention in Mrs. Prey's class, were you?" asked Pies's voice.

"I hated history," said Vicki's voice.

"The French ran that country for years before we started bombing it," said Pies's voice.

Pies's eyes scanned the stadium for his target, but he still couldn't locate the actual woman whose words he heard playing presently in his ears.

"Mr. Zielinski's cousin was there, too. He didn't come home," said Pies's voice, which was followed by a long lull in the conversation. The cheerleaders on the running track below again filled the void with their vocal cacophony.

A middle-aged man, decked out in the home team's colors, slid into a seat next to Pies and nodded to him before turning his attention to the football game being played out on the field.

For a brief moment, Pies leaned back against the safety fencing at the top of the stadium seating and took in his surroundings. He watched as a linebacker on the home team made a great, hard-nosed hit on a running back that sliced through the center of the defensive line. The home crowd erupted in cheers and applause.

The visiting team had gone for it on a fourth down and six yards to go without gaining one single inch. After the linebacker made the hit, his teammates mobbed and congratulated him as he made his way to the sidelines.

Pies's eyes wandered and he began to admire the athleticism and grace of the varsity cheerleaders doing their thankless job of pumping up the home crowd and keeping the energy alive.

Then he noticed the water boys sprinting up and down the long row of uniformed team members on the sidelines and offering them squirts of Gatorade from the bottles they lugged.

There was so much cooperation in motion, and in action, and in practice. And all of it, every little bit of energy and cooperation, was provided by a bunch of motivated teenagers who were not being paid for their efforts. This amazed Pies.

Instantly, he respected their endeavors. He didn't know what was coming over him, but it came on suddenly. He felt immediate gratitude for even being in close proximity to the schoolkids doing their best, either on the field of play or in support of those frontline team members.

Could the rush of emotion that washed over him at that moment be due to the fact that he, Pies, never had a childhood of any sort? He'd never really been close to honest, motivated teenagers in his life, and, as he viewed all of the cooperation in motion at the school's football field, it impressed him.

Growing up, his mother was drunkenly absent most days, and his father worked overtime whenever he could—just so he could be away from his alcoholic wife. Pies only went to high school for a year or so, before Stan Zielinski got him out of school and into a well-paying job. Not exactly a legal job, but it was very, very well paid.

Vicki's voice broke his thoughts wide open, "My God, the food has to be awesome. The spices? They use some great chilies. Have you been to the new Vietnamese place on Harlem? Harlem and Irving. It's excellent."

"Not yet. Let's go tomorrow," said Pies's voice.

Vicki kept the conversation going by not answering his request for a date. She simply ignored his ask and continued on with her own response, "Oh, hell yeah, I'd live in Vietnam in a heartbeat. It'd get me away from the 'rents, for sure."

"If you need your own place...you could stay here until you find one," said Pies's voice.

At that very moment, Pies caught sight of the woman who he had been tasked to watch over by his boss, Bast. Pies tapped a button on his smartphone, and the recorded conversation in his ears ceased.

Vicki stood on the field level next to the chainlink fence that separated the running track from the people in the stands.

Even as she stood in partial illumination, under the edge of where the stadium lights were aimed toward the football field itself, she was still beautiful. He could see her splendor from two hundred feet away. She was decked out all in black, her face was perfectly made up, and a portion of her beautiful, dark hair framed her left shoulder with the other half tucked behind her right ear.

From this distance he understood that he'd never be able to drink in the color and contour of her gorgeous blue eyes, but he knew they were there—all those two hundred feet away. Vicki was always beautiful to Pies.

She appeared full of energy, too, as she playfully danced up to a group of five cute little girls—maybe seven or eight years old—who all hopped excitedly in place along the fence near the north end zone of the football field. The little girls gazed in awe as the varsity cheerleaders did their routines on the running track, and then they tried to mimic the older girls' moves.

Pies observed as Vicki leaned into the middle of the group of girls and spoke with them. The little girls all whooped and hollered with joy at whatever Vicki had told them.

Pies, still with the earbuds in place, pushed the smartphone's play button and listened as he watched Vicki teach the little girls cheers and dance moves of their own. Vicki would do a move, and the little girls would try for themselves.

Pies's own voice on the earbuds said, "We're seeing what this guy wants us to see, right? How do you trust this guy? He's some TV asshole. Could you imagine traveling all the way to Vietnam based on his show and finding out he was full of shit? I don't know. Remember when this guy had a half-hour show? It was all about touring around the world as a cook?"

"I was the one who told you about that. I watched that all the time on demand," her voice said in his earbuds.

Pies's voice said, "If it's as cool as this guy is making it look, yeah, I'd go for sure. But if he's bullshitting me, I'll find him, man."

"Yeah, what would you do?" giggled Vicki's voice. "You don't fight, Pies. You're one of the good ones."

Pies noticed that after nearly every move Vicki showed the little cheerleader wannabes, she rubbed at her nose. Feverishly rubbed, not a gentle brush-off.

"Oh, no," said Pies, aloud. "Damn it."

"What's that?" asked the middle-aged man sitting next to him.

Pies ignored the man and observed as one of the little girls' mothers, and then another, and another, advanced quickly toward the group. Just then, Vicki demonstrated a high kick that caught a little girl on the side of the head. Not a very hard blow, but the little kid went down to her knees and rubbed her head in pain.

"Damn it," said Pies again, and he launched himself from his seat and down the stairs of the stadium. When he got to the walkway that led him around to where Vicki and the girls stood, he could see a few fathers entering the fray—they all loudly jawed at Vicki as they tried to guard their children.

Pies sprinted between fans, shoved a few that wouldn't yield, and made his way into the middle of Vicki and the parents.

"Are you on something?" asked the mother of the kid who got kicked.

"Oh, kiss my ass," said a now-frantic Vicki.

"Watch your mouth," squealed one of the mothers.

Pies waded into the middle of them all and forcefully ushered the belligerent Vicki away.

"Not the place for this," said Pies. "Come on."

Pies led her under the main stadium seats and toward a gate on the west side of the stadium. But as he pushed her along, he could see the mother of the kid who had been kicked speaking with a uniformed, stadium security officer.

He peered toward the exit gate he wanted to use, and it was locked. Anyone who left the stadium was funneled toward the gates at the south end of the stadium.

"Man, come on, I didn't mean to kick her," said Vicki when she saw the interaction between the mother and the man in uniform.

Pies noticed an equipment manager, a student, who drove a golf cart full of supplies along the outside of the main fence that surrounded the stadium. The equipment manager was headed in the other direction of where people could come and go, to a twenty-by-forty-foot building that stood just inside the stadium gates on the north end. Pies knew that the home team used the building during halftime to regroup and go over the game plan for the second half.

"Let's go," said Pies as he tugged Vicki in the direction of the locked gate that the equipment manager was headed toward.

Pies and Vicki arrived at the gate at the same time the golf cart did. As the equipment manager got off his cart and unlocked the gate with a key, Pies and Vicki scooted out the open gate and into the expansive field next to the football stadium. The equipment manager hopped back on the golf cart, drove inside the stadium perimeter, and then got off to relock the gate.

"Hey, you," yelled the security officer, who was now fifty feet away and locked inside the stadium after the equipment manager drove away. "Get back here. Unlock this," ordered the security officer of the equipment manager.

Pies and Vicki never looked back.

"Where's your car?"

"I walked here," said Vicki.

"You walked all the... You have a lot of extra energy tonight, huh, Vicki."

"Don't start," she said.

"Time and place, Vicki," said Pies.

"Don't tell him," she pleaded. "Pies, you can't tell him about this."

Pies softened his tone and said, "Let's get you home."

He hurriedly led her to his car, which was parked on a narrow side street across Talcott Road. Before the equipment manager could open the gate and before the security officer could call for help from any other officers on his radio, Pies and Vicki faded into the darkness where the football stadium lights could no longer reach.

Inside the stadium, the harried security officer pawed for his shoulder-mounted microphone, fully turned around, and bumped directly into—Naomi Gott.

"Excuse me, ma'am," said the security officer.

"Oh, I am so sorry, officer," said Naomi as she got out of his way. She then stood there and regarded the darkness for any sign of Pies and the pretty woman he ushered away in such a hurry.

*

PIES PULLED his car, an inexpensive, gray two-door Toyota, in front of Vicki's parents' beautiful brick home on North Shore Avenue. Pies didn't drive a BMW or Mercedes. He kept it low-key with a conventional Japanese-made model. For Pies, there was never a need to attract any undue attention to himself. That would only invite trouble. Stan Zielinski had taught him that when he was still a teenager.

After placing the car in "park" he turned and stared at his beautiful passenger.

"Thanks, Pies. I know Bast doesn't want you talking to me, but he doesn't know us like we know us, right? Thanks for watching out for me," said Vicki. "That was pretty stupid, huh?"

Pies let out a little chuckle. "Yeah, it was."

She leaned across the front seat and gave him a peck on the cheek.

Vicki gathered herself, took a deep breath, and said, "Have to act casual when I get inside."

"Why don't I take you over to the apartment, then?"

Vicki said, "No, my mom wants me to go with her in the morning to do some shopping, so it's better here."

"Right," said Pies.

"I just don't want them freaking out, too, you know." She caught sight of Pies's face when she said her last comment and knew immediately that she had hurt his feelings. "You know what I mean. You were only looking out for me."

"So are they," said Pies.

Vicki's face went to stone. "I'm not a damned kid anymore, okay?" The coke still seethed through her and had its hold. She grabbed at the handle and flung the door open, got out, slammed the door closed, and walked up to her parents' home without a look back.

"Come on," said Pies.

He sat there and made sure that Vicki got inside the front door before he slowly drove on. A block away, he decided to circle around and drive past the Chlebeks' place once again to make sure everything was okay.

Halfway down the block that led directly to the Chlebeks' front yard, Pies could see Vicki walk through the park next to her home. She was headed across the railroad tracks toward a row of lively taverns and eateries.

"What the hell is wrong with you?" he said to no one. Pies slowed down and pulled into a space in front of a fire hydrant—it was the only spot available at the time. He watched to see if he could identify which nightspot she entered. After she crossed the tracks, Vicki turned left and waded through throngs of pedestrians as she headed into the very popular Olmsted Inn—a two-story bar and restaurant that catered to the sports-loving crowds.

Pies angrily turned off his car, got out, and jogged toward the Olmsted Inn's front door.

Just inside the door, a cool-acting muscular doorman, who never even made eye contact said, "ID." The doorman finally raised his gaze, lost his cool-guy attitude when he recognized Pies, and waved him right in.

The place was very crowded that Friday night. The clientele was usually a mix of neighborhood regulars and folks from Park Ridge.

Pies scanned the multitude of faces but couldn't locate Vicki. He elbowed his way to the right side of the bar area, took another glance, and then worked his way to the left side of the massive space.

"Pies! Yo, Pies," yelled a man's voice.

Pies finally caught sight of the bartender, a white guy with blonde dreadlocks. "Vicki?" asked the bartender.

When Pies nodded yes, the bartender pointed upward. The blonde bartender looked like an utter fool with the dreadlocks, but at least he helped Pies in his search.

Pies nodded thanks and waded through the crowd to the second floor stairway, which led to a large area set aside for private parties. There were some drunken people going up and down the stairs, and Pies knew that meant only one thing. There was actually a private party in progress on the top floor of the establishment.

At the upper landing of the stairs, a bouncer with the physique of a WWE wrestler stood watch. He hadn't fully recognized Pies when he said, "I'm sorry, sir, this is a private… Oh, hey, Pies. They got some work thing going now. A copier company sales event or some bullshit."

"I'm not going to stay, I just want to…" And that's when Pies saw Vicki. She was already at a back table of the crowded room seated with a handsome man in a suit. Without another word, Pies rushed toward Vicki.

The bouncer trailed him. "Pies, buddy, you can't be in here." The bouncer sounded stern, mostly for show for the copier company clients that they waded through and around, and who had paid for the private room—but his heart wasn't into giving a Zielinski crew member the boot. "Pies, man. Please?"

Pies angled to the table as the man in the suit surreptitiously handed Vicki a rolled-up, hundred-dollar bill and held up his Amex Black Card with a single line of coke on it.

Pies knocked the coke-covered card out of the man's hand and gently took Vicki's elbow and got her to her feet.

"What the hell is wrong with you?" demanded the man in the suit. "She's with me."

"Your boss know you're putting the company profits up your nose?" asked Pies as he began to lead Vicki away.

"I am the boss, asshole," said the man, as he caught Pies with a right to the side of the head.

Pies gathered Vicki in tightly as the man took a few more swings. Pies took the beating without returning one single punch.

The bouncer, conflicted by not knowing which person to protect —the copier company boss, or the Zielinski crew member—chose correctly when he popped the man in the suit with a single punch to the ear. The man in the suit's eyes rolled back in his head and he fell to the sticky floor.

And that's when the downed man's workmates all piled onto the bouncer.

Pies shoved Vicki through the crowd of drunken copier salespeople and got her to a door that led to the back stairway—the one the public didn't know about. Once on the back stairs and away from the fight, the decibel level diminished rapidly, and Vicki began to lead the way. She knew the buildings of Edison Park as well as Pies did.

"You're going to get some unsuspecting fool killed acting like that," said Pies. "If Bast saw that up there, the dude in the suit would disappear. He had no idea how close he came."

"You're being dramatic," said Vicki as she opened the back door of the building and entered the alley directly behind the Olmsted Inn. "And why are you following me?"

"Vicki, you know why," said Pies as he trailed her across the alley to the locked metal door of the building across the way. Vicki grabbed a small ring of keys from her front pants pocket and unlocked the door. She swung the door open and walked inside the building. Pies caught the door before it latched shut.

"Hey look, I'm all safe and sound and in one piece. And no bad men are having their way with me. Pies, go home."

Vicki giggled heartlessly as she quickly hopped up the back stairs of her parents' bakery building to the second-floor apartment she and Bast kept.

Pies accelerated up the stairs and barged into her apartment before she could close the door. They stood nearly nose-to-nose in the tiny kitchen of the spartan apartment.

"Goddamn it. Get out of here," she said.

Pies ignored her and leaned toward the sink. There, he snatched up a tall glass off the counter and poured her some water from the sink tap. He handed the water to Vicki, who refused to take the glass.

Pies said, "It'll help dilute the coke and get you feeling right."

"I am feeling right—right now. You're the one messing that up."

She spun and walked into the main living area of the apartment. Pies trailed after her, still holding the glass of water.

To the street side of the room were three old-fashioned sash windows, which looked out and over busy Northwest Highway. The only furnishings in the room were an expensive, leather sleeper sofa with an equally pricey leather recliner and a bargain-store coffee table. A forty-six-inch, flat-screen television was positioned opposite the furniture and on top of an old rickety, wooden table.

On the coffee table, Pies saw an open box of condoms, a half-full bottle of whiskey, a bong, and a small mirror laid flat with white cocaine residue on it. He turned away as soon as he recognized each item.

On the floor near the window were a few folded men's shirts and pairs of boxer shorts. Pies figured they were Bast's for when he had to freshen up before going home to his wife and kids.

The reason for so few furnishings was quite evident, though. Positioned in nearly every other open space were easels—each with a finished painting or a work in progress resting on them. Other finished canvases were piled on the floor and leaned against every available wall. They were all Vicki's paintings, and the apartment space was being used as one of her studios.

Pies admired Vicki's artistic vision and messages. Her work was violently playful with a cynical flair that Pies, along with almost anyone else who came in contact with the work, admired.

Like the pieces she was currently working on—a series of colorful paintings depicting high school football games. The human subjects in the paintings were all portrayed as robotic creatures being controlled by a shadowy figure housed in the press box at the top of the stadium seats. On the field of play, the football players were armed with sledgehammers and giving each other head shots as a robot doctor smoked a cigarette on the sidelines and viewed the action with utter delight.

"Too much?" Vicki asked Pies when she caught him staring at one piece. She laughed at his confused, nonverbal response.

She was a master for her age, Pies thought, even if he didn't truly understand everything that she created. She was born with immense talent, like most artists are, but she had been getting even better at attacking the blank canvas of late.

"I think it's awesome, Vicki," said Pies.

"I sold that today. Some guy from Northbrook paid me $250. His buddy saw one of mine at the Olmsted Inn and asked around," she said as she pointed to a darker piece depicting an old man in a baker's apron who was taking a tray of cooked baby-doll heads from a hot oven. "You messed up my celebration."

"You should be showing at the galleries in River North. You're selling yourself short, Vic. You should be getting a few thousand for these. Maybe more. Not a few hundred."

Vicki's face froze for a moment, and her nose twitched as anger boiled up inside.

"So I'm never good enough for you, either?" asked Vicki.

Now Pies felt like a complete fool. "What? No. That's not what I'm... I'm sorry, I just..."

"I'm just a poor little lost girl who can't do for herself, that's what you're saying. Know what? I'm sick of being treated like a little kid, Pies."

Pies took a step back and lowered his gaze.

"You can't be doing the blow, Vicki. That's what I'm getting at. It changes you. The coke really changes you. You're not yourself, you know? You're going to get hurt. You just... Don't do the blow."

"Or hang with other men," she said.

And that stumped him. As he dug around in his gray matter for a way to continue the conversation, he noticed a painting Vicki had shown him before. The piece was partially obscured by another football field painting. He took the two steps to where the painting was peeking out, put the glass of water on the coffee table, and gently pulled the football piece away so he could pick up the one he really wanted to look at.

Pies scooped up the green-hued painting and held it at arm's length. The painting was of a tiny village where children kicked a soccer ball near an anciently constructed building that had jungle foliage climbing all over it.

"Vietnam?" he asked.

Vicki stood there, and her right eyelid twitched. She was so angry, but she was silently seething instead of voicing her anger.

"Go home, Pies."

"I could stay and..."

"Thanks for looking out for me. I'm here. I'm good now," she said as she picked up the glass of water and chugged. After she emptied the glass she said, "See?"

*

AT FIRST, Pies noticed the flashing yellow lights, and then he saw the tow truck that was backed up to his car across the tracks from the Olmsted Inn.

He sprinted toward his ride as a Chicago patrol car pulled away from the tow truck, leaving the driver to do his work. As Pies got closer he noticed that the tow truck driver was a guy Bast and Stan loaned money to on occasion.

"Hey, man, not tonight," said Pies.

The tow-truck driver, a hulking man of forty-five, didn't even turn as he knelt to chain up the front axle. "Sorry, bud. Don't know what the hell you were thinking. A fire hydrant, brother? Dude..."

"You're the one who always goes heavy when it's the Packers and the Bears."

The tow-truck driver quickly spun and landed on his ass. He was a tough, tattooed-covered man, and he recognized Pies right away— like most residents in the Edison Park neighborhood would. Pies was Zielinski dirty, and dangerous royalty, and tonight, like other nights, he had used that advantage as much as he saw fit.

"Oh, I wasn't, ah... I wasn't hooking this car. I was only... The cop said to move it to the lot over there," he lied.

"Great," said Pies. "Well, I'm here now."

The tow-truck driver stood, brushed himself off, smiled, and then noticed the ticket under the windshield wiper. He leaned over the car and snatched the ticket away. "Don't know what that's all about, but I'll figure it out for you. Promise."

Pies nodded, got into his car, started it up, and stopped cold—his eyes stared straight ahead.

Dana Banasik, obviously drunk and barely able to walk a straight line, exited a dive bar next to the parking lot to the east of the Olmsted Inn. Right behind her was the angry bartender, a stocky middle-aged man, who yelled as she stumbled down the sidewalk. The bartender flipped her the finger and stomped back toward his business.

The tow-truck driver stood in place and waved like an idiot as Pies drove his car over the tracks and took a left.

Pies slowed as he paralleled Dana, and he rolled down his passenger window. "Dana."

Dana Banasik stumbled along, in a world of her own.

"Hey, Dana. Dana," said Pies loudly, as he stopped his car.

She finally halted, teetered, turned, and stared for a long moment. "Jakub? Jakub, that you?"

"Dana, come on, I'll get you home."

Dana staggered forward to his car, nearly fell off the high curb, but managed to make it to the passenger door. She grasped the door with both hands to steady herself, leaned into the car, and said, "I saw you today."

Pies froze.

He didn't think she was sober enough to notice that it was Pies who had peeked through the fence. But Dana was ever so intelligent and observant—even while drunk. Unfortunately, she wasn't able to complete her studies at Dartmouth. Once her father died, she was forced to move back home and take a crappy customer service job at a call center in Schaumburg so she could help her mother pay the bills. Two years ago, she lost that job and hadn't worked regularly since.

Pies said, "I just wanted to make sure you were okay."

Dana drunkenly squinted at Pies and slowly nodded. "You like po... poking around. I've seen you," she said.

Pies wasn't sure how to respond so he said "Come on, get in."

Dana studied Pies in her drunken-hard manner for another long beat, before she said, "Thanks for checking up on me, Jakub. But I'm okay. Look now. I want to walk. Need the air."

"Dana, please."

She gently tapped the door of Pies's car with both open hands, pushed away, and stumbled onward.

"No. Wait. Ah, damn it," said Pies. He sat there for a moment before he slowly drove away. He knew Dana enough to understand that once her mind was made up, it was made up. She was extremely strong-headed—and she wasn't going to get into his car tonight.

10

"DEVIN? HEY, asshole, you pressed mute again," said Zielinski burglary crew member Andy Peters, who casually maneuvered a dark-blue minivan through the beautiful North Shore neighborhood, Bluetooth headset on his ear.

The fully bloomed, manicured foliage of the area was visible, even at this darkened hour, because most of the moneyed homes had fantastic up-lighting systems to show off their wonderful McMansions, even as the owners slept. It was no wonder that movie directors such as John Hughes and his ilk often chose this area to showcase the more upscale suburbs depicted in their films.

"That's the second time. You get in trouble and ask for help, no one hears you. That's a hard lesson, dude," continued Andy.

It was 3:42 A.M.

Andy and Crick were supposed to be steering clear of any illegal activities, but this morning they worked against everyone's wishes, including Stan Zielinski's, Noretti's, and even their lawyer's, and they actively supervised a B&E with Crick's nephew Devin working as their muscle.

Bast knew what they were doing, though. Bast Zielinski had lied and advised Stan and Noretti that only Devin would be on the job.

Bast was also the one who had served up Crick and Andy with the information from the Northcomm 9-1-1 Center that the alarm of the elegant clothing and jewelry boutique, located in downtown Winnetka, was on the fritz.

The minivan Andy operated looked like any other suburban parental automobile, complete with a properly installed baby seat in the back, toys scattered about, and a couple of pairs of tiny, muddy soccer cleats strewn on the floorboards. There was even one of those "family of four and a dog" stick-figure caricatures on the rear window. But in Andy's case none of the child or family items were from his kids or family, because he didn't have either. Andy would much rather screw anything with a beating heart than settle down with one woman. And kids? No way.

He and Crick were operating nearly identical vehicles, the only difference being that Crick's was red and Andy's was blue. Both vans were similarly outfitted to make the men appear to be what they were not—honest and hardworking fathers.

The interior design of each vehicle was simply stagecraft.

The thoughtful crew member who had created this, as well as the many other ruses the Zielinskis currently employed—one Pies Jakubowski—had also fashioned oddly shaped and reusable magnetic strips in the same reddish hue the state of Illinois used for its license plate numbers. The magnetic strips would be utilized for areas where too many surveillance cameras had been deployed by municipalities or businesses and homeowners. The design of the magnetic strips was ingenious—it made the Ps and 3s on the Zielinski vehicle license plates look like Bs and 8s. The strips could be removed shortly after leaving the area of the cameras so that, if stopped, the driver wouldn't be arrested for altering the plates. The ruse could be just enough to throw doubt into any eyewitness accounts. "I think the plate had a B in it, officer...I think. Maybe..."

If any Zielinski crew members were ever pulled over by the police while using the minivans, their chances of talking their way out of a search and possible arrest increased quite a bit with a, "Gee, officer, I was lost." Once the cop swept a flashlight across the interior of their vehicles and illuminated the children's items strewn about, they'd likely let them go, mostly out of a sense of pity for the poor bastards.

Andy and Crick had used the vans in the past but had been getting sloppy and cocky of late—especially since Bast quietly took over from Stan and began to run the operation. Crick and Andy had mostly used their own vehicles on their jobs for the past couple of months, but on this early morning, with some pressure on them to lay low, Bast decided that they should go back to utilizing the vans for now.

Before this particular job, Bast seemed to like to take chances. He was hoping to make a bigger splash with his Outfit overlords that way. Larger jobs equaled bigger paychecks for Noretti and his people. Huge paydays meant more of a percentage for Bast, Andy, and Crick. Bast thought that if he placed enough supplementary dough into Noretti's pocket, the Outfit underboss would someday offer Bast and his crew an even larger area to operate within.

However the recent sloppiness was most likely the real reason for Crick's and Andy's fresh arrests near the kitchen and plumbing supply business. Crick had used his own car the day he got pinched.

Bast's, Crick's, and Andy's collective egos had allowed them to drop their guards. And that was not good for business.

Pies had always used one of the minivans when he was assisting on a job. His fellow crew members thought the minivans were overkill and not necessary and would bust Pies's stones for using them—sort of like a badass biker who gives a guy shit for wearing a helmet. Sometimes it's the geek in the helmet who survives the pileup.

Crick and Andy secretly berated themselves, though, for not using the vans and ultimately getting arrested two weeks ago. They would never admit that to Pies—or Bast or even to each other, for that matter. They'd appear weak if they did.

"Sorry. Damn, I must've tapped mute when I popped the door," said Devin's young voice in Andy's ear.

Crick's voice on the other end of the three-way, cell-phone call said, "So, you're good?"

Devin's phone voice said, "I'm good. I'm cool."

Crick's voice in Andy's ear said, "There's no need to cover your face now."

"Right," said Devin's voice. "Thing's hotter than hell, man."

Crick and Andy could hear Devin's deep breaths as he gently grunted while apparently pulling off a mask.

The burner cell phones that they used for these specific jobs would never be traced to them. The used phones were delivered through an Outfit-controlled retailer and were completely untraceable. The devices even arrived to the Zielinski crew preloaded with a scanner app that allowed the burglars to listen in on local police radio traffic, if needed. Once this gig or any other illegal task they completed was over, the phones would be destroyed and tossed into a storm drain. New disposable burner phones would be used for the next job.

Andy turned his minivan down a side street off of Sheridan Road and leisurely proceeded toward Lake Michigan. His eyes expertly scanned the homes that he passed, and he noticed that every one of them had a small alarm company sign near its front door.

"The dough these assholes have. Christ. Copper gutters on this one. You know how much copper gutters cost?" he asked no one as he spotted a huge brick home, mid-block, that was in the process of an expensive rehab, its brand-new copper gutters glinting in the home's fabulous up-lighting. "Dude, they'll be green in a couple of years."

Crick, wearing a wireless headset as well, drove a slow loop around the tiny downtown area of the posh suburb of Winnetka and kept an eye out for patrol cars. All was quiet because towns like Winnetka usually had no trouble at this hour.

Most low-level criminals kept their distance from high-class suburban downtowns like this one, believing that they'd be spotted in a nanosecond at this time of night.

Crick and Andy weren't most criminals. And they had an ace in the hole in the form of Pies's alarm-out-of-service information. They'd get Devin in and out of their targeted boutique in a matter of minutes.

On his latest pass around the area, Crick spotted Devin, his tall, muscular, nineteen-year-old biracial nephew, as he pulled a large wheeled, plastic container from inside of a parked utility van. Crick could also see that his nephew had the back door of the boutique propped open slightly for ease of access.

When the door was initially jimmied, the alarm silently activated at the provider's headquarters in Dallas. Because the system had been placed out-of-service for repair by the shop owner through the Winnetka Police and Northcomm, the operator in Dallas noted the activation and made a nonemergency courtesy call to Northcomm. The communications officer on duty had acknowledged the security company's call and relayed the message that the alarm had activated to the Winnetka Police through the MDT (Mobile Data Terminal) in their squad cars. This particular alarm had been going off six times a night, and Winnetka PD was tired of responding—so the officers on duty chose not to investigate.

Devin had parked the van, as instructed by Crick, in back of the upscale clothing store on the southeast corner of Elm and Chestnut Streets. The van was painted red and had signs with big white block letters across each side that read "Giovanni's Fine Produce."

There was no Giovanni, and he didn't sell any vegetables, but the vehicle was properly licensed to a front company, Otsego Industries, that the Zielinskis owned. Otsego Avenue was a street in their Edison Park neighborhood. The Giovanni signs were really just large rubberized magnets that could be applied and removed in a moment's notice. If anyone got a look inside of the red van and dug under the green tarp inside, they'd also find signs for Ralph's Plumbing and Jen's Custom Wallpaper. The magnetized signs were yet another ploy that the burglary crew had fashioned over their years of successful operation. The crew also operated a tow truck and a pickup supposedly owned by a landscaping company.

In the days before a job was going to be pulled off, one of the crew members would drive the produce van or one of the other "front business" vehicles around the area to simply acclimate the vehicle and make it seem as if it belonged in the area.

Across the alley from the high-end clothing and jewelry store, in this instance, was an upmarket restaurant. If a cop drove past at any point while Devin was inside ripping off the top-shelf-quality wares of the boutique, the patrol officer would probably think that the produce delivery person was making a late-night delivery to the restaurant.

When he first arrived, and immediately after he pulled down his mask over his face and spray-painted the two surveillance cameras that were angled toward the back door of his intended target, Devin had piled two four-high stacks of fresh, boxed tomatoes next to the van. To gild the lily, one of the stacks of boxes had a hand truck tucked underneath it. "Got to keep it a hundred," Devin said to himself when he stacked the tomato boxes earlier. The tomatoes were real and only borrowed for the night from a friendly grocery store manager in Niles.

A half hour before the boutique closed for the night, Crick put on an expensive-looking pressed shirt, painted on his best fake smile, and ventured out to pretend-shop for the wife that he didn't actually have. The lady who owned the targeted boutique, a pretty sixty-year-old blonde with what appeared to be an excellent face-lift, happily assisted Crick, especially when he became interested in the jewelry. By her hasty, eager movements toward the jewelry cases, Crick immediately picked up on the fact that the diamonds and gold were Mrs. Face-lift's bread and butter. But earlier, when he looked directly at her eyes, Crick couldn't tell if the owner was as excited as her voice and quick movements betrayed, because the work done on her mug made it impossible for him to recognize when, or if, she was actually emoting. She seemed to have one expression for every occasion.

Once Crick left the targeted retail outlet earlier that evening—sans an actual purchase, of course—he took a leisurely stroll around the block and scoped out other businesses in the vicinity.

That's when he noticed the restaurant that shared the alley, the surveillance cameras, and also another boutique on Oak Street one block away that was probably nicer than the place they were going to rip off. The store on Oak would usually be their first choice, but since its alarm was in proper working condition, they would pass this time.

Devin Nowak nimbly glided about the interior of the smallish, but finely appointed, boutique and grabbed up the best clothing labels. He was only nineteen years old, but Devin knew what he was looking for. His Uncle Crick, who understood how truly intelligent the young man was, had put him through a B&E crash course, and Crick had taught him well.

Devin shuffled from rack to rack of designer dresses and blouses and snatched up entire sections of wares an armload at a time. Once he did that, he turned and put the stolen goods inside a clean plastic container like the ones used by hotels to collect linens. The wheels built into the base of the container made it perfect for this type of work. All Devin had to do was push the cart around the boutique and go shopping.

In his ear he heard Andy say, "How goes it, mutt?"

Devin smiled at the invective because he knew Andy was kidding. He replied, "You won't be calling me that when the tests come back. It's good. Almost done."

"Have you looked in a mirror, friend?" said Andy's voice in Devin's ear. "I'm going to win this one." Devin was actually looking into one of the shop's mirrors when Andy said that. What he saw was a six-foot-two, two-hundred-pound, handsome young man. Devin puckered a kiss at himself in the mirror and snickered.

"What's so funny?" said Andy's voice.

"Don't get so cocky, Andy, I bet he has more Polish in him than you do," said Crick's voice just as Devin picked up his heavy pry bar, moved behind the counter, and started to pop open the secured cabinet the boutique's owner used as a safe.

"Bullshit. Peters was changed at Ellis, asshole. It's Piotrowski. Yeah, you heard that right. Pea-Oh-Trow-Ski," said Andy.

It took two attempts, but Devin successfully accessed the locked cabinet and picked up half of the velvet-lined jewelry trays stored inside with his rubber-gloved hands. He tossed the jewelry trays into the wheeled plastic bin where they landed quietly on top of the clothing. He reached for the other half of jewelry, tossed that in the bin too, but he stopped when something caught his eye.

Dangling off the side of the top jewelry tray in the bin was a pair of distinctive-looking, palm-tree-shaped, diamond-encrusted earrings. Devin gently picked the earrings off the tray and slid them into his front pants pocket, and then he wheeled to the back door.

"I'm going to love taking that $500 from you, Pea-Oh-Trow-Ski," said Devin. "Wait, $600. Whoever loses pays for the tests, you said."

"You almost there?" asked Crick.

Devin wheeled to the rear door of the retailer and said, "Yeah. All set."

"Okay, hold there. We'll do another loop," said Crick.

"I'm on it," said Andy.

Andy slowly drove his van down Sheridan Road but didn't see any movement at all, north or south. "Good to the east," he said.

Devin stood patiently inside the rear door of the boutique and awaited further instruction.

Crick circled around the short blocks of Elm to Chestnut, and then around once again—slowly. When he completed his loop he said, "Go."

Devin shoved his way out the back door of the boutique, rolled the plastic bin to the rear door of the produce van, popped the doors open, got up and into the van, and reached back to pull the heavy bin up and inside of the vehicle.

The kid was so powerful that he performed his task in seconds. He hopped back out of the van, tossed the tomato boxes inside, and then the hand truck. He was out of the boutique's door, fully loaded into the van, and gone in forty-five seconds. Crick had indeed taught him well.

Crick and Andy drove past one another on Elm Street, and Crick through the glare of the streetlights that played off of Andy's windshield could see the other man's raised middle finger. He laughed.

Andy turned northbound on the next side street and disappeared from view.

"Nice work, dickhead," said Andy's voice in Crick's ear. Crick smiled knowing that they were almost home free.

And then in his rearview mirror as Devin pulled the van away from the alley, Crick noticed a Winnetka police car speed up with its lights off and come within twenty feet of the van's rear end. The patrol car, which was totally blacked out and running dark, continued to follow Devin as he rolled west on Elm Street after turning from Chestnut.

"Shit. Be cool, Devin," said Crick.

"What?" asked Andy.

"He's got a friend," said Crick as he drove away and turned the next corner. "Andy, do that thing and then head out."

"Damn it," said Andy's voice in Crick's ear. "Okay."

"I'm good, guys," said Devin's calm voice. The kid was acting like a seasoned pro. "I'm not stopping. I didn't do anything wrong, right, fellas?"

"Own it, mutt," said Andy.

Devin continued to drive west on Elm Street and headed out of Winnetka—he proceeded along at the prescribed speed limit.

Crick pulled up in front of the other, even higher-end, boutique that was located around the corner from their target store. He parked, lowered his mask to partially cover his face, and got out holding a large brick in his gloved hand.

Crick quickstepped to the front of the high-end boutique and launched the heavy brick through the plate-glass window. The window glass exploded and came cascading down and out onto the sidewalk. The alarm instantly activated with a rhythmic and electronic whirring sound.

Crick casually got into his car and headed east toward Green Bay Road. He lifted the mask up and off his face. He turned left and headed north and away from downtown Winnetka.

Andy skidded to a stop back on the quiet street in front of the house with the expensive copper gutters. He partially lowered his mask and jumped out of his vehicle and hustled up to the front door of the house. When he got there he reared back and kicked as hard as he could right under the doorknob. The door splintered and burst open, and the very loud alarm shrieked into the predawn darkness. As Andy retreated and got back into his van and slowly drove away, neighbors' lights began to come to life all around the rehab house.

"He pulled a u-ey. He's gone," said Devin's voice in Crick's ear.

Crick smiled and said, "See you at the shop."

"Hey, mutt, what should I spend my $600 on? I was thinking of getting a new toilet. Maybe one with a heated seat," said Andy's voice in Crick's and Devin's ears. "That way I can flush all of your 'I'm more Polish than you are' bullshit."

"DNA tests will be back soon, Pea-Oh-Trow-Ski, so you'll see. You will see," said Devin's voice in Crick's ear.

"Okay, let's lose them," said Crick.

"See ya," said Devin.

"Buh-bye," said Andy.

After he drove for another half mile, Crick pulled to the side of Green Bay Road, parked, snapped his phone in half over the steering wheel, got out, and tossed the broken bits down a storm drain opening.

He got back into his minivan and rolled away—headed to Edison Park.

LA QUINTA
INNS & SUITES

Florence
Kraco
2/7 Remainder

11

NAOMI WAS away from their communications pod, and Pies sat alone for the time being. The phone switch was toggled to the inactive mode so that Pies wouldn't receive any calls from the public in Naomi's absence.

He had only a few minutes to get the alarm information that Bast required while Naomi was preoccupied—but one of the other communications officers, a thirty-five-year-old, chubby man named Tim Ketmen kept staring in Pies's direction.

On his first day at Northcomm, Pies had pegged Ketmen as a probable cop wannabe from the very moment they met. There was something about the portly man and the way that he tried to act tough that was very comical to Pies. He figured that Ketmen was most likely a high school nerd who was trying to reinvent himself as some sort of a badass in adulthood. Pies guessed that Ketmen got the job in emergency communications to be close to the action—just not too close. With his experience working at Northcomm, Ketmen would still know enough about emergency services to talk shop in the cop bars that dotted the area, maybe even impress a couple of unsuspecting barflies.

"Hey, where did you work before coming here, broham?" asked Ketmen, but Pies did his level best to ignore the man. "Jakub? Can I call you Jake? Jake-Jake?"

"It's Jakub."

Ketmen made a "screw-you" face when Pies offered nothing further. Ketmen finally spun back around in his seat and seemed to have given up on the conversation.

Naomi had been called to the shift commander's office space, an open area on the outside of the main communications room. Pies could see her and the commander, a stern-looking fifty-year-old woman who the Northcomm employees all called "Soup," through the glass wall. Neither woman looked happy to be in the meeting.

"So you get your frilly written commendation certificate, she gets the opposite for leaving the phone in active mode. That could've gotten really ugly, really fast," said Ketmen without fully turning to Pies. "Stupid move on her part."

When Pies quickly glanced over and confirmed that Ketmen still had his back fully turned away, he used the keyboard to call up the alarms-out-of-service page on the computer system and tapped his pant leg to activate the button camera.

Pies noted that a few of the alarms had been out of service for each of the days he recorded the page, but every time he accessed the program there always seemed to be freshly listed targets, too.

Pies kept his left forefinger and thumb on the button camera in his shirt as he recorded the monitor for a few more seconds, but he turned his head toward the shift commander's office to make sure Naomi wasn't on her way over to the pod.

Naomi's head was canted downward and she nodded to what the commander said. When Soup finished speaking, she handed Naomi a piece of paper and motioned for her to go back to work.

Naomi stood—and Pies let go of the button camera and turned off the recorder in his pocket.

Pies glanced over as Naomi, paper in hand, walked out of Soup's office and then down the outer hallway and in the direction of the break room. Once there, she stepped from view.

Pies pressed the Escape button on the keyboard, and that cleared the alarms-out-of-service page from his monitor. As an added measure to make sure his digital tracks were covered, Pies also simultaneously pressed the Control-Shift-Delete keys to eliminate the cached history on the computer system, something he neglected to do the first few times he'd accessed the alarms-out-of-service page. A deeper, more expert, inquiry into his computer history might show what he'd been up to, but Pies figured his plan would be in full effect and he'd be gone by that time.

He leaned back in his seat and noticed that Ketmen and another communications officer, a forty-year-old woman named Bev, who also wore a dark-blue golf shirt, regarded him as if he were a caged zoo animal. Ketmen smiled and nodded to Pies. "I guess what I was trying to say was nice work yesterday. That was slick, you know, the paper stuffed in the bank bag," he said.

"Yeah, thanks," said Pies as he wondered if they'd seen what he was doing with the alarms-out-of-service page.

"How did you come up with that idea? The bank bag and all that?" asked Ketmen.

Pies didn't want to engage in any further conversation that seemed unnecessary to his task, so he ignored Ketmen's question. Pies was at Northcomm to get alarm information, and that was that. If he had to participate in chitchat or engage Naomi in any way that related to the job, so be it. That would all be part of his grander purpose. But Pies was not going to go out of his way to make any friends at the communications center.

He pretend-studied the computer screens on his and Naomi's communications pod so that no other questions, or conversation, would come his way.

At that point, the other six communications officers in the center saw the exchange between Pies and Ketmen, and they all turned to each other, even the ones currently on phone and radio calls, and shrugged it off. Everyone went back to what they were doing.

"Hey, guys. Be aware that we've had two more calls from the drunk guy on the Wilmette and Evanston border," said Lori, another female communications officer from across the room. "He was over near Central a while ago."

"Thanks," said Naomi as she entered the glassed-in room, this time without the paper in her hand. "Jakub, are you ready to take some calls today?" she asked as she sat next to Pies and put on her own headset.

"Yeah, sure, I guess," said Pies.

Naomi sat and said, "I'll mute my mic and tell you what to say if you get stumped. I'll do the computer commands, too. All you have to do is get used to speaking with the public."

Pies's face said it all. He was a bit terrified by the prospect.

"You'll be fine. I'll be right here with you," said Naomi.

"Yeah. Sure."

"You did okay with the phone yesterday, huh?"

"I didn't know that you'd get in trouble..."

Naomi waved away his comment, and said, "That was all on me. I'm glad you were there to pick up the pieces. After that robbery call, I don't think you're going to have too much trouble with this part of the job," she said. "You're a natural. Okay. Plug in."

Naomi and Pies both plugged their headsets into the communications pod, and Naomi activated the switch so they would receive phone calls.

"One tone for non-emergency calls and three tones for 9-1-1 calls, remember? For one tone you answer 'police and fire administration,' and for the three tones you say 'Northcomm 9-1-1, where is your emergency?'—if you can. Sometimes you're not even able to say that much because the caller will be frantic."

Pies nodded, and they waited. Naomi studied Pies's intense hazel eyes as he scanned the computer monitors in front of them, and she badly wanted to ask him about the beautiful woman she saw him with at the high-school football game the night before. But instead she kept her mouth closed.

Thirty seconds later, three tones sounded in their headsets. Pies took a deep breath to ready for what he was going to hear. Would it be a terrified caller stating that his house was on fire, an auto accident with injuries, or something even worse—a choking child call, perhaps?

"Northcomm 9-1-1, where is your emergency?" said Pies.

"Ah, yes, so dramatic. You, there, what time will the street festival start this coming Saturday?" asked the elderly woman's voice.

Pies was so surprised by what he heard that he froze for a second. "Um, what?" he asked.

"The street festival soirée with the food and face painting. You know. What time? My grandchildren will be in from Santa Fe Friday, and I want to take them," said the elderly woman's voice.

"Tell her this line is for emergencies only and disconnect the call," said Naomi.

"This is an emergency line, ma'am," said Pies.

"Don't you dare hang up on me," ordered the woman. "I'm paying your salary."

Pies wasn't sure what to do, and Naomi could see it on his face. She nodded for him to hang up on the rude woman. He pressed the button to disconnect the call. When he reached to reactivate their position, Naomi stopped his hand.

"One of the strange things about this job is that sometimes the callers with no real emergency are the most belligerent, and the ones with a life-threatening situation are super calm. It happens, and it can throw you off. You may think the caller with an actual emergency is messing with you. So be aware of that. You have to try and even your emotional keel for whatever may come your way. But take each call seriously, okay?"

Naomi reactivated their communications position, and instantly they heard one tone in their ears.

"Police and fire administration," said Pies.

"Hey, yeah. I got a parking ticket near Botanic Gardens last night and I wanted to talk to someone about that," said the man's voice.

"Tell him you're going to transfer him to the traffic court line," said Naomi as she hovered her fingers over the phone number keypad on their communications pod.

"I'm going to transfer you over to the traffic court line, sir," said Pies. He watched as Naomi pushed the pound key and then three digits and then the pound key again on the phone dial pad. The phone line went dead when the caller was successfully transferred.

"Okay," said Pies. "Got it."

"All the extensions are here on this card," said Naomi as she motioned to a laminated phone number list that was affixed to the pod. "Press pound, the three-digit number, and pound again to transfer the call."

From nearby they heard, "Sir, please, the police are going to arrest you if you don't cease this activity." Ketmen, flustered, and becoming somewhat emotional, continued, "What? Please, sir, there's no reason to use that type of language with me. I won't do that. No, sir, I will not. Hello?" Ketmen flicked his phone to the deactivated mode. He appeared shaken and as if he was about to cry. He composed himself and spun in his chair to address the room. "He's definitely on the move today. That one came from the copy shop near Green Bay and Central."

"What did he say to you?" asked Bev.

Ketmen hesitated and then said, "Nothing I want to repeat. The guy has a mouth on him."

Naomi said to Pies, "This guy's been on a rampage for a few weeks. He's a nut who goes into businesses and picks up their phones when the people working there aren't paying any attention. He likes calling in fake emergencies."

"Why can't they find him? They'd have to have him on video, too, right?" asked Pies.

"He's sneaky, and he knows how to work the system," said Naomi.

"Most businesses have video surveillance, especially during their open hours. After hours the cameras are mostly motion activated," said Pies with an expert's tone. "I'm sure they can figure out who he is." The moment Pies made the comment, he knew he had said too much.

Naomi didn't pick up on Pies's gaff. She said, "This guy? It's like a big game for him. He wears hats, fake beards. Like I said, he's a nut. He thinks what he's doing is funny. It took us four fake calls to figure out that it was all the same guy's voice."

Pies took it all in and thought that Naomi was going to offer more, but she had suddenly stopped talking. She stared at him blankly.

Naomi thought to herself that, sure, she received a written reprimand for leaving their communications position activated with a newbie alone at the controls the day before, and she could live with that. If her shift commander Soup, or any of the other Northcomm 9-1-1 officials, knew that she had accessed the personnel file of one Jakub Jakubowski from her home computer, she'd be up for possible criminal charges, though.

When she was first hired at Northcomm from the Evanston Police Department, Naomi caught site of Soup's log-in information for the Northcomm administration's computer system scribbled on a post-it note on the boss's desk one day.

Naomi hadn't seen a need to use the access to the personnel information, other than to check to make sure all of the other regular employees were being paid the same amounts, which they were.

That was until Pies had been hired.

She could not shake her infatuation with the man from the Edison Park neighborhood. She had become so inexplicably interested in Pies's life that she had been following him home for the past few days without him even noticing. Naomi knew that it was wrong for her to get so personally involved with a coworker, especially one that she was training, but she couldn't help herself.

She didn't actually have to follow Pies to learn where he resided, either, because she knew exactly where his address was located. She knew Pies's home and cell phone numbers, too. It was all in his computerized personnel file, along with the fact that of the 750 people who applied for the latest job openings at Northcomm, Pies tested into the top spot. He truly did have a knack for this type of work.

Jakub Jakubowski was made for the job he currently had, she thought. Nearly all of the other current employees, with the exception of Pies and another woman who had recently started on the night shift, were grandfathered into the Northcomm 9-1-1 Center from the individual municipalities where they worked before the inception of the facility.

A single tone rattled Naomi from her thoughts.

"Police and fire administration," said Pies into his headset.

"This is Skokie 2. I already turned my radio off but wanted to let you know that I'm two-seven remainder," said the woman's voice. "Sorry about that. Should've done it on the radio."

Pies looked a question at Naomi, and she nodded that it was okay.

"Okay, thank you," said Pies and the line went dead.

Naomi typed a command onto the pod's computer keyboard, and Pies noticed as a data line listed under "Skokie Units" as "Skokie 2" disappeared from the left-side computer monitor.

"Most police departments use radio ten codes, like ten-four as an acknowledgment, that type of thing, but we use a lot of plain English dispatching here. A robbery is a robbery, not a ten-thirty-one, or whatever they use in other departments. We just say on the radio what the call is in plain language. But sometimes we still use codes. Mostly two-six and two-seven. Two-six means the unit is done at their previous call and available for another. But two-seven can mean a few different things."

"How's that?" asked Pies.

"The man who started this center worked in the Cincinnati area, and a few of the codes he used there made their way into Northcomm. In the Chicago PD a ten-twenty-seven means that the officer would like a driver's license run on the computer. Here, though, two-seven usually means the unit is not available for any calls presently. They're too busy to break away."

"Okay, I'm following," said Pies.

"The code can also be used when an officer goes home for the day. They'll say they're two-seven remainder. Like that Skokie unit did."

"I got it," said Pies.

"But, say, when the police come up on a scene like an accident scene where there's a dead body, they use two-seven remainder as a secret code to let everyone not already on that scene know that there's no reason to hurry. They also use the two-seven remainder code so that any civilians around or listening on a police scanner won't truly understand what the officer is saying, especially when it comes to using the code at a death scene. Make sense?"

Pies nodded. "Yeah, it does."

"I've heard them say two-seven remainder on the radio when they're at scenes where the deceased person's spouse is standing right next to them. They don't want to exacerbate the stressful situation by saying the person is dead, so they use the code."

"That would make sense, sure," said Pies.

"Could you imagine if your wife or girlfriend called 9-1-1 because they had found you unconscious and you were not waking up, and the moment the police or paramedics show up, they say on their radios, 'this guy is dead'? Your significant other would be crushed. That's why they use two-seven remainder."

"Yeah, I'm not really with anyone, but I get what you're saying," said Pies.

Naomi almost smiled, but kept her cool. "Right. Okay, here we go. Ready for another call?"

She reactivated their phone position, and immediately three tones sounded in their ears.

"Northcomm 9-1-1, where is your emergency?" asked Pies into his headset.

But all they heard was heavy breathing.

Naomi pointed to the bottom of their middle monitor and Pies saw a data-line display: The Blue Marble Diner, 1923 Central Avenue, Evanston, IL.

"That's right at Green Bay Road and Central in Evanston," said Naomi.

Pies nodded, and said into his headset, "Hello. Is anyone there? This is 9-1-1."

"I know it's 9-1-1, dipshit," said the man with a heavily slurred speech pattern. "That's why I'm calling. I got an emergency. I got a big fat emergency."

"Go ahead, sir. What's the problem?" asked Pies.

Naomi spun in her seat and said to the other communications officers, "We got him at the Blue Marble on Central. Send a car somebody, would you?"

Ketmen shrugged, and said, "What's the use? He'll be gone by the time they get there." He looked away and acted bored.

In Pies's ear, the drunken man said, "The problem? Oh, I got a problem, all right. That's what the ladies call it. A big fat problem." The drunken man laughed.

Naomi whispered to Pies, "Try to keep him on the line." She unplugged her headset from their pod, got up, and scooted over to Ketmen's communications pod—where she plugged in again.

"Hey. What the hell?" asked Ketmen as she gently shoved his rollerchair away from the pod.

Naomi pressed a radio transmit button and said, "Evanston 2, Evanston 3. Evanston 2 and 3, we have that repeat caller on now. He's at the Blue Marble on Central."

"What's going on, sir?" asked Pies into his headset.

"You're a bunch of assholes, that's what," said the drunken man. He followed that up with more raucous laughter. "There's a fire. No, no. There's a murder happening right, fricking, now. Capone's men are killing a guy right there on the street. They got Uzis, man. They're killin' him good. Blam. Blam."

Pies heard the drunk man's laughter begin to fade as he started to hang up the phone—and Pies hurriedly blurted out, "Hey, asshole?"

"Wait. Wha..."

"You think you're some sort of a tough guy, huh?" asked Pies.

"What was that? What did you say to me?" asked the drunken man's voice as it came closer to the receiver once again.

"Going around and calling us, putting people in real danger because we have to deal with your dumb ass. What if someone has an actual emergency and they can't get through because you're screwing around, huh? I've got to say, you sound like a punk to me," said Pies. "You're a punk. You hear me, coward?"

Ketmen sat up straighter in his chair as he watched Pies go to work.

"I called you out. You're a coward. You're a punk-ass bitch," said Pies. "Let's go. Name the spot, asshole. I'll go with you right now. We'll dance."

"You wait one damned minute. You can't talk to me like that," said the drunk. "I'll tear you up, man. I'll knock you out."

"Sure you will. You're a pathetic drunk. Beer muscles don't count in a real fight," said Pies, who caught Naomi's eyes as he said his last remark. He smirked a little and shrugged a shoulder. She laughed out loud.

Pies said, "You'd be easy to take care of."

"No, no, no...," said the drunk. "I'll mess you up! You can't talk to me like... What the hell? Oh, shit... What did you do? Damn it..."

In the background of the phone call, Pies could hear a male Evanston police officer talking to the drunken man, "Put the phone down. Put the phone down and step over here, now."

There was a whiff of a hesitation before Pies could hear as the Evanston officer wrestled the drunken man to the floor. The phone on the other end of the line bounced around on the floor and made a loud racket. "That guy can't talk to me like...I got rights," said the drunken man.

"Evanston 3, I have one in custody," said the officer. Pies could hear the officer, both through the phone and the radio console where Naomi sat, all at the same time.

Ketmen gave Pies another "screw-you" expression as Naomi slipped away, and he rolled his chair back to his own communications pod.

Naomi extended her fist, knuckles side out—and Pies noticed her offer of a congratulatory fist bump. At first, he wasn't sure what to do. After a couple of seconds, he finally made a fist of his own and gently completed the fist bump with his training officer. They were ready for their next call.

12

"YOU WERE so weird," she said just before she sipped from a bottle of water. "Something was going on, I know it. I mean you completely stopped talking to me. You didn't even come over for a few weeks. Do you remember that?" asked Vicki—the image of her face, videotaped a few months earlier, visible on the twenty-six-inch, color monitor on Pies's basement workbench.

Vicki's eyes were not focused on center-frame. They were angled slightly upward at the off-camera Pies as he secretly taped this session with a hidden video camera.

Pies's voice on the video said, "I wasn't that quiet."

"You were weird, Pies. Really weird. You have no idea how weird you were that whole summer. I knew something was up," said Vicki on the tape.

"Nothing was going on," said Pies's voice, off camera.

"I wonder if those murders got to you. I bet that was it, because that was the summer when Dana's dad and that other guy, the one who never talked, were blown up, remember now?" asked Vicki. "That was probably too close to home for you. Well, shit, the cops talked to you after Dana's dad was killed. I bet that was kind of scary."

Pies was in his basement workshop area to perform a specific task on his computer systems, but he'd gotten off track, which happened every time he saw any video images of Vicki.

The finished product from his work here today would eventually be delivered to the Chicago police. The multimedia creation was going to be Pies's fail-safe method of making sure that no one from the Zielinski crew would ever come after him and Vicki once his escape plan was initiated.

There was a lot of work still ahead, which included piecing together all of the video he'd taken of Bast and the Zielinski crew meetings and burglaries. Pies had hours of incriminating evidence to edit and transfer. All of the video had the faces of the guilty plainly visible and excellent audio quality, as well. In a court of law it would be slam-dunk proof for the prosecution. Any defense attorney taking one of the Zielinski crew member's cases would be fighting an arduous legal battle for the entire trial.

Pies and Vicki would be safely in Vietnam, and the Zielinski crew would be behind bars. And, of course, Pies would be in the clear because Vietnam was still without an extradition treaty with the United States.

Pies hit the Pause button on the playback controls of his desktop computer, and Vicki's movements froze in place on the monitor.

Pies stored the moving images and some audio-only recordings on numerous 32GB memory cards that he locked into an eighteen-inch cubed wall safe his father installed into the foundation of the basement when Pies was a young boy.

It wasn't the most ideal location for electronic equipment storage due to the high humidity levels during the summer months, but Pies needed a secure place that only he would have access to. He regularly tossed tiny packets of silica, like those found in the shipping boxes of computer equipment, into the safe to soak up excess moisture and keep the humidity levels as stable as possible.

For a time he considered transferring all the video and audio data files he'd obtained to a secure online server facility, but the notion that his most intimate life situations, including nearly every criminal activity he'd participated in since the video technology had become so miniaturized, could be accidentally delivered to the world through some bored hacker's efforts just didn't work for him—not yet, anyway.

Pies needed secrecy for now, and he also required the security of knowing that the recordings were nearby at all times, so he could view them at his leisure.

The current stacks of memory cards on his workbench were six high and ten across. Every one had a bold letter *V* scribbled onto it.

There was an even larger stack of memory cards off to the side of the workbench, triple the amount with a *V* on them. These memory cards had the letter *Z* emblazoned on each.

Pies knew that the *Z* memory cards were the ones he should be working with presently. He was supposed to be in the process of transferring all the Zielinski memory cards onto a series of external hard drives.

But then he saw Vicki's face and was sidetracked—yet again. Pies rested his elbows on the workbench, and then his chin into his hands. He studied Vicki's frozen image on the monitor in front of him. He had one ultimate goal and that was to get Vicki away from Bast and all that he epitomized.

When the incriminating data from the memory cards was finally transferred to the small, palm-sized external hard drives, it could be easily dropped off for the police property crimes division through any number of delivery services.

After he finished editing and transferring the video of the Zielinski crew's illegal exploits, Pies needed to find a way to convince Vicki to come with him. As he sat there and studied her image, he mulled over a few different methods, finally deciding that a direct approach would probably be best.

It didn't really bother Pies that he was videotaping his criminal cohorts—Stan, Bast, Crick, and Andy—over the past couple of years. He was the low man in the group and, over time, treated poorly because of it. The nickname he endured, "dog," illustrated that point perfectly. And being in that diminished situation he understood he was constantly in a position of being disposable—if not physically, then emotionally left out. He was nervous about the tapings, sure, but the feeling of empowerment he had as he continually added to his video/audio insurance policy kept him moving forward toward a successful completion of his overall plan.

The members of the Zielinski crew were a part of his journey now that he had documentation on video. Pies began to liken the Zielinski crew to nothing more than passing tourists at a roadside attraction who had accidentally wandered into the frame of his roving camera lens. Emotionally, they meant nothing to him. Well, that wasn't entirely true. Pies still had powerfully conflicted sentiments when it came to Mr. Stan Zielinski. It was a difficult emotional equation to reconcile, but Pies both loved the man for taking him in and hated him for turning him into a murderer.

The police would have much more interest in the Zielinski crew than Pies ever would from here on out. Once he was finished using the crew to obtain his and Vicki's freedom, he would never think of them again.

Again, Pies realized he should be placing the Zielinski video onto the external hard drives now so he could eventually put the crime family away, but he just could not help himself from procrastinating his way through several of the Vicki memory cards. Viewing her videos was a bit addictive.

Whenever he was alone with Vicki, in person, he would not put up as many emotional walls. Around her, he would be more open and honest. More himself. Pies knew that the videotape sessions that existed, where it was just him and Vicki alone in a room, would yield some personal inner truths he didn't see in himself at the time the session was initially taped. Watching the videos over and over again and searching for those "tells" was part of this viewing process. In Pies's mind there was a deeper purpose to his studies of the videotape sessions with Vicki—it was a journey of self-discovery for him.

The stress and pressure of the new 9-1-1 job had torn away at his psyche over the last few weeks. He began to feel quite similar, as far as he could remember, to the way he did that moment in time right before he murdered two unsuspecting men. It was a sickening feeling that had kept him up at night these past days.

Pies listened for patterns in his own self while he examined the taped sessions. He hunted for the verbal confirmations that would point to prompts that could have lead him to doing something radical, like possibly killing another human being. It was something he wanted no part of ever again. If he spotted the triggers in time, maybe he could stop any violence from escalating. Pies couldn't stomach the idea of killing another person.

If only he had videotaped himself during that horrible moment when Stan compelled him to murder the Bs, he might have been able to recognize, and understand, what his mental condition was by examining his physical state at that time, and then not felt so duty bound to kill the men.

Was he an angry person at that time of those killings? Or was he simply a confused teenager, who, after losing both parents, was emotionally prompted into killing two people? He didn't know. But if he could discover now why he did what he did all those years ago and stop it, all the videotape study sessions would be well worth his time.

What seemed to scare Pies the most was that he knew deep down at his core that he probably was some sort of monster.

Who else would kill two men, one within an hour of the other, and simply go back to living his life—other than an unrepentant, and evil, person?

Being a murderer didn't empower Pies—it frightened him. He'd sooner not defend himself and take a physical beating than risk unleashing his lethal anger on another person—and that's exactly what he had been doing for the past decade. He'd been in a few barroom scrapes over the past years, like the one involving Vicki after the football game, and each time he chose not to defend himself and instead to curl up and take the punches.

But his anger did brew and bubble every now and then—especially as he noticed Vicki's physical and mental state declining through the videotape sessions. On a day-to-day basis when speaking with her in person, her decline didn't seem so severe, or noticeable, because it was so gradual.

Seeing it happen over an hour's worth of time through the magic of video recording, though, jarred Pies. It shocked him.

Vicki's vibrant blue eyes faded as the memory cards played from meeting to meeting, her beautiful skin became more pallid, her hair became more unkempt, her daily hygiene, in general, disintegrated as well. She was still beautiful, but she didn't look the same.

Pies placed the blame for Vicki's decline squarely on Bast's shoulders. Bast was the one that kept Vicki dependent on cocaine, booze, and the promise of an exciting lifestyle. Pies realized that Bast Zielinski was a romantic and a social dead end for Vicki, but she couldn't see it for herself.

Pies knew that surreptitiously taping Vicki was wrong, but he couldn't help himself. Other than looking for patterns in his own behavior, he loved replaying the videos over and over again. That voyeuristic re-watching could've stemmed from his Generation X habit of viewing television shows over and over again. He remembered that his own mother allowed him to watch the same cartoons on a seemingly endless DVD loop. She could've just been placating her kid while she got her drink on, though.

The people in Pies's age group came into existence at the dawn of the DVD and, slightly later, DVR systems. Repetitively watching programs seemed to be in their blood.

Pies had observed this particular segment of video of Vicki many times over, and he pressed the Play button once again.

"I had only seen you get that quiet for that long one other time, and that was after your parents died. Pies, what happened that summer? Something was going on, I know it." Vicki's video image spoke on the monitor—and then it froze in place again.

Pies was aware that he would become quiet around Vicki when he was troubled, but he didn't realize that he'd given her the silent treatment for as long as he did after both his parents' deaths—and the murders.

Again, he really needed to know how he was acting before the murders—that could be the key to identifying his violence trigger.

As soon as he thought about how he should look for tells in his own behavior, though, Pies shook himself back into performing the job he initially set out to do—digitally transferring to the hard drives the footage of the Zielinski meetings and burglary jobs that he had taped over the past few years.

He had to focus.

Pies ejected the Vicki memory card that was inserted in the mini-DVR he used for playback and slid a Z card into the device.

Instantly on the screen appeared Andy Peters, dressed casually, a ski mask partially pulled down over his nose, and the cell phone headset on his ear. He wore black, baseball batting gloves and was standing in a small and darkened retail store of some sort.

Off camera, Pies's voice said, "We have ninety more seconds before the silent alarm is activated. The ringer override will kick on right after that, so it's going to get loud."

Andy smiled, and said, "Dumbass needs to upgrade his system, right, dog?" He smashed the top of the glass case he stood next to and began to lift expensive timepieces out of the display case and place them into a plastic garbage bag. "We'll be gone before those seconds tick away, dog."

The camera swung to the right and quickly panned around the interior of the pricey jewelry store. The view settled on an angle of the street-side, plate-glass window. Pies's gloved hand reached out in front of the camera, a rubber mallet clenched in his fist. It was dark outside on the sidewalk, and a streetlight illuminated the painted—backward—business name on the front window: J. Thompson & Sons, Jewelers. Official Rolex Dealer Since 1955.

Pies's hand quickly lifted and swung down hard, and the mallet smashed the display case nearest the front window. His free hand reached into the case and began to snatch up high-end timepieces—and the video image froze in place.

Pies tapped a few keys on the keyboard on his workbench and sent the entire portion of the burglary video to the external hard drives. He ejected the memory card and placed the next Z card into the mini-DVR and continued the file transfer process.

13

PIES STROLLED quickly toward the heart of Edison Park. Finally the file transfers were finished, but now the most crucial portion of his escape plan needed to be completed.

It just had to.

He wasn't sure how much longer he had before he was unmasked at the Northcomm 9-1-1 Center.

The stress was evident on Pies's face. His features were completely wracked with worry, and it seemed to have aged him. He had texted Vicki several times throughout his latest day shift at Northcomm, but he never received a reply. That usually meant that she was on a bender of some sort. Probably out drinking shots and snorting coke, or using the coke alone. She never just drank booze, but blow was fine by itself. He hated that she treated herself the way she did. Once he had her to himself and away from Bast, she'd get better. She'd get clean. He was sure of that.

He mulled over the exact words and the approach he was going to take with Vicki to persuade her to go along with his escape plan. If he messed up and frightened her away, though, he'd likely lose her for good. He probably had only one chance to get this right. But once that was successfully done, and she was on board, he'd have to act decisively—and run.

As his worry and anxiety grew, he walked over the railroad tracks, through the tiny park, and up to the brick bungalow where the Chlebek family lived. He had assumed that his best chance of finding Vicki would be at the apartment over the bakery, but she didn't answer the door there a few minutes prior, and Pies could hear that no one was inside when he put his ear to the back door. If she was on a bender, like he presumed, the apartment would be the most likely place she'd hang out until she sobered up. Once lucid, she usually headed back to her parents' house.

Something was off today, though, and it worried him. He didn't locate her in any of the open taverns and restaurants on Northwest Highway, and she wasn't in the apartment, so Vicki's family home was his final option for now.

As Pies stood at the base of the front porch steps at Blaze and Milena Chlebek's home it gelled in his mind that a direct approach would be best when he confronted Vicki. She had always seemed to respond best when Pies didn't try to play her in any way. He'd explain to her that both of their lives were in a free fall, and the only way to fix things would be to leave for good.

On the surface it probably all seemed rather cowardly, and rather drastic, but it was their chance for a clean break. They were both not-even thirty years old. They had plenty of life to live, and they'd live it somewhere else where the Zielinskis couldn't get to them.

And as soon as those thoughts pinged around in Pies's mind—as he stood there at the base of the Chlebeks' front porch steps—he wondered if he was being delusional. Why in the world would Vicki ever want to come with him?

She had her life here in Chicago.

As screwed up as it was, it was still hers to live—rather than one that Pies wanted to create for her out of sheer desperation.

Pies took a deep breath and nearly broke down in tears at the thought that Vicki wouldn't go along with his plan. He sucked in a few more quick breaths and controlled his emotions.

"Can't happen," he said aloud to no one. "No. She'll see it my way."

He hopped up the stairs two at a time, and as he rang the doorbell, he turned and noticed a young mother playing with her toddler at the park next door. The young woman gently kicked a soccer ball to the little boy, but instead of kicking it back, the little guy picked up the ball and ran away with it as he giggled.

Pies wanted to smile at the cute display by the little boy, but his overwhelming, and still blossoming, angst wouldn't allow him to get there. His mission to get Vicki to go along with him overruled all else. Enjoyment could wait until she was safely out of Edison Park. There was work to do.

He rang the doorbell once more and leaned his ear toward the front door and listened, but all was quiet inside. He knocked to make sure that no one was there, waited, and then slowly descended the steps and walked around to the side of the house.

As he unlatched the chain-link-fence gate that straddled the side walkway, he stopped abruptly and tucked his chin to his chest as a memory collided with his conscious mind—a memory from back when he was a fifteen-year old boy, the summer before he became a murderer.

He recalled unlatching the same type of gate back then, on his fifteenth birthday, as it happened. It occurred at Vicki's other house, the one she lived in before her parents began making more money and moved here to the other side of the tracks.

He remembered that he had been in a better mood because Vicki said she had something very special planned for him that day. Over the phone she said, "Get your butt over here. It's going to be something you'll never forget."

The pending surprise from Vicki that day had sparked just the hint of a lighter feeling in the young man that he hadn't experienced since both his parents had died. He recalled it being a powerful emotion. It was the first time in a long time that he had experienced something that felt like joy, and he could hardly wait to find out what she had planned.

Since the time they were small children, it was Pies's practice to go through the side gate—on either her old or new house—walk down the stairs, and simply enter the basement of the house. The

Chlebeks always trusted Vicki with the basement spaces, where she worked on art projects, so they never bothered to check on her when she was down there.

When Pies walked into the basement that day, all those thirteen years ago, he was met by a robe-clad Vicki. Her hair was done in a stylish fashion, and her face had a splash of makeup on it.

"Oh, sorry," said Pies. "I'll wait outside until you're ready."

"You will not. Close the door," she said.

Pies was pleasantly confused by the mischievous grin she aimed his way, and he sensed that the energy in the basement was very different that day. Sexual energy. The look in Vicki's eyes was something Pies had never seen before. She held the emotional upper hand and brimmed with excitement because she knew what was to come —he did not.

Pies closed the basement door.

"Sit," she said.

Totally confused by the moment, Pies kept his eyes on the young lady and sidestepped to the beanbag chair and plopped down into it.

"Happy birthday, Jakub," said Vicki as she gently untied the sash and let gravity take hold of the robe's fabric. It fell open but remained on her shoulders.

Pies's breath caught in his throat as he took in the sight of the beautifully naked young woman. Her skin appeared so smooth to Pies, like soft, pliable porcelain. He'd never witnessed anything like what he saw there in the basement that day. Not in person, anyway. She had a lacey red ribbon wrapped around her taut waist with a single bow tied over the top of her belly button.

She said, "Ta-da!" and placed a hand on her hip, playfully lifted a shoulder, and giggled. "Happy birthday, big boy."

Pies was utterly dumbstruck.

He had no expectation of something like that ever happening that day, or really any day. Sure, he had constantly fantasized about the love of his life, but Pies was a bit naïve when it came to actually acting on his carnal instincts. Bast, Crick, and Andy teased the teenage

Pies about his lack of knowledge when it came to the opposite sex. A seemingly flippant remark by Andy just the week before about how Vicki was checking out the others in the crew, and being "ripe for action" began to bounce around in Pies's mind. It wasn't that he didn't want to experience what Vicki had to offer; he was just painfully shy when it came to girls in general.

An intimate relationship would never, could never, happen until Vicki and Pies were a bit older. At least, that's how the young Pies saw his relationship with Wicktoria Chlebek evolving. That's how it always worked out in his teenaged fantasies, anyway. Pies was an unlikely and steadfast romantic, but it would cost him this day.

Vicki immediately sensed his apprehension and closed her robe.

Pies wanted to say something, but his mouth wouldn't work.

"Pies?"

He stammered, but couldn't say actual words.

"Pies? I wanted it to be you. My... My first," said Vicki. Her hands began to tremble, and anger and embarrassment slowly simmered as she tied the sash tighter around her waist.

"I... I'm, uh," was all Pies could get out of his mouth.

"Get out," said Vicki, forcefully. "Leave. Go, Jakub."

Pies scrambled from the basement—his own embarrassment was so heavy that he never even looked back.

He remembered going home and sitting in his basement for a time, trying to figure out what had happened at Vicki's house. He had feelings for her, sure, but when he really dug down and considered their relationship, he didn't think that she was sexually interested in him. He thought that he was the one with designs on Vicki, not the other way around. Her surprising—and after he finally had time to fully consider it, quite sweet—proposition an hour ago was a gift. She was offering Pies her ultimate gift, and he was too naïve to understand it in that moment. Too stupid and confused.

Later the same day, after he had more time to ponder what happened in her basement, Pies went back to apologize to Vicki and to profess his love to her.

At his house, he created and memorized a speech that laid out his goals for their relationship going forward from that day on. If she loved Pies as much as he loved her, they could wait for a sexual relationship until they were both ready. And shit, he knew how stupid he would sound saying all of this to her. Most guys his age would've jumped at the chance to be with Vicki. Pies wanted her to know that he was her man for all time—not only for a teenage romp.

When he hurriedly ran back down the steps and opened the Chlebek basement door, he found Vicki and a sixteen-year-old Andy naked, and all wrapped around each other on the futon.

"Dude," said Andy. "Get out of here. Close the door, man."

Pies leaned away and began to shut the door, but at the last moment he caught sight of Vicki's expression. It was one of sorrow and embarrassment.

The gate latched back into place with a loud clink, and Pies heard the toddler in the park call out, "Look, Mommy. Look! I'm kicking the ball."

Pies finally hopped down the cement stairs two at a time, leaned forward, and knocked on the basement door. There was no answer, so he made his way around the house and back toward Northwest Highway and the Chlebek bakery building a couple of blocks away.

Instead of using the front entrance, Pies worked his way down the narrow alley that led to the back door of both the bakery and the stairway to the apartment above.

He had to try again, to see if Vicki had arrived at the apartment when he was at her parents' house just now. He had to find her.

But he didn't want the Chlebeks to see him. It always led to an awkward situation where Mrs. Chlebek would corner Pies and discuss how bad Bast and his cohorts were for Vicki.

Blaze and Milena Chlebek had no reason to believe that Pies was working right alongside the crew for the simple reason that Pies didn't hang out with Bast, Crick, and Andy on a regular basis. Mostly though, the Chlebeks had been gently deluded regarding Pies's involvement by Vicki, and Pies himself, throughout the years. There was no use in causing upset, they had figured. Pies worked with the Zielinski crew, sure, but that occurred mostly at night when no one really saw what they were up to. In the daylight hours Pies would usually steer clear of the other crew members.

As he had done earlier, he arrived at the shared rear door of the bakery and the apartment. Like before, Pies could hear faint music coming from a radio that played inside the kitchen area of the business. He went inside the tiny rear vestibule—and instantly the music became louder and he could hear Blaze Chlebek toiling away in the work area of the bakery. Blaze hummed along with the tune and sang in Polish as he clanked about.

"Do we have more baguettes?"asked Milena in her clipped Polish accent.

Pies stopped moving. He couldn't see Blaze, Vicki's stocky sixty-five-year-old father, or Milena, for that matter, but he was only a few feet away from them with just a wall blocking their view.

"No more. And I'm not making no more," said Blaze in the same clipped accent. "You tell them they want bread to get here early, not right before dinner time. They think this is supermarket?"

"Okay, okay," said Milena's perturbed voice as it trailed away to the front of the store.

Pies gingerly tread up one stair at a time and made his way to the top without Blaze hearing him, just as he had done twenty minutes prior.

At the landing on top of the stairs was only one doorway and that led into Vicki's apartment. Pies knocked gently, and, when no one answered, he stooped over to retrieve the door key from its hiding place under the welcome mat. This time he was going inside to make sure Vicki wasn't home.

It wasn't the most creative spot to hide the key, but no one in their right mind would ever dream of messing with an apartment sometimes occupied by Bast Zielinski. Other than Pies, that is.

He slid the key into the lock and opened the door. Once open and inside, he quickly and quietly closed the door behind him and stood still—and listened. There were no sounds in the apartment other than the low murmurs from Milena, Blaze, and an angry male customer loudly discussing baguettes below in the bakery.

Pies felt comfortable in the apartment when he was alone. He had been here a few days earlier to retrieve Vicki's passport. She probably still didn't even realize that it was missing. She'd have a new one soon—waiting for her at their first escape-plan destination of Half Moon Bay, California.

By that time, he and Vicki would be safely away from Edison Park and Bast's dangerous ways.

He shifted toward the bedroom and made sure Vicki wasn't there napping. The room was very messy with clothing and shoes tossed about, but there was no other sign of the woman.

As he shuffled backward and out of the bedroom he couldn't help but notice a pile of cocaine centered on a tiny mirror on the coffee table. Pies angled toward the coke, leaned over, and snatched the mirror off the table. He walked to the bathroom, kicked up the toilet seat with his shoe, tilted the mirror toward the toilet bowl—and stopped.

Pies saw his own reflection in the bathroom mirror and lost his will to flush the drugs. Vicki would know for sure that Pies had been in the apartment, and she'd become unglued. It had happened in the past.

He needed her to be open to his escape plan. Making her angry by flushing her coke would shut her down from the beginning.

Pies would find another, softer, approach to getting Vicki clean. Hopefully it would be a method that would make her sobriety stick this time.

He put the coke-covered mirror back where he found it and padded through the kitchen and out the back door again.

The door was set to automatically lock when it closed. He gently pulled it shut and allowed the lock to quietly snick back into a secure position. He returned the key to its hiding place and took one slow step at a time as he quietly descended the stairs.

When he got to the back door that led to the alley, he took hold of the doorknob and gently twisted it.

"Jakub? Hey, Jakub. How are you?" asked a smiling Blaze in his accented English. The late-middle-aged man stood three feet away and had a large plastic bag of garbage in his flour-covered hand. "We don't see you much anymore, Jakub. How have you been?"

"Hey, Mr. Chlebek. I've been okay. Thanks. I was on my way over to..."

"And I hear you have a new job. Important job, Wicktoria says to me," said Blaze.

"I'm taking 9-1-1 calls. It's stressful, but exciting," said Pies as he did his best to make small talk and get the hell out of the building.

Blaze motioned to the stairway that Pies had descended, and said, "She's not home right now. Come. Come say hello to Milena. Say hello. She loves seeing you, Jakub."

"I, ah... I'm just going to..."

Blaze put the garbage bag down and grabbed Pies by the wrist. He wasn't going to take no for an answer.

He led Pies to the front area of the store, where Milena Chlebek pulled empty aluminum trays out of the glass display cases. "Blaze. Blaze, my sweet one, *niech maja schabowe na obiad.*"

"Forget pork chops," said Blaze as he stood proudly next to Pies.

Milena's face lit up when she finally recognized Pies. "Jakub. My little Jakub, how are you?" She put the trays down, wiped her hands on her apron, and charged forward to grab up Pies into a tight embrace.

"I'm great, Mrs. Chlebek," said Pies.

Milena broke the embrace, but held Pies at arm's length. "I'm making Mr. Chlebek pork chops for dinner. You come home and eat with us, yes?"

"I said forget pork chops," said Blaze as he nodded his head toward Pies. "Jakub has that new job now, Milena. Wicktoria said, right?"

"It's nice, but why always so many new jobs, Jakub? You do repair of appliance, the fixing of air conditioners, the carpet cleaning stuff.

What? You get bored easy?" asked Milena as she playfully poked his ribs with a finger.

Pies did his best to act the part of the neighborhood kid all grown up, done good, and out in the world fending for himself, but deep down he knew the Chlebeks would hate him for what he was about to do. He was on track to take their baby away from them forever. She'd be safe but completely out of their reach for good once everything worked out as planned.

Pies noticed the small, child-sized, wooden chair that was situated in the corner behind the front counter. It was the chair that Vicki sat in from time to time when she was a little girl. Pies remembered when he would sit right alongside her when he was a wee one. Seated there, her parents could keep an eye on young Vicki while they worked in their bakery. A well-used teddy bear with both eyes missing and matted faux fur occupied the chair nowadays.

"No, not bored, Mrs. Chlebek. It was just a good job that opened up and I took it," said Pies.

"I kid you, Jakub," she said. "I'm so proud of you. You help people with this thing you do now. Really help. You save them."

Both Blaze and Milena looked Pies up and down for a long moment. Finally Milena broke the silence again.

"She'd be better with you, Jakub. You'd be good to her. You know how to treat our little girl, yes?" said Milena Chlebek.

"Milena, don't. It's not your place," said Blaze. "Jakub, she doesn't mean to poke around like she does. She put nose where it don't belong."

"But I do mean it, Blaze. Jakub would treat our Wicktoria like a princess. I'm sure of it. He'd keep her safe from people like, like those people," she said, nearly spitting the word "those" out like used chewing gum. In her invective was both anger and fear, an unspoken acknowledgement of the position the Zielinskis occupied in Edison Park and desperation about their daughter's romantic choices.

"Milena?"

"No, I won't stop saying these things, Blaze. I will not. She needs to change her ways, and Jakub could help her. Jakub can help her like he helps people in this new *praca* he do," she said. "He could save our Wicktoria."

Pies looked at his shoes, and Milena knew then that she, indeed, had gone too far.

"Jakub, you're a good boy."

"Good man, Milena. Man," said Blaze happily.

"A good man. A very good man. And you come tonight for pork chops, yes?"

"I really can't, but thank you, Mrs. Chlebek," said Pies.

"Please come by more often, yes?" she said. "We miss talking to you. We see you in the neighborhood, but you always seem too busy, and we don't want to get in your way."

"I'll do that. I'll stop in more often," said Pies.

Milena nodded sadly as she realized that Jakub only wanted to leave.

"If you see Vicki today, tell her..." Pies didn't know how to finish his own sentence.

"Yes? What should we say?" asked Milena.

"It was nice seeing you both," said Pies as he gave Milena a brief hug and shook Blaze's hand. Blaze walked Pies out and picked up the bag of garbage along his way.

When the back door shut, Milena stood pat, a sad smile on her face. She gazed at the closed back door for a long beat before the smile melted completely away. Her eyes cast downward, she shuffled back to her bakery duties.

14

Vicki Chlebek dodged and nimbly shoved her way through and around the scrum of weary, nighttime rush-hour pedestrians who all lumbered to make their train rides home on time. She was headed in the opposite direction, and she zigzagged her way to the exit doors on the Madison Street side of the Ogilvie Transportation building in downtown Chicago.

After she pushed through the doors and out into the fading sunshine, she made a left and headed east. She crossed over the Chicago River, and when she got to Wells Street she made another left and walked north.

Vicki wasn't coked-up, or drunk and high, as Pies assumed during his search for her an hour earlier. She was on a mission for personal betterment.

She knew Pies so very, very well. So well that she could easily recognize the look on his face when he was distressed and thought she was up to no-good. She caught a glimpse of his expression when he charged through the tiny park, past a mother who played with her toddler son, and to her parents' home an hour earlier. She had a perfect line of sight on Pies as she waited at the Edison Park train station for her ride that would carry her downtown. She detected this all as Pies knocked on the front door and then went to the basement door, before he exited and walked toward her parents' bakery once again.

She wanted nothing to do with Pies when he was in a mood like the one displayed on his mug an hour earlier. He would condescend during those moments and act like a third parent, and she hated that. She'd experienced this from Pies several times in their lives. She couldn't stomach it today. She had important work to do.

Vicki wanted to make this trip downtown of her own free will—and of clear mind. At least that's how she sold it to herself the moment she decided to come this way.

Something Pies had said to her in her apartment after that entire high-school football game/bar fight fiasco had gotten to her. It hit a nerve so deep, and so sharply, that she couldn't shake Pies's words from her head.

"You're selling yourself short, Vic. You should be getting a few thousand for these. Maybe more. Not a few hundred," Pies had said of her paintings.

At first, his offhand remark made her angry, but then what he said to her that night began to sink in. Hard. Her lifelong friend had more than insinuated that she should be actively taking her career, and her artwork—to another level, that her work was so very worthy of greater exposure.

He was right.

She was humbled by his backhanded compliment and hated that Pies was right all at the same time.

In her early teen years, Wicktoria Chlebek's life changed rather dramatically when her parents enrolled her at Maine Township High School in neighboring Park Ridge. She was perfectly happy with the idea of attending a Chicago public high school with the kids she had grown up with, but that wasn't going to happen.

On the surface, and to her immigrant parents, enrolling at the suburban school seemed like the right educational move for their artistic fourteen-year-old daughter—especially since the Chicago public high school in their area lacked a decent arts program.

Mr. and Mrs. Chlebek didn't even consider trying to enroll her into one of the performing arts schools in the city. They knew that the suburban school would fit the bill, and it was conveniently close to their home.

Blaze and Milena Chlebek would have to work longer hours and sell an even greater volume of creamy pans of *sernik* and loaves of *makowiec* to make it happen, but if their daughter were in the highly regarded suburban high school, the extra tuition money would be well spent.

They wanted so badly for their first-generation child to succeed in America. An outside observer may have thought the Chlebeks pushed Vicki toward excellence because they didn't want to be embarrassed by a possible lack of achievement on their child's part. But nothing could be further from the truth. Blaze and Milena would die to make sure Vicki became a good person, and a good citizen of the country, and the world. Growing up in Poland they saw too much strife and failure before things changed and Eastern Europe transformed so dramatically in the early 1990s.

Blaze and Milena had already immigrated to the United States by that time, so they didn't enjoy Poland's resurgence. They were very glad for it, but so proud to be American citizens now, too.

The Chlebeks wanted Vicki to have a better chance to do well for herself. Once she left the nest, they had hoped her life would be her own, mostly. That was their initial plan for her anyway.

In adulthood though, Vicki Chlebek had challenged Blaze and Milena's overall strategies. She needed a bit more nurturing, and a bit more oversight.

The Chlebeks also didn't factor into their daughter's high school educational plans the awkward, and sometimes brutal and dangerous, position they had placed Vicki in by having her attend the suburban school. They thought that nothing could go wrong because the school was in Park Ridge. What could go wrong in a place like Park Ridge, with its pretty, tree-lined streets, and vibrant, Art-Deco-influenced, commercial district that the locals called Uptown? The Chlebeks would've moved to Park Ridge initially when they arrived from Poland, but they were drawn to the Edison Park neighborhood because they had so many friends and acquaintances from the old country nearby. They simply fit in better in Edison Park.

Some of the students at Maine Township High School—not all, but a small and aggressive minority—were so territorial that anyone who was not from their side of the tracks and didn't live within a few blocks of the swanky country club on Prospect Avenue was deemed sub-human. And any fellow students living outside of Park Ridge proper were considered below even the sub-human grade—and treated accordingly.

Because of this, some of the students from outside Park Ridge city limits had a tendency to band together. It was simply a matter of finding strength in numbers.

Vicki was a complete loner who didn't want to be part of any clique, no matter how safe they were, or where their members were from. Unfortunately, that made her high school years even worse.

As it turned out, Wicktoria Chlebek had been systematically brutalized by a few of those well-heeled, female classmates. The boys in the school tended to warmly gravitate toward her, at first due to her natural ease hanging out with the opposite sex—something she did with the guys back in Edison Park daily—and also because she was so damned cute.

Surprisingly, early on in her freshmen year a junior classmate had asked her to the homecoming dance. She was so excited to finally be accepted into the high school's social hierarchy after only a month or so at the new school, especially since the junior was a popular kid and an athlete. Her joy was quickly dashed the night of the dance when she discovered that the boy had only asked her because he heard that girls from Edison Park were easy to bed.

The week after her refusal of the boy's advances, two of the girls from the "right side" of town, jealous that Vicki had been asked out by the popular athlete, pummeled her with fists and feet in the girls' locker room following gym class. As one of the larger girls violently held Vicki down on the floor, the other girls took all of her street clothes from her locker and shoved them into a nearby toilet.

Instead of alerting a teacher, or calling her parents and requesting dry clothes, she spent the remainder of the day going from class to class in wet, urine-soaked clothing.

Vicki knew that her parents had gone out of their financial way to get her enrolled into the high-ranking high school. She understood their sacrifice, and she didn't want to rock the familial boat in any way. It would've crushed her parents if they knew what she had to put up with.

Vicki applied herself and graduated in three years. But she never told her parents how she was treated during the course of her time there, and they never questioned her as to why she didn't hang out with kids from school.

The Chlebeks were so proud that their daughter would graduate from the school in Park Ridge. If only they understood the psychological and physical damage done to her while she studied there, they would have been deeply hurt.

Vicki kept it all inside so that they'd never find out.

She didn't even let Pies in on what was going on through those three years. She grew adept at acting happy and upbeat when she was at her lowest points.

She had tricked herself into thinking that the weed and booze she secretly consumed daily helped, too.

Vicki knew that when she was initially brutalized in the locker room her freshman year she could've said something to Pies, or even Bast, who was a year older, but they, particularly Bast, would have overreacted, and one of the nasty girls from Park Ridge would've caught a beating. Vicki was sure of that, so she did her three years like a prisoner in general population. She kept her head low and did her time. The locker-room beating had been only the beginning of the abuse she endured.

But the psychological damage was done, and these days, years after graduation, Vicki couldn't stand being around anyone she perceived to have been a domineering girl when she was younger—even if the woman had matured and apparently grown out of her abusive ways. Those girls, even now as full-grown women, when faced with a stressful situation, would let their nasty-girl flags fly. Vicki had seen it time and time again.

Once while working the counter at her parents' bakery a few years after high school, Vicki was berated by an entitled, snippy suburban woman for what she considered the lack of quality in their baked goods. Vicki completely lost her temper with the woman and physically shoved her from the store. Nothing more had come of the volatile situation, but Vicki's anger boiled barely beneath her artistic surface at nearly all times.

Those violent bubbles of emotion were also the reason her artwork was so visceral and appealed to people. Viewers could nearly feel Vicki's anger, hurt, and deep-felt emotions through her brushwork.

As Vicki walked along on Wells Street she crossed over the Chicago River and continued north toward Superior Street. The area where she was headed was a good, long, trek on foot from the train station, but the movement, the setting autumn sunshine, and the vibrant downtown scene helped clear her head and get her ready for what she was about to do.

She'd never done this type of thing before—ask a high-end art gallery to look at her work. She was wildly anxious. But thankfully her excitement seemed to overrule all her other emotions. It was a good thing she didn't do a bump of coke before her trip to downtown, because she would've been so wired, and on edge, that she would have probably talked herself out of the trip altogether.

In the past, she'd sold pieces of her work in piecemeal fashion, but that was usually through neighborhood word of mouth and for chump change. The galleries on Superior and Huron Streets in River North were the main destination for any artist of note in the Chicago metro area.

Vicki checked her watch, a Rolex that Pies gave her as a gift a few months before, and saw that she had plenty of time before any of the galleries closed. She knew that the timepiece was probably snagged from some job the Zielinskis pulled off, but that was okay with her.

The only ones getting hurt by the burglary crew's activities were the insurance companies, she presumed, incorrectly.

She didn't know about, or get involved in, the crime crew's day-to-day operations, but she knew enough to understand what Bast, Pies, and the rest of them did for money. It didn't bother her too much. In fact, she kind of thought that being Bast's side woman was glamorous in its own way. The crime boss provided her the party lifestyle she'd become comfortable with, and her freewheeling ways worked to fuel her creative process.

But she still yearned for something all her own—something that she, and only she, had set up and worked out by herself. Sure, she was the mistress of a criminal, but she still had some pride.

Vicki slowed her pace and took in the sights of the city. Edison Park was located within the limits of Chicago, too, but it was absolutely nothing like downtown. Downtown was a weirdly magical place for Vicki, where beauty and sadness mixed at the street level. Her senses were assaulted from all sides by sights, sounds, and smells. Where the sweet fragrance of freshly popped, caramel corn and other enticing cooking smells mingled with the sewer gasses emanating from the river and storm drains, and where thousand-dollar suits slipped past the fetid, huddled homeless.

At every street corner she found visual seeds that could grow and become future paintings, both in the faces and actions of the downtown inhabitants and visitors—but also in the soaring architecture that rose all about her. There was so much to take in.

As she walked, she was amused by the absolutely frantic nature of some of the people who scurried about. The primal expressions on their faces, as if their lives were in danger if they didn't get the hell away from their offices, were enough to make her nervously smile and giggle out loud.

She stopped and took in the view of the sun as it dipped between two buildings. The purple-hued, elongated shadow the buildings cast on the sidewalk below intrigued her. Pedestrians walked from the dark purple shadows to the blast of sunshine that cut between the structures. People seemed to disappear into the burst of sunlight for a brief moment, as if being teleported to another planet, only to reappear into the shadow cast by the next building. She stored that image away in her creative brain bank where it would, someday, become an actual painting.

Finally, at the corner of Wells and Superior, Vicki paused to collect herself. This was the location of choice, and this cold-call situation she placed herself into involved being on her best behavior. The galleries she approached would have no idea she was coming through their doors. It was chancy, she knew, but she had to expand her boundaries and maybe, hopefully, even her career.

"Hey, pretty lady," said a man's voice.

Vicki flinched because the man surprised her. He was a well-dressed, handsome man, about thirty years old or so, and he was armed with a confident, sexy smile.

"Need help with anything? You look lost," said the man.

"I'm cool," said Vicki. She wondered what the man's angle was going to be. She'd been approached numerous times since she was a teenager and began to blossom, so she was an old pro at deflecting unwanted advances.

"There's no doubt you are definitely cool," said the man. "Want to get a drink?"

Vicki simply ignored the man for the moment and turned her head east and then west, as she scanned Superior Street. The first gallery that looked promising, and there were many in her line of sight, was the one she'd go to. After a couple of eye sweeps, she spotted a sign with white and red lettering—the colors of the flag of her family's origins. That would be the one. It was the signal she was looking for.

She began to move toward her chosen gallery, and the man said, "You know that everything old is new again, right?"

Vicki hesitated for a moment and caught the man's eye.

"I have you pegged as a fellow traveler. I'm never wrong about these things. We could bump, bump, bump. I'll give you the Roger discount. I'm Roger, if you hadn't figured that out. Hello," said the man as he pretended to doff an imaginary hat.

Vicki, slightly confused, tilted her head to the side and noticed as the man pulled a small, cocaine-filled, clear plastic baggie from his shirt pocket and then replaced it. He tapped at his pocket and winked. "I can set that up for you."

Vicki kept moving toward her chosen gallery.

"I'm not going anywhere. I live in that high-rise right there, so if you're interested, I'll be around, pretty lady."

The man with the coke walked in the other direction and leisurely window-shopped the galleries as he went along.

Even through the din of passing traffic, Vicki heard her phone ring in her purse. She stopped, dug it out, and saw on the phone's display that it was Bast calling. She answered and pressed the phone to her ear.

"Hey, baby, I was just—"

"Where the hell are you? We're supposed to be getting dinner at the Olmsted Inn," said Bast. "You know she's with the kids at her mother's tonight."

"Bast, I had something to do downtown, but I'll be back in an hour. I promise. I've checked the train schedule, and if—"

"You're coked up, aren't you? You get your ass back here now," Bast urged over the phone. "I told you, you can only use when you're with me. You act crazy when you do it. You can't be alone."

Vicki held the phone away from her ear and nearly ended the call. Instead, she pressed the phone back against her ear and said, "I'm not coked... I'll meet you in an hour or so. I have something that I have to do."

And she disconnected the call.

"Shit," she said loudly right as two women walked past. "Sorry. Sorry about that," said Vicki to the women.

She collected her wits and continued to her desired destination.

Vicki gently pulled open the door of the gallery with the white-and-red-colored sign and slipped inside.

The hum from the street traffic faded the moment the door softly snicked closed behind her. The place was Monday-church quiet. Vicki rocked a little on her feet and could tell, even through her shoes, that the carpet underfoot was quite cushy and top-notch. The air smelled faintly of lavender, and the art pieces displayed were breathtaking.

Each private gallery is curated by the dictates of the owner's own tastes, and the owner of this particular establishment would appreciate Vicki's work, she was certain. She wondered if other galleries in the area would have the same sensibilities, or if she had simply gotten lucky by choosing this establishment first.

The pieces inside were a mix of abstract and modern art. Vicki's football-game pieces with their juxtaposition of wholesomeness and violence would fit in well here.

Vicki advanced a couple steps farther inside and leaned forward to check a price tag on the piece nearest the front window—$15,750. "For a forty-by-twenty-eight canvas?" Vicki asked herself, nearly inaudibly. "Holy hell," she whispered.

"Hello. Let me know if I can assist you in any way," said the blonde-haired, thirty-five-year-old woman, the gallery owner, as she walked from the back and into the showroom area. The owner wore the look of a well-maintained woman, extremely polished, dressed in an expensive ensemble—and she never even glimpsed at Vicki directly.

Vicki immediately picked up on the gallery owner's dismissive nature, and she wondered if choosing this place was actually a mistake. She closed her eyes, took in a deep breath, let it out, opened her eyes, and moved toward the antique oak desk the gallery owner had taken a seat behind.

"Hello. My name is Vicki Chlebek, and I'm an artist..."

"Oh, really? That's nice," said the gallery owner through a toothy, faux smile as she tapped away on her computer keyboard and basically ignored Vicki.

Vicki wasn't going to stop now. "I think my work would fit here in your gallery. It's a blend of styles, but it would fit, I'm sure of it."

The gallery owner finally gave Vicki a brief once-over, let out a breath, and said, "I am so sorry, but I am truly swamped right now. There's a big showing Saturday. If you can go to the Web site and follow the contact link, that'd be great. E-mail me, and I'll take a look from there. How's that sound? The address is on the card right there."

"But I'm right here. I have pics on my phone of some of my pieces," said Vicki as she nervously fumbled in her bag for her phone.

The gallery owner did her best to remain professional, but she physically stiffened. "Please, if you can go to the web address and follow the procedure, I'll make sure to take your work under consideration," said the gallery owner, who had now completely lost her smile. "I am truly busy."

That stopped Vicki. Her eyes glazed over, and she wanted so badly to come back at the woman like she had done to so many other entitled, rich girls since her high school days, but she pulled up short. She needed to get used to dealing with perceived elitists if she was going to make any headway in her artistic pursuits.

"I'll navigate the phone for you. You won't even have to—"

"Have a good day," said the gallery owner, the fake smile returning.

Vicki lowered her head. And just like that, what little confidence she had mustered for this foray to downtown was instantly depleted in that very moment. Gone. She stopped fumbling for her phone, turned, and walked toward the front door.

When she got to the door, though, she spun back around. "How do you know my work isn't up to your standards? You have no idea what it looks like," said Vicki.

The gallery owner looked up from her computer and said, "I'm sure your pieces are wonderful. Please, I have work. Have a good day." She went back to typing on her computer.

Vicki then noticed her own reflection in a tall floor mirror that sat propped against the wall to the side of the front door. What she saw was a very pretty, twenty-eight-year-old woman dressed in a modest, white button-up blouse and nice blue jeans. No pizzazz, no over-the-top style at all. She was simply a girl from Edison Park.

She tilted her head back toward the woman and said, "I'm an actual artist. I'm not some wannabe selling other people's work and making a buck off their talents because I don't have any myself."

The gallery owner's head snapped in her direction, and her face reddened. Vicki's outburst had hit its mark.

"Your loss, sweetie. You talentless piece of..." said Vicki as she shoved her way out of the gallery and did her best not to allow any tears to fill her eyes. "Shit."

"We meet again," said Roger. "I have time if you still want to get that drink."

"Leave me alone," said Vicki as she charged back in the direction of the train station—past gallery after gallery.

Her mind was filled with so many angry thoughts, and all at once she began to hate what her life had become. This was the usual course for Vicki, though, when things didn't go her way.

She knew something was probably wrong with her mind. Her parents loved her deeply she realized, but they never recognized her psychological issues and that she required professional help. She'd been left to emotionally fend for herself all these years.

And damn it, she was an artist, not some piece of property for Bast, or the jerk at the gallery, to order around.

She checked her Rolex and saw she could easily make her train ride home if she kept walking at the same pace back to the station—and as quickly as that thought came to her, another did, too.

Why had Pies's comment about her artwork gotten to her? She wanted to work at her own pace and be her own person. She really didn't want to expand her career at this time. Not right now, anyway. She was so sick of doing things for others—her parents, Bast, and Pies.

"Damn it, Pies," she said aloud. "Why can't you let me be?" If she wanted to stay in Edison Park and paint what she wanted when she wanted, that should be more than enough. Why had Vicki allowed these two men, Bast and Pies, to push-pull her in so many different directions over the years? The directions that they wanted for her were theirs, not what she wanted for herself.

Vicki angrily ripped the Rolex from her wrist and spun on her heels. She accidentally collided with a woman in a windbreaker who was a few feet behind her at the moment, and said, "Sorry."

She walked-jogged in the direction of the man who wanted to party with her. She had a trade she needed to set up with him—a Rolex for the baggie in his pocket.

The woman that Vicki collided with straightened her windbreaker and covered the stitched police badge that was woven into her dark-colored work shirt.

Naomi Gott observed as Vicki walked briskly down the sidewalk. She waited for a moment, and then followed.

15

Bast was pissed off. It was all about his body language—shoulders bunched, head leaned forward, his mouth tightly closed. It was there for all to see at the crowded Olmsted Inn.

Crick nudged Andy with an elbow and nodded toward Bast as the two men walked to the back booth where their boss sat.

"Ah, man. Great," said Andy when he finally noticed Bast and his moody posture. "Hey, almost forgot. I'm supposed to get an e-mail with those DNA results back today. Let Devin know that I only take cash," he said with a laugh. "Six one-hundred-dollar bills works for me, but I will takes twenties in a pinch."

"Focus, asshole," said Crick, as they steadily moved between and around, the occupied tables to Bast's back booth. Crick watched as a waitress brought a drink to their boss, set it down, and turned back to the bar—just as Bast took his first sip.

"Hey? What the hell is wrong with... Rum and Coke—not Diet Coke," said Bast.

The waitress bowed her head a little, returned to the table, and retrieved the drink as Andy and Crick slid in across from the Zielinski crew boss.

"How hard is that, huh? Shit," said Bast to no one, really.

Bast finally leaned back, relaxed a bit, and took in the sight of Andy and Crick.

"Did you see her outside?" he asked. "She does that sometimes until she knows I've cooled down. She'll walk up and down the sidewalk."

Andy asked, "Vicki, or one of the other ones?"

"What? Vicki, asshole," said Bast.

Both Andy and Crick shook their heads.

"You know what? Screw it. Listen, there's no slowing down. We amp up. We ramp up. And we go to town on those lists. Are we cool?"

"Yeah, sure," said Crick.

"That nephew of yours will be fine until you two are free to do the heavy lifting again. How many do you think he can pull in a night?" asked Bast, as he reached into his pants pocket and pulled out a wad of cash.

"A night?" asked Crick, concern showing on his face.

Andy said, "Bast, I think we're good to go now, man. We can jump back in. No one's been following us, I'm sure of it. Screw that lawyer and his shitty advice."

"But what's a few weeks to make sure?" asked Crick. "Let Devin take some of these layups we've been handed, maybe do a couple a week, and..."

"A week, Crick? No. You'll do a few every night. We're not going to have Pies for much longer. That place is going to find him out sooner than later. We have to move now, as fast as we can pull them off," said Bast as he slid a piece of folded paper across the tabletop to Crick.

Bast looked around to make sure no one was paying them any attention, and he said, "You've got a medical supply and an office supply that will be out all week. Benny's Liquors on Golf Road is out for the next two nights. The fine wine room there will be gold. There's a kitchen supply and an antique jewelry place in Skokie that will be out tonight only."

Crick said, "Kitchen supply? What, like utensils? Why would we..."

"High-end mixers are the specialty there. I checked online. An easy $150 each for us on the market," said Bast. "They're a grand retail, asshole."

Crick nodded and acted as if the slight didn't sting.

Andy scooped up the paper and saw the kitchen supply business name and added, "Shit, the knife sets alone will bring some nice ched-dar. Easy to carry. You can haul a ton of those at one time."

Crick nodded in agreement but wanted so badly to slap Andy for overriding him in front of Bast.

"Do the interference thing and let your nephew..."

"Devin," said Crick.

"Sure. Let Devin do the heavy lifting," said Bast.

Crick leaned forward and lowered his voice even further. He said, "Bast, man, we need to hit a place that's not on that list. If we're only taking out spots that Pies is handing us, he'll be in a cage in a couple days, not a couple of weeks or months. It won't be hard to figure out."

Bast violently slapped the table, and other patrons around them all looked before they turned away. Bast settled down but kept his eyes angled angrily at Crick. "We're doing this."

Andy broke the tension. "What about more space? How's that go-ing? We're up to the ceiling, and Lou isn't ready yet for the last wave of merch. He's still selling off the stuff from a week ago."

Bast leaned back and said, "I have a lead on another closed school in Niles that'll be renting space soon."

"The Touhy building is almost full, so..."

"I'm working it, Andy," said Bast. "Okay?"

Andy leaned back and put his palms out in surrender.

"This is how we're going to officially introduce my leadership to the boys in Oak Park and beyond. We earn for them. We earn and we become indispensable to them," said Bast. "Pies? I'm not worried about Pies any more. If soldiers fall, soldiers fall. We just need to set the tone."

"Sure," said Crick, his eyes cast on the tabletop.

"It's an awesome idea, Bast," said an uncertain Andy.

As the waitress brought over the correct drink order, Bast grabbed her wrist and stopped her before she could leave.

"Sorry about my attitude. Been a stressful week and I shouldn't take that out on you," he said as he seductively slid a hundred-dollar bill into her palm. She smiled and walked away.

Bast took the glass from the tabletop, raised it in a toast, and then chugged it down.

Crick dug his cell phone out of his pocket and began typing a text message addressed to Devin. It read: tnite @1.

Crick pressed the button that sent the text message and raised his hand for the waitress to return.

16

VICKI WAS high, and Naomi could tell immediately as she took one of the last remaining seats across from her on the train at the Ogilvie Transportation Center. The doors hissed closed, and the nine-car train slowly rolled out of the station as the other passengers settled into their chosen seats.

Vicki sat farthest from the middle of the car, where the end seats are locked in a backward-facing position. That allowed Naomi to look at Vicki head-on, knee-to-knee.

Vicki's eyes fixed onto Naomi for just a second before they darted about. She used the fingers on her right hand to tap out a tune that played only in her head on the seat cover.

"Hi," said Naomi. When Vicki didn't respond, she asked, "Headed home?"

Vicki's eyes flitted about as she rubbed under her nose with her left forefinger. But then her eyes locked and briefly held on Naomi for a moment, before they went off on another herky-jerky mind journey.

"It's home to Arlington Heights for me," said Naomi. She lied because the zone ticket she purchased would only bring her as far as Park Ridge, one stop after Vicki's, where she knew the pretty woman would be exiting the train. Naomi knew all of this because she'd been following Vicki this entire time. Earlier, she even had to quickly bolt into the Edison Park train station to hide from Pies when he walked past so she wouldn't be seen.

The train continued to make headway over the crisscrossing switches just outside the station. Each switch passed over made the car tilt from side to side, and the noise created was such that conversational volume had to be adjusted to match the racket.

"I love going downtown. The shopping and the..."

"Why are you talking to me?" asked Vicki.

Naomi smiled and bowed her head. "Nervous traveler, I guess."

"I know you're making *me* nervous," said Vicki.

"Sorry about that."

The train picked up speed as it chugged along.

Naomi stared out the window, but she could see Vicki staring directly at her in the reflection of the train's window glass.

The train lurched and rolled along through the cavernous set of buildings that made up the West Loop, and Naomi saw that Vicki's stare never left her.

"Edison Park," said Vicki. "That's where I'm going."

"I'm really sorry. I didn't mean to bother you," said Naomi.

"No need to apologize," said Vicki.

Naomi knew the opening was made, and she dove right in. "That's a great neighborhood," she said while still looking out the window. "I had friends in high school who lived there. They went to Loyola."

"Yeah? Cool," said Vicki.

"And a guy who started at my work lives around there," said Naomi as she turned to face Vicki.

"Is that right? I've lived there my whole life. What's his name? I may know him," said Vicki as she pulled her phone from her purse and began to rapidly slide through the photos of the paintings that she wanted the gallery owner to see.

Naomi saw what she was doing and said, "Wow, those are colorful."

"I was just... I had to try and make something happen. Probably too soon," said Vicki, absently.

"What's that?" asked Naomi.

Vicki put her phone away and said, "Nothing. What's the guy's name?"

"Guy?" asked Naomi.

"From your work. The new guy," said Vicki.

"Jakub. Jakub Jakubowski," said Naomi.

Vicki's mind raced at an even faster rate than the coke allowed for. Her eyes fluttered a little as she tried her best to come up with a response to this strange lady on the train. Vicki knew that something was really off.

She said, "Jakubowski? No, never heard of him."

Naomi was a bit shocked at first that Vicki offered up the lie, but then she played it cool. She'd already launched a Hail Mary and knew that it didn't connect. "Big neighborhood, Edison Park," said Naomi.

"Not really," said Vicki as she got up, walked to the other end of the car, and found the last remaining seat available.

Naomi looked out the window and pretended as if Vicki's verbal slap didn't get to her. "Damn it," she quietly said to herself.

Thirty minutes later, when the train stopped in Edison Park, Vicki hopped off and Naomi looked out her window as the coked-up woman strolled toward her parents' home.

Naomi exited the train a mile down the road at the Park Ridge stop. She'd have to hoof it back down Northwest Highway to where she parked her car in front of Chlebeks' Bakery before she would be able to drive back to her shitty trailer home on the northern edge of O'Hare airport.

17

"THE MALL just opened at ten, and... Hey, sit down.... He's starting to get agitated. You have someone coming, right?" asked the woman's voice over Pies's communications headset. "Sit down. Sit."

"They should be there any moment," said Pies.

"Ask if they searched him," said Naomi, who sat right next to Pies, thighs touching, in their Northcomm communications pod.

"He doesn't have any weapons, does he?" asked Pies.

"I don't have police powers to search, so I don't know if he does or not," said the woman's voice. "I'm private security here at the mall. He came into the office upon request, so my guess is no."

"Okay, hang in there, I'll keep you on the line until the police arrive to make sure everything is okay," said Pies.

"Will do," said the woman on the phone.

"Perfect. Good work, Jakub," said Naomi.

Pies nodded to Naomi, but he kept his eyes on their supervisor Soup's see-though, glassed-in office across the hall from the phone and radio room.

Soup had a uniformed police officer in her office. Pies couldn't make out the department name on the patch—and it appeared as if they were locked in a serious discussion. At that very moment, four other officers walked down the hallway and into Soup's office, all of them in different uniforms, a mix of men and women, who all wore sergeant and lieutenant stripes and insignias. That much he could see.

"Big doings, huh? Not sure what happened, but it can't be good," said Naomi when she noticed where Pies's eyes landed.

"Heard there's been a shit-ton of B&Es in the past few days," said Ketmen as he eavesdropped in on Naomi's comment to Pies.

Pies's heart rate quickened, and he did his best to act as if there were no problems. He fiddled with his button camera and asked into his headset, "Everything still okay, ma'am?"

"Yeah, we're good here. He seems to be settling down now," said the woman's voice in Pies's headset.

"On overnights? I don't remember hearing about any reports on days," Naomi asked Ketmen.

"Oh, hell yeah. Pounds and Poulsen both took one each this morning. A jewelry place in Skokie, and a kitchen supply somewhere, I can't remember where exactly," said Ketmen. "The Ps could tell you. They're on break."

Ketmen's use of "the Ps" for Pounds and Poulsen sent a deep wave of nausea washing over Pies. He instantly thought back to that horrible, bloody day those many years ago when he took care of the Bs.

"Oh, got to go, got one coming in," said Ketmen as he tapped his headset and sat upright and turned away. "Northcomm 9-1-1."

"Sit down, sir. Damn it. He's getting riled up," said the woman in Pies's ear. "Sir, you are being detained for shoplifting, I told you that."

Pies had stopped paying any attention to his caller with the shoplifter. His eyes were glued on Soup's office across the hall. One of the police officers turned and stared directly at him.

Pies froze in place, his eyes widened slightly, and then the uniformed cop looked away.

"Hello? Are you there? Northcomm? Hey, I told you... Sit down, and be quiet. Damn it. No. Hold— Hold his arms," said the woman, loudly.

Naomi nudged her knee into Pies's, and he snapped out of his trance.

"Are the police on scene, ma'am?" asked Pies, but there was no answer, only the sound of a struggle and a cacophony of loud voices.

Naomi turned and yelled, "Carter, they're fighting at the Court's
security office. Tell them to step it up."

Carter, a female communications officer, who sat on the opposite
side of the room, put her hand to her ear and motioned that she
didn't understand what Naomi wanted.

"Damn glass," said Naomi as she stood and leaned out and away
from the noise-reducing partition that enclosed her pod. "They're
fighting at the Court, tell them to step it up."

Carter instantly spoke into her own headset. She then gave Naomi a thumbs-up and called back, "On scene now."

Naomi nudged Pies's shoulder and said, "They're on scene. Tell
her the police are there."

"Ma'am? Ma'am, the Northbrook police are there now," said Pies
into his headset, but all he could hear was the fight going on in the
security office of the Northbrook Court Mall.

"They're in real trouble," said Pies to Naomi.

"Only so much you can do, Jakub," said Naomi. "Listen for anything that can help the police before they get into that office."

From across the room, everyone heard one of the communications officers, a man named Jerry, voice loudly, "Be advised, Skokie
2 is in pursuit of an older, blue-colored Chevy on Dempster Street,
and they're headed into Evanston."

The other communications officers, even the ones on radio and
phone calls of their own, nodded to acknowledge Jerry's comment.
This was part of the job. Even as they dealt with one issue, the communications officers might be called upon in an emergency to help
another employee at any moment's notice.

"Shots fired! We got shots fired," called out Jerry.

"Shots fired on the Skokie and Evanston line," yelled out Naomi,
as she made sure that everyone in the room heard Jerry.

Pies immediately saw that the uniformed officers in Soup's office,
all with shoulder-mounted radios, and even Soup herself, looked

into the communications room. They were listening into to Jerry's radio traffic, too.

Two more frantic male voices came over Pies's phone call line and the fight briefly escalated in his ear.

"Hello? Hello?" asked Pies, to no avail.

But then the fight he heard quickly settled. One of the Northbrook officers closest to the open phone line said, "Calm the hell down."

"He's hooked," said the other.

"You can disconnect," said Naomi. "It's over. Let's get ready to help Jerry with anything he asks for. He's got a hot situation now."

Pies disconnected the call, and before Naomi had a chance to deactivate the phone, three tones sounded in their ears.

"Shit," said Naomi.

"You tell them to back the hell off, or I'll do it, man. You tell them that," said the frantic man's voice in Pies's ear.

He and Naomi both checked as the enhanced 9-1-1 locating system displayed data at the bottom of their monitors: 2201 Greenwood Street, Evanston, IL.

"What's the trouble there, sir?" asked Pies.

"I'll shoot her, man. Tell them to leave me alone. You tell them now."

From across the room, Jerry shouted out, "Skokie tried to stop that vehicle at Greenwood and Hartrey in Evanston, but the guy bailed and ran into the house on the corner. He's armed with a semiauto pistol."

"That's him," said Naomi, as she nodded to the monitor and the address displayed at the bottom.

An emotional switch had been immediately flipped in Pies's mind. He needed to help the woman being held at gunpoint by the man being pursued by the police. Nothing else mattered. Not even Vicki and the pending escape from Chicago.

He said, "Do you know her?"

"Of course I know her, you idiot. She's my girl," said the agitated man as he panted out ragged breaths over the phone line.

Naomi took a couple of short steps from Pies and called out across the room to Jerry, "Tell your units we have the subject on the phone. He's saying he has a female hostage. The name at the address is," she leaned over to read from the data displayed on the monitor and then straightened, "Benjamin Johnson."

"Benjamin, why would you want to hurt her?" asked Pies. "What did she do to you?"

"How do you know my damned name, man? Just tell... You tell those dudes to back way off and no one'll get shot, you feel me? I'll do it...."

"Benjamin? Hey, Ben, you hear me?" asked Pies. "Hey."

"Yeah, yeah, I hear you," said Benjamin Johnson.

"Do you really think the police are going to leave?" asked Pies. "You feel me, Benjamin?"

Naomi's face froze for a moment. She wasn't sure Pies had this call in hand.

"What the hell, man?" said Benjamin over the phone line.

"Think this one through, Benjamin. Whatever you did is nothing compared to hurting that lady," said Pies.

"Aw, man... Come on," said Benjamin.

Naomi sensed at that very second that Pies had gotten through to the man. The assailant on the other end of the phone had softened his tone a minute fraction. She knew from experience that could be all that was needed to peacefully end a situation like this. She also could not believe how cool and calm Pies was under extreme pressure. How determined he was to settle the situation. She and the other communications officers who had the chance to overhear his side of the conversation observed the rookie handling the call like a seasoned professional.

"Skokie and Evanston units are requesting a SWAT call out to their location. Who wants to handle that for me?" asked Jerry.

Pies heard Jerry because his loud voice carried around the noise-reducing partitions. He placed his finger over his mic and said, "Wait. I think I can get him to come out."

Naomi said, "Pies, I don't think..."

Pies shot a look Naomi's way that froze her.

"Someone do the SWAT notification," said Jerry, as he lost some of his patience. "Now. As requested!"

"Ben, they're going to call out a SWAT team. Is that what you want? It's going to get ugly for you," said Pies. "The lady could get hurt, too."

"Come on, man, I wasn't doing nothing. The cop pulled me over for rolling through a stop sign. I stopped, man."

In the background, Pies heard a young woman cry out, "Benny, what've you done? Benny? Baby?"

"Stay down," answered Benjamin. "Come on, girl, they could shoot through the damned windows."

Pies gave Naomi a knowing look and a grin. He put his finger over his mic and said, "He's not going to hurt her." He took his finger off his mic and said, "What do any of your screwups have to do with hurting your girl?" asked Pies. "So you screwed up, pal. That's on you. Why bring your girl into this? She didn't do anything wrong."

Silence from the other end of the line as Pies and Naomi stared at each other and waited for something from Benjamin Johnson.

"SWAT's been activated," called out Ketmen.

"Thanks," said Jerry.

"You're right, bro," said an even meeker-sounding Benjamin. "I'm sorry, shorty. I'm didn't mean to scare you like this. I wasn't thinking," said Benjamin. "Okay, I'll come outside. I'll do it."

"It's the right move, Benny," said Pies. "Okay, you'll need to put the gun down, and let me tell the police that you're coming out, okay?"

The woman in the room with Benjamin cried, and Pies could hear her step closer and embrace him, their voices muffled as they hugged.

Naomi called out, "Jerry, he's coming out."

Jerry didn't hear her.

"Benjamin, you hear me? You have to put the gun down first, man. Benjamin?" asked Pies.

"Tell him again to stay put until we let the police know he's coming out," said Naomi. She called out again to Jerry, "He may be coming out."

Jerry still didn't hear her, shook his head, and turned away to quickly write something on a pad. He turned back around and motioned for Naomi to try again.

Pies called out, "Benjamin, we have to tell the police you're coming out first. Don't go out until—"

"Jerry, he's coming out," called out Naomi.

Then Pies heard through the phone as the front door opened, and a single gunshot cracked in the background.

The woman in the room with Benjamin screamed.

"Shots fired! Suspect down," bellowed Jerry from the other side of the room. "Need an ambulance."

"Got it," said Ketmen as he began typing on his computer keyboard.

"You didn't have to shoot him," sobbed the woman on the other end of the line. "He was coming out."

Pies heard a male officer demand, "Roll over. Hands behind your back. Do it."

"You killed him," shrieked the woman's voice.

"Sit down. Sit over there. Where did he put the gun?" asked the male officer.

Pies and Naomi, once again, looked at one another and couldn't believe what they had been audio witnesses to.

"Shit. What the hell? I told 'em I was coming out," said Benjamin.

"The gun? Where's the gun?" called out another officer's voice as she entered the house.

"It's on the couch, man. Right there. I dumped the clip out. It's empty," said Benjamin.

Pies raised an eyebrow, and Naomi showed a hint of relief.

"I got one in custody, you can cancel that SWAT call out. We'll probably need that ambulance just to check him out. Looks like a minor leg wound. Grazed him," said the male officer into his radio, which Pies and Naomi could hear over the phone.

"Minor, my ass," said Benjamin. "Tore the shit out of my drawers."

The female cop at the scene said, "Where's the gun, ma'am? Where? Okay. Got it. Gun's secured."

Then the line went dead as one of the cops disconnected the call from inside the residence.

Naomi deactivated their phone immediately.

"You handled that well, Jakub," said Naomi. "Holy crap. Nice work."

"He got shot, how the hell...?"

"Things happen very fast sometimes. You did nothing wrong. You tried to warn him. That's all on the suspect, not you. The tape will show that you handled that perfectly. I'm sure of it. Let's take a break. I could use a cup. You could probably use a shot and a beer."

They both peeled their headsets off and stood in unison, but then Naomi hesitated, smiled at Pies, and deactivated the phone switch once again. "Have to make sure, right?" she said with a grin.

"Nice job, Jake-Jake," said Ketmen. "You rocked that, man."

Jerry heard Ketmen's comment from across the room and added, "You're the man, Jake-Jake."

Pies looked at Naomi and narrowed his eyes.

"I didn't have anything to do with the Jake-Jake thing," said Naomi. "They're just being assholes. It's what they do here."

Pies ignored the other communications officers in the room, and he and Naomi stepped out of the door and into the hall where they headed in the direction of the break room. Pies noticed that Soup motioned for the officers in her space to quiet their conversations.

As Naomi and Pies walked past Soup's open office area, not a word was spoken by those inside—all eyes were on Pies, though.

"Hey, rook?" called out one of the uniformed brass in Soup's office.

Pies stopped, sucked in a deep breath, and cocked his head toward the male officer who had addressed him.

"Soup plugged into your phone. We all heard. That was a great job," he said.

Pies nodded thanks and said to Naomi, "Give me a minute, would you?" He then angled toward the restrooms that were located near the front exit door.

He turned back and could see that Soup and the officers no longer looked his way, and then Naomi stepped out of view and into the break room.

Pies knew that the police were all there in Soup's office to take him down. He just knew it. Why else would they be there? They would act supportive just to rope him, get him close, so that they could arrest him without incident.

He walked past the restroom doors and shoved his way through the front exit door instead. Once outside, he jogged to his car while he disconnected the camera button and began tugging on the hidden cable through the fabric of his shirt. No other employees were in the lot, so Pies pulled the mini-DVR unit out of his front pants pocket, and the camera wire slid right out with it.

The sweat began to sprout along his forehead as he reached his small car and opened the trunk with his keys. He tossed the camera apparatus in the trunk, slammed the trunk closed, and, with his head down, began to step to the driver's door, keys still in hand.

His mind raced, but he knew his next step would be to get to a sporting goods store for a duffel bag, or something similar, and then to the banks where he kept various safe-deposit boxes. It was still before noon, so he had plenty of time. He would have no chance to go home, though. Hell, for all he knew, the police could already be there. He wondered why they hadn't already arrested him right there in the radio room.

Maybe he could convince Vicki by phone to meet him in California, and then once there, he'd be in a better position to tell her about Vietnam. And as soon as he thought that, he knew it would never work. She'd think he was screwing around and making a joke or something. He needed to be face-to-face with her when he offered up the escape plan. She'd see that he was deadly serious.

"Hey, what's up?" asked Naomi.

Pies almost fell against his car from the startle. "What the...?"

"Oh, my God, I am so sorry," she giggled. "I didn't mean to..."

"Wow. You got me good," said Pies as he painted on a fake smile. "I was, ah...I needed something in my car."

Pies noticed that the uniformed officers who had been huddled into Soup's office all began to shuffle out of the building and get into their cars to leave. Not one of them gave him a sideways glance.

Pies let out a long breath as he shifted away from his car and put his keys into his pocket.

"What about the thing you needed?" asked Naomi.

"Yeah, um, I think it's inside anyway," said Pies as he began to walk back into the building alongside Naomi.

Once back inside the Northcomm 9-1-1 Center, Pies and Naomi went down the hallway toward the break room. As they reached the room and entered, two other men, fellow communications officers Pounds and Poulsen, ushered themselves out.

"A full audit? Oh, hell no," said Pounds. "Hey, Naomi. Hey, new guy."

As the men slipped from view, and their conversation faded, Poulsen said, "How long would that take? The entire alarms log?"

"Go ahead," said Naomi to Pies as she motioned with her chin to the coffeemaker and the cups.

Pies grabbed a clean cup off a shelf located over the coffeemaker, poured some black coffee, sat at one of the four round tables, and watched as Naomi did the same.

"You okay, Jakub?"

Pies shrugged and nodded.

"Jakub?"

Pies flinched and then saw that Soup had poked her head into the break room. "That was one hell of a job just now," she said.

Naomi said, "It was, Soup. Very professional."

Soup nodded to Naomi but looked like she wanted to say something more substantive to Pies—then she pulled up short with, "Good work. Naomi, the ride-along is today, yes?"

"We're all set," said Naomi.

Soup gently tapped her knuckles on the break-room doorjamb and said, "You get to see how the police actually operate on their shifts. You'll enjoy that, Jakub," as she backed her way out and into the hallway.

Naomi studied Pies for a good, long beat. She couldn't really explain why, but she was falling in love with the thoughtful man, and the way he'd been handling the phone calls over the past couple of days only sealed her feelings. She knew that Pies had the type of kind-hearted temperament that she yearned for in her life. Others at Northcomm had picked up on Pies's thoughtful ways, too—she was sure of it.

She believed she knew what was troubling Pies at that moment and said, "This is the job, Jakub. You take a call, handle it the best you can, and then move on to the next one. All. Day. Long. One right after the next. We rarely get to be involved in the outcomes of the calls we take. Sure, we can ask the police or fire departments what happened to a person we spoke with, but there will be so many people that you'll stop asking after a while. You'll get those calls like the one at the mall all the time, too. You send the police to a potentially violent situation, and you have to sit there and listen in until they arrive on scene. It can get brutal sometimes. Once, about ten years ago, I took a call from a woman who said she was having a problem with her seven-year-old daughter. When the lady called she asked for the police. She sounded very angry, but wouldn't get specific, so I sent the officers to be safe. I wasn't going to argue with her. She wanted the police, I sent the police. Let them figure out what the problem was when they get there. The entire time I was listening to the lady complain about her young daughter, I could hear her grunting a little. Little grunts, not too dramatic, right? The cops get there, and they find her holding the kid's limp body in a headlock and actively stabbing her with a ten-inch kitchen knife. The grunts? The kid was already dead by the time the cops entered her residence. She was probably already dead when the lady called me."

"Why did you tell me that?" asked Pies, as he still tried to fight an earlier urge to puke.

"I'm not trying to freak you out. I'm saying that you have to ready yourself to hear all sorts of situations unfold. Yes, even on the fancy

North Shore, in the best of neighborhoods. The shit happens in every neighborhood. Day after day you'll be an audio witness to the worst moment someone will ever have. You may also get a call of a live birth in progress and hear the baby cry for the first time, or help someone with a successful CPR run, or save a choking victim. These things have happened to everyone in that room, if they've been on the job for any length of time. The job is more stressful than air traffic control, and after we take a horrible phone call, the only debriefing we get is a ten-minute break and a shitty cup of coffee." She sipped from her cup and added, "If that's not something you can handle, now actually is the time to hit the road."

Pies blinked a few times at Naomi's candor.

"There's no shame in leaving, Jakub. Most people they hire for this job don't last too long. That's why departments keep long lists of applicants," she said. "It can sometimes become a revolving door."

Pies looked at the floor and took a deep breath or two.

"But...leaving would be a mistake for you. You are made for this job. You're a natural," said Naomi.

Pies pretended to take a sip of his coffee. "I'm not sure about..." Pies shook his head and put the coffee cup down.

He did want to leave.

He wanted to run.

He wanted to sprint back to his car, start it up, and peel out of the lot.

But if he did that, it would be so painfully obvious to anyone at the communications center that he was the culprit who was stealing alarms-out-of-service information.

Pies was in real trouble, but he hadn't gotten Vicki to go along with his escape plan yet, so he had to be composed and see how long he could stay on the job before he hit the panic button.

He had to get to Vicki.

That was the key to his plan. Get to her alone so that he could sell her on his—their—escape plan.

"And, boom, you've been debriefed. That's it. You took a crazy call, and this is your debriefing. Welcome to Northcomm," Naomi said as she raised her coffee cup, again, in a toast.

"Great," said Pies. He gently shoved his coffee cup away with the back of his hand.

"Oh, speaking of hitting the road," said Naomi with a grin as she took another sip of coffee.

Pies barely paid any attention to her, but when he saw the cute expression on her face, he asked, "What's going on?"

"Every newbie has to do a ride-along with a beat cop for a half shift. Today is your lucky day," she said.

Pies stared hard at Naomi. He wanted nothing to do with driving around in a squad car. He'd done it so many times with his own father when he was a boy. It was against the CPD rules to have someone that age do a ride-along, but Pies's father made sure to patrol only in Edison Park, where violent crime was nearly unheard of.

A ride in a police squad car would be a four-hour-long reminder of his deceased father and the total shit that Pies's life had become since his demise.

"Is there a way to get around it?" he asked.

"It's required, sorry," said Naomi.

"What if I told you that I know exactly what happens on a shift in a car? What the police actually do, what they look for, all of that," said Pies.

Naomi gave Pies a dubious stare.

"My dad was a sergeant with the Chicago PD," said Pies. "I've been in a lot of squad cars, Naomi."

"My father-in-law was a detective in homicide for years. He's retired now. And he's actually my ex-father-in-law. Where does your dad work? Or is he retired now?" asked Naomi. "Maybe they know one another."

"I doubt it," said Pies softly.

After a quiet moment she said, "Well, now I know why this job is so easy for you. You grew up in the business."

"I lived with a scanner my entire life," said Pies with a sad smile on his face. "That thing was on most of the day in our house."

Naomi noticed the time on the wall clock. She slowly stood, "An Evanston unit will be meeting you in the lot in five. It's a requirement. Sorry."

Pies nodded, resigned to the fact that the ride-along was all a part of his official training. He got to his feet, angled to the sink, emptied and rinsed out his coffee cup, placed it on the counter, and headed to the parking lot.

He had to keep this ruse going a little longer until he could get Vicki safely out of town. He could do this.

18

Pies used his cell phone to call Bast while he waited in the parking lot for the Evanston officer to arrive, but he got voice mail. He had already sent five coded text messages to arrange a meeting—all without a reply. He was livid.

He had to keep his emotions in check.

Things were closing in on him.

He needed to get out of the situation—now.

Pies didn't leave messages on voice mail systems, never had, and he never would. He had learned over the years of operating with the Zielinskis that there was never any good reason to leave behind evidence that could self-incriminate. He had to let Bast know that the police were definitely onto their scheme, but they had not recognized Pies as the culprit—yet.

Pies had to relay to Bast, or Mr. Zielinski, that the crew must stop the burglaries and get Pies out of the 9-1-1 job at once.

But he couldn't leave for the day to warn away the Zielinskis. If he left, the authorities would definitely look at him more closely, if they weren't already doing that now.

Next, he texted Vicki yet again, and for the tenth time. The simple message read: Must see you today!

He then slid the phone into his pocket and acted as calmly as he could as the Evanston Police car pulled up to the curb outside the building.

A timely reply message with a meet time from Vicki and getting through to the Zielinskis were all that mattered to Pies at that moment. He'd do his training ride-along to appease the Northcomm people and to keep his subterfuge going for the time being, but he had real work to do after his shift here ended.

"Are you Jakubowski?" asked the Evanston police officer with the sergeant's stripes on his sleeves. He was a tall, handsome African-American man of forty, and he stood from the driver's side door and looked over the roof of the car at Pies.

"Yeah. Hello," said the apprehensive Pies. Could this be a setup? Is this how they would take him down for his crimes? Gently lure him into a police car? He wondered. But as soon as he thought that, he knew he was being ridiculous. If the police were going to arrest him today, he'd be facedown on the cement right now with a knee on his neck and a gun to the back of his head.

After Pies worked himself into the passenger seat, the Evanston sergeant sat back down and reached across the seat to shake Pies's hand. "Jay Meager. Let's go then."

*

THE TWENTY-MINUTE ride to downtown Evanston from Northcomm had been a silent one. Meager didn't really have much to say until he got into his own jurisdiction, and Pies didn't want to talk at all.

"You ever done anything like this before? A ride-along," asked Meager.

Pies could've lied and said no, but he didn't know if Naomi knew Meager personally, especially since he was an Evanston officer, and she had told him she worked for that department before she came to Northcomm.

"Yeah, I have. My dad was a cop in Chicago," said Pies.

"Great. Then you probably know what we do. No need to bore you, right?"

"Huh?"

"I have a ton of paperwork to do," Meager said with a smile.

"Okay, I get it," said Pies.

"Let's find some food. You can ask any questions that you have, but I'm sure you won't because you probably understand the job, and I'll get some work done. How's that sound?"

Spending the next few hours not driving around in the patrol car and relaxing in a restaurant instead?

"Sure, sounds good to me," said Pies with a hint of gratitude.

✳

MEAGER AND Pies sat tucked into a booth in the rear corner of a crusty diner on Chicago Avenue near Church Street in Evanston. Meager sat with his face to the door.

"That was quick thinking. Real nice. What made you come up with that approach? The man was dangerous. He'd already shot at the police," said Meager. "I haven't heard the tape yet, but my boss said you laid into the guy—gave him a sweet little verbal one-two, and it worked."

Pies pushed a cold French fry through a puddle of catsup on his plate and said, "I don't even know. I used the guilt of putting his girl in danger to send it right back into his lap. It seemed like the right angle to take."

"My lieutenant is at the Greenwood scene now, but that's mostly a Skokie situation over there. Their chase, and they're the ones who launched the projectile at the mope. Those poor coppers will be bogged down in more paperwork than this," said Meager as he hovered his open hand over an array of paper on his side of the table.

Pies wanted this part of his training to be over with as soon as possible. Small talk was not on the agenda.

"You should see some of the people I've had over the years on ride-alongs. Man, the majority of them are clueless when they get hired," said Meager. "They have no idea what they are in for. And they're, like, immobilized with fear and anxiety when they get in my damned car. I can almost smell the fear coming off of them."

"Hmm," said the uninterested Pies.

"But not you. I knew the second you sat in my squad car that you had this figured out. I've done this long enough to get good reads, you know? I knew you'd be okay with the job. I bet your old man showed you some fun times on those ride-alongs, huh? In Chicago?"

Pies knew that he had to respond to Meager, but he wasn't sure of the right words to use.

A loud tone sounded over Meager's shoulder-mounted microphone/radio transmitter. His facial features hardened and he sat up straighter.

"Any Evanston unit in the downtown area, report of a man with a knife, corner of Davis and Hinman. Possible hostage situation," said Jerry's voice over the radio from the Northcomm Communications Center.

"Stay here," said Meager as he quickly launched out of the booth. "I'll be back when it's secure."

Pies advanced, too, and he wasn't even sure why. Why should he get involved in a potentially violent situation? But, inexplicably, he began to follow along.

Meager, without noticing Pies's movements, motioned to the diner owner, a seventy-year-old man, and said, "Pauly, I'll be back for my paper. Keep an eye on that and my friend here, would you?"

"Sure, Jay, no problem," said Pauly.

Meager shoved his way out the door, and Pies was ten feet behind him.

Pauly called to Pies, "Hey, what the hell…? Where are you going?"

Meager headed south on Chicago Avenue, then turned east on Davis Street. He pulled his service weapon from his holster and cried out to passersby, "Get away! Get the hell away. Everyone back. Back!"

Pies was right there with Meager, and that's when he saw the man and his hostage. They were standing in the very middle of the intersection of Davis Street and Hinman Avenue—in broad daylight—and it wasn't exactly a knife that the assailant brandished.

The three-hundred-pound man wore a tattered T-shirt and blue jeans. He held a crude, homemade machete, point end to the throat of a much smaller man who had already been hacked with the blade along both of his arms.

The smaller man bled profusely and appeared as if he were about to pass out. The large man, who also bled from a wound to his own shoulder, had a handful of the smaller man's shirt. He kept his victim upright with his left hand while with his right hand he held the machete.

People scrambled out of the way and backed off to safe distances. Some onlookers took out their cell phones to record the situation.

Meager got within twenty feet of the assailant and his victim and aimed his gun at the large man's chest with his right hand, while he used his left to speak into his shoulder mic, "Roll an ambulance, but have them stage up the block." When he noticed Pies he said, "9-1-1, goddamn it, I told you to stay back there!"

Pies could hear a multitude of sirens wail in the distance. He was unarmed, but strangely, he was ready to help if need be. When he saw the smaller, helpless man yanked back and forth violently like a rag doll by the large man with the machete, Pies's instinct was to get the victim free no matter what it took. There was no time for consideration, Pies was ready for a fight.

Meager quickly turned back to the matter at hand.

"Let's take it easy, okay, buddy," said Meager, rather calmly, to the large man. "Looks like you already tagged him pretty good. You can let him be now. He's learned his lesson."

"He still owes me, mon," blurted the large man with a thick Jamaican accent. "Pay me, asshole."

"How's he going to pay if he's in tiny pieces, huh, man? Come on, put it down," said Meager. "Can you do that for me, big man? Be cool."

The large man locked eyes with Meager and said, "He shot me, too, mon. See?" He nodded once to his shoulder, "He made me so very angry. I defend myself now."

"Where's the gun?" asked Meager, emphatically.

"Took it from him and tossed it back there somewhere," said the large man, as he nodded to the north.

Three other Evanston police cars, one after the other, flew into the intersection and skidded to halts. Immediately, six police officers were out of the cars with guns drawn and aimed at the large man.

"Drop it, now. Drop the damned thing or I'll shoot," ordered one of the other cops.

"Rondy, come on man, put that thing down," said a second officer. "Don't do this."

"Let's all take it easy," said Meager to his own officers. "Everyone calm the hell down, okay? Thompson you check north, he said he tossed a gun up the street."

Thompson, one of the newly arrived officers, jogged northbound.

Meager said, "Chris? Chris, you know him?"

Chris, a forty-five-year-old beat cop said, "Rondy Clarke. He just got out for doing five on a manslaughter."

The large man's eyes frantically scanned about and took in the sight of each of the armed officers who pointed their guns at his head and chest. He had killed before, and he could easily do it again. One hack from his machete across the neck of the small man and it would all be over—for his victim and himself.

Then the assailant locked and narrowed his eyes when he took in the sight of Pies, and his shirt with the woven gold badge over the heart. He grinned a little and said, "Dude don't have no gun. You stupid, or real brave. One or t'other."

"Stay back, 9-1-1," said Meager.

Pies took three steps back but was still only thirty feet from the large man.

It was imperceptible to everyone except the assailant, but Pies's expression hardened, and he refused to look away. His piercing eyes tore into the assailant's own—and that seemed to set the big man off. He said to Pies, "I'll cut you up, player. I'll take you apart, mon."

The bloodied victim's eyes rolled back in his head and he began to drop. The large man hoisted him back into an upright position once again, but his eyes did not leave Pies's eyes.

Pies never blinked. His inner monster had fully returned.

He stared with a cold, deadpan expression, and the large man's own facial emotions slowly began to melt from anger to apprehension and, then, to outright terror.

Something in Pies's eyes, and his eerie poker-faced expression, had frightened the large man. No one else saw it, or even noticed the visual exchange, but it was all there, and it played out as a non-verbal altercation between Pies and the assailant.

"Look around, my man. You're dead if you don't drop the blade. Do it now," cautioned Meager, and the large man's eyes finally snapped off of Pies and onto Meager. He scanned about again, saw the other Evanston cops all there, armed and ready to kill.

He tossed the blade aside and let go of the victim, who tumbled to the pavement. The large man then got onto his knees and then his massive belly and put his hands behind his thick neck.

Meager pinched his shoulder mic button and said, "Evanston 5, tell the ambulance we're secure now and to step it up. Have one in custody."

The Evanston cops quickly and aggressively converged, and Meager said, "Hey, 9-1-1, the blade. Stand over there, don't let anyone touch it until we get this guy squared away."

Pies quickly jogged to where the blade had skittered to the asphalt, nearly fifty feet from the altercation, and he straddled it with his feet so that no one else would try to pick it up or even touch it. He peered down at the bloodied machete blade and then slowly raised his gaze to stare directly at the freshly handcuffed, prone assailant.

Meager had leaned in to wrestle the man's arms behind his back, and it took two sets of handcuffs to secure him. The large man lay on his belly, but he looked directly at Pies. His eyes began to plead and his face curled up as if he was nearing tears.

"No, mon. You can't do me like that. I gave up, bro. I'm not doing nothing, mon. You can't do that," said the large man, his terror-stricken eyes locked onto Pies, who stood pat over the machete blade.

Meager, confused by the man's outburst, turned to Pies and said, "You okay?"

"I'm good," said Pies.

∗

MEAGER KEPT an occasional peripheral eye on the silent Pies as he drove back to Northcomm.

"Thanks for keeping cool today," he finally said. "It can turn to shit quick, can't it? But you knew all of that."

Pies still hadn't received a return text from Vicki or Bast, and he was nearing panic mode again. Luckily for him, he was able to hold it together outwardly so that no one else would notice that he was actually freaking out.

"Who's your training officer?" asked Meager. "I need it for my report."

"Gott," said Pies. "Naomi Gott."

Meager turned to fully look at Pies. "You're kidding?"

Now it was Pies's turn to look Meager's way. "Why?"

"She's good at her job. Probably one of the best I've ever seen."

"Yeah…"

"That copper, Chris, back there on the scene who knew Rondy, the guy with the blade? Chris used to be a lieutenant on the PD when Naomi Gott jammed him up. Lost his insignias."

Pies didn't follow Meager's line of conversation, and he really didn't intend to get involved any deeper.

"He was married. She was married…."

"Oh, right," said Pies, finally, as understanding washed over him. He feigned interest, but actually he only wanted to get the hell out of the car and into his own so that he could go and find Bast—or Stan Zielinski—and then Vicki.

"Chris's wife found out when Naomi kept snooping around their house. She was kind of creepy about it. Lurking. Kind of weird, you ask me," said Meager.

"Huh," was all Pies offered.

"You married?"

"No," said Pies.

"Be careful, is what I'm offering to you," said Meager. "She got booted from Evanston because they caught her hanging around other officers' homes when she was off duty. She had things going with a few of the guys, and she scared the shit out of a few wives. Chris lost his rank for breaking the no-fraternizing rule. He was a fool, but he's lucky he still has a job. They forced her to resign."

Pies looked Meager's way and said, "Why are you telling me this?"

"Hey, trying to look out, is all," said Meager. "Hell, you won't have any problems with her because she's more of a badge bunny, anyway. Has a thing for coppers with badges and guns."

19

PIES, STILL dressed in his uniform shirt, rattled the handle and then knocked hard on the glass door of Zielinski's Insurance Agency. He cupped his hands around the sides of his face and peered through the window, but the place was empty. There was no light emanating from under the wooden door that led to the back room. No one would be coming to open the door today.

Pies had already tried to open the shared, inside metal door between Zielinski's and the shoe store, but the results were the same —a locked door, and only silence from within.

He backed away from the storefront, got into his car, and drove around the block to the Olmsted Inn. He double-parked facing the wrong way, left the engine running, hopped out of the vehicle, and entered the front door of the restaurant.

The friendly hostess met Pies at the door, "Hi, are you meeting someone?"

Pies peered about, and he angled his gaze toward the back of the room where Bast liked to sit in a booth. The booth was empty.

"No, I'm good," said Pies as he backed his way out of the place and to his idling car. He got into his car and sped away—headed toward Stan Zielinski's house on North Shore Avenue.

That was that.

He was going to go against Bast's earlier wishes and he was going to confront Stan Zielinski directly about their pending troubles. If he couldn't locate Bast, and the man wouldn't even return his phone calls or text messages, he had to get the Zielinskis to understand the gravity of the situation they had placed him in. The entire burglary operation was in jeopardy of being torn to pieces by the police sooner than Pies needed for it to be. He had to get the Zielinskis to slow down or to stop hitting businesses on the lists altogether—at least until he and Vicki could get away from Chicago.

*

"GET THE hell off of me, I'm Jakub, I told you. Mr. Zielinski knows... Let me up!" said Pies as he lay face down on the living room floor just inside the front door of Stan Zielinski's house.

Luke, Outfit member Donny Noretti's dangerous body man, had Pies held firmly in place with a knee positioned to the middle of his back.

"Stay put, asshole," said Luke as he searched Pies's pockets for weapons.

Stan Zielinski and Donny Noretti, both with unlit cigars in their hands, came running into the kitchen from the backyard when they heard the commotion in the house. As Stan rounded the corner that led into the dining room, he saw Luke and Pies in the living room.

"Okay, okay, he's a friend," said Stan. "He's a friend."

"Luke take it outside," said Noretti. "That's the dog. You haven't met."

Luke straightened and Pies got himself off the floor right away.

Luke tossed the faintest of grins Pies's way and walked outside.

"Jakub, you okay?" asked Stan.

"I'm fine," he said. "I've got to..."

Pies froze.

He didn't really know Noretti, even though he understood who he was and he'd seen him around Zielinski's house from time to time. What he had to say to Stan, Pies did not want to share with anyone else just now, so he kept mum.

"Looks like the man needs to unburden himself," said Noretti. "I'll be out front. We'll finish these and our talk when you're done," said Noretti as he displayed his unlit cigar. "Let me know when Bast gets here if I don't see him first," he said as he slipped from the house.

Once Noretti exited, Pies suddenly couldn't get the words out of his mouth. He was frozen in the moment, afraid to broach the subject of shutting down the 9-1-1 job. Pies knew that the older man who stood in front of him had taken advantage of him during his fragile teen years, but, inexplicably, Pies still had a kind of respect for the man that he couldn't explain. As his conflicted emotions roiled, his hands began to tremble. Pies cupped one hand over the other to stop the nervous shaking.

Stan sensed Pies's reticence and said, "It's been a while, huh? We haven't talked, you know. I miss that."

"Mr. Zielinski—"

"You should call me Stan, Jakub. Come on, it's time. What's the problem, huh?"

"Mr. Z—Stan, you have to call this off," said Pies. "You can't do this anymore."

Stan motioned with his cigar to the two chairs that framed the front windows, and he and Pies took seats.

"Call what off, Jakub?" Stan asked.

"The 9-1-1 center job. I know that it could be good for us, but you're—"

"What? What is it?"

Pies had never gone against Mr. Zielinski in the past. He had always done as he was asked, without question or worry for his own security. At that same moment he also knew he probably shouldn't feel anything for the man who turned him into a criminal. He took a deep, cleansing breath to try and clear his head, but it didn't work. If Stan knew what Pies had planned for him, and that there would be incriminating evidence sent to the police soon that would put him in prison, he would be infuriated with Pies.

Pies was at odds with himself over the man seated in front of him —but he had to save Vicki, and if that involved getting over on Stan

Zielinski, that's what would happen. Stan would eventually fall. He leaned forward and locked eyes with Stan.

"You have to slow down the jobs from the lists I get. No. No, you have to stop them. Probably for good. We have to stop it. Now."

Stan began to speak, "Whoa, kid, why are you telling me this? I'm not the one who's—"

"The police..."

"The police?"

"At work today, there were cops from a bunch of different departments for a meeting. That's not normal, you understand? And then I heard a couple of people talking about an audit of who accessed the alarms log on the computer system. They're going to find me."

"Oh, shit," said Stan. "Jakub?"

"You know me. You know that I watch out for you and the crew, but you have to do this for me. This time you have to really watch out for my best interest."

"Now hold on a—"

"You have to stop using the alarm information."

Pies looked long and hard at Stan because what he was about to say, he had never done anything like it before.

"It was a mistake to do so many jobs. You made a bad mistake. We have to stop, or—"

"I didn't push this, damn it. Bast did. That brain-dead kid," barked Stan as he got to his feet and paced. "I told him to be smart about it. Smart would be to use the info every once in a while."

"They've been pulling jobs nearly every night since I got them the info," said Pies. "Two last night."

"*Kurwa,*" said Stan. He almost tossed his unlit cigar against the nearest wall, but he stopped himself.

Pies was confused to learn that Bast was in charge of the operation.

"He's been the man for what, a couple of months, and now this shit?" asked Stan.

Pies lowered his head and said, "He never...I thought you were still in charge."

"What?" he barked. "Why the hell wouldn't he tell you? Doesn't even make sense."

A chill washed over Pies. He knew in that instant that Bast saw Pies as disposable. The less he knew about the operations moving forward was okay, because Pies probably wouldn't be around too much longer. Stan was obviously clueless as to Bast's motivations.

"It's that whore. That artist—damn whore!" yelled Stan.

Pies's eyes hardened and snapped toward Stan, and held tight. "Don't."

But Stan didn't notice what Pies had said or that his employee's emotional state had suddenly turned to fury.

He was too wound up in his own anger as he said, "She gets him putting that shit up his nose with her, and it all goes to...mother-fucker!"

Out in the front yard, Noretti and Luke casually leaned against Noretti's BMW and could hear nearly every word that was spoken through the front screen door.

Luke turned to Noretti and raised an eyebrow. "Was wondering about the badge on the dude's shirt," he said.

"I told you that was the dog. The guy at the new 9-1-1 place," said Noretti.

From inside the house, Noretti and Luke heard Stan say, "I want you to stop giving Bast any more information, hear me? No more lists. Shut that down."

Pies said, "What do I say if he asks?"

"Tell him to see me," said Stan.

"I have to get out of there," said Pies.

There was a moment of silence from the living room, and then, "No. You can't do that. No, don't leave. The cops will know it's you right away. They'll take you down. I don't want that to happen, Jakub. I can't have you in custody. Stay for now," said Stan.

Noretti lit his cigar with a match—puffed a couple of times to get it going. "I bet it's good to have an inside man," he said. He nodded, and smiled, and nodded some more.

20

NAOMI, STILL in her work shirt, opened the back kitchen door of her ex-in-law's home in the Sauganash neighborhood. "Hey, it's me," she called out. "I have groceries."

"Mommy," squealed the little boy's voice from the next room. Immediately, four-year-old Jason scrambled into the well-appointed kitchen, and Naomi put down the two grocery bags and scooped up the little guy.

"How's my big boy today, huh?" she asked as she tucked her nose into his neck and snorted playfully. The boy giggled and began to wriggle free, so Naomi put him back down. "What are you doing today, buddy?"

"Bumpa and me are building a car," said Jason.

"Wow, that sounds pretty cool," she said.

"It's just a model, Mommy. It's not real."

"Oh, is that right? I thought you were ready to drive for real?" Naomi tickled little Jason, and he laughed and laughed.

"Hi Naomi, boring shift, I hope?" asked her ex-father-in-law, Mike, a seventy-year-old bull of a man, as he walked into the kitchen.

"Hey, Mike," she said as she reached into her purse and came back out holding a small stack of twenties.

Naomi's ex-mother-in-law Emma, a sweet-looking woman of seventy, shuffled into the kitchen and said, "Hi, there, darling. How was your day?" She and Naomi leaned in to embrace one another.

Naomi handed the cash to Mike and said, "Here's for last month."

Mike took the money but gave it a suspicious, quick glance before he laid it on the countertop.

"It's not what you think," said Naomi. "I got paid."

"He wasn't thinking anything, Naomi. He rarely does," said Emma with a chuckle.

"Bumpa, let's do the car. Come on," said little Jason as he yanked Mike by the thumb and tried to lead him back into the den area of the attractive ranch house.

"Hey, Mike? I, ah..."

Mike halted and turned back, "What's that?"

"On the job, do you remember a cop named Jakubowski? Probably worked in Edison Park or somewhere on the Northwest Side," said Naomi.

Mike made a face as he pondered. "That's the 16th. No, doesn't ring a bell," he said. He slipped out of the room and said, "Let's do this, little man."

"Yeah!" yelped Jason from the other room.

Naomi felt that Emma was staring—and she was. When she fully turned her attention toward the older woman, Emma said, "He broke up with her, you know. She was too controlling. He's been talking about you a lot lately."

"I don't want to get into this...."

"There's always a chance, Naomi. Always," said Emma. "You're a good team when you're both present, you know. People get divorced and remarried all the time."

Naomi lowered her head and said, "I love him dearly, but your son and I are not meant for forever." She smiled sadly and backed her way out of the house. "There are a couple more bags out here."

"Wait. Hey, Naomi, hold on," said Mike as he moved back into the kitchen.

"What's up?" asked Naomi as she stood in the doorway.

"Jakubowski is familiar. I remember the name, but I'm not exactly sure from where. Let me check some of the basement stuff, and I'll let you know."

"Thanks, Mike, appreciate that," said Naomi.

"What's it about?" asked Emma.

"Nothing, really, only curious. This guy, Jakub at work said his dad was a cop, and I was nosy about it, I guess. That's all," said Naomi.

"A guy at work...?" asked Emma.

Naomi shook her head. "I have to get the groceries, Emma."

She stepped through the doorway and exited.

21

PIES PULLED his car from Stan Zielinski's house and crossed the railroad tracks, and that's when he spotted Vicki. She saw him, too, and she didn't appear to be too happy about it. She was on foot and rounded the corner from the street to the alley that led to her apartment above the bakery.

Pies goosed the gas pedal and accelerated into the alley in time to see Vicki step over a garbage bag that propped open the back door of the bakery and move into the building.

He pulled his car to the side of the alley, turned it off, and got out. He ran to the door and yanked it open, kicked the bag out of his way, and heard her close the door at the top of the stairs.

"Leave me alone," said Vicki through the closed door above.

Pies ignored her plea, charged up the steps two at a time, and tried the knob, but the door was locked. He tapped his knuckles on the door and said, "Come on. We have to talk," said Pies.

When she didn't respond, Pies found the hidden key and opened the door.

Once in the apartment, he heard Vicki slam the bedroom door closed. "Go away."

"Come out of there."

"I'm kind of pissed at you right now."

"What the hell did I do?" asked Pies.

"Please go home," said Vicki.

"I need your help," said Pies. "Please. Vicki? There's not much time."

The bedroom door flew open, and Vicki launched herself toward Pies until they were chest-to-chest.

"I don't get you, Jakub. I don't look for anything from you. I don't bother you. I don't ask anything of you, but you stick your nose into my life and everything turns to shit. Total shit."

"Whoa, what the hell?" said Pies. "What's going on?"

"I like my life. No—I love what I do. What I paint, I love that. On my time. My time, Pies. Not yours. It's my goddamned life," she screamed.

"Vicki?"

"You can't come into my place, where I work, where I create, and tell me what's what, okay? You can't do that. I was perfectly happy with the path I was on."

Pies's eyes did a quick scan of the coffee table. The mirror that she used for snorting cocaine was not on it.

"I'm not high, asshole," said Vicki. "God, you are...really something. I'm pissed off that you stuck your nose where it didn't belong, I'm not high," said Vicki. "Have you figured that out by now?"

"What did I do, exactly?"

Vicki angled to one of her paintings—the one Pies had alluded to when he made his comment about her selling herself short. She picked up the painting and punched her fist right through the canvas.

In a mocking tone she said, "You should sell these for a few grand, Vicki. You should be selling these at galleries in River North, Vicki."

Now he understood.

"Okay. Okay, I got it. What happened? Something happened. Obviously."

Vicki locked her eyes on her lifelong friend but clammed up. She stood there and seethed.

Pies nodded. He got it. Someone had embarrassed Vicki. "You went to River North."

"Get out."

"Okay, I'll go. But I was serious when I said I needed your help," said Pies.

Vicki reached out, grabbed Pies by his shoulders, and spun him toward the back door. She shoved him along to the kitchen area and the door that led to the back stairway.

"I planned a really cool trip and I was hoping you'd come with me," said Pies. So much for the direct and honest approach he planned in his mind earlier.

"You've got to be kidding?" said Vicki. "Get out."

"I've never been to California, and I know that you haven't either. I got a deal on the Internet for a three-day trip to Half Moon Bay, and I was—"

"Let me demonstrate what you can do with that travel deal," said Vicki as she pushed him onto the landing at the top of the stairs and slammed the door shut.

"Vicki?"

Through the door she said, "California? You're insane."

Pies let out a long exasperated breath and loped down the stairs. At the bottom landing, Blaze stepped into view.

"Jakub, is everything okay?" he asked.

"Yeah, we're just goofing around," said Pies as he moved through the alley door.

22

"SPACE THEM out. That's all I'm saying. Why is that so difficult? You maybe do one or, maybe, maybe, two off the list every couple of weeks," said Stan Zielinski.

"So you're not backing my call," said Bast loudly.

"I'll back you, but you have to be smart about—"

"Now I'm a dumbass," said Bast.

"You got me wondering."

"Am I doing this, or not? Am I running the show? It's mine now, right? Is this mine now, or not?" yelled Bast.

Stan opened his mouth to say something, but came up empty.

Bast filled in the blank, "This is my call, not yours."

Stan and Bast stood toe-to-toe in the kitchen of Bast's beautiful brick home on Oliphant Avenue. Bast never showed up at Stan's house for their meeting with Noretti, so the elder Zielinski had to come here to talk it out.

The place was tastefully decorated with expensive bric-a-brac, highly polished wood floors throughout, and fine Oriental rugs dotting the spaces within. None of the interior elements were purchased items. All of them, even the plumbing and lighting fixtures, had conveniently "fallen off a truck."

"You have to be smart, Bast. Smart isn't getting Jakub pinched and us looked at after only a couple of days," said Stan. "This is a gold mine, kid. But only if it's played right. Patience."

Bast turned away and completed the task he was in the middle of when Stan barged through the kitchen door a minute earlier. He successfully trimmed the crust from the peanut-butter-and-jelly sandwich that was on the cutting board next to the sink.

"I've got this," said Bast.

Stan was about to rebut, but he caught sight of Bast's cute little daughter, Itty-Bitty, who wore a colorful dress as well as a frightened expression on her face. She peered around the kitchen doorway from the dining room.

"Oh, sweetie, it's okay. Your grandpa and daddy are playing," said Stan as he extended his arms and took two steps forward so he could scoop up the little girl in a tight embrace. "We're play-yelling, that's all. It's a game."

Bast shook his head in disgust, turned, and cut the sandwich in half. He placed it on a paper plate and brought it over to the kitchen table.

"Here you go, honey," he said to Itty-Bitty. "Do you want pretzels?"

The little girl shook her head, and Stan put her down. She hopped up and into a chair at the kitchen table and immediately chomped into the sandwich.

"Slow the roll, Bast. That's all I'm saying. Do the jobs, space that shi…"

Itty-Bitty, mid-bite, looked Stan's way and raised her eyebrows.

"Stuff out, is all. That's all I'm advising," continued Stan.

Bast lowered his gaze. The fight was instantly out of him, especially with his daughter in the room.

"Okay, I'll handle this, Pops," said Bast. "I got it. Slow is better, sure. This will all work out."

"Good," said Stan as he leaned over and gave Itty-Bitty a little peck on the top of her head. "You be a good girl, okay? I'll see you tomorrow." He straightened, nodded to Bast, and exited through the kitchen door.

"Is that yummy?" Bast asked Itty-Bitty.

"It's delicious," she said.

Bast chuckled sadly and repeated her words, "Delicious, huh?"

"Yup," said the little girl and she chewed and chewed.

Bast pulled his cell phone from his pocket, dialed, and waited. Someone on the other end answered after two rings.

"On that paper there's a place with golfing supplies and shi..."

Itty-Bitty snapped her gaze up at her father.

"Stuff. Yeah, like golf—golf, and...stuff. What did you think? That place made the top of the list. Tonight. I already have a buyer," said Bast into his phone. "Cool, okay. Yeah, yeah. Hope you boys are up to the task at hand. I can put the feelers out if you're not. What's that? Dude, I was just fu..."

Bast stopped himself, didn't even bother to look his daughter's way, and continued, "Of course you're the man. I was messing with you."

He disconnected the call and finally smiled at Itty-Bitty, who by now had PB&J all over her face.

"Good?"

"Super delicious," said the little girl.

23

PIES WATCHED as she barged her way out of the back door of the bakery, and he realized then she was high on cocaine. He'd seen her under the influence of the drug so many times before that the telltale signs were easy for him to spot—even from fifty feet away.

It wasn't particularly warm out but Vicki was sweating along her forehead, and as she plodded down the alley a deliveryman wheeled a hand truck full of boxes and nearly sideswiped her. Instead of getting out of the man's way, though, Vicki began to argue with him, becoming so aggressive in her outburst that the deliveryman had to fend her off with one hand while he maneuvered the hand truck with the other. After a few steps, Vicki gave the man the finger and peeled off toward the railroad tracks.

Pies started his car and pulled a quick u-turn. He had a good idea where she was headed, especially after he noticed her jogging through the park.

By the time he found a spot and parked, Vicki was already down the walkway to the side of her parents' home and in the basement.

When Pies finally made it to the back basement steps, he heard Milena Chlebek through the closed door say, "*Moja slodka*, what is wrong? Sweetheart, are you okay? You look like you're burning up."

"I'm fine, Mom, just tired," said Vicki. "I'm okay, leave me alone for a minute, would you? I want to paint."

Pies waited until he heard Vicki's mother ascend the interior stairs before he opened the basement door and went inside.

"You're joking, right?" asked Vicki. "Leave me alone. Leave."

"I wouldn't be here if it weren't important, Vicki. I'm asking a favor. A favor from one friend to the other, come with me on this trip. It's a couple of days, and I hear it's really something special. Supposed to be very beautiful there. I bet you'll find a ton of inspiration in the scenery and the people. It's California, Vic. Come on," said Pies.

Vicki was still sweating and a bit fidgety as she sat on the futon.

"Why? Why now, Jakub? What's so important now, huh? Didn't you just start a new job?" she asked. "How the hell are they going to let you go for a few days now, huh? Doesn't make sense," she said.

"They know it's the chance of a lifetime, you know, winning this trip," said Pies.

Vicki gave Pies an odd expression and said, "Wait. Winning the trip? What are you..."

"From the radio station," said Pies.

"I thought this was some sweet Internet deal?"

Pies, his mind a confused mesh of intersecting thoughts of late, was caught in his own lie.

"What the hell are you up to?" asked Vicki in a soft voice.

"I didn't want to spoil the surprise that I won the trip. Come on, it's just three days away from here," he said as he tried to smooth over his obvious gaff. "It's California. You've never been. I've never been."

"You're really pissing me off right now. I'm already not happy with you, and now...this."

She grabbed up her leather purse and rooted around inside but couldn't locate what she was looking for quickly enough. Then a faint smile formed on her mouth when she pulled out a vial—but it was empty. She tossed it back into the purse and took in a sharp breath of disappointment.

"I have things going on here, Jakub, that I can't leave right now. Not even for a few days. You'll have to find another friend to go with you," said Vicki. She knew that Pies had no other friends. She had quickly designed her word choice to emotionally injure the man who had, unwittingly, helped to embarrass her in front of the woman at the art gallery. It was an experience so painful to Vicki that it would not fade with time—or cocaine.

An angry calm washed over Pies's face as he watched Vicki dig farther into her purse to locate another vial of coke.

"They have dealers in California," said Pies. "You won't be without."

Vicki stood up straight. "Get the hell out of here. Get out, now," she shrieked.

"Wicktoria? Wicktoria, what's wrong?" yelled Milena from the first floor.

Pies backed his way out of the basement. He had pressured her too hard, and now he was at a total loss as to how to proceed. He needed Vicki to come with him, but he had blown this chance.

"Wicktoria, I'm coming down," said Milena.

"No, stay up there. I'm fine. Everything is okay," said Vicki.

Pies turned and didn't look back. He left without another word.

24

"EVERYTHING LOOKS right, mutt. Good to go. Oh, wait, shouldn't I call you Polish mutt now?"asked Andy with a chuckle into his cell phone headset as he drove westbound on Touhy Avenue.

This particular area of Skokie, where they were currently operating early this morning, was the portion of town that experienced a mass swap out of low industrial buildings for strip malls over the past decade or so.

"How's that $600 feel in your pocket, D?" said Crick's voice in Andy's headset.

"We told you I was more pure than you," said Devin.

"My mom never mentioned that she was that much Irish, so piss off," said Andy. "What the hell. Took a DNA test to get it out of her. Believe that?"

"Tests don't lie, my mick mutt friend," said Devin.

"Was she embarrassed to tell you about her true heritage, McAndy?" asked Crick's voice in Andy's ear.

"Yeah, man. McAndy," howled Devin's voice in Andy's ear. "Awesome. Love it. Good one."

Andy grinned at the ball-breaking banter but remained vigilant for any suspicious appearing cars, police or otherwise.

"You beat me by two percentage points, mutt, don't get cocky there. I paid you. I held up my end of the deal," said Andy as he slowed his minivan to a stop at the red traffic light that bisected the shopping district that straddled both sides of the avenue.

"We're more alike than we're different, dude. Point proved," said Devin's voice in Andy's ear.

"Get off your horse, man. Focus," said Andy with a grin on his face.

The golf specialty store from Pies's latest list had ornate golf-centric signage and sat facing the street in the dead center of a huge strip mall that was located along the usually busy Touhy Avenue. At this very early hour, though, traffic was light.

Directly across the street from their target was a chain restaurant, with a gaudy white and red striped motif, that was closed for business but was still open in the back of the house to accommodate the overnight prep and cleaning crew of five employees. The night-shift crew had parked all of their vehicles in the rear of the building, and that's where Devin sat presently, parked in the Giovanni's Produce van among the workers' cars. Hidden in plain sight.

Crick drove eastbound on Touhy slowly and passed Andy's minivan with his own as the traffic light changed to green.

"You're good here," said Crick. "There's no need to make that stroll."

"It's a big lot, unk. Lots of places for the five-oh to hide out. I'm doing the look-see," said Devin's voice in Crick's ear.

"Dev, you're good. Just go," said Crick, with a bit of eroded patience. He pulled into a parking lot a block away and observed the front of their targeted store from there.

"Too late," said Devin's voice. "Is this job even worth the trouble? Golf shit, come on."

Crick could see Devin dart across Touhy Avenue on foot and slow his pace as he made it to the front walkway of the golf specialty store. It wasn't a big place, but it held some extremely expensive gear within.

"Let's stick to the play, man. Get the van and do it right," said Crick.

"Mutt, what the hell, bro. Let's do this," said Andy's voice in Crick's ear. "Hey, Uncle Crick, did he get away from you? Control that kid."

"Out of our hands now, Andy," said Crick. "It's worth it, D. They have a back room full of high-end stuff. Very high-end," said Crick. "Some of those sets go $8,000 retail, each."

"Well, okay. Now that I have my DNA results back, maybe I'll be more interested in this golf thing, ya know," said Devin's voice.

Andy's voice laughed in Crick's ear.

Crick grinned at his nephew's comment and watched as Devin casually strolled past the front of the outlet. When the young man was just past the target, he spun on his heels and then walked by the door again.

"Ah, shit. They're on me. Dark four-door to the west," said Devin's voice. "They know I saw 'em, too. Damn it. Here they come. Here they come."

"Movement," said Andy's voice. "Get out of there."

That's when Crick saw what Andy and Devin were talking about—a nondescript, four-door car began to slowly roll through the parking lot from the west of Devin's position. Then Crick saw a second car pull out from behind a low building located farther back in the massive parking lot on the south side of Touhy Avenue, between him and Devin.

"Don't run, D, be cool. They're coming from both sides now," said Crick.

Devin was a young man, but he was extremely professional and levelheaded. And he breathed a sigh of relief knowing that he had no burglary tools whatsoever on his person. What could the cops do to him?

He saw the cars coming, lights off, and each traveling at a steady rate—but not too quickly. He casually peeled off his headset, making it appear as if he scratched his ear, and searched his immediate surroundings. That's when he saw the large storm drain located in the high curb on the edge of the massive parking lot nearest Touhy Avenue. It was only twenty feet away. He advanced deliberately toward Touhy and slid the cell phone from his pocket, palmed it and the headset, and then dropped them both at the same time along the side of his leg. He twisted slightly and instantly kicked them toward the storm drain, where they skittered along the asphalt like a puck off a perfect slap shot.

It was dark at this hour, so to the occupants of the approaching cars it looked as if he was simply walking along, but his quick actions knocked the cell phone and headset tumbling down and into the storm drain where Devin could hear them plop with a hollow echo into the water eight feet below.

"Un-ass, Andy, he's on his own now," said Crick as he casually pulled back eastbound on Touhy Avenue.

"I'll go past the expressway and come back by," said Andy.

"Okay. I'm going to circle around to the south and then back," said Crick as he slowly drove along.

"I don't want to say it, man," said Andy's voice over the cell phone.

"Then don't," said Crick.

"You have to think about it. You just do, man. Is the dog screwing us over, Crick? You got to wonder," said Andy's voice in Crick's ear. "He's been acting weird lately, bro."

"I know. I know," said Crick.

"Ever since he took that 9-1-1 gig. Did they get to him over there? The cops?"

"Okay, I heard you," said Crick. "We got problems here, Andy, for Christ's sake."

Crick didn't want to believe that Pies had turned them over to the authorities—or to talk about the possibility any longer. Crick knew that Pies, although believed to be a coward when it came to throwing down in a fight, had helped them all to make a good living for the past several years through his excellent planning. Why now? Why would Jakubowski mess up his own way of life only to turn on the Zielinski crew members now?

Devin slowed to a halt as the two unmarked cars pulled right up to him and stopped. Four plainclothes police officers, three men and a woman, all piled out of the cars simultaneously.

But they didn't have their weapons drawn, and Devin showed a hint of relief as he said, "Hi, officers. How's your night going for you?"

"Hands on the hood, Slim," said the female police officer, the one in charge. She followed that up by shoving Devin face first down on the hood of her car. "What's your story? Why are you out here?"

"No story, miss, just the truth like my mom taught me. I'm out for a walk. I live nearby," said Devin, which was sort of true. He lived in Lincolnwood, only a mile away.

One of the male officers took Devin's wallet from his back pocket and pulled out his driver's license and read, "Devin Nowak. Yeah, Lincolnwood."

"You a golfer, Devin Nowak? You were sniffing pretty hard around this place," said the female officer.

"Tiger Woods is my hero, officer," said Devin, as he turned sideways and grinned. "He's an inspiration to us all."

"What a wiseass," said one of the male cops.

Devin eyed the other cop and said with a grin, "There's no need to belittle me or my hero, sir."

The female officer didn't appreciate Devin being an asshole so she kicked his legs farther apart.

"Hey, come on, man, there's no need for this," said Devin as he lost his cool and started to stand and turn around.

That's when all four officers converged and took him to the asphalt in a violent heap.

"Come on, I didn't do anything, man," said a defeated Devin. "Get off of me."

"Arms behind your back," ordered the female officer.

When Andy finally turned his vehicle back in the direction of where Devin was stopped, he saw the nineteen-year-old being loaded into the backseat of one of the four-door cars.

"They got him," was all he said into his headset.

Crick drove along and sadly shook his head.

"Someone is going to be pissed," said Andy's voice in Crick's ear.

"Lose it. See you at the shop," said Crick as he drove north and back to Touhy Avenue. He pulled to the side of the street, snapped his cell phone into pieces, got out of the minivan, and dumped the remnants down a sewer opening. "Shit," would be the only word he continuously repeated for the remainder of the night.

25

STAN, DRESSED in another expensive workout suit, mopped his soaked brow with a dishtowel as he stepped into the living room.

"He's out now. It's going to be fine, Pops," said Bast. He sat in one of the chairs near the front windows of Stan's living room.

"Which lawyer did they use? Not DiNizio, right?" said Stan as concern washed over him. "They use DiNizio and the cops know for sure that the kid is connected. Tell me they didn't use the Outfit's guy. Damn it, did I leave the heat on?" asked Stan as he wiped his sweating face once again. He stepped over to the wall thermostat and made sure it was in the "off" position.

"They got it handled, Dad. Crick worked it all out himself, okay? His sister got her own lawyer. His sister has a different last name so the kid has a different name than Mazur. It won't come back on us. If they ever figure it out—and they won't, trust me—it'll take them a while to do that. They got nothing on the kid. Nothing."

Stan paced as he wiped his face and forehead, nodded, and continued to pace.

"Jakub was here," said Stan.

"P-yes? What did he want? I never ordered the dog to see you."

Stan's eyes flashed with anger and then softened. "Jakub came to me. He said that the police know about the alarm information being used. They're onto what's happening. They aren't stupid. He's been trying to get in touch with you, but you ignore him."

Bast said, "It won't matter. We're going to be okay. Don't worry so—"

"How do you think we got all of this, huh? We own this entire area. You think it came to be by flitting along without a care in the world? Worry? Worry is what got us here. Worry is what keeps us in business, Bast. We live on fear. Worry and fear keeps bread in our mouths," said Stan softly as thoughts began to rush into his mind at a faster pace.

Stan knew his son was a bit raw when it came to his management skills, but with this latest blunder Stan was having severe doubts that the younger Zielinski actually had what it took to be in charge for the long haul. And it was Stan who made the ill-conceived decision to place the younger man in charge in the first place, so he had to live with that. Shit. He quickly began to think through the options of how he would approach Noretti with the idea of possibly replacing Bast. It was all going to illustrate how Stan had lost a step, though, and it was going to be a tough sell to the Outfit's man.

"They charged him with disorderly and resisting, not burglary," said Bast. "Crick said the kid spotted them first so they had to move on him. He never even touched the building. It all went down fast, so the kid had no time to get out of there. But that's all they had on him. We're good."

Stan slowly made his way to the front door and tossed the towel on an end table. He said, "Come on. Let's get those eggs." He held the front door open for Bast, and they both exited the house. "I have to eat. My head's been killing me." He coughed twice and added, "That flu's been making the rounds again. You think Itty-Bitty picked up that shit?"

Bast shrugged as he stepped from the house. "Maybe," he said. "Her nose is always running."

Once on the sidewalk, they went toward the heart of Edison Park and Stan's favorite diner. They walked for a block in silence, but as they entered the tiny park that was located alongside the Chlebeks' house Stan said, "I think that we're going to have to shut it down."

"What the hell are you…?"

"Just for the time being. No more jobs from Jakub's lists. We go back to the old methods."

Bast, angered, pulled up to a stop and grabbed Stan's sleeve. Stan stopped, too, and faced his son. The blood seemed to have washed from Stan's face during the short walk.

"This is my party, Pops. My business to run. This is how Noretti and his friends, North Side, and South Side, finally get introduced to how I'm different than you. And believe me, they'll never forget the way I came into this thing—the way I poured cash into their pockets right from the start," said Bast as the self-pride oozed from of him.

"You can't run shit when you're in a cage."

"I'm not going to be…"

Stan coughed again and said, "I've got to consider what the next move's going to be. Give me a few days."

"Noretti won't like this," said Bast.

Stan took in the sight of his son for a long beat and said, "He'll understand. I'll make him understand."

"This is bullshit."

Stan began to walk once again. He cleared his throat and spit into the grass.

"Pops, come on, you can't do this," said Bast. "What will the other guys think of me?"

Stan shrugged and absently shook his head.

Bast couldn't believe what he was hearing. Absolute rage began to boil up within him. He and his father had been at odds nearly from the start of his taking over the operation, but Bast figured it was mostly because of his involvement with Vicki.

He supposed that some of the acrimonious issues caused by management changes were probably normal—the man exiting the post giving grief to the new manager for his lack of experience. But to Bast, this was ridiculous. It was his show now, goddamn it. Why would his old man pull this shit now?

Stan lowered his head and quietly said, "I'm thinking of putting Jakub in charge. Temporarily."

"What?"

"I'm not losing what I built. That's not going to happen, Bast. I'm sorry," said Stan.

Bast pulled up to a stop once again and placed his fists on top of his head. This couldn't be happening. What would Crick and Andy think of him now? They'd probably stop respecting him the moment they heard the news—that's what. How would he be received among the residents of Edison Park? He'd be laughed at—that's what would happen. His mind was made up. He was truly taking over. Now or never.

"You know what, Pops? Fuck you," seethed Bast.

A few people strolling through the park looked toward Bast and Stan as the elder Zielinski leaned in and grabbed his son by the shirt, aggressively at first, but then he let go and gently patted his son's chest with his open palms. He regarded his son's eyes and then leaned in closer still and lowered his voice. "Jakub runs it for now. Jakubowski is the guy in charge. I'll let Noretti know after we eat. Let's go."

Bast violently pulled away and squared off for a physical fight. "You son of a bitch. What the hell is wrong with you? P-yes. P-yes running the show? Are you kidding me?"

Stan stood there and tossed out a weak grin. He then coughed through his grin. "I made a mistake. I was wrong to bump you up so soon," he said, softly, as a pure sadness washed over his facial expression. "You need more seasoning, Bast. You'll get there, just not now."

Stan and Bast stood there and eyed one another. Neither wanted to make a move.

"You are such an asshole, Pops. Pump me up all these years, tell me I'm the one who's going to run—"

Stan's eyes showed concern, then sudden terror, as he clutched at his left elbow.

"Pops, what?" said Bast.

Stan stopped breathing and fell to his knees and then to his face. "Dad? Pops!"

Bast rolled Stan over on his back and slapped gently at his face, which had turned a purplish blue.

"Help! Someone call for help. Fuck! Get 9-1-1," called out the terrified Bast.

26

UNDER BRIGHT sunshine, Pies, in suit and tie, deliberately strolled through a throng of mourners and made his way to the side door of the funeral home on Harlem Avenue. On his way he caught sight of Vicki, dressed inappropriately in a short skirt and plunging neckline ensemble. She looked so uncomfortable and out of place, Pies wished that he could walk up and escort her away from the building and to the airport, where they'd fly away to freedom. But now wasn't the time or place.

Milena and Blaze Chlebek, both in conservative attire, stood next to her. Neither of them appeared particularly pleased to be at the funeral home, but they both seemed to speak kindly, and respectfully, with the other funeralgoers around them.

Pies saw Rebecca Zielinski, Bast's beautiful wife, along with their daughter and Rebecca's parents. Rebecca's mother held Rebecca's infant son in her arms. Rebecca was in a tasteful black dress, as was Itty-Bitty. Rebecca was a seemingly classy woman and always looked the part of the pampered housewife, but the expression on her face this day registered annoyance. Pies noticed the look and then took note of the direction that she stared—her line of sight was angled directly at Vicki. Rebecca's eyes never wavered from Vicki, and Pies could tell by the way that Vicki only engaged with her own parents that she knew she was being watched.

The funeral of Stan Zielinski was an uncomfortable situation made even tenser and more untenable by two jealous women locked in a silent struggle over one Bast Zielinski.

Pies couldn't understand the attraction to Bast, but money and power were both potent aphrodisiacs. Bast reminded Pies more of an arrogant, pampered Neanderthal-like, high school jock than a true man.

Finally, Rebecca's eyes quickly scanned the crowd and locked onto Pies. He nodded his condolences from fifty feet away, but Rebecca's lips tightened and she quickly turned away.

Pies let out a breath and wondered why he, too, got an icy stare from Rebecca. He shook it off and stayed on task.

Bast advised him on the phone earlier that morning to meet him in the office of the funeral home at 10 A.M. Pies was fifteen minutes early. He headed in anyway. Just as he was about to melt into the side door, he met Vicki's eyes. She, too, turned away the moment she saw him, though.

Noretti with Luke at his side, both wearing dark suits, observed Pies work his way through the crowd and enter the side door of the funeral home. Noretti and Luke shared a knowing glance, and Noretti then patted Luke's back once.

*

A THIN line of finely crushed cocaine was swiftly vacuumed off the backside of a credit card through the shortened, clear-plastic drinking straw between Bast's thumb and forefinger and traveled upward, directly into Bast's left nostril.

Bast, Crick, and Andy sat in the funeral home's main office. Bast was positioned behind the owner's desk, Crick in a side chair, and Andy sprawled on the couch. The door was open, but no one else milling about in the hallway dared enter the room.

Bast leaned his head backward and sniffed hard, once again, to make sure he got every delicate flake of the drug into his nostril and, soon, his bloodstream.

"This changes nothing," Bast said. "We're a go. We don't slow down, you hear me?"

When the two subordinates didn't reply, Bast repeated himself, "You hear me? He wanted me to ramp this up. It's what he wanted."

"Sure," said an apprehensive Crick.

"Yeah. Got it," said Andy.

"Pies isn't long for us. A few more lists, and then…"

Crick and Andy shared an uncomfortable glance that Bast picked up on.

"He's going to get grabbed up, I can see it coming. It's happening soon. Won't be difficult for the coppers to piece together," said Bast. "We get what we can while we can." He nodded sadly. "He won't talk. Don't worry about that."

"Sure," said Crick. "Whatever."

Andy nodded, too, but both he and Crick fought to understand what Bast meant in his last comment about Pies.

"The kid can still operate," said Bast. "Have him give me a call tomorrow or the next day. I have a side job for him that I want to discuss directly."

"I think he's done," said Crick.

Andy gave Crick a confused look.

Bast said, "No, he's not done. Not yet. I'm bringing on another player to assist your nephew. It's temporary. We'll make do without your direct involvement until you're free to roam about without the prying eyes. It'll be your nephew and this other dude."

Crick sat up a bit straighter and said, "Maybe we should lay low for a—"

"He's a guy I know from the Olmsted Inn. It'll be a temporary thing, like I said. He's the one who delivers," said Bast as he tapped the side of his nose. "He's done work like ours before. He's cool."

"Wait. Is that smart?" asked Crick.

Bast shot him a deadly look that stopped Crick cold.

Andy tried to defuse the situation, "I told you, no one's following us anymore. We're good right now. Today. Crick and me, we've been watching for tails, Bast, and there's nothing going on. Those Skokie cops would've stopped us instead of D if they were onto us. We don't need help on these jobs. Maybe we use Devin, sure, the kid's good, but no one else."

Bast still eyed Crick for another short beat and then said, "Devin and his legal shit won't be a problem as we go forward, right?"

"What do you mean?" asked Crick. "I'm not following..."

"You know," said Bast, coldly. "He's not prone to doing really stupid things. Like talking to a cop."

Crick said, "No. Why... He's family, Bast, he won't—"

"Losing family is a tough thing to handle," said Bast. He gave a stare that Crick had never seen before. It was a murderous glare. Cocaine had a way of changing Bast's entire demeanor and his outlook on life—and Crick wanted nothing do to with the man this day.

Crick slowly cranked his head side to side and stretched, which was the reason for his nickname, and it portended that he was not in a good mental space. He said, "What are you getting at here?"

But then Bast deteriorated into tears and his body was immediately wracked by violent sobs. "My pops..."

Crick and Andy looked at one another, but neither moved to comfort the man.

Crick mouthed the words, "What the..." to Andy.

Andy mockingly mimicked the snorting of a line of coke and shrugged.

Rebecca and Itty-Bitty both rushed into the room and angled over to the desk so they could comfort Bast.

"Honey. Oh, sweetie," said Rebecca. "It's okay. It'll be okay," she said softly. She hugged Bast and gently brushed his hair with her fingers. Itty-Bitty leaned against her father's leg and rested her head on his shoulder.

"It's okay, Daddy. Don't cry," said the little girl.

Bast grabbed both of them in a tight embrace and continued to sob.

Crick turned away and looked out into the hallway. Pies stood with his back to the opposite wall. His eyes never faltered from Crick as he shoved off the wall and walked out of view.

Crick launched himself from his seat and went into the hallway.

"Hey, Pies. Hey, man, wait," said Crick. "How long have you been here?"

Pies shrugged and stopped so he could turn and face Crick. Crick leaned in a little closer as mourners moved about, and he kept his voice low.

"You heard about my nephew? Devin?"

"No, what?" asked Pies.

"Skokie PD caught up with him," said Crick. When he saw the blood drain from Pies's face, he added, "Yeah, they were all over that specific spot. The golf store you got."

Pies froze—this is what he feared the most, that the police would quickly locate the source of the leak at Northcomm. The sudden urge to turn and run washed over him, but he fought to remain cool.

"He's out now, but I'm going to ask you straight-out, man. How would they know...?"

Bast's loud sobs stopped their conversation, and they both turned and watched Rebecca escort the inconsolable man from the office. Bast came to an awkward halt in the middle of the hallway to try and compose himself, but it didn't work at all. He grabbed up Itty-Bitty in his arms and hugged her closely—and cried.

Andy slipped from the office and aimed a shrug Crick's and Pies's way. He didn't know what to do for the man, either.

Crick nudged Pies and said, "Call me after this. We got to talk, you hear me?"

Pies immediately knew he was off the hook with Crick for the time being. If Crick thought that Pies had set them up, he would either be already dead, or have caught a major beating for his misstep. Crick requesting a later conversation meant only one thing—they still didn't fully suspect that Pies was up to anything. Not yet, anyway.

Vicki, along with Milena and Blaze Chlebek, slowly stepped from the front outer doors and through to the interior hallway and headed toward where Stan's body lay inside.

When Vicki saw Rebecca and Bast she stopped, which allowed her parents to go past her by a few more steps.

A contrite Milena leaned forward and gently touched Bast's arm. She said, "I'm so very sorry for your loss, Sebastian."

Bast, through his tears, made an angry, ugly face, which Milena reacted to by taking a half step backward.

Blaze noticed the exchange and softly said, "Let's go, Milena. You said what you said. Now we go."

Bast deliberately sniffed and a menacing hardness overcame him once again. "Oh, here she is. The voice of reason in Edison Park. The lady who thinks that she's the one who runs the show. You coming to make sure my old man's really dead? Is that it? Making sure that the guy you despised is really gone. Don't worry, Chlebek, he's no more. Go on in, he's there in the box. He's dead and cold. Go on," yelled Bast, as he placed Itty-Bitty down and angrily advanced closer to Blaze and Milena—each frozen by the embarrassment of the awkward situation.

Crick and Andy swooped in to take Bast back to the office, but the new boss twisted his arms free in a violent fashion and said to Milena, "You can see his cold body for your own damned self and go back and talk and talk and talk all your bullshit about me and my family to those assholes who come into your shitty bakery every day for what you call food."

"Milena, please. We go," said Blaze.

Bast spread his arms out wide and motioned to everyone in attendance. His voice rose louder still and he said, "Look around, huh? Take a good, goddamned look, because if not for the Zielinskis, you would have nothing. All of you. You heard that, you stupid sheep. Nothing! We built this goddamn neighborhood. You all came over here without a piss pot and needed cash to start a business. Who gave you the loan? The bank? Shit... You needed a favor for this or that we're the ones who made it happen for you. The Zielinskis did that. We made all of you."

People, now angry and embarrassed, began to file out of the funeral home.

Vicki, silent until now, leaned into the fray and took her mother by the elbow, "Mom, please. Come on. We'll go home."

That's when Rebecca tucked in alongside Bast and said, "Yeah, you really should go, Wicktoria. He's done with you. And you know what? He got bored, just like he did with the others. He always comes back to me. You know why? Because you're all trash. You're a whore, Vicki. You're disposable."

"Enough!" yelled Pies. Bast, and everyone else except Vicki, turned in his direction. Vicki was so embarrassed and mortified by the situation that she was rigid. But the tears began to flow down her cheeks.

Rebecca ignored Pies and never lost momentum. "You'll be nothing more than that, Vicki. He will always come back home to me. Because he loves me."

"Mommy," shrieked Itty-Bitty. "Mommy, stop."

Bast stared hard at Pies, but Pies never looked away. He was at the end of his rope, too. A hazy fantasy image came to his mind in that very moment of the arrogant Bast nonchalantly walking through a labyrinth of crisscrossing lines of filament that activated a series of shotgun-shell booby traps—too many to count.

But then Pies remembered, in that same instant, that he needed to keep his head. He blinked his angry daydream away and moved toward Vicki but stopped himself. He couldn't be seen too close to her. Bast may become suspicious, and Pies couldn't take that chance right now.

Milena and Blaze were finally able to shake their frozen state, and they walked briskly out of the funeral home with the many others who also exited at that time.

Vicki was left on her own in the hallway. She couldn't quite locate the words to defend herself, so she stood still—terrified and mute.

Pies wanted badly to scoop her up and run out of the place and back to his house, where it would be safe. There he could comfort Vicki. But he didn't. He remained mute, too, as the funeral home continued to empty out.

"He's all done with you, you...you...sex toy," said Rebecca. "Yeah, that's right, you're just a sex toy."

"Rebecca. Stop," blurted Rebecca's own mother as she moved in to grab her daughter and spin her back toward the office. "That's enough."

Rebecca broke down in tears in her mother's arms as they padded along. Bast held Itty-Bitty's hand, and they both followed Rebecca and her mother into the office. The door slammed closed—and the hallway became tomb quiet.

It was over.

Pies scanned the faces of the hushed people who were leaving the funeral home and caught sight of Noretti and Luke as they looked directly at him. Even as they slowly stepped along, they never took their eyes off of Pies.

Noretti winked.

27

PIES COULD see Naomi seated at her pod as he entered the North-comm 9-1-1 Center for his shift. He noticed her glance and wave his way, but he ignored her. As he stepped down the hallway toward the door that led into the radio room, his cell phone vibrated in his pocket. Pies slipped the phone free and saw that it was Crick calling —most likely to get more information about how the police knew to keep an eye on the golf-supply store on Touhy Avenue.

It had been Crick's fifth call just that morning, and Pies had to keep the dangerous crew member in the dark, at least for a little while longer. Pies pressed the "ignore" button as he shoved through the doors and made his way over to the pod.

He took a seat.

Naomi said, "How was your day off?"

Pies, in no mood for small talk, shrugged, opened the drawer that contained his headset, lifted the apparatus out, and slipped it over his ear.

Naomi probably would've surreptitiously gathered firsthand knowledge of how Pies's day off went, if she hadn't taken her son to Lincoln Park Zoo the morning before.

"We all have access to that file," said Ketmen, in mid-conversation with Jerry, as he looked toward the pod where Pies and Naomi sat. The alarms-out-of-service log was displayed on the middle monitor of the pod's array.

"So, really it could be any one of us," said Jerry, who sat three pods away. "As many times a day as those files are accessed? Come on..."

"How in the world can they tell who's taking the information?" asked Ketmen smugly, as he leaned back in his chair. "What are they going to do, start searching us when we leave? Good luck with that."

The Northcomm 9-1-1 Center was unusually quiet this morning —tense and quiet.

Without Ketmen, Jerry, or even Naomi noticing, Pies had activated the button camera on his golf shirt and was already recording the alarms-out-of-service page right then and there. It was a brazen move, but he had to keep his plan in motion the best he could.

This was Pies's last day in the 9-1-1 communications center.

Stan advised him they were going to shut down the B&Es for the time being, most likely until things calmed down. But Stan was gone now. Pies made the decision—the moment he angrily slogged out of the funeral home the day before—that he would do this last shift, get a new list so he could keep Bast happy and off guard, and then he'd be gone for good.

He would now have to force Vicki to come with him to Half Moon Bay and, ultimately, to Vietnam. Both of their lives would change for the better the moment they landed in that far-off country, Pies was sure of that.

Pies pressed the "off " button on the mini-DVR in his pocket and stopped taping the page. To the others it looked as if he tapped his pant leg with his forefinger. They were none the wiser.

"The way that lieutenant from Winnetka was eyeballing you the other day, man, as he came down the hallway, damn," said Naomi, playfully, to Ketmen. "I don't know. Don't be surprised if you get a subpoena. You may be their number-one suspect."

"What about your new guy, Naomi? Jake-Jake, you ripping off the fine citizens of Chicago's North Shore?" asked Ketmen.

Pies turned and stared down Ketmen, but the chubby man smiled and continued, "Pulling your chain, my man. Take it easy."

Jerry leaned back and away from the glass partition at his pod. He laughed and said, "Just look for the one with a gambling problem, and, bam, you got your crook. Boom. Done. Over."

A painful wave of acid rose in Naomi's throat. *Shit,* she thought to herself. One of the first things the police probably would do is look for someone with a gambling problem. Her bad habits could cause even more unintentional upheaval in her life. She'd already lost a marriage and almost her son over her addiction.

"Maybe there's a reward for turning in the person?" asked Ketmen with false hopefulness. "I need new wheels."

"And some liposuction," added Jerry with a chuckle.

"Fuck you," said Ketmen through a faux grin.

Naomi peered at her shoes and said, "Maybe it's Soup." Her hope was to deflect the conversation away from herself.

And it worked.

Jerry and Ketmen laughed hard at that remark, then Jerry tapped his headset and sat up straight and said, "Northcomm 9-1-1." He still looked at Naomi, though, and mouthed, "Good one." He turned away and took care of his emergency call.

Naomi leaned toward an open binder with laminated pages that was splayed out on the pod desk. She said to Pies, "Okay. We're going to go over the SWAT notification protocol between the calls you take today, Jakub. It's a fairly simple procedure, so you'll have it down by the end of the shift."

Pies wasn't listening to Naomi. His demeanor softened and he said, "How will they figure out if someone is corrupt? Can they even do that? Is it even possible to actually know who stole the alarm file information?"

Naomi hadn't seen Pies act so vulnerable before, and it took her by surprise. "I'm not sure. I mean any one of us can access that alarm file from any terminal in this building. Alarms are placed in and out of service all the time," she said. "Some of the supervisors can access the files, all the files, from their home computers with a remote entry point." Naomi knew this because that's how she found Pies's home address after she stole Soup's remote-access password and log-in information.

Three tones went off in their ears, and Pies absently said, "North-comm 9-1-1, where is your emergency?"

"He's not breathing," said the frantic woman's voice. "My God, he's not breathing. What do I do?"

Simultaneously, the address imprinted at the base of the computer monitors: 1004 Washington Street, Kenilworth, IL.

Naomi immediately typed a quick, three-digit command onto her computer keyboard and hit the send button. She leaned away from the glass partition and loudly said, "Non-breather, coming over."

Carter, who sat today at the fire communications pod, straightened and nodded. She checked her computer monitor and pressed activation tones on a keypad to alert the appropriate ambulance.

Pies asked, "Are you at 1004 Washington Street?"

"Yes. Yes! Get here. Get here now!"

"Who isn't breathing?" asked Pies.

"My son. He's twelve," said the woman. "He's only twelve. Are you sending someone?"

"Yes, ma'am, we've already dispatched them," said Pies.

"He's cold and blue. His arms are stiff. What do I do? Tell me what to do?" she asked, and then she broke down into uncontrollable sobs.

Naomi leaned in and whispered, "Tell her that the ambulance has been dispatched and to wait outside for their arrival."

"Is he right there, ma'am? Are you right with your son now?" asked Pies.

"Jakub?" said Naomi in a whisper.

"Yes," said the woman on the phone line as she wept loudly. "How do I help him? I have to help him. Please."

"Is he on a bed or the floor? Where is he?" asked Pies.

"Jakub, what are you doing?" asked Naomi, a bit louder, but Pies ignored her.

"He's in his bed. He's been sick with a cold or something, and—Are they coming? Please, hurry."

"Yes, they've been dispatched," said Pies with a professional reassurance in his voice. Something, again, clicked in Pies's mind—like when he was thrust into the situation with the man with the machete while on the ride-along in Evanston. Or when he took the robbery call a few days before.

He had to help. It was an instinct that he never knew he possessed.

During his first day of training, Naomi had instructed Pies on how to talk a caller through the CPR process. There were specific steps that had to be followed to do the procedure in the proper fashion. It was one of the first training sessions they had when he started working at Northcomm. The verbal prompts were housed in the computer system files, accessed through some simple keyboard commands. But as a backup, the CPR verbal prompts and instructions were also printed on a laminated, eight-by-eleven-inch card in case the Northcomm center ever lost power to their computer systems and the files couldn't be accessed.

Pies grabbed up the laminated CPR card on the desktop and said, "Ma'am, listen to me. Are you alone with him?"

"Yes. Are they coming?!" shrilled the woman.

"Do you want to help him, or not?" said Pies. "You have to listen to me."

"Yes. Yes, I want to help," said the woman's voice.

"Here's what I want you to do. Get him off the bed and onto the hard floor surface. Can you do that?" asked Pies.

"Send someone!"

"Ma'am, are you going to help or not?" yelled Pies. "He needs your help now!"

The verbal slap worked. "Yes, yes, I want to help," said the woman's quieter voice.

Over the phone Pies and Naomi could hear the twelve-year-old's body slump to the floor with a sickening thud. Pies lowered his gaze for a moment, took a deep breath, and then dove right back in.

"I'm going to have you do chest compressions, ma'am. This is crucial," he said. "You do not need to do breathing for him. No mouth-to-mouth, just the chest compressions."

"Pies, he's gone. She said he was cold and blue," whispered Naomi as she placed a gentle hand on his shoulder.

Pies shrugged her hand away.

"I'm ready. What do I do?" asked the woman's voice.

"With the heel of your hand locate the spot near the center of his sternum. His chest bone. Place your other hand on top of your first hand and interlock your fingers—"

"I can't do it. I can't!"

"You said that you wanted to help him. Listen to me, and do as I say," said Pies rather forcefully. "You have a speakerphone?"

"Yes," said the woman's voice.

"Activate that and put the phone down next to your son," said Pies.

Ketmen and Jerry looked toward them, and Naomi dropped her gaze. She had lost control of her trainee.

"Are your hands in position?" asked Pies.

"Yes. Yes, I'm ready," the woman replied.

"Lean over his chest, straighten and lock your arms at the elbows, and depress down two inches and repeat. You'll be pushing down hard. About two inches down. You're going to do that over and over again. Don't stop until someone else takes over. I'll count with you. We're going to go fast. Ready?" asked Pies.

"Yes."

"One, and two, and one, and two, and one, and two, and one, and two. Keep it going at that rate. And one, and two, and one, and two. Don't stop. They're on the way."

Pies and Naomi could hear the woman's quick breaths as she beat the rapid rhythm out on her dead child's chest with the heels of her hands.

Naomi said, "You can't help him, Jakub. He's gone."

He locked eyes with Naomi, placed his finger over his mic, and said, "I'm not helping him."

Naomi, a bit dumbfounded, sat back in her seat. Being a parent herself, she understood immediately.

"She'll remember that she tried to save her son," said Pies. "That's how she'll remember this day."

Carter yelled from across the room, "They're on scene."

Pies and Naomi could hear the doorbell chime in the background. The woman shouted, "It's open! We're in here. Back here!"

The rattle of a paramedic's bag could be heard getting closer to the phone.

"Okay, ma'am, I've got it now," said a commanding woman's voice. "Get me oxygen and start a line."

The caller's voice said, "He's been sick. I came in to check on him, and..."

"Ma'am, please, can you take a seat there," said another voice in the room, this one a professional and patient-sounding man.

The line went dead.

28

"SIR, YOU'LL have total privacy, I assure you," said the middle-aged woman at the third bank Pies had visited since leaving Northcomm. He had feigned illness and bolted from the emergency communications building an hour after the non-breather call. It was time to go. He was done with the 9-1-1 job. It had served its purpose.

Today was the day that he left Chicago for good.

The nicely dressed woman carried the long, metal safe-deposit box to a small, closet-sized room that was positioned off of a hallway in the back of the beautifully decorated building in Glenview, Illinois. She glided into the room and placed the box on the waist-high table within.

Pies had had a savings account worth a few thousand dollars and a safe-deposit box at this bank since he was in his early twenties. That was when he initially deposited the $100,000 into the safe-deposit box, all in hundred-dollar bills. It was essentially the first $100,000 he earned as a Zielinski crew member, and he recalled, with pride, the day he brought the cash to the bank. The cash had been in the box, untouched, safe and sound, ever since.

Pies readjusted the backpack that was angled off his shoulder and said, "Great, thank you."

The backpack had seen the inside of two other banks' safe-deposit vaults that morning, and it was already $200,000 heavier for those efforts.

Pies thought $300,000 sounded like a lot of money, and, if used in a place like Vietnam, it could last a lifetime. But it wasn't all that bulky when carried in one backpack.

"Please let me know when you're all finished, Mr. Jakubowski," said the woman.

Pies stepped into the small room, and the woman moved back out and into the hallway before she softly closed the door behind her. Alone now, Pies shrugged the backpack off his shoulder and onto the table alongside the box.

He opened the safe-deposit box first and then reached over to unzip the backpack. He reached inside the bag and took two envelopes off the top of the cash that was already inside. He placed the envelopes on the table and got to work. The envelopes contained two one-way airline tickets to San Francisco for that very evening. Pies had purchased the tickets at a Northbrook travel agency, in cash, prior to arriving at the bank. One ticket was in his legal name and the other was in Wicktoria Chlebek's.

Pies transferred all of the cash from the safe-deposit box into the bag. It only took a few seconds. He placed the plane tickets back on top of the money, zipped the bag closed, and left the small room.

When he exited the bank and got into his car, he didn't notice the blue minivan with the "family of four and a dog" stick-figure decal on the back window that was parked facing away from the bank's front doors. Andy observed Pies through the rearview mirror of the vehicle.

Pies started his engine, backed up, and then pulled his car onto busy Waukegan Road and headed south.

Andy put the blue minivan in reverse and began to follow.

29

THERE WERE four of them—external hard drives that were digitally loaded with all of the video and audio evidence that Pies had gathered over the past few years. They sat on the workbench in his basement. He probably could've fit everything on one hard drive, but he wanted to make sure nothing was left off due to any unforeseen storage-space issues. Better to be safe. It was the evidence that would put the Zielinski crew away, hopefully for good. He'd already destroyed, and disposed of, the many 32GB memory cards from which he had initially gathered the information.

Pies gently loaded the hard drives into a two-by-two-foot box that was lined with Styrofoam and sealed it with a roll of clear tape.

The overnight delivery label that he preprinted was still sitting in the printer's tray. Pies grabbed it up and securely taped it on top of the sealed box.

He backed away from the workbench and quickly leaped up the steps and into his kitchen, as he remembered something else.

He rounded into the dining room and hopped up the stairs that led to the second floor. Once upstairs, he entered his bedroom and leaned over the bed to grab up the pants he had worn to work that morning. He reached into the right front pocket and took out the mini-DVR.

He hurriedly moved back to the basement, and his phone vibrated in his pocket. When he grabbed the phone and saw that it was Crick calling, yet again, he pressed "ignore."

He plugged a USB cable into the mini-DVR and then into his desktop computer. Once attached, he turned the power on the mini-DVR unit and waited for the images to upload to his desktop computer.

When the few seconds of video flashed onto his monitor, Pies pressed the space bar on his keyboard, and the frame froze in place.

The alarms-out-of-service page that he recorded early that day was in plain view. There were at least forty lines of information, addresses, and notations.

Pies leaned over and took a piece of paper from the hopper of his printer. He grabbed a pen off his workbench and copied down one line of address information. Below the information he wrote: B-Man's Pawn. I know this place. Jewels. Coins. Guns. No alarm and no watchman tonight only.

He underlined the word "only" twice.

Pies got online and did a map search of the pawnshop's address and then clicked to get the aerial satellite view. He printed the image that was displayed on his computer monitor, waited for the page to come out of the machine, and then quickly snatched it out of the tray. He used the pen to circle something on the roof. He wrote a note next to the circle: Roof access. Front and back doors are gated off after-hours.

Pies folded the pieces of paper, checked the time on his computer monitor, and said, "Damn, damn, damn."

On the monitor, plainly seen, was the single data line that was videotaped at the Northcomm 9-1-1 Center for B-Man's Pawn.

It read: Alarm out of service, night watchman on premises until service is repaired and due to unsecured roof-hatch access.

He hovered his mouse over the corner of his computer screen and pressed to exit out of the images and maps, unhooked the cable, turned off the mini-DVR unit, and then bolted up the stairs. He had a schedule to keep and a plane to catch.

30

Pies was under considerable duress as he drove through his neighborhood. There were so many pieces to his escape-plan puzzle, and they had to all fit together right now—today. He could pull it all off. He had to.

His eyes nervously darted about, but he really didn't see anything. At an intersection crossing Ibsen Street, he nearly clipped a turning car. The other driver honked, but Pies just kept going. He couldn't help but think that he had forgotten something important, something crucial to his overall plan. He ran through everything once more to make sure he was still on track, and everything still seemed to fit together.

He arrived at his destination and parked his car near the alley that led to the apartment above the bakery. He got out of the car with the folded map and note in hand and jogged around the block to Northwest Highway. Once on the busy street, Pies proceeded to the front of Zielinski's Insurance Agency and opened the metal mail slot. He flipped the folded pieces of paper into the storefront where they hit the tile floor with a click.

Pies then sprinted back around the block to the alley opening that led to the bakery. He turned the corner and entered the alley—and skidded to a stop.

He took two steps back and watched.

Bast emerged from the rear bakery door and moved into the alley, followed by a silk-robe-clad Vicki. They passionately kissed one last time before Bast patted her ass, turned, and walked in the other direction, presumably toward his own home. Vicki waved after him and then slipped back inside the building.

Vicki was high. She only had that ultra-aware expression on her face when she was flying, and Pies knew it.

Pies waited for Bast to exit from view and then hurried to the rear bakery door, where again a bag of Blaze's garbage held it open. He went inside and ran up the steps, when he heard Vicki say through the closed door at the top of the steps, "Did you forget something?"

Pies made it to the landing at the precise moment Vicki opened the door. When she saw him, she tried to close the door, but he wedged his way inside.

"Goddamn you. What the hell is wrong with you?" asked Vicki. "Seriously, what the hell? Leave me alone."

Pies slammed the door shut and made sure that it was locked so that if Bast did come back it would take him a minute to unlock and open the door again. Pies thought that could possibly give him just the time needed to get Vicki to come along with him.

Pies tried to find the right words as he studied Vicki. Her face was overly made-up, and she was wearing an expensive stockings-and-garter-belt combination under the short robe. Pies, embarrassed by what he saw, tried not to gawk. Her hair was tousled, and she had that crazed, cocaine-induced expression that Pies, unfortunately, knew too well.

He came here to make her come along with him. A gentler approach would probably be his best bet, but something struck him the moment he saw Vicki and Bast together in the alley. It enraged him how quickly she would fall into bed with Bast even after the fiasco at the funeral home. What in the hell was she thinking?

"Is he back home with his wife now?" Pies asked, trying to get a rise out of Vicki.

"Get out!"

"Vicki, you're not thinking straight about any of this...shit with Bast," said Pies.

"He wants to be with me," said Vicki.

"Bullshit," said Pies, and Vicki's eyes flew open. He could tell that she was working out a way in her head to bolster her argument, but Pies wouldn't allow that to happen. "This isn't a good thing, Vicki. This life you're leading isn't much of anything. It's a dead end. You have to get out of here. He doesn't love you."

Vicki tried to puff up a bit of self-pride and said, "It's a glamorous life, and it's mine to live."

"Glam— Glamorous? It's pathetic, that's what this is. You know it. I know it. Everybody knows it. Bast's wife knows it."

"Don't you mention her again. Get the hell out of my apartment," said Vicki.

"You're delusional. You think that Bast would ever be with you and only you?" asked Pies.

"He told me that he's leaving Rebecca. Just now, he did."

Pies gave her a weary look of his own and said, "Vicki...when did that ever matter to you? Now you want to be a housewife to Bast? Really...?"

"Not especially, no. But he's leaving her, that bitch.... Did you hear her at the funeral? My God!"

Pies let out a slow and exasperated breath. He looked at his shoes, gathered some steam, and said, "Do you actually think he'll leave the woman who had his children? The same woman who allows him to mess around whenever he wants, with basically whoever he wants?"

"Shut up!"

"He's not leaving her. You've got to understand that. He probably has a couple of women like you on the side at all times," said Pies, sadly, knowingly.

Vicki quick-punched Pies in the gut. He bent forward to catch his breath but did nothing to retaliate.

Vicki locked her gaze on Pies and said, "You're jealous. That's it, isn't it? You messed up your chance to have me, and now you don't want him to have me, so..."

"It's not that."

"What then?" asked Vicki.

"I want you to have a better life. A good life," said Pies. "I want you to be away from the Zielinskis altogether."

"Good life? Great, now you sound exactly like my parents. Haven't we been over this before?" asked Vicki. "I told you. I told you that I am my own person. I'm doing things my way. No one is dictating my life to me, Jakub. No one, do you understand? Not my parents. Not you, and not even Bast, okay? He loves me and lets me do my own thing. He lets me live my own life. I'm free to paint, to create, to live, and do the things that I want. Once we're always together—"

"You'll allow him to screw other women? You may not realize that yet, but that's exactly what you'll be doing."

"You're such an asshole," roared Vicki. "You always try to control me somehow."

"How is that even possible...?"

"How about the lady on the train who followed me, huh? I'm sure you set that up."

"What are you talking about?" asked Pies in confusion.

Pies wasn't going to get through to her. Not until the majority of coke passed through her system, anyway, which shouldn't be too much longer, Pies reckoned. He shuffled past the sofa so he could take a look out the windows and down onto Northwest Highway. As he did, he saw the handgrip of a 9mm pistol that poked out from under an open magazine on the coffee table—next to the mirror with cocaine residue on it.

Vicki saw where his eyes landed. "I know how to use it, okay...dad?" she said mockingly. "Bast wants me to keep it around, you know, in case."

Pies wanted badly to grab her up and force her into the car parked at the mouth of the alley. Once in the car, they'd escape. He wanted so, so badly to do that, but he knew it wouldn't work. He had to try to negotiate with her so that she saw clearly how things really were. Pies had to allow Vicki to decide, on her own, to come along on the travel adventure that would change both of their lives for good. He could guide her down the right path, but she had to allow herself to understand that it was best for the both of them to get the hell away from Edison Park.

There would never be a normal, or even peaceful, existence for either of them here, or anywhere in the Chicago area for that matter. Bast Zielinski would always make sure of that. He "owned" each of them in his own screwed-up way—Vicki through free cocaine and financial support and Pies through blackmail. There was no other course of action then to run. Vicki, unfortunately, did not understand the situation as clearly as Pies did.

Vicki took a couple of deep breaths, and her tone softened a notch. "I'm in control of my life, Jakub. Okay? It may not appear that way to you, but I am. In fact, I have an appointment in Lake Forest about my artwork. A very nice gallery there is interested in my work. He's more than interested. He's already been talking about how to price my paintings. Can you believe that, Jakub? Me, selling paintings. In Lake Forest!"

Pies studied her for a good long moment. In that instant, as Vicki and Pies stood staring each other down, the tension was lifted from the air. They had known each other for so long that they could never really stay angry with each other for any extended period of time.

"That's great," said Pies, softly, as he moved closer, leaned over the coffee table and snatched a tissue from the box on the table, and tenderly reached out toward Vicki's face.

She didn't move. "I'm sorry that we never, you know," she said. "I remember that being your choice."

Pies stopped his hand, smiled, bent forward, and kissed her cheek. He gently wiped some of the gaudy red lipstick off her mouth with the tissue, and she didn't stop him.

Vicki grinned, took the tissue out of his hand, and turned to walk to the bathroom. "Okay. Okay, I'll go a little more conservative."

"I think Lake Forest may require that," said Pies with a fake chuckle.

Pies watched her get ready from the living room. She quickly adjusted her make-up to appear a bit more subdued. As she worked, Pies shifted back to the windows and said, "Where in Lake Forest? I can drive you, if you'd like."

"It's right in the town, across from the train station. You don't have to do that. It's a long way," said Vicki from the bathroom. "Too bad it's on the other rail line, otherwise I'd just train it, you know. I'll get a car service or a cab," she said.

"That'll cost you. I've got nothing going on right now. In fact, I have a couple of days off that 9-1-1 job Bast has me doing," he lied.

"Are you sure?" asked Vicki.

"Yeah, it'll be fun. A nice car ride. Why not?"

"What about that California trip? Aren't you supposed to..."

"That all fell through," said Pies.

"Oh," said Vicki. "Sorry to hear that."

"Does Bast know you're going to Lake Forest?"

He caught Vicki's reflected expression in the bathroom mirror as it froze in place, and her eyes locked onto his. After a second, she looked away and got back to fixing her makeup. An answer never came.

31

As Pies and Vicki, who now looked professional in an attractively cut blouse and pencil skirt, drove through uptown Park Ridge on Touhy Avenue, she said, "Why not go the other way and take 94? It's probably closer."

"I'll do 294 north," said Pies. He lied because he had only this one more chance to get through to her while he had her as a captive audience in his small car.

"This Mr. Roer, the guy in Lake Forest, he's very influential in the North Shore art scene. I emailed him photos of some of my pieces, and he said he can sell them. But he still wants to meet with me first, to make sure we can work together."

"Work together?" asked Pies.

"He's got wealthy clients who are willing to pay, but the buying customers sometimes like to interact with the artists. It makes them feel closer to the pieces they purchase," said Vicki. "He wants to spend an hour with me to make sure that we are compatible as we move forward. If Mr. Roer and I get along, things will work out. That's what he said, anyway. I can't believe this is happening, Jakub."

Pies's mind raced.

He had to broach the subject of Vicki coming to O'Hare, hopping on a plane to San Francisco, and leaving Chicago behind for good, but he couldn't get his mouth to say the words.

"I've been waiting a long time for this, Jakub," she said. "Could be my break."

The coke had dissipated, but her upbeat nature remained. She turned and smiled his way and continued, "I have you to thank, you know."

"Thank me, why would you do that?" asked Pies.

"I know I got mad at you the other day because you pushed me toward downtown, but if you hadn't of done that, I would never have looked up Mr. Roer and emailed him. I would have given up," she said.

Pies wasn't an educated man, but he was smart enough to realize that Vicki had peculiarities in her psyche that sometimes made her thoughts and actions vacillate from one extreme to the next. He wondered how she could go from striking him violently with her fist to gently thanking him for something he didn't even realize he'd done—and all within minutes. As he drove onward he thought that now, though, was not the time to discuss her idiosyncrasies.

"Yeah? Sure. I'm glad this is working out for you," he said quietly.

To Pies, Mr. Roer sounded like a person who could change her life for the better. But as soon as the pleasant thought of Vicki selling pieces of her artwork to wealthy clients came to mind, it vanished.

Pies began to imagine a future where Vicki became successful— so successful that she would never choose to leave the area. The images accelerated, too. The visuals were of Vicki and Bast, still together, locked in their sordid relationship with no end in sight. Vicki would snort copious amounts of the cocaine that kept her chained to Bast, her free source of the drug and the outlet for her misguided "glamorous" lifestyle.

What Pies finally visualized in the future for Vicki was her becoming even more of a pariah in the neighborhood than she presently was. He could see a miserable woman, prematurely aged by drug abuse, moving about the neighborhood and causing trouble at every turn. And if Pies was being honest with himself, he didn't really have to imagine some of this. He had already witnessed her physical decline in the videotapes. She was well on her way, and she would continue to spiral down her woeful path as the woman who screws a married man for drugs and a feeling of power in her little corner of the world.

Beads of sweat sprouted on Pies's brow when he saw the highway interchange ahead. There was only one way to get onto I-294 from Touhy Avenue, and that was southbound, away from Lake Forest.

"Where are you going?" she asked.

"Vicki," said Pies, but he stopped. He couldn't get the words out of his mouth.

"What the hell is this?"

Pies went under I-294 and looped to the right. They entered the ramp to the southbound lanes of the toll road.

"Jakub? What are you doing? I have to be—"

"We'll get you some clothes in California, so don't worry about that," said Pies. "There's got to be some great places to shop there."

Vicki's face showed unmitigated confusion."California? Is this a joke? What do you…"

"I have money in my backpack, enough for a lifetime, and two tickets to San Francisco," he said.

"How can you travel with that much money?"she asked, confused by the whole line of conversation.

"We'll stay in a place called Half Moon Bay for a few weeks until the passports arrive—"

"Jakub. Jakub, take me back home."

They were only on I-294 for a minute before Pies took the connector that led directly into O'Hare Airport.

As Pies drove along, a FedEx van blasted past them doing eighty miles an hour in the high-speed lane. The passing van jarred Pies's mind from his current task and to something truly terrible.

It had suddenly dawned on him that his plan had a major flaw.

When the hard drives arrive at the Chicago PD, sure, Bast and the other crew members would be grabbed up by the police within a day or two, but Pies wouldn't be out of the country for another few weeks. The Zielinski crew would be in custody, but the first thing that they'd do would be to rat out Pies. He would be a wanted man—who still had to hide out for weeks on U.S. soil until his new passports arrived in Half Moon Bay.

How could he be so goddamned stupid?

Pies became even more frantic as the flaw manifested and fully bloomed in the back of his mind. Why the hell didn't he delay the shipment of the hard drives? Why didn't he ship them from California the day he left for Vietnam? *Shit! Goddamn you, man,* he thought. *What have you done?*

"It's okay. It's okay," he said aloud, mostly to calm himself.

He fought hard to console his inner thoughts, and he quickly began to see that he had to simply go through with the plan anyway. He'd take his chances that everything would work out. There was no other choice now.

"Vicki, I love you. I love you so much that I'm doing what's best for you, and what's best for me."

"My God, you're crazy."

"No one will look for us in Vietnam."

"Vietnam...?"

"And if they do, and they try to arrest me, it won't work, because there's no extradition from Vietnam to the United States."

"Jakub, pull over and stop. You're not thinking clearly. You're scaring me."

"You won't make it here, Vicki. You need help and I want to help you."

Vicki, at first, reeled, but she worked hard to collect her thoughts so that she could act more reasonably. "Jakub, I'm not the one who needs help here."

Pies turned to her as he took the exit ramp that led to the airport's long-term parking area. He saw that Vicki was wild-eyed with fear, her right hand on the door handle.

And he knew.

He had lost her.

Pies knew, as he slowed the car on the ramp, that it was all over. Vicki would never come with him.

He'd simply...lost.

As he finally stopped the car on the shoulder of the exit ramp, Vicki opened the door and scrambled from the car. She waved frantically at passing taxis, and the third one stopped for her.

Pies glanced to the side, in defeat, as the love of his life got into the back of a taxicab, and the car pulled out and onto the roadway where it quickly rolled from view.

32

NAOMI SAT, quiet and with her eyes downcast, at the kitchen table of her ex-in-law's Sauganash home, and ate a family dinner. Pot roast. Little Jason was there, along with her ex-in-laws, Mike and Emma.

Naomi ate, but her mind was on the non-breather call that Pies had handled earlier. She simply couldn't shake how the trainee dealt with the situation. His instincts were incredibly keen. He was completely off script, but later in the shift, after she advised Soup of the call and the supervisor listened to the recording of the incident, the boss agreed that Pies's actions were obviously not effective in saving a life, but heroic in their own special way.

An hour after he took that call, Pies told Naomi that he wasn't feeling well and that he had to leave for the day.

"Oh, I found something," said Mike.

Naomi was lost in her own thoughts, and she flinched as he made his comment. She said, "What?"

"He was rooting around in those old, case file boxes all morning, Naomi. Jason even got to help," said Emma.

"I had to take a bath afterward," said little four-year-old Jason. "Bumpa said the boxes had a shit-ton of dust on them."

"Jason?" said Emma. "We don't talk like that."

When the chagrinned Jason looked down at his plate and flicked a pea with his fork, Emma gave Mike and Naomi a quick smile.

"Jakubowski. That name. After you left the other day, it stuck with me. I knew I'd heard it before," said Mike. He stood and moved over to the countertop where a stack of old files lay. He picked up the stack and brought it back over to the table and placed it next to his plate.

"No crime scene photos at the table," said Emma, and then she pretended to shiver. "Please."

"So you said there was a cop by that name, Jakubowski, but that's not why I remembered. Here, look," he said as he opened the file and spun it around for Naomi to read.

It was a typed report titled: Suspect Interview, Jakub Jakubowski.

Below that was a note that read: Double murder, 16th district.

Naomi lifted her gaze, and Mike could tell she was thrown off guard completely.

"Looks bad, I know, but the kid was probably only in the wrong place. He had nothing to do with it," said Mike.

"What happened?" asked Naomi.

"Two burglary experts, Mobbed-up guys, went to the great beyond on the same morning some twelve years ago. It looked sort of like the Outfit being the Outfit to us at first, but it was more intricate than their usual tactics. Kind of a complicated set-up was used there. It was a weird, shotgun-shell, booby-trap device. A lot of trip wires and the like. There's pictures in there..."

"Not...at the table," said Emma.

Naomi shook her head and said, "Of course not, Emma."

"The two hits happened a few minutes apart, and a few blocks apart in Edison Park. That's your guy from work, Jakub, I figured. Right?" asked Mike.

Naomi nodded but kept her eyes angled toward the typed report that was laid out before her—and the photo the investigative team had snapped of sixteen-year-old Pies. In the photo he was obviously younger, and thinner, but his intense hazel-colored eyes, that she'd grown so fond of, still shone through.

"The Jakubowski in there was near the scene of both locations, but it was a coincidence, that's all. The kid, he was like sixteen then,

I guess, was out riding around on his bike. We cleared him pretty quick."

Naomi stared at the photo.

She couldn't take her eyes off of the photo.

Naomi was a lot of things, but an idiot was not one of them. She knew right then that Jakub Jakubowski didn't leave the Northcomm center early because he felt poorly after the non-breather call.

He was the leak.

And he was a killer.

33

CRICK, IN the red minivan, was parked in a fast-food lot, a block away from their target. He had a clear view of B-Man's Pawn from his vantage point. The business was housed in a two-story brick structure and bracketed by two one-story retail outlets on Oakton Street in Skokie. The low-roofed business on the right of B-Man's Pawn had easy access to the permanently affixed maintenance ladder on the side of the pawnshop's wall above its own low rooftop.

"Yeah, one bank to the next and then to the next. Three in an hour. It was weird, man, that's all I'm saying," said Andy's voice.

"I've been calling him all day without an answer," said Crick as his voice trailed off.

"I thought he had a full work day. And why would he go on those bank runs?"

"He's definitely up to something, man, but I don't think he'd screw us over. Come on, everyone's been off these past few days since Stan dropped," said Crick. "Hell, Bast wanted some coke dealer helping us here tonight. Had to be kidding me, right?"

"I don't know. The more I thought about that, would it be so bad?" said Andy. "It's good to have help, you know."

"Bast's losing control. You heard him talking his weird crap at the funeral. Took some doing getting only the three of us on this here tonight. He says he has to have these jobs done, it's a must, you know. And we'll do 'em, but we have to do what we're comfortable with," said Crick. "None of this risky bullshit just to make him look good."

"Bast's the main man," said Andy. "His game to run."

"What's that, dudes?" asked Devin. "What's this all about? Sorry, had the mute button pushed."

"Nothing, mutt. How goes it?" asked Andy as he turned a lazy corner in the blue minivan and drove along in Skokie, not a police car or any other car, for that matter, in sight at this late hour.

"Well, McAndy, this will be a piece of cake," said Devin. "That's all the news from here."

Five minutes earlier, Crick, after he had Devin climb from the top of his van to the low rooftop next to B-Man's Pawn, drove across the block and backed his vehicle in among the overnight cleaning crew's vehicles at the restaurant so that any passing patrol car wouldn't look at him twice.

"Okay, I got him," said Crick. He could see Devin, dressed in dark clothing, including black rubber gloves, scale the ladder from the low rooftop and over to the top of B-Man's roof.

"I can see my house from up here," said Devin. "You feel me?" he asked with a laugh.

Crick smiled to himself. His nephew had been a great addition to their team, and he'd do anything to keep him safe—especially from Bast.

"No lock," said Devin. "Our lucky day, and not too smart for them, huh?"

"A can of corn," said Andy.

"Okay, hold up. Don't pop it yet. I'll give you the go-ahead when the van's in place," said Crick.

Crick got out of his minivan and leisurely sauntered across Oakton Street and moved a half block away where Devin had parked the red utility van in an auto-repair parking lot, this time with the "Ralph's Plumbing" sign on the sides. Crick hopped into the driver's seat, started the vehicle, and with the lights off drove down the rear alley that led directly to the back door of the pawnshop.

He got out of the parked van and said, "Okay, now."

He walked back toward the red minivan and could plainly hear Devin creak open the hatch on the roof thirty feet above him.

"So far, so good, fellas. No alarms. No nasty pooches," said Devin. Andy and Crick could hear Devin's heavier breathing as he climbed down a ladder and descended a stairway inside the building.

"Andy, where are you on your loop?"

Andy said, "On the downside and heading back around."

Crick waited patiently at the curb ready to cross Oakton Street as a single car passed him by. He placed his right foot out and into the street, when—

"Back the hell off, man," said Devin's voice in Crick's ear. "Crick. Uncle Crick!"

"Andy," called Crick as he ran to the front door of the pawnshop.

"I'm rounding back," said Andy. "I'm on the way."

Over their headsets both Crick and Andy could hear Devin struggling with someone.

"Devin, where are you?" asked Crick.

"Back the hell off, brother," demanded Devin.

A man's rather low voice said, "I ain't no brother."

"Shit," yelled Crick as he frantically peered through B-Man's front-door window. He couldn't see much, though, only a partially lit showroom full of expensive goods.

The struggle escalated and sounded quite violent in Crick's and Andy's ears.

"Back room. First floor," yelled Devin. "You motherf—"

"Back door," yelled Crick as he headed in that direction.

"Got it," said Andy's voice.

In the still darkness, Crick could hear Andy's minivan accelerating toward the pawnshop. Its engine's powerful whine cut through the quiet night air. Crick rounded the corner into the alley behind the pawnshop and hurried to open the rear door of the produce van. He reached inside and grabbed up a thick length of chain. Crick scrambled to the back door of the pawnshop and wrapped the chain around the back door handle.

Then the sounds of the fight got even uglier. Both Devin and the other man could be heard shouting and grunting, but neither was making any sense. Blows could be heard, followed by animalistic grunts.

Andy pulled up in his van and Crick motioned for him to come closer and back up, which he did. Once Andy's van was in position, Crick wrapped the other end of the chain to the trailer hitch on the rear of the minivan and patted the side of the car.

Andy slowly pulled forward but the chain slipped off the shop's door handle.

"Damn it," said Crick.

Things had become suddenly quiet inside the pawnshop.

"Devin? Devin, what's happening?" asked Crick.

Nothing.

Crick's eyes showed all his emotions. He had to get to his nephew. "Come on, come on," he called to Andy.

Andy backed up again, and this time Crick anxiously wrapped the chain around the door handle as many times as he could before he looped it into a knot. He pounded on the van once again, and Andy pulled forward and the door slowly popped and peeled open.

Crick yanked his ski mask partially down over his face and hurriedly wedged his way into the back room of the pawnshop and saw… Devin, mask down, breathing heavily, as he aggressively loomed over the body of a large, muscular, biker-looking man whose arms were covered in tattoos.

The man was dead.

"D, you okay?" asked Crick.

"What happened," asked Andy, mask down, as he slipped inside and saw the bloody carnage of Devin's lethal battle with the biker.

Devin's eyes were wide open as the adrenaline pumped through his system. He said, "I think I got 'em."

Devin kicked gently at the dead man's ribs.

"You got him, buddy," said Crick, softly, sadly, as he shifted closer and guided Devin outside.

Once out and into the alley, Crick peeled off his mask and phone headset and said, "Scrap 'em. We're done. You good to drive?"

Devin nodded and said, "Came out of nowhere, man."

"Go. Let's go," said Crick. He bent to pick up the chain. He tossed it into the back of the produce van and closed the back doors of the truck.

Andy and Devin drove away simultaneously. Crick did his best to calm his breathing and casually stroll back to the minivan parked in the fast-food restaurant's lot. If any police were patrolling in the area, he didn't want them to stop and have a chat with him simply because he moved in an agitated way from the adrenaline pumping so freely through his system.

When he got to his minivan, he took the cell phone from his front pocket. He snapped the phone into a couple of pieces and chucked them across the lot. He got into the driver's seat, closed the door, leaned his head back, and screamed as loud as he could.

He settled down, started the van's engine, and said, "Pies...."

34

Pies sat at his kitchen table and stared at the pre-labeled box with the external hard drives inside.

It was nearly 4 A.M. and he hadn't slept.

He had allowed his entire world to crumble in the past several hours—all on his own accord. It was all over. Done. His downfall lay squarely on his own shoulders. He let his emotions overrule his logical mind, and it cost him. Everything.

Vicki would never speak with him again—he was sure of that. The final look she gave him as she got out of his car on the exit ramp near O'Hare clinched it. Vicki thought Pies had lost his mind. She was probably right, too. How could he ever think that she would go along with his plan to leave Chicago for Vietnam?

Vietnam?

What the hell, man?

She would surely tell Bast all about his plans to get her away from Edison Park and the weird car ride to the airport. Bast would make Pies pay for his missteps, even though his plan to take Vicki away from the boss didn't work.

And then there was the box on his kitchen table.

That damned box.

Not only had he screwed up the timing of the delivery date of the hard drives to the police, he had forgotten, altogether, to actually even send the damned box with the evidence inside.

Pies couldn't keep his head together and do anything right.

His ultimate escape plan to get away from the Zielinskis and Chicago had failed.

And Vicki was gone.

That was the most difficult piece of this broken dream for Pies to handle.

Vicki was gone.

His eyes were heavy from the lack of sleep, but he couldn't help but stare straight ahead at the box full of hard drives.

Then the back kitchen door was forcefully kicked inward.

"Knock, knock," said Bast as he advanced into the room. His eyes were wild and wide open from extended cocaine use. His smile was more of a snarl, and his shoulders were bunched as if he was ready for a fight. He smelled of cheap perfume, dried sweat, and sex.

Pies just sat there as Bast took over his kitchen. There was nothing left to do.

"No sleep tonight, buddy?" asked Bast, rhetorically. "Everything okay?"

He angled to the fridge, opened the door, and peered inside. He didn't see anything he liked, so he slammed the door closed so hard that the contents within rattled about. He then shifted to the cabinets. He opened a few, but he still didn't find what he was looking for.

"Are you a monk? Where's the booze?" asked Bast.

"Do what you have to do," said Pies, resigned to his fate.

Bast turned and gave Pies a goofy expression. "What the hell's wrong with you? What's with the pouting, huh?"

Pies became instantly confused. He thought Bast was here to punish him for any one of the crimes he had committed in the past few hours against Bast or the Zielinski crew.

"Didn't think I'd catch you awake. I was cruising by and saw the light," said Bast. "So..."

Bast pulled a chair out from under the table and took a seat. "I got to ask? What's up with Vicki today? I was by earlier and she was acting super weird, man. Did she say anything to you?"

Pies looked Bast in the eye and shrugged.

"She's a beautiful, sexy woman, I don't have to tell you, right? But she gets on my nerves, you know? Is that all part of being artsy? I don't know," said Bast. "She can be a real pain and she's probably a little crazy, but that ass, am I right?"

Pies was in no mood at all to talk so he kept silent.

"And look at you. Everyone's acting all messed up for some reason. What the hell's wrong?"

Pies's eyes darted away.

"P-yes, it was really something having the old man drop like that, huh? Shocking, you know. He was all fit and trim and all that crap. You know that he didn't eat red meat. Can you imagine? Eggs, sure, every once in a while. But he was mostly shoving veggies in his mouth, that man."

Pies ignored him.

"You and him, though, right? You and old Stan had a nice relationship. Sort of, right, wouldn't you say? Father and son-like." Bast sported a demented smile and continued, "Except for when he had you blow up those two assholes."

"Bast, I don't—"

"You ever call him Dad? Daddy, maybe?" asked Bast, mockingly. "He took you under his wing, and you loved it, you piece of... You fuck!"

Bast slammed his open hand on the tabletop.

Pies's eyes locked onto Bast.

"I'm the one running this now. You do as I say, you understand me, right? You get me the information I need. The right information. The correct information, P-yes."

Pies stared and offered nothing else.

"If you ever fuck me over like you did tonight..."

Pies looked at the floor. He was fuming. He wanted so badly to attack Bast and beat him into submission, but he did nothing. And who was Pies kidding? Bast was physically a much stronger man. He could kill Pies with his bare hands if he wanted to.

But in that moment, when Pies was at his lowest, yet another plan sparked to a start. Pies narrowed his eyes slightly as the immediate visuals associated with his new idea grew to full completion in his mind.

Bast noticed a slight change in Pies's demeanor. He smiled maniacally and said, "Anyway, I guess there is something that needs to be addressed right now."

Pies looked a question at his boss.

"Oh, it's not me who wants to do the addressing," said Bast as he stood. He said, "Okie-doke, guys," and the back door pushed opened once again.

Crick, Andy, and Devin quietly, but forcefully, moved into the kitchen—all of their eyes were locked onto Pies. Devin still wore the same clothes he had on during the burglary, and the bloodstains were large and still visible on the dark material.

All three men had cold and static expressions on their faces.

"You guys work this out," said Bast. He turned to Crick and continued, "Not the face. I don't want any questions at his work. There's enough heat there already. I've got to find a drink," said Bast as he backed his way out of the house. "Good talk, dog. See you soon."

Crick nodded to Devin and the young man bashed Pies with a right fist to the center of his chest. Pies fell out of his chair and hit the floor. He coughed and tried to catch his breath, but Devin wasn't done. He rained down several quick punches to Pies's midsection.

As Devin straightened and took a break, Andy came in and pounded Pies with a three-punch combination to the gut. Crick shoved Andy aside, reared back, and kicked Pies in the ribs. The kick hit its mark. Hard.

Pies painfully struggled to get any air that he could.

Devin leaned close, nose-to-nose with Pies, and said, "Stay there."

Andy headed down the stairs and into the basement while Crick marched up to the second floor.

Pies heard Crick rifling through the bedroom drawers and bathroom above, but things were quiet in the basement.

Devin stood guard, observing Pies without saying another word.

Pies got to a seated position on the floor and silently seethed as his breath finally came back. He looked away when he heard Andy in the basement say, "Woot! Here we go, fellas. Crick! Pay-fucking-day!"

Pies heard Crick scramble down the stairs and watched as he rounded into the kitchen and then went down the basement stairs.

After a short moment, Crick said, "D, get the cart from the van. We're going to score tonight after all."

Devin finally smiled a little. He said, "You move, I'll kill you, too."

Pies, confused by the remark, narrowed his eyes at Devin as the young man walked from the house.

He then heard Andy and Crick begin to climb back up the rickety basement stairs. They emerged with their arms overloaded with Pies's most expensive computer equipment. His high-end monitors, the desktop computers, his mini-DVR and button camera. They were going to take everything of value that he owned.

As Crick set a fully loaded $5,000 desktop computer on top of the kitchen table, he finally noticed the pre-labeled box full of external hard drives. Without even looking at the label, he torn the box open and smiled when he saw what was inside. He scooped the hard drives out of the box, placed them on the table, and carelessly tossed the empty cardboard aside.

The box landed in the corner of the kitchen, the address label plainly visible: Head of Detectives, Chicago PD, 3510 S. Michigan Avenue, Chicago, IL 60653.

Pies sat on the floor, defeated, and watched as the crew members took every last shred of evidence that he held over the Zielinski burglary crew. They didn't even realize what they were taking. They only saw dollar signs. But it was worth so much more than money to Pies.

Once they were gone, and the house was quiet, Pies stood up. He painfully leaned forward onto the chair that he'd been knocked out of. For a long moment he stared straight ahead.

Tears formed in Pies's eyes—tears of anger and frustration...and defeat.

He lifted the chair over his head and slammed it onto the kitchen floor where it broke into a few pieces. Pies picked up the longest hunk of broken wood and began violently swinging it into anything and everything within his sight. He cried out with each blow.

He obliterated the table, the glasses and plates on the countertop, the cabinet doors. As he gained momentum, he advanced throughout the first floor and inflicted heavy damage to the walls, furniture, lamps, and anything he could take a swing at.

When the wooden chair piece finally splintered under duress, he went back to the kitchen and picked up the next-largest piece.

He ran upstairs and annihilated every framed painting, photo, and piece of artwork in the home as he moved along quickly.

He screamed loudly and flung the hunk of wood toward the small, attic access door in his bedroom. The piece of wood embedded into the three-foot-tall attic door like an arrow.

Pies fell to his knees so that he could catch his breath, but he kept his eyes focused on that attic access door—and he thought about what was inside.

He scrambled to the door and flung it open. He reached inside and pulled out a rolled blanket that was heavy and difficult to lift.

He unfurled the blanket on the floor and revealed the cache of handguns, mostly revolvers that his father had taken off of criminals while he was on the job all those years ago.

Pies leaned forward and studied a chrome-plated .38 snub-nosed revolver. He reached out, lifted it, and scrutinized the gun very carefully. He gently rubbed his thumb along the metal where the serial number had been filed away.

Pies opened the gun's cylinder to confirm that it was fully loaded. He snapped the cylinder back into place and stood. And when he did, he caught his reflection in the closet-door mirror across the room. He immediately looked down and away.

35

DEVIN, DRESSED in boxers and a rumpled T-shirt, awoke and sat up in his bed at his mother's house in Lincolnwood. He reached over to his ratty side table and picked up his phone. He began to thumb-swipe through his smartphone and chuckled loudly. He said, "Damn right, I'm a real player."

He had only placed the posting on Twitter six hours earlier, and so far three of his measly eleven followers had clicked the "favorite" button of his photo of the palm-tree-shaped, diamond-encrusted earrings—the earrings that he had kept for himself when he broke into the Winnetka boutique.

The caption on the photo with the earrings read: Making bank.

The loud crack of the rear kitchen door violently and loudly splintering inward caused him to drop his phone onto the carpeted floor. Instead of retrieving the phone, the stupefied young man took a hesitant step toward his closed bedroom door.

"Who are you? Wait. Stop," yelled his mother from the first floor kitchen of the modest home. "Devin, honey! Devin!"

"Mom?" said Devin as he stood frozen in the moment.

The heavy thumping of large men running up the stairs literally rattled the home. All at once, four burly uniformed police officers, two wearing dark-blue Lincolnwood uniforms, the others in Winnetka uniforms, barged into his room, guns drawn.

The first Lincolnwood officer in the room said, "Down! Get down!"

Devin took a step back and slowly raised his hands as the other Lincolnwood officer tackled him to his bed, spun him around, put his gun in his holster, and asked one of the Winnetka officers, "Cuffs?" The closest uniformed Winnetka officer handed him his cuffs, and the Lincolnwood cop roughly hooked the suspect. The same officer did a quick body search of the arrestee before he straightened and said, "He's all yours," and took a step back.

A fresh-faced, thirty-five-year-old, suit-wearing man, Winnetka Police Detective Bill Dempsey, slipped into the room and said, "Devin Nowak, you're under arrest for burglary and receiving stolen property."

After his rights were read to him, Devin sat on the edge of his bed as Dempsey leaned in super close. He said, "You are a special brand of stupid."

Devin sneered at Dempsey and said, "Lawyer."

"Those earrings were one of a kind, dipshit."

"Lawyer," said Devin as he tried to thrust his shoulder into Dempsey's chest.

"Let's get you back to Winnetka and have a nice sit-down. Some other jurisdictions, like these officers here from Lincolnwood, may want to have a word with you, too, in the very near future. And I bet you could tell us who your friend at Northcomm is. It's time to unburden yourself," said Dempsey through a faux grin.

Devin looked to the door and saw his skinny mother, Cindy Nowak, with tears in her eyes and an expression of pure defeat on her pallid face.

"Mom, you got to call—"

Devin stopped when he noticed the hopeful look on Dempsey's face.

"Call him. Do that, Mom."

Cindy Nowak looked away without uttering a word.

"Mom?"

Detective Dempsey finally got a good long look at Devin, and the fresh cuts and bruises on his face and arms from the fight in the pawnshop. "Someone push you down some steps?"

The remains of the dead biker-looking man from the pawnshop probably hadn't been discovered as of yet. Devin understood that simply by Dempsey's response to his injuries. The police hadn't put it all together—yet.

Devin's face screwed up in anger and he said, "Lawyer."

"Get him to the car," said Dempsey.

"Mom?" screamed Devin as he was yanked from the room, still dressed only in his T-shirt and underwear, and wrestled from the home by the uniformed cops.

"Mom," said Dempsey in a condescending tone, "Devin's been very stupid. We're going to tear this shithole apart, ma'am, and when we find more stolen property, there's a good chance you'll probably be joining your kid."

Cindy sobbed openly and cried out, "I don't have anything to do with them."

"Them?"

Cindy shook her head.

"Ma'am, who's 'them'?"

But Cindy remained silent.

"If you help us, we can work something out, I'm sure," said the Winnetka detective.

*

Two of the four uniformed officers led the handcuffed Devin to the back of a Winnetka squad car. One opened the door, and the other stuffed the young man inside. As Devin sat side-straddle, before he tucked his legs inside, his eyes locked on something in the distance. He lowered his head and slowly shook it.

"I know, man. You'll be cool," said Crick as he sat in his own vehicle, a black Dodge Charger, parked a half block away on the tree-lined Lincolnwood side street. His jaw muscles worked overtime as he continued to peer through the windshield of his car. All he could do at this point was watch as Devin was locked inside a cruiser.

Three squad cars and an unmarked vehicle remained at the house. The three uniformed officers still at the residence stood around in the front yard and conversed among themselves.

A few nosy neighbors were out on the sidewalk and observed the goings-on.

Crick grabbed his cell phone from the center console and dialed, pressed it to his ear, waited, and kept his eyes on the house.

Detective Dempsey was the next to step from Crick's sister Cindy's house. He turned and motioned for Cindy to step outside as he waved the uniformed officers into the house. Cindy came out holding some folded clothing for Devin. She handed the clothes to one cop who walked them over to the car with the suspect inside. Cindy then took a seat on a porch step, where she tucked her chin into her chest and sobbed.

Crick leaned his head back on the rest and said, "Turned to shit..."

"Troubles, my man?" asked Andy.

"D got grabbed," said Crick. "Winnetka."

There was a long silence on the other end of the line.

"Pies? That son of a—"

Crick shook his head and said, "No. Not Pies. You online?"

"Hold on." After a few seconds Andy's voice said, "Okay."

"Check D's Twitter," said Crick. "I was on my way over to have him take it down. He and his mom wouldn't answer their phones this morning."

"Ah, shit, man..."

"This is bad," said Crick.

"He's got to know," said Andy's serious voice.

Crick knew that Bast would have to be briefed, but he couldn't wipe away the Bast-getting-revenge-on-Devin images that immediately began to flash through his mind. The acid in his stomach began to churn.

"Work on that, would you? I'll wait here until they clear the place," said Crick as he disconnected the call.

One of the uniformed officers stepped outside and opened the trunk of his car. He pulled out paper and clear-plastic evidence bags, tucked them under his arm, and went back inside Cindy's house.

Crick let out a slow breath and settled back into his seat.

36

THE OVERLY made-up, possibly underage blonde in a low-slung blouse that publicized how fantastic Mother Nature had been to her, slowly kissed Bast's neck. They were seated in a back booth of The Merc, a smallish, darkly lit, high-end eatery on Northwest Highway, a few blocks from Zielinski's Insurance Agency.

Bast raised an empty beer bottle, and the waiter nodded and turned to the bar to fill the order.

The restaurant was nearly empty, it being a weekday at lunchtime. Edison Park's commercial strip was not an area where corporate offices were located, so during the midday usually only the locals frequented the restaurant. Later in the day, The Merc would fill with a good-sized happy hour and dinner crowd as area residents arrived back in their neighborhood.

Bast only came here when it was nearly empty like it was presently. The Merc was a fantastic, and cozy, place to hide out from his wife— or meet with new friends, as it were.

"You want another?" asked Bast.

The blonde whined with the voice of a little girl, "No, baby, I just want to go. You said you were sad since your old man died, and I wanted to cheer you up. The way you like."

"Okay, we'll get there, sugar. But I got to eat."

"I know," she said as she snuggled his neck again.

Bast smiled, but lost it the moment he saw Andy, stone-faced, approaching the booth's table.

"What?" was all Bast said.

*

PIES LEANED with his shoulder blades against the back interior kitchen wall at The Merc. It was a busy spot to post up, as the staff darted about, clanked pans, chopped produce and the like, as they prepped for the later dinner rush. The noises didn't faze Pies at all. He was laser focused.

Every time an employee shoved through the swinging kitchen door that led to the dining room, Pies got an excellent view of the back of Bast's head and the blonde bimbo who kept her lips on his neck.

The .38 snub-nosed revolver was tucked into the back waistband of his pants, and his button-up shirt was untucked and pulled over the weapon to conceal it.

Pies arrived here after he observed Vicki leave the back-alley door of her apartment and walk the few blocks to her parents' home. He watched from a safe distance as she simply sat on her parents' front porch. When a delivery truck arrived fifteen minutes later, Vicki signed for the large, flat boxes the driver unloaded and carried them around to the basement door. Pies knew from their odd dimensions that the boxes contained canvases. He made sure that she was inside the basement door before he made the trip to his current location.

"Pies, hey my friend," said Javier the cook with a Honduran accent. "You hungry?"

"No, Jav, but thanks," said Pies.

"Lemon chicken is the special tonight. I know you like that, man," said Javier. "I'll get you a plate. You can eat right there."

Pies never took his eyes off the door as Javier spoke with him.

It swung open again, and Pies could see Andy sitting across the booth from Bast and the blonde. Andy didn't look too happy.

"I'm good, Javier," said Pies. "Thanks."

*

ANDY EYED the blonde and wondered about her. Except for the big boobs, she looked like a damned kid, he thought.

Bast caught Andy's expression and he said, "She's legal." Personally, though, he didn't really care one way or the other.

The blonde smirked and reached down to cup Bast's zipper. He roughly shoved her hand away and said to Andy, "You get that asshole on the line."

"Baby, come on, let's go," said the blonde.

Andy pressed the button on his cell phone that would call Crick. He watched as Bast brusquely reached below the table with his right hand. The blonde's eyes slowly closed and she tilted her head back a little. Andy immediately stood, let out a breath, and walked toward the front door to get away from Bast. Right then Crick answered.

"Yeah," said Crick's voice.

"He wants you," said Andy as he spun and shifted back to the booth.

"Great," said Crick's exasperated voice.

Andy handed the phone to Bast, who took it with his free hand.

"What have you done, Crick?" asked Bast as he raised his other hand back to the table top and the blonde straightened in her seat.

"He took photos," Crick replied.

"What? What does that even mean?"

"He posted pics on Twitter from a score in Winnetka, okay? He messed up," said Crick. "They found more stuff in Cindy's place, too. I didn't know he was skimming."

Bast angrily launched himself from the booth and began to pace. "You've got to be shitting me? Who would do that?"

"He's a kid, man. He kept some stuff. He's good at this, but he's still a kid. He didn't think," said Crick. "That's all. He didn't think."

"Crick, man?" said Bast as he rubbed his forehead. "Crick? Crick, I—"

"I paid for a lawyer. No one we know, so it won't come back. My sister can bail him out. They haven't set the amount yet, but I'll cover it. We're hoping they don't put two and two together with last night anytime soon," said Crick. "They got his DNA now that he's in the system. I know he left some last night, so..."

The waiter stepped closer with a tray and the fresh bottle of beer.

"Goddamn you. What have you done?" shouted Bast.

The waiter U-turned and went back to hide at the bar.

"He won't talk. He won't, Bast. I know this kid. I helped to raise him. You know that. He's not going to jam us up. He wouldn't do that to me," said Crick's voice in Bast's ever-reddening ear.

Bast lowered his gaze as he paced. He suddenly stopped and then sat at the empty booth nearest the front door. He leaned forward and closer to the tabletop and whispered, "Well, now we have no other choice, do we?"

There was nothing but silence from the phone. Bast leaned back in his seat and observed as the blonde applied a new coat of lipstick. In that moment, Bast was downright confused—bewildered, really. He wanted nothing more than to screw the blonde and to weep —all at the same time.

"Crick?"

Silence.

"Okay," said Crick's sullen voice.

"No sign."

There was another long hesitation.

"Gone," said Crick.

Bast watched as an employee carried a tray full of fresh ice from the bar and pushed his way into the dining room. As the door swung back and forth, Pies was no longer leaning against the interior wall. He had left a second before. Bast would never even know he'd been there.

Bast slipped back to his own booth and sat. He eyed Andy for a long beat.

"You're going to..." He stopped and just shook his head in disbelief that it had come to this.

"What?" asked Andy.

"With Crick and the kid, you'll have to... You have quality control," said Bast as he handed Andy back his cell phone. "Okay? In case he can't..." Bast let out a breath.

Andy took in a sharp breath of his own, and his right eyelid twitched a little. He knew Bast had just made the ultimate call to erase Devin for good. "I'll make sure," he said.

"Good," said Bast.

"Hey, what about the dog? What did you decide there?" asked Andy.

"He's got a few more days of usefulness left in him before he's put down," said Bast. "There may be a payday in there for you now that Devin's gone. Was going to have him do the dog."

"Right," said Andy. "I can do that, too."

"Well. Okay, let's get you out of here, baby," said Bast to the oblivious blonde as he stood again and helped the young woman to her feet. He pulled a hundred-dollar bill out of the wad he yanked from his pocket and dropped it on the table, and he and the blonde exited through the kitchen door.

Andy looked after Bast and the girl until they completely left his field of vision. He turned and motioned the waiter back over, the one with the bottle of beer still propped on the tray.

37

PIES WAS livid.
He silently seethed.

He'd warned Vicki about Bast, that she was not his only one. That she had absolutely no future with the sleazy man. If only she could see this for herself, she would understand. Then she would come with Pies to Half Moon Bay and then...on to Vietnam. She would willingly go at that point, he was sure of that. He could get some grainy video or snap photos with his phone, but the lack of picture quality wouldn't prove anything, especially from this distance.

He despised doing this. He watched from the line of manicured bushes at the edge of the huge private parking lot next to the railroad tracks, as Bast and the young blonde had sex in the backseat of what he assumed was the blonde's SUV. They had backed the car into the far end of the lot where it was mostly empty of other parked cars, but Pies could still see, from 150 feet away, exactly what they were doing. It wasn't too difficult to notice under the midday sun.

A few minutes earlier, when Pies walked past the bearded, parking-lot custodian, who stood in the rickety wooden booth at the lot's entrance, the man gave him a knowing grin and shrug as he moved past. As if this was a usual thing—Bast having sex with women in the parking lot. Bast could do whatever he wanted in Edison Park without many repercussions.

Pies could shoot Bast right now with the revolver that was currently tucked into his waistband. He would be able to cover the 150 feet of gravel parking lot in no time, aim, and deliver a round to the side of Bast's sweaty head. That would be too obvious, though, in too open of an area. He'd be recognized.

The parking lot attendant, who knew him by face, had already seen him, of course. Pies didn't want to get caught, and he didn't have a death wish. He only wanted Bast to cease to exist. If Bast were out of the picture maybe Vicki would have a chance at a happy life, even if it wasn't with Pies.

If he killed Bast right now, he'd still have Crick and Andy to contend with. Pies was sure that they would not appreciate their meal ticket being put in the ground.

The monster inside him had truly awakened again when he knew he had lost Vicki. So after dispatching Bast, Pies wondered if he could keep the demon awake for a while longer until he took care of Crick and Andy—and Devin, too.

The other Zielinski burglary crew members would never expect any violence from Pies, so he'd be able to basically sneak up on them one at a time and take care of each of the men without much trouble.

But as soon as that violent notion washed over his mind, he was struck with a much better idea—a murderous idea that carried with it more nuance and finesse, just the way Pies liked to operate.

Bast would have to shower after his tryst with the blonde girl.

Sure, Rebecca allowed for his transgressions, but she still didn't want the reminders of the affairs in her own home. That's why Bast kept extra clothing in the apartment above the bakery. Bast would have to freshen up before he went back to his own home and the wife who foolishly stood by him.

Pies backed away from his observation spot in the gravel parking lot. He would get to the apartment above the bakery before Bast. He'd get set up and be ready to kill the man who had made his life miserable for the past decade or so.

When it was over, some in Edison Park might possibly mourn the shocking suicide of Bast Zielinski.

38

A LOUD HARLEY motorcycle growled below on Northwest Highway. The windows were closed in the apartment above the bakery, but the bike was still extremely noisy. It startled Pies, who stood just inside the front doorway—revolver in hand, hammer back in the cocked position.

When Bast used the apartment if Vicki wasn't around, he most times used the front door, not the one out back because he didn't want to cross paths with the Chlebeks coming in and out of the bakery's kitchen. Pies knew this from past experience.

He was sweating profusely, his eyes twitching uncontrollably.

This was it.

He thought, *Why couldn't the Harley drive by when Bast came to the apartment? The engine noise would cover the sound of the gunshot.* But it wasn't going to be that perfect, nothing ever was. His plan would work, but he had to be prepared if it went sideways on him.

He wouldn't miss, that he knew. His plan was to fire the gun as the muzzle contacted Bast's skull.

His worry was that the loud report would instantly alert bystanders, maybe even Milena and Blaze below in the bakery, to come and investigate.

There were two ways in and out of the apartment, so that doubled his opportunities to escape once Bast was dispatched. He liked those odds.

If he was discovered immediately, he could claim self-defense. With the history between him and Bast, that could easily play out with a jury.

"No, no," he said aloud as he made himself concentrate on the job at hand. He had to focus.

He would stick the barrel of the gun into Bast's ear the moment he walked through the front doorway, pull the trigger, and silently rejoice that his troubles had vanished right in front of his eyes.

He'd take Bast out, wipe the gun clean, put the revolver into the dead man's hand, and leave through the back doorway. No, no, the front doorway. Blaze and Milena never used the front doorway, he remembered again just now.

It would be loud, but he hoped that the equally noisy and busy, midday vehicle traffic on Northwest Highway would, at least, partially cover for his misdeed.

He heard the twelve-window-paned, street-side, vestibule door squeak open at the base of the front steps—and he stopped breathing for an instant. His breath then quickened, and he fought to slow his lungs down.

Focus.

He heard the distinctive sound of a city bus as it rumbled near and as Bast ascended the sixteen creaky, wooden steps. Bast seemed to be approaching carefully, treading lightly as he climbed the stairs.

Pies knew there was a bus stop directly across from the bakery. Pies couldn't believe his luck. By his quick calculation, the bus would pull over and apply its airbrakes at the very moment Bast stepped into the apartment.

He nearly smiled as a bead of sweat trickled from his forehead and into his left eye. He blinked the sweat away as the door unlocked and opened.

As the door swung inward, the bus released its airbrakes and came to a noisy stop—and Pies raised the gun, extended it, and...fired.

The report was loud.

Very loud, and Pies's ears rang instantaneously.

When he completely cleared the sweat from his eyes with the back of his hand—Vicki's body toppled forward. Her heart had stopped beating a nanosecond after the bullet knifed through her brain.

She limply bounced sideways and against the partially opened door, and the door, in turn, rebounded off the wall and arched back to slowly close.

Pies was all alone in that shoddy apartment with the dead body of the woman he loved, the woman he would kill for.

Her body lay chest down, her face canted toward Pies. Her eyes were locked in place, staring at nothingness. And the blood flowed, forming a wide pool around her upper body.

Pies stood there and blinked the sweat away. Then he began to shiver slightly and convulse. His mouth opened and he screamed, but no noise came out, only spittle.

He bent forward, dropped the pistol, and dry heaved. He crumbled to his knees, reached out to touch Vicki's face, and stopped his movements as he saw clearly the gore. He put his open hands on his thighs and then made fists. He pounded his fists into his thighs—hard—over and over again. His mouth was open in a permanent scream, but still he made no sound other than a guttural gurgle.

He frantically tried to settle himself, and he listened, but no one was coming. All the sounds he heard were normal ones that emanated from the street and bakery below. He reached out to grab up the pistol—but stopped cold. He couldn't bring himself to touch the weapon. He wiped tears from his eyes with the sleeve of his shirt, which was now soaking wet with sweat.

After a good long moment spent staring at Vicki's face, he stood. And when he did, he could see out the window, and across the street as Bast walked along, a stupid smile on his face, headed toward the insurance agency office—where there was also a bathroom...and a rudimentary shower.

Pies gulped in great breaths of mournful air as he observed Bast. He could not take his eyes off the man.

39

Naomi Gott had to find Pies.

He'd not shown up for work, and she left the communications center early to look for him.

It wasn't all that difficult for Naomi, now, to solidify her suspicions that Pies was the leak—especially when he left early the day before and didn't show up for his shift that morning.

Before Naomi feigned illness herself and left "sick" for the workday, Soup had advised her that several police jurisdictions wanted to have a word with her new trainee.

Naomi also knew that Pies was a killer. She realized that the minute her ex-father-in-law spun the file on the table for her to see.

She just knew.

Still, she had to find the man with the stunning, hazel-colored eyes.

But on her way to Pies's neighborhood her cravings had tightly grabbed hold, and she was sidetracked, as if she was switched to autopilot.

Without remembering much of the actual drive, she found herself parked in the massive blacktop lot of the casino on River Road. The only thing she recalled was her addiction softly yet firmly recommending to her that it was okay to gamble first—simply to calm her nerves. To an outside observer it would seem counterintuitive— callous even—for her to slide a few twenty-dollar bills into the frog slot machine first before finding Pies. But her addiction gently expressed to her that it would be the perfect tonic to settle her mind and allow her to successfully find the man. She had reluctantly agreed.

As she turned off her car's ignition switch she caught sight of her own eyes in the rearview mirror—and she didn't like what she saw. *What the hell am I doing?* she thought to herself. Immediately, and as if she'd just lost a staring contest, she looked away from the mirror. A queasy feeling rose up, and she placed her elbows on the inside edges of the steering wheel and then her chin into her hands and sat there for a moment.

"What is wrong with me?" she asked aloud.

As she leaned back and reached to start the car and leave, a dark-colored, unmarked police unit slowly drove along two rows farther down, near Devon Avenue, the driver peering her way. She recognized the operator of the car immediately—Winnetka Detective Bill Dempsey.

She'd known him since he was a twenty-seven-year-old patrol officer in that suburb and she was a communications officer at the Evanston PD. They'd met at police functions over the years, and recently she'd seen him more often when he came to the Northcomm center to retrieve audiotapes and speak with communications officers for his investigations.

In that instant, she knew she'd been followed here. Did they place an electronic tracker on her personal car? Her close, one-on-one work as Pies's training officer had obviously marked her for questioning in the burgeoning, leaked-alarms-out-of-service investigation.

She took a couple of cleansing breaths when she saw the unmarked police car slowly circle back toward the front of the casino building and park.

If they could follow her here, they'd continue to follow her all day long, she presumed.

Naomi got out of her car and walked steadily to the front door of the casino, as if she hadn't a care in the world. She casually squared her eyes forward so not to give herself away that she knew she was being tailed. As she was about to pull open the glass door and enter the building, she happened to notice another unmarked police car parked directly in front of Dempsey's.

Once inside, she moved quickly, dodging around other patrons and through the entire gaming floor to the back exit that led to a rear parking lot. Naomi pushed her way out the glass door. As she looked over her shoulder, she saw Dempsey enter the casino with another man she didn't recognize. Both men looked here and there, but never in her direction.

Naomi ducked out and jogged around to the side of the building where she had parked her car.

She needed to find Pies, but she wouldn't be able to use her own car right now. The authorities were obviously on her tail, but what incriminating evidence would Naomi have, other than her assumptions about Pies's criminal history? She concluded that she was the investigator's way of getting more information on Pies, maybe even leading them to the man. She was not about to offer them any further assistance.

She raised her hand when she noticed a taxi begin to pull away after dropping off two young women. The taxi halted, and Naomi got inside.

"Edison Park," she said after closing the door.

∗

NAOMI HAD visited four businesses in the neighborhood so far. No one at any of the locations knew a Jakub Jakubowski. At least that's what they told her. In her frazzled state, she had left her windbreaker in her car and was wearing her golf shirt with the emblazoned badge on it. Perhaps, the people she talked with were simply averse to speaking to someone wearing a badge.

She began her search for Pies at his home, but didn't get an answer at the front door. When she went to knock on Pies's kitchen door, she discovered it was wide open—and she saw the extensive damage within.

Her anxiety grew, and grew. Naomi had to find Pies.

She had to let him know that she would never give him up to the authorities. It would be a stupid move on her part, but she couldn't help herself from breaking the law to save him. Perhaps they could work out an escape plan to get him away from the area until things settled down—until they could figure out how to maybe fix things.

There was no doubt in her mind that she understood who the real Jakub Jakubowski was, the person with a deep, emotional understanding of other human beings. His depth of emotional knowledge was like none she'd had ever experienced with any other man.

And she wanted so badly to say the words—though she knew it would scare him away, like it had with other men in uniform—that she loved him. She'd wait until the time was right.

It was all so crazy, but she understood they had a special connection. She felt it, and she knew that he felt the same about her, too.

If she could locate him and get him alone so they could talk it all through, he'd see that she was the one for him. It could work. It would work.

"You a cop?" asked the friendly male voice.

Naomi stood at the bar of the Olmsted Inn, a half-full glass of water in front of her.

"How's that?" she asked.

Andy tossed an insincere smile her way and said, "Your shirt. The badge. You a cop?"

Naomi pushed the glass away and reached into her purse for some money. "No, not really. I'm a communications officer."

"Yeah? What's that mean? Communications?" asked Andy, the ex-Chicago cop, knowing exactly what it meant.

"I'm a 9-1-1 dispatcher," she said.

"Wow. Cool. Must be stressful, huh?"

"It can be," she said as she placed a five on the bar and motioned for the bartender with the blonde dreadlocks to keep it.

"Water's free," said the man with the dreadlocks.

Naomi nodded for him to keep it anyway, and he did.

"There's a guy from the neighborhood who does that kind of work. Jakubowski's his name," said Andy. "A great guy."

Naomi spun around, and her startled expression confirmed to Andy, who had followed her here after noticing her Northcomm shirt when he passed her earlier on the sidewalk, that she was up to something. The way she reacted to him just now was not natural at all. She was definitely looking for Pies.

"You know him?" asked Naomi.

"Sure. Everyone knows Jakub. He's the pride of Edison Park," said Andy with a wink.

"You wouldn't know where I could find him, would you?" asked Naomi.

Andy made a face, shrugged, and said, "Not really. The business area's not too big, though. I bet if you keep looking, you'll find him soon enough. I see him around all the time."

Naomi walked to the door. "Thanks," she said over her shoulder.

Andy waited a five count, got off his barstool, and followed.

40

PIES STOOD naked in the tub of his upstairs bathroom, his forehead pressed hard against the faucet wall, and showered. The hot water cascaded off his head and washed Vicki's blood from his face and hair. He couldn't stand the idea that her blood was sprayed all over his person. It was beyond maddening, so he had to shower.

He had already cried himself out.

Now his mind worked around the notion, and logistics, of turning himself into the Chicago Police so that he could do his penance for killing Vicki.

The shirt and pants he wore when he fired the shot were neatly folded on his bed. He'd bring the clothes with him when he turned himself in so as to more tightly lock in his guilt.

Turning himself in was really the only mission he had left in him.

He would admit to the police the murders of the Bs, too.

It would only be right.

Pies's life as a free man would be over anyway, so why not cleanse his soul? The monster that was created when he was a sixteen-year-old kid, and kept under wraps for the past twelve years, would finally be caged where it belonged. He could hurt no one else.

Pies turned off the shower water, and he stepped out of the tub to towel dry. He moved into his bedroom for a set of fresh clothes when he was tackled to the floor and hit hard in the head by a flying fist.

One blow. One very hard blow.

It was enough to get his attention and make him curl up and cover his head with his arms.

When he finally laid eyes on his attacker, Pies gulped in a couple of deep breaths.

Luke, Noretti's dangerous bodyguard, kneeled over him and gave Pies the briefest of smirks.

"Get dressed," said Luke. The formidable man stood and adjusted the holstered .38-caliber revolver that dangled under his right arm.

Pies tried to cover up with the towel and get to his feet at the same time, but Luke kicked him hard in the bare buttocks and said, "Now, sunshine."

Pies stumbled toward his closet and reached inside for clothes to wear.

*

ON THE ride in Noretti's large BMW, Pies stared through the passenger window at the tree-lined streets of Park Ridge. He sat in the front seat while Luke drove, and the cordial Noretti, pen in hand, his nose in a crossword-puzzle book, took up the deep backseat of the automobile.

"Relax, Jakub, this is a good meeting," said Noretti. "If Luke was a bit rough, he should apologize."

Luke turned to Pies and said, "Yeah, real sorry about that." His statement was purposefully comical in its lack of sincerity.

As they drove down Belle Plaine Avenue, westbound, toward the massive, high-school grounds, Pies had a sense of déjà vu. He'd taken this same ride on his bike back when he was much younger and had tested the shotgun-shell booby traps in the woods. He shook the thought away and tried to focus on exactly where they were taking him—and what in the hell Noretti wanted with him.

Luke merged the BMW onto Talcott Road and then made a left on Dee Road. As they slowed at the entrance to the Dam No. Four Woods-East parking lot, Pies felt the urge to vomit. He half turned and caught Noretti grinning at him over the top of his crossword book.

The desolate, tree-filled location was where Pies had, indeed, tested the shotgun-shell booby traps, and it was the same place where—

"Your dad liked this spot, right Jakub?" asked Noretti.

Luke parked the car deep inside the preserve and cut the engine. There were no other cars or people anywhere in sight. The thick, lush foliage blocked out most of the sunshine.

Once the car was stopped, both Noretti and Luke seemed to relax even further. Luke leaned against the driver's door and stared off into the trees. Noretti kept penning in answers on his crossword puzzle.

"What's this about?" asked Pies as he turned in his seat to face Noretti.

Noretti peered over his book and said, "What's a four-letter word for 'snakes of Egypt'?"

Pies turned and faced forward.

"Asps," replied Luke without hesitation.

"Ah, good. Thanks," said Noretti as he scribbled the answer in his puzzle.

"Any time," said Luke.

"Jakub, you'll be working for me now," said Noretti.

He allowed that to fully sink in and watched as Pies gulped a few times.

He continued, "I know that you're the Zielinskis' brain. I now realize that you're the one who has made them so successful."

Pies's stomach sank even further.

"Bast is no longer running the crew. He doesn't know that yet, but he'll find out soon enough."

Luke smiled at the remark, but kept his eyes forward.

"The best part is that you'll no longer go on night runs. You'll be white collar all the way from now on. You provide the insight, and the know-how, and I'll gather the crew to do the heavy lifting."

"I didn't show up for my shift today," said Pies.

"Nothing I can't smooth over with the folks running that place. There are people we know. Let me take care of that," said Noretti.

"I don't think so, because I'm not going back," said Pies.

Pies turned and stared directly at Noretti. He tried not to show any emotion, but the anger boiled up deep down inside.

"You're going to make triple what you do now, and you'll get the Northcomm salary on top of that, too. Not too bad, huh, for an orphan from Edison Park. This is a good thing, Jakub. We'd hate for you to end up like your old man, right?"

Noretti made a big deal of looking out all of the car's side windows, as if he were a sailor looking for land. "Wasn't this about the spot where your old man, you know...?" he asked.

Pies's left eye twitched a little. Noretti didn't catch it, but Pies's entire demeanor was slowly changing right before his eyes.

41

"HE'LL BE fine," said Crick as he sat on the sofa in the lawyer's office. "I'll keep him where the cops won't find him."

His sister Cindy and his nephew Devin, dressed now in a crisp, button-up shirt and black pants, sat in chairs next to the large desk in their lawyer's Glenview office.

"Ma, they may get me on other stuff," said Devin. "Crick will keep me free for now. If I'm home, they'll grab me whenever, you know?"

"Crick, please. Crick, don't let them take him away. Please," pleaded Cindy.

Crick stood, went over to where his sister sat opposite the lawyer, a stern-looking man in an expensive suit, and leaned in to hug his sister. "I got him, okay. I got him." He tenderly kissed her forehead.

Crick straightened and caught the eye of the lawyer. The lawyer nodded once, and Crick tapped Devin on the shoulder. "Let's go."

"Where? I have to know. Where, Crick?" asked Cindy.

"There's a place in Wisconsin. Twin Lakes. He'll be fine," said Crick. "He'll call you soon. We have to get a jump, Cindy."

Devin stood, and he and Crick exited the office.

When they reached the lobby of the small office building, Crick stopped Devin so he could scan the parking lot through the windows from within the building. Nothing looked out of the ordinary in the parking lot. There were not any marked or unmarked police vehicles anywhere in sight.

"Once Winnetka starts releasing more information about the shit at your mom's place, you're going to have a bunch of coppers up your ass," said Crick. "We're lucky we got you out in time. That lawyer knows his stuff."

"Cool. Cool. Thanks, Uncle Crick," said Devin as they walked out into the parking lot.

They hurriedly got into Crick's Dodge Charger and drove away. They were headed north, toward Wisconsin.

Neither of them spoke as they drove along, until...

"Pretty messed up, huh?" asked Devin. "I'm sorry, man. Wasn't thinking straight."

Crick sported a crooked smile, but he remained silent. He had a job to do. He had to keep on point and complete the task in a timely fashion.

They got on I-94 north and headed to Wisconsin—but veered off where the road met Highway 41. At Lake Cook Road, Crick exited Highway 41 and went west.

"What's up?" asked Devin. "Where you going, Uncle Crick?"

The kid did screw up and must be taken care of. Crick, of course, didn't want to verbally broach the subject with the nineteen-year-old—that he was marked for death by Bast.

He kept driving westbound on Lake Cook Road toward a place where no one would find Devin.

"You still have your phone?" he asked his nephew.

"Sure." Devin turned and stared hard at Crick. "Really, man?" he asked.

Crick nodded, and Devin slipped his smart phone from his pants pocket, rolled down his window, and tossed the phone out of the moving car—where it smashed into several pieces as it spun along the pavement at fifty miles an hour.

"People can track those," said Crick.

42

NORETTI LEANED back in the seat of the BMW and grinned and grinned. He was the lord of the Zielinski crew now. And Pies was, once again, placed into a slave-like position.

"It'll be a seamless transition, Jakub. You'll just go on doing what you do. Making money. We'll keep an eye on you. Keep you safe and sound. Right, Luke?" said Noretti.

"Sure," said Luke, bored, as he lazily scanned the trees. "You'll be super safe."

"Once you do some more time at the Northcomm place, you know, show that you can handle the workload, and all that, you'll be ready to take a job at Chicago's 9-1-1 center. I've got it all set up when you're ready. Give it a year. Can you image the alarms not working in the city? Found money, you ask me."

There was still no one around them in the desolate corner of the forest preserve property. No cars had even driven past.

"There's times when you have to clean the pool out, you know what I mean? You have to freshen up things so they don't get stale. People make mistakes when things get stagnant. I've seen it," said Noretti. "Happens all the time. Bast? Bast is stagnant."

Pies's eyes were searching the car for something, anything that could be used as a diversion to simply get away.

Noretti reached both hands out, one with the ballpoint pen in it, the other with the crossword-puzzle book, and hoisted his head and

276 * MATT HADER

most of his shoulders over the seatback. He was uncomfortably close now, and there was nowhere for Pies to hide. Noretti's hot and pungent espresso breath wafted across Pies's face, but he didn't dare turn away.

"You remember when Stan took care of Banasik and Bartosz, right, Jakub? Wasn't really that long ago. I'm sure you remember, though."

Pies's breath caught in his throat for a moment. It wasn't lost on Noretti, who smiled wide.

"Things had been getting stale, and those two assholes got bored. Then they got caught because they were bored and lazy, and they decided they could sell what they knew to the cops for their own freedom," said Noretti. "Stan took them out like the man he was. That happened, all of that, because the pool wasn't cleaned in a timely fashion. Stagnant, you see?"

"That's not...," said Pies before stopping himself.

"How's that, Jakub?" asked Noretti.

"That's not exactly how it happened," said Pies.

When Noretti's head cocked sideways, and he looked a curious question at Pies, Pies snatched the pen from his hand and jabbed the pointed end—hard and deep—into Luke's right eye.

Luke let out a yelp like none Pies had ever heard before. It was a resonant and guttural sound, like that of a large, wounded animal.

Noretti tried to punch Pies in the head, but the men were both so close to one another that the multiple blows had no effect.

Pies let go of the pen as Noretti leaned back in his seat and fumbled to open the rear-center console.

As the injured, confused, and bleeding Luke awkwardly pawed at the embedded pen in his eye socket, Pies grabbed Luke's gun from his shoulder holster and shot the big man twice in the ribs. The gun had barely cleared the holster before it went off and killed the man.

Luke instantly went motionless.

"You piece of shit!"

But that was all that Noretti said. Those were his last words.

Pies twisted the gun—still caught up in Luke's holster straps—

and fired three times, rapidly, right through the edge of the front seatback. The bullets struck Noretti dead center.

The Outfit underboss's head lolled to the side, and his eyes remained open as blood trickled from the corner of his mouth and nose. His arm went limp and his hand that was inside the console slipped out. There was a small .380 pistol nestled in it.

Pies's ears rang from the gunshots. He wiped the gun clean with the tail of Luke's shirt and dropped it on the seat. He quickly scanned the car and tried to remember which surfaces he had touched. He grabbed the now-crumpled, crossword-puzzle book from the seat and ripped out a page. He used the paper to wipe the dashboard and the inside door armrest and handle. He used the same piece of paper to wrap around his fingers to pull the passenger door handle open. Once he stepped from the car, Pies used the paper to cover his hand to close and wipe the outside, as well. He opened the crossword book and shoved the piece of paper inside, and he walked away without even looking back. He would throw away the book somewhere in Park Ridge.

The monster had overruled once again.

Before he turned himself into the police, Pies had to travel the two miles back to Edison Park and Zielinski's Insurance Agency.

He was all-in now, and he had one more thing to take care of.

43

Bast, his cell phone pressed tightly to his ear, angrily paced in the back room of Zielinski's Insurance Agency. He stopped for a moment and said, "How should I know? I got stuff going on here. I got a situation I'm handling, baby."

He walked to the rear door, opened it, and looked side to side, up and down the back alley. Nothing was out of the ordinary.

"Maybe she walked to my old man's house. Why? She doesn't understand, that's why. She's little. She probably thinks he's coming back. I know it's getting dark."

He turned and kicked a chair out of his way, and then he heard a soft knock on the metal door that led to the shoe store. He narrowed his eyes in the door's direction and said, "You have one job. One. Okay. Okay, I'm coming. I'll be there in a few minutes."

He disconnected the call and moved to open the door.

Pies, soaked in sweat, his eyes locked on Bast, entered and shut the door hard behind him.

"Andy's already told me. That 9-1-1 place had some broad out looking for you. She's gone now," said Bast as he hit the speed dial on his cell phone. "He needs to get back here so we can figure this all out. I hope they don't fire you for not showing up. We can't lose this. Dog, you really fucked this up."

Pies inched closer to Bast, but the larger man was so wound up in his own angry little space that he didn't even notice how close his subordinate stood to him. He turned his back and kept pacing.

"You got some balls, P-yes. I need more lists. Today," ordered Bast. "We have to ramp up now because I need this. We'll need to hit two or three places a night. That's goddamned right—a night! Shit, now I'll have Noretti up my ass if he finds out you messed this up. I don't care how you do it, but you're going to go back and do the job. We need this...."

Bast stopped his rant short and sensed that Pies was being too quiet. When he fully turned to see why—Pies punched him hard in the nose.

Bast dropped to his ass on the concrete floor, and his phone skittered away and broke apart when it struck a metal desk leg. The blow stunned the crew's boss, so much so that he just sat there as the blood flowed from his right nostril and onto the front of his shirt.

Pies advanced for the kill.

He rained down fists on Bast as the larger man tried to squirm away and crawl toward his desk.

"Dog! Dog, stop," was all Bast said as he tried to move forward, but Pies struck him with blow after blow—a punch to the side of the head, one to the neck, the next to his shoulder. Wherever he could land a fist, Pies landed a fist.

Bast, bleeding from his ear and over his left eye, finally reached his desk where he opened the side drawer from his kneeling position. He shakily rooted around inside as Pies struck him repeatedly, and he withdrew a 9mm pistol with his right hand.

Pies kicked the pistol away. It bounced off the back of the expensive, Italian leather chair and clattered to the floor.

Bast spun around, put his palms up in surrender, and sat still as he tried to catch his breath. He looked into Pies's raging eyes, and he said, "I'm going to rip you apart, P-yes."

Sirens could be heard in the distance as the rear door opened and Crick slipped inside from the nighttime air. He had a .40 caliber semiautomatic leveled waist high.

"Christ," said Bast. "Do it, Crick. Shoot him!"

Crick didn't aim at Pies. His gun was angled toward Bast.

Crick said, "You shouldn't have asked me to take care of him. He's my blood. Like my little brother."

Pies didn't understand what Crick was getting at, and he didn't care. He leaned in and punched Bast again, but this time Bast was having none of it. He launched to his feet and struck back, a hard right to Pies's face. Pies tumbled backward, and Crick squeezed off a round from his pistol, which missed the boss.

Pies was focused only on killing Bast with his bare hands and didn't even flinch when Crick's gun went off.

"Back off, dog!" yelled Crick.

Instead, Pies tried to dive forward and tackle Bast, but the big man spun away and in back of the desk to successfully retrieve his own gun. Pies stumbled but kept his footing.

Crick squeezed off another shot, and it grazed Bast's upper right leg. Bast winced and fired back three times, and he struck Crick once in the left elbow.

Crick, his arm a bloody mess, fell to his side and quickly ducked behind some large boxes full of stolen, commercial-grade, kitchen mixers.

Bast turned the gun on Pies, but Pies was too quick and splayed himself out in front of the desk as the shot went off. Pies scrambled on his belly around to the other side of the desk as Bast limped forward so he could kill Pies or get another shot off at Crick. The desk was the only cover Pies had available.

All three men were less than twenty feet apart.

The sirens grew louder and closer still.

Two quick shots went off and Bast tumbled backward, hit once in the lower left abdomen. The other bullet hit the wall in back of him. Bast returned fire in the direction from where the shots came, behind the boxes of kitchen mixers, and he struck Crick in the lower left leg.

"It was either Devin or the both of you. I figured Andy would follow up if I couldn't get Devin done. That asshole," said Crick. "Time to flush the bowl..."

Bast screamed out in anger as he fired twice into the boxes. Crick let out a yelp and all grew silent.

Pies was doing a quick analysis in his mind. If he were to spin left from his narrow hiding spot, keep his head down, and accelerate, he might surprise Bast and take him out at the knees. But Bast would probably be expecting Pies to do that—come at him from the left and away from his gun hand.

Bast began to train his gun on Pies, whose only cover was still the desk between himself and where Bast stood. Bast heard Pies's shoes scuffle on the floor.

Even Bast was surprised to see Pies rotate around the desk, head low, and angle directly in for a frontal assault.

Bast lifted his foot and stopped Pies cold with the sole of his shoe on Pies's shoulder. He raised the gun to fire point blank—

"She's gone! Bast! It's Vicki. She's dead, man," said a winded Andy as he entered through the rear door and panted out quick breaths. "She's dead. Her parents...they found her."

Bast's face went ashen and then slack. But then the anger returned once again. He peered downward at Pies, and all Bast had to do was squeeze the trigger one time.

Crick rose from in back of the boxes and fired twice. The rounds struck Andy in the chest and head with two quick, expert shots. Andy's dead body hit the concrete floor with a sickening thud.

Crick winced from the pain he endured, rotated, and fired once at Bast—but missed.

Bast planted both feet and quickly returned fire and tagged Crick twice, in the gut and chest. Crick fell against the sidewall and slid to the floor, and his gun tumbled away, about three feet to his right side.

Bast looked down at the kneeling Pies and asked in a childlike tone, "What did you do? What did you do, Pies?"

Pies was beyond exhausted and he figured that this was his end. An eerie peacefulness washed over him and a nearly imperceptible smirk cracked his lips.

Nothing mattered any longer.

It was over.

He glanced back to where Andy's body lay and to the blood trail on the floor that led to Crick. When he finally turned his attention fully to Bast, he had just enough left in his tank to get one last confession out. He let out a caustic chuckle and said, "This here... Damn, man. Are we a bunch of assholes, or what?"

Bast's face screwed up in confusion as he tried to understand Pies in that moment.

The sirens wound down and went silent—they were for Vicki across the street and down the block, and not for this active-shooter crime scene.

Pies was resigned to his fate, but then the faint sound of scuffling and movement by the back door caught his attention—in his left peripheral view, near Andy's body. He instinctively and hastily threw himself toward the rear door.

Bast squeezed off two shots as Pies moved ten feet and crouched down—both bullets struck Pies in the upper left back. As soon as Bast fired his gun though, he winced and said, "Oh, no! No! Please!"

Another shot rang out, and Bast stumbled as blood poured from his chest.

Crick, still barely alive, had somehow retrieved his gun and now leaned against the sidewall in a seated position, blood pooled all around him.

Bast raised his gun in Crick's direction and staggered backward, but he no longer had the strength to pull the trigger. He plopped down heavily in his leather chair and lazily turned toward Pies, in time to see...

Pies slowly spun away from his awkwardly crouched position and revealed a cowering Itty-Bitty, Bast's beautiful little daughter. Her eyes were locked wide in terror, and she had gathered up the hemline material of her dress into her tightly balled fists as the tears began to silently flow.

"She okay?" asked Bast, lazily, his eyes already at half-mast.

"Yeah," said Pies as he let go of the girl and she ran to her father.

Pies, bleeding profusely, began to lose consciousness. He leaned back on his elbows and watched as Crick and Bast both slowly bled out, neither strong enough now to even raise their weapons.

The room was filled with the ragged breaths of the dying and the metallic smell of fresh blood and cordite.

"Crick? Hey, Crick," said Pies, his voice weakened like the rest of him.

Crick slowly and fully turned his head in Pies's direction.

When their eyes locked onto one another, Pies grinned and said, "Woof, woof."

Crick appeared as if he wanted to rebut, but as he attempted to speak, the life finally left him.

Itty-Bitty hugged at her father's waist and said, "Wake up. Wake up, Daddy."

Pies listened as the little girl wept. He grunted in pain as he lay back on the dirty floor and turned his head. In a corner of the room, stacked one on top of the next, were the external hard drives that were taken from his house by Crick.

Pies's vision grew a gray haziness around the edges, and his eyelids became heavy as he saw the hard drives slowly fade from view.

44

PIES THOUGHT that he heard the words "waste of time," but in his mentally diminished state, he wasn't sure.

He tried desperately to blink and will himself to full consciousness, but the going was tough.

"You understanding any of this, Jakubowski?" said a man's baritone voice.

Pies finally saw the man, but his vision was blurry at best. He concluded that if he closed one eye, his right one, he could stop the room from spinning and be able to focus. His surroundings looked slightly clearer, too. If he focused, maybe he could stay awake for a longer period of time.

Stu Von Bargen, a fifty-two-year-old Chicago Police detective—all pasty, balding, six feet, four inches, 250 pounds of him—leaned over Pies's bed at the Park Ridge hospital and trauma center. The man wore an off-brand suit and smelled faintly of Italian beef sandwiches and French fries. But he sported a friendly, reassuring smile that seemed to sit right with Pies.

"Waste of time?" asked Pies, weakly. "What are you...? Who...?"

"And he's back. I think he's actually in there this time," said a different man's snarky voice.

Pies painfully tilted his head and saw another large man in a suit —this one had chestnut-colored skin and slicked, dark hair. The second man spoke with an extremely hard-edged Chicago accent. He leaned against the room's open doorjamb and appeared bored by the proceedings.

"Jakub, come on, pal, we asked around about you. You're going to try and tell us you don't know anything about Sebastian Zielinski and the other cold slabs of beef we found with you?" asked forty-six-year-old Chicago Police Detective Sony Brar.

Pies blinked his one open eye a few times and muttered, "What did I tell you..."

Von Bargen interrupted, "Like we were saying, you're either brave or stupid to be in that back room, because Zielinski was a bad, bad man."

"What? What did I say...before?" asked Pies, still confused from the cocktail of medications coursing through his body. The detectives knew his mental capacity was temporarily reduced, but they didn't give a shit. They had a job to do.

"You were out of it last time we visited, but the docs think you'll be able to head home in a day or two," said Brar. "Maybe your selective memory will come back by then, huh? Man, oh, man, you are one lucky asshole, aren't you?"

Pies kept his right eye closed and stared hard at the detectives.

His voice nothing more than a croaking mumble, Pies said, "Vicki. Vicki. She was..." He stopped himself, utterly confounded, when he finally realized he wasn't even handcuffed to the bed. He noticed that there was a hep-lock IV inserted into the back of his left hand, which protruded out of a sling, but no handcuffs left or right. In his overly medicated brain he just couldn't figure out why.

"It's a shame, but her parents said she'd been distraught over some break up. A fight with Zielinski's wife? Something. We're not completely sure at this point. That mope Zielinski had her all tangled up," said Von Bargen. "You know anything about all of that?"

Pies just stared with his one open eye, but he began to slightly drift away.

Brar added, "Hey! Wake up. You heard she offed herself, right?"

Pies's eye shot open and then shut again as tears began to form and squeeze around his closed lids.

"So you didn't know?" continued Brar. "Or you did?"

There was only silence from Pies.

Brar looked at Von Bargen before he said, "Her parents showed us her paintings. Good stuff. Talented, you ask me. Creepy, but there was talent there."

Pies opened his good eye a little. He wanted to come clean on his terms and he tried to talk—to tell these two cops to go fuck themselves and leave him alone for now—but he coughed violently instead. Von Bargen placed a cup of water with a straw into his right hand. Pies's left arm was wrapped tightly in the sling to keep the left side of his upper body immobile. Pies sipped and blinked his one open eye.

Von Bargen said, "Her parents said you looked out for her. Just another of the many reasons the DA isn't following through on any charges on you."

"Not right now, anyway. We think the DA's got her head up her ass on this, just in case you were wondering, Lefty. We'll keep that between us friends here, you know," said Brar with a wink. "For now."

"Brar?" said Von Bargen.

"What? They suspect he had something to do with the alarm information leak at that new communications center, right? Am I out of line?" asked Brar with a knowing grin that didn't sit well with Pies.

Pies was confounded by the entire conversation. What DA were they talking about, he wondered? Why couldn't he form his many thoughts into words and make them come out of his mouth cleanly? And with all he'd done, why the hell wasn't he handcuffed to the bed? He'd done horrible things.

"And what a big hero you are," added the sarcastic Brar. "Maybe I should ask for an autograph, then sell it on eBay. You're not left-handed, are you? That'd be a shame, you not being able to give your adoring public what they want."

Von Bargen gave Brar a look to back off just a hair and added, "That little girl's fine. Not a scratch on her."

Pies tried to speak, but all that came out was, "I'm not..." And to the detectives it sounded like he was clearing his throat.

"You're lucky to still be breathing and blinking, that's what you are," said Brar as he feigned concern.

Pies's one open eye began to sag, as he nearly drifted off again. He fought it, though, and bellowed, "Vicki."

"I know. I know, Jakub. She was your friend," said Von Bargen. He pushed gently away from the bed and continued, "We'll talk again when you're off the high-octane stuff."

"Because we think you're fucking dirty and you need some serious locking up," said Brar. When he caught Von Bargen's stare, he added, "Oh, I'm sorry. Just trying to add to the scintillating conversation." Brar looked into the hallway and smirked. He and Von Bargen had been playing these good cop/bad cop roles as partners for the past seven years, and their conversational dance was usually fast-paced and well-rehearsed.

Pies was so puzzled, and frustrated, and in physical pain, that he hadn't been able to focus very well, but he was beginning to come around. Neither of the detectives seemed to notice, though. That was just fine with Pies. The sooner they left, the sooner he could get himself more awake and on the mend—and out of the hospital.

"You take care," said Von Bargen as he began to exit the room. He stopped and looked over his shoulder and continued, "We'll probably see you around."

"That's my guess, hero," added Brar. "Don't be surprised when coppers from the suburban departments you screwed over come calling, either. You know, once they get their investigative shit together. You're not fooling anyone."

As he and Von Bargen stepped into the hallway, Brar said to an unseen person, "He's all yours. You can go back in now." He and Von Bargen moved from view.

The haze began to lift more rapidly as his anxiety over the cops' visit grew, and Pies finally realized why he wasn't cuffed to the bed. Could it be the Chicago Police hadn't found any evidence that Pies had fired a gun when they discovered him unconscious among the dead bodies? There were no weapons near him before he passed out, he was sure of it. Crick dropped Andy so quickly when he entered that room, the dead man never had a chance to pull a weapon, if he even had one on him at that moment. That lack of evidence and Itty-Bitty's recounting of how he shielded her must have carried some weight. The little girl had obviously spoken with the police since the detectives kept bringing her up just now.

In his foggy state, Pies assumed that he had sweated enough of the gunshot residue off his hands and arms, both on his trek back to Edison Park after he took out Luke and Noretti and during his fight with Bast. That was the only explanation he could conjure up in his state of mind as to why he hadn't been arrested. No, wait, that wouldn't be it. The results for tests like that probably took months to get back—not minutes like in the corny TV shows.

He didn't really know why he was still a free man.

He was so damned confused.

Pies turned his head toward the window and squinted out at the painfully bright sunshine. He didn't know what to think right now. He didn't know what his life would be like now that Vicki was gone and the Zielinski crew was no more.

Should he go to the Chlebeks and confess to them what really happened with their daughter, or would that only hurt them further?

He tried to adjust his eyes to the brightness, but the sunshine began to hurt his one open eye. He turned his head toward the hallway door, and that's when he finally noticed that Naomi was standing there.

"Hey, Jakub. It's good to see you awake. How are you feeling?" she asked, hopeful. "The doctor said you're going home in a day or so."

Pies looked to the ceiling and let out a long breath of frustration.

He cleared his throat, and his voice felt stronger for some reason. "Pies," he said.

"You're hungry? I can get the nurse..."

"That's my name. Call me Pies. My name is Pies."

Naomi was taken aback, but a lot of things that she learned about Pies this past week had confused her. Deeply.

His violent actions over the past decade were so antithetical to what she saw in him. His gentle demeanor, the way he handled people's emotions during stressful situations—all of that pointed to the type of man that she had to have in her life. She wanted to know Pies outside of their working relationship, and she was here, now, to get that process started.

When she learned of Pies's heroics during the harrowing gun battle, it had completely cinched it for her. She was now willing to forgo reconciliation with her ex, something her ex-mother-in-law had always wanted, and to take up with Pies, so that he could help her raise her son Jason. Jason would love the man lying in the hospital bed in front of her, she was sure of it.

"They've been talking about you on the news. Because of the little girl."

Pies only grunted.

"I know about the other stuff you've done, Jakub," she added. "I don't care about any of it. A few of the police departments at Northcomm interviewed me, but I didn't tell them anything."

Pies squinted his one open eye and studied Naomi for a good long while.

"What are you talking about?" he asked.

Naomi peered into the hallway to make sure no one was listening and then turned back in Pies's direction. "In Edison Park. The booby traps. That," she said. "I don't care about any of it. Or any of the alarm stuff that happened recently. I know if you and I were together, that we'd..."

"You don't want that," he said. "You have no idea."

"I can see past it all."

"Get out," he loudly begged.

Pies had truly found his voice. He had to use it to warn Naomi. He couldn't risk hurting another person—even one as obviously and equally delusional as himself.

Naomi blinked and stared and didn't understand why Pies's attitude had changed all of a sudden.

"If you need your rest, I can come back..."

Pies opened both eyes, angled an angry look her way, and said, "Get the hell out of my room!"

Naomi stood there for a moment, shocked. Finally, she grabbed her purse off the shelf near the door, but she stayed where she was. She appeared as if she were about to say something else, when...Pies threw the cup of water that was still in his right hand in her direction. It bounced off the wall.

Naomi exited without looking back.

"Get out. Don't come back," cried Pies. "Get out!"

Pies laid his head back into his pillow and let out another long breath. He painfully raised his right arm and covered his eyes.

And he wept.

45

PIES, DRESSED in blue scrubs and disposable cream-colored rubber slippers, carefully stood upright from the wheelchair and
nodded good-bye to the orderly who had pushed him there. The orderly rolled the chair away without a word. Pies's left arm was still
housed in a tight sling.

He waited at the cabstand of the hospital's circular front drive.
In his good hand were the folded, hospital-release documents and
two prescription bottles—one filled with prophylactic antibiotics,
the other with pain pills.

An appreciative discharge nurse, earlier, had ordered up a cab for
Pies on her own dime telling him, "It's my treat, Mr. Jakubowski, for
what you did." It was okay with Pies because the police had taken
every shred of his clothing and belongings shortly after he was ad-
mitted to the hospital. He had no money at all and no one to call for
a ride. Once he got home, he'd probably have to break in because
the police probably also had his house keys.

Pies had been all over the news for the past few days. One of the
investigative reporters at Channel 7 dubbed him "the Blemished
Hero" because the police figured he was criminally involved somehow with the dead men at the insurance agency, and yet he had also
saved a young life. The name stuck across the media board. He had
watched some of the television reports from his hospital bed over

the past two days. A few of the reporters said they were tipped by un-named sources that Pies was under suspicion by North Shore police authorities for some sort of crime, too, but that no arrest warrant had been issued yet. The alleged criminal act or acts hadn't been re-leased, either. Pies was embarrassed by the attention and his shitty new moniker, and he thought to himself, *If they only knew the real me. The killer. The Blemished Hero? What a bunch of idiots.*

The discharge nurse had worked diligently to conceal Pies in an interior office while she went through the release process. She made sure that no one would tip off the media and possibly cause a circus atmosphere at the hospital when he walked out the door.

Pies fought to remain standing because the pain in his left side was intense. As he waited for the cab to pull up, a small gaggle of hos-pital employees congregated thirty feet away, admiring him, taking photos with their cell phones, and waving.

Pies ignored them.

When the cab arrived, the driver, a tall and goofy-looking man with crooked teeth, cheerfully hopped out and raced around to open the rear door. "I got it. I got it, mister," he said with a smile. "Where to?"

"Edison Park," said Pies.

As Pies painfully tucked himself into the backseat, the cabbie added, "And you just relax, sir. We'll keep an eye on you this time. You've done enough good deeds for a lifetime."

Pies released an apprehensive breath as the cabbie gently closed the rear door and then jogged around the car and got back into the driver's seat. Once off the hospital grounds, they headed east on Dempster Street.

"It's an honor, sir. A true honor to have you in my rig," said the cab-bie. "Have to be honest, I wouldn't of recognized you if the lady at the hospital hadn't of told the dispatcher about who you were when the run got called in. Glad she told us, though. It is a pleasure."

The cabbie took a right on Greenwood Avenue and headed south.

Pies thought he should reply, although he didn't want to. He fi-nally said, "Yeah, um, thanks for the ride."

"No problem," said the cabbie, who could barely keep his dancing eyes off Pies in the rearview mirror and on the road ahead.

"I don't mean to... Could we not talk, if that's okay?" asked Pies.

"Sure thing. No problem, mister. I understand perfectly if you'd like your privacy. No problem at all," said the cabbie.

Pies looked out the right side windows as they crossed over Oakton Street. When his eyes quickly glanced back at the cabbie in the mirror, the driver's demeanor had changed dramatically to a more worrisome expression, and the cabbie's eyes were locked on the road in back of them.

"Ah, mister?" said the concerned cabbie.

"Yeah?" asked Pies as he painfully tried to turn his head back to see what was behind them. That's when he heard the police-car siren burp twice.

The cabbie pulled the car off of Greenwood and onto a side street and stopped. He lowered his window and waited for the approaching police officer.

Pies was startled when his door was flung open. He looked up and saw Detective Stu Von Bargen holding the handle. "Hey, Jakub. We'll take you the rest of the way. Come on, let's go."

Detective Sony Brar moved to the cabbie and leaned over to address him, "You get paid already, or does this mope still owe you?"

The cabbie was confused by the situation but answered, "No. No, we're good. Someone at the hospital already paid me."

After Von Bargen helped Pies from the backseat, Brar patted the top of the cab and motioned for the cabbie to move along—which he did without hesitation.

Von Bargen motioned for Pies to step toward their dark, unmarked vehicle as Brar moved quickly to get behind the wheel of the car.

When Von Bargen opened the rear door and nodded for him to get in, Pies said, "I'm good. I'll just walk from here."

"Don't be an asshole," said Von Bargen. When Pies didn't move to get into the car, he added, "Jakub, please?"

"Why no cuffs?" asked Pies.

From inside the car Brar playfully called out, "Cuffs? You need to unburden yourself?"

"Just to talk, that's all," said Von Bargen. When Pies still didn't get into the car, Von Bargen tossed him a reassuring smile and nodded once again to the backseat. When Pies leaned toward the car, Von Bargen quickly patted along Pies's waist and his sling to make sure he didn't have a weapon of some sort.

"Officer safety," said Von Bargen with a grin.

Pies painfully, slowly, got into the car, and the detective closed the door.

Once Von Bargen got into his seat, he said, "Let's go and get something to eat. You hungry, Jakub?"

Pies shook his head, and Brar drove to their destination—a hot dog place on Harlem Avenue located a couple of miles away. Not a word was exchanged until they arrived. As they rolled into the parking lot, Brar asked, "A dog and fries?"

"Through the garden. You sure you don't want something, Jakubowski?" Von Bargen asked Pies.

Pies stayed quiet.

"Whatever, mope. We were buying." Brar got out of the car and stepped inside the small, boxy, yellow-painted restaurant building.

Von Bargen and Pies sat for a few minutes in awkward silence while they watched Brar order and pay for the food.

"We saw the videos you gathered on the hard drives," said Von Bargen. He just sat there and allowed it to sink in.

After a long pause Pies finally said, "I'm not going to talk to you."

"You collected a lot of juice on those boys over time, didn't you?" said Von Bargen as he canted sideways to get a better look at Pies. "Impressive."

Pies locked eyes with Von Bargen, hesitated, and then nonchalantly looked away.

"I'm sure you've heard the news, you with nothing to do but watch TV for the past few days. The Cook County state's attorney thinks

Zielinski is the one who did Noretti and his driver before he also nosed in for his final journey," continued Von Bargen. "What you didn't hear was that Noretti had been talking about retiring Zielinski from your crew. Noretti's second-in-command offered that up to an informant of ours yesterday. We figured that young Sebastian Zielinski caught wind and got to Noretti first."

Pies directed his chin toward the restaurant and said, "Chapin's up the street is a better place. They hand cut their fries."

That stopped Von Bargen for just a second. He adjusted his angle to more fully gaze at Pies. "We caught the bodies, so CPD gets the lead on this case for now, but you and I both know all those suburban agencies that Northcomm takes care of have their leak sitting in the backseat of this car. You did some seriously stupid shit, but you tried to take the Zielinskis down all by yourself, didn't you?"

Pies remained silent.

"And that, along with the little girl, helps muddy up the waters for the DA and any possible case she had. With a good defense attorney at your table who'd toss in a lot of doubt, maybe even say that the cops told you to get the juice on that crew, she'd be fighting uphill the entire time. Probably lose. She's a climber, so there's no way she'll take on something that doesn't result in a victory at the end of the day. But because you've been gifted this get-out-of-jail-free card, I was hoping you'd help me to clear up a few things. Like, of the three dead bodies, who fired first? That'd be a solid start."

Pies just stared for what seemed an eternity before he said, "You know my history. Who my dad was. You and your partner here can cut the bullshit and take me home." Pies studied Von Bargen's angry eyes and continued, "I bet it's eating you up to be the good cop this time around. After spending time up close like this, I get the feeling you're the real son of a bitch, and Brar's a teddy bear."

That halted the detective's movements completely. Von Bargen stared hard before he quietly spun back around to face forward.

Brar exited the eatery, bags of food in hand, and re-entered the car.

"Take me home, or let me out here," whispered Pies.

Brar looked Von Bargen's way, and his partner shrugged a little. Brar turned to Pies. "Asshole," he said.

Von Bargen nodded for Brar to drive on. They headed toward Edison Park in silence. Pies just stared out his rear passenger window and watched as the neighborhood houses slid past. He wanted nothing more than to get into his own bed and sleep.

When they arrived on Northwest Highway, and after driving for a couple of blocks, Von Bargen said, "Here's good."

Brar pulled to the curb. Neither of the detectives looked to the backseat, but Brar said, "Bye-bye, shit bird. You can walk the rest of the way. Do you some good."

Von Bargen had to actually exit the vehicle to open the secured rear door from the outside. As Pies laboriously straightened up after getting out, Von Bargen, jaw muscles fixed, stared him down without blinking. "There's one thing the DA did go to bat for," said Von Bargen.

When Pies didn't bite, the detective continued, "Your passport is being temporarily revoked. Settle in, asshole." Von Bargen got back into the passenger seat and the vehicle took off.

Pies stood for a moment and peered down the street. The detectives had dropped him off next door to the Chlebeks' bakery.

Pies slowly backed away, turned, and hobbled toward his home.

46

FORTUNATELY, THE back kitchen door was unlocked. Pies swung it open and slowly worked his way inside. The occasionally excruciating pain from the injury to his upper left back had now migrated to his entire left side, including his hip for some reason, and the pain pills he'd been prescribed were barely making a dent. The doctors told him that one round from Bast's gun had passed through his back muscle, nicked his rib, and exited out the left side under his armpit. The other bullet, because he had been crouched over the little girl, ricocheted off of his left shoulder blade and up and into the ceiling. Each wound had to be surgically opened to clean and repair major muscle damage, so Pies was left with two eight-inch incisions, now closed with staples, on his upper left back and left side. In the next week or so, the staples would be removed. His left shoulder blade, miraculously, didn't fracture when the bullets struck him. If it had been broken, Pies would have been looking at an even more painful surgery. And thus far he was infection free, so there was that.

The sling that housed his left arm and kept it immobile so that his back muscles could heal properly hindered his movements, but he managed.

Once inside, Pies shut the door and was astonished by what he saw. The place had been cleaned up. All the remains of the damage he'd done that early morning before the shoot-out were now gone. There were still holes in some of the walls and cabinets and such, but

298 * MATT HADER

the splinters, drywall debris, and shattered glass were swept clean, and the remnants of the broken chair were gone.

There was a simple note on the countertop that read: Wanted to help before you got home.

It was signed, N.

Pies put the prescription bottles and hospital paperwork on the counter, pushed the note away, and opened the drawer nearest the sink. Inside were his car keys. He reached into the drawer and placed the keys on the countertop where he could easily get to them. He was going to need those soon enough.

He slid the drawer closed and walked to the stairs and went up to the second floor. Once in his bedroom, he saw that Naomi had put away the blanket with the throw down weapons on it. The upstairs was cleaned up, too. The folded shirt with Vicki's blood splatters was gone. He had no idea who had taken it.

He went to the attic doorway, opened it, and could see the blanket tucked neatly inside. Naomi had, rightly, assumed that because of its position on the floor near the open attic access, the blanket belonged back inside that space.

Pies grunted as he laboriously stooped and with his right hand felt that the remaining guns were under the fabric of the blanket. If the police had been through his house, they must've missed the weapons. But then he realized that there was no evidence tape anywhere on his house, so was it possible the police hadn't searched his home? That seemed unlikely, but maybe they hadn't searched yet because Pies appeared to be a victim of the shooting at the insurance agency, not the perpetrator. If they had searched his home, they obviously hadn't discovered the weapons in the blanket—that was a certainty. They'd be gone otherwise. Or maybe he had simply caught a break. He straightened and closed the attic-access door.

Pies plopped down heavily on the edge of his bed and sat very still. For a good long moment, he didn't move a muscle.

Then he agonizingly got back to his feet and opened his closet door and saw fresh shirts and pants on hangers. He stepped inside.

47

CHLEBEKS' BAKERY had been closed for the past week so that Milena and Blaze could mourn the loss of their daughter, Vicki. Most would've stayed away from their jobs for a second week, but not the Chlebeks. Their incredible work ethic guided them to opening sooner rather than later. The neighborhood needed their baked goods, they would tell each other as they plodded around their quiet house, needing something to busy themselves with. In trying times, like the Edison Park neighborhood had experienced this past week, the neighbors would rely on them to be there, open for business, they would say. At least those were the lies the couple began telling one another a few days ago.

In reality, they each realized on their own that the relentless grind of their everyday existence—baking, cleaning, and greeting customers for twelve-plus hours a day—would help them to forget their pain, if only for five- and ten-minute intervals. Work equaled a forward moving life, and they had to keep living. It was already coded into their every fiber to keep working away and to not dwell on the pain. Work helped them when they first immigrated to America and went through many years of strife with no family or close friends to lean on. Their work was that important to them.

All the bakery goods they had prepared to sell the day of Vicki's death still sat, moldering, in the refrigerators in back, as well as in the display cases out front.

Once they learned about what happened in the apartment above, the Chlebeks simply locked the doors and stepped away.

*

BLAZE CHLEBEK opened the rear alley-side door of the building with his key and slipped into the darkened back vestibule. The moment that he entered the space, tears began to fill his eyes. He stopped to peer up the steps that led to Vicki's apartment. Then he unlocked the bakery's kitchen door. The usual smells of the kitchen, even after being left dormant this past week, seemed to brighten Blaze's mood just a hint.

Then Milena came through the same outer door, but she couldn't make herself look up the stairway. Her head was down because she had important work to do. They had to get their lives back on track today. They just had to. She walked into the kitchen area of the business, strode past Blaze, and went out to the front retail space.

There were no words spoken between the couple the entire time they began to fire up ovens, turn on lights, and get sheet pans ready for the day's food preparation and baking.

Heads down, they both worked, and worked away.

As Milena began the process of throwing out the rotted food in the display cases, something made her freeze in place.

In the tiny child's chair in the back of the counter—the chair that Vicki had sat in when she was very young, so that her parents could work and keep an eye on her—there was a simple backpack.

Milena, confused by the vision, slowly inched closer. She lifted the backpack and hefted it a few times and gauged its bulk.

She placed the backpack on the front countertop, unzipped it, and tilted the bag. Stacks of banded hundred-dollar bills tumbled out. Stunned, she counted $300,000 worth.

In the kitchen, Blaze hoisted a forty-pound bag of flour onto his worktable, when—

"Blaze... Blaze, come here," screamed Milena. "*Moj Boze*, Blaze. *Moj Boze!*"

48

ON THE pristine Market Square in the beautiful and exclusive Chicago suburb of Lake Forest sat Roer's Gallery. The tony storefront was nestled in with several other high-end businesses.

With its traditional Tudor style, it fit in perfectly with the landscape of quaint Lake Forest. It wasn't a large retail space, but the paintings and sculptures sold within were top quality, by top-flight artists, and the gallery's patrons willingly paid exorbitant prices.

A FedEx van pulled up in front of the business and parked. The driver, hand scanner at the ready, moved to the back of his van and opened the doors. He reached in and pulled out a thin, four-by-four-foot box and scanned the package.

As he closed the van's door and carried the box to the front entrance of the gallery, the name on the return label of the package could be plainly seen. It read: Wicktoria Chlebek, 7699 W. North Shore Ave., Chicago, Illinois 60631.

49

DANA BANASIK awoke that day with a killer headache. It was almost 11 A.M., and she'd been out the night before, like all the other nights before, getting drunk.

Dana lived in an awful, depraved state of constant inebriation, sorry circumstances for such a brilliant woman. Her health had suffered greatly for her addiction, too.

The neighbors, most of whom had known her since she was born, were heartsick over the turn of events that led to Dana's decline into alcoholism. It was days like these that they also hated living nearby.

"Damn it, Mother. Damn you," shrieked the tattered-robe-clad Dana as she walked away from the garage and through the backyard of her Edison Park home, the one that she shared with her remaining parent. "You keep taking them away, but you don't learn, do you. They won't stop making the stuff, Mother."

Dana was on her way back inside the house after going to her liquor hiding place in the garage. The sweet spot was located above the parked car, up in the rafters. She required a short ladder to get to her stash, but, no matter the weather outside, it was always worth the trip to the garage.

Through the kitchen window Dana could see her mother seated at the table. Her mother's face showed confusion as she turned away, shook her head, and drank a cup of tea.

Dana opened the rear door, angrily advanced through the kitchen past her sulking mother, and headed to the basement stairway.

"You think you're so smart," said Dana with a goofy grin on her face. "You have no idea who you're playing with here. I went to Dartmouth."

"Yeah, you said," said her mother, not impressed with her daughter one little bit at the moment.

Dana inched down the creaky basement steps and into the dank area. It was mostly an open cellar, with the exception of one closed-off room where the utility apparatus was housed—the HVAC system, water heater, and the like.

Dana went in the other direction, to three stacks of cardboard boxes that sat on top of a series of three wooden pallets, all lined up one next to the other.

She leaned over and grabbed the exposed slats of one of the pallets and pulled it slightly away from the other two. The space she created was about a foot across, and it exposed the open side of a hollowed out area in the second box down from the top of the middle stack.

She reached inside her other hiding spot, and her face screwed up in confusion. There were no bottles in the space.

"Damn it," she said softly, as she wondered if her mother had finally found this other stash.

"Mother, what did you do?"

She rooted around inside the seemingly empty box, and then her hand came back out with a manila envelope and a small metal box of some sort.

She turned the box this way and that and quickly surmised that it was an electrical box, like one of those used for electrical outlets in homes. But this box had been altered, with the sides cut and angled toward the middle of the box—where a copper tube held a single shotgun shell in place.

Dana's hands began to shake as she placed the metal electrical box on top of the other cardboard ones, and she opened the envelope. She shook out the contents on top of the cardboard box right next to the little metal contraption with the shotgun shell in it.

There were old photos inside the envelope.

They were photos of her when she was still in high school. She was fresh-faced and full of energy and hope for her future. There were photos of Bartosz and of her mother, but mostly the photos were of Dana. Her father must've taken the photos, she mistakenly concluded, in her confused state.

Tears began to form in Dana Banasik's eyes as she kept shuffling through the envelope's contents and got to a series of photos of the device that was sitting on the box in front of her—or at least a device that looked the same. Only, the device in the photos was displayed on a workbench. There were four different photos with four different views of the device.

In the background of each shot were old television sets and similarly old, dated computer equipment. It was equipment that hadn't been used in the last ten or fifteen years.

In the last photo Dana could see, in the near background, a Chicago Police Department uniform shirt that hung on a hook near the workbench. The uniform shirt had sergeant's stripes on it.

The uniform nameplate read: Jakubowski.

Her voice trembling, Dana called, "Mother...Mother!"

50

THE FAINT smell of photo-development chemicals still wafted in the air of Pies's basement as the police investigative team searched the premises.

A police photographer took digital still shots of the workbench, but it didn't look, presently, anything like it did in the photos that Pies had staged and left in Dana's basement.

Pies had taken the time to remove the newer devices that had survived the raid by Crick and Andy, and he replaced them with whatever items were left in his basement from twelve or so years ago, as many as he could locate. The photos had to look right.

Detective Stu Von Bargen, wearing white rubber gloves, anxiously roamed among the investigators and checked on their progress.

He walked to the stairway and went up to the kitchen, where more investigators were milling about, taking prints, and going through the cabinets and drawers.

Detective Von Bargen slipped through the living room and out the front door—the street was full of police vehicles. News crews and bystanders crowded the sidewalk and gawked at the goings-on.

Von Bargen yanked the gloves off his hands and dropped them onto the grass. He pulled the car keys from his pocket and moved past uniformed Chicago PD officers standing guard by the crime tape across the front walkway.

Von Bargen said, "You see him, you get help. He doesn't look dangerous, but looks are deceiving with this one, okay?"

"Got it," said one of the officers.

As Von Bargen sat in his unmarked unit, Detective Sony Brar stepped from a home across the street with a notepad in hand.

Before Von Bargen shut the car door he said to Brar, "I have that mother and daughter meeting me at the 16th. I'll be back in two."

Brar nodded and walked in the direction of the next house down as Von Bargen shut the car door, started the engine, and drove away.

The 16th police district on Milwaukee Avenue was only a ten-minute ride away.

When he arrived and parked his vehicle, he made his way to the back door and then to the interior window-lined conference room that he used as an office for the now substantial Zielinski crew/Bs murder case investigation. His usual office was on South Michigan Avenue, but with this case out here in Edison Park continually expanding its scope, it warranted a temporary move to the 16th.

He stepped into the conference room, and Dana Banasik, dressed properly and with a hint of makeup on her face, sat expectantly alongside her mother at the long table in the center of the room. Dana's eyes showed a strong and sober determination. She was on a quest to finally catch, and put away, the person responsible for killing her father.

"No sign of him," said Von Bargen as he took a seat at the table, too. He leaned back in his chair and said, "You've known him a long time, Dana. Where do you think he'd want to go? You know, if he were running? Anything you can tell me? A city? A country? Maybe to some friends you both had back in the day?"

"We mostly knew each other as kids, and he never really had any other close friends that I can remember, except for Vicki, of course. So...no, I don't have any idea. I still can't believe he's the one," she said. "Why would Daddy have those photos, or that shotgun-shell contraption? How could Jakub have worked with my dad? I just...I don't understand."

Von Bargen didn't want to answer because he wasn't sure who had taken the photos or had left the booby-trap device so conveniently located. Sure, the photos looked old, all of them, even the photos of the shotgun-shell, booby-trap device, but the lab would have to check the chemical components to see if the photos were twelve or so years old, or just taken last night. For now the detective was glad they had a huge break in the old double-homicide case.

Dana's mother reached out and lightly held her daughter's forearm. She said, "Finding that evidence, you're the hero here in all of this, Dana. You're our hero."

"Don't," was all Dana could say. She gradually pulled her arm free of her mother's gentle grasp.

At that moment, Detective Stu Von Bargen peered through the interior windows of the conference room and to a bank of eight video monitors that were lined up over the desk sergeant's head across the hallway.

The street-facing portion of the sergeant's desk was too high for Von Bargen to notice if anyone was seated in the line of chairs on the other side.

But the center two monitors above the desk sergeant's head displayed live images of the entire area in the 16th district's front lobby.

Seated, alone, left arm in a sling, was Jakub "Pies" Jakubowski.

Pies sat there and looked right at the middle-monitor camera lens —the one pointed directly at his position. He rarely blinked, and he showed absolutely no emotion.

He then deliberately—and obviously quite painfully—pulled his left arm free of the sling and grimaced as he agonizingly lifted both of his arms up and over his head.

He carefully interlocked his fingers behind his head, cast his eyes downward at the floor—and awaited his fate.

MATT HADER'S circuitous route to becoming a professional writer followed an unlikely path through post-collegiate classes at The Second City, on-air shifts in Chicago-area radio station studios, and work as a 9-1-1 communications officer. He's had numerous screenplay options and production deals over the years, and in 2011 his first novel, *Bad Reputation*, was published, followed by six more stories that expanded the *Bad Reputation* universe. Matt served for a time on the board of directors of the nonprofit American Screenwriters Association, and he's a current member of the International Association of Crime Writers (North American branch). He and his wife make their home in Barrington, Illinois.

Made in the USA
Lexington, KY
31 October 2016